WHAT KIND OF MOTHER

BOOKS BY ANNA-LOU WEATHERLEY

Detective Dan Riley Series
Black Heart
The Couple on Cedar Close
The Stranger's Wife
The Woman Inside
The Night of the Party
The Lie in Our Marriage
The Housewife's Secret

Wicked Wives
Vengeful Wives
Pleasure Island

Chelsea Wives

WHAT KIND OF MOTHER

ANNA-LOU WEATHERLEY

bookouture

Published by Bookouture in 2025

An imprint of Storyfire Ltd.
Carmelite House
50 Victoria Embankment
London EC4Y 0DZ

www.bookouture.com

The authorised representative in the EEA is Hachette Ireland
8 Castlecourt Centre
Dublin 15 D15 XTP3
Ireland
(email: info@hbgi.ie)

Copyright © Anna-Lou Weatherley, 2025

Anna-Lou Weatherley has asserted her right to be identified as the author of this work.

All rights reserved. No part of this publication may be reproduced, stored in any retrieval system, or transmitted, in any form or by any means, electronic, mechanical, photocopying, recording or otherwise, without the prior written permission of the publishers.

ISBN: 978-1-83618-481-2
eBook ISBN: 978-1-83618-479-9

This book is a work of fiction. Names, characters, businesses, organizations, places and events other than those clearly in the public domain, are either the product of the author's imagination or are used fictitiously. Any resemblance to actual persons, living or dead, events or locales is entirely coincidental.

For SP, one four three x

If you tell the truth, you don't have to remember anything.

MARK TWAIN

PROLOGUE

I saw her that night; that fateful evening before my life became unrecognisable. Before *I* became unrecognisable.

She came to me in my dream, suspended somewhere between fantasy and reality. She looked different though, older, more in keeping with the age she would've – should've – been now. Her cheeks had thinned out slightly, that delicious puppy fat I used to pinch between my thumb and forefinger giving way to the faintest outline of cheekbones.

I used to wonder, in all the years since she died, why she so rarely infiltrated my dreams. I felt guilty about it. Why did I never dream of her when for so many years I found her in every waking thought I ever had?

I know now, with the bittersweet benefit of hindsight, why she came to me in my dream that night. It was an omen. She was warning me of the dangers that lay ahead.

'Cora?' I called out to her. 'Baby, is that really you?'

I felt no fear as I sat up, turning to glance at Ed, who was sleeping peacefully next to me. Could he see her in his dreams too? I knew he would've given anything to be able to.

'You look different,' I said. 'All grown up.'

Though she remained forever an infant in my memory, that night my subconscious placed her around the age she should've been had she lived. Twenty-one. The same age I'd been when I'd expelled her, bloodied and screaming, from my body, not much more than a child myself.

She looked to me like the beautiful young woman she should've lived to become, not the precious child I had loved so fiercely and yet so fleetingly in the flesh. In that moment, I felt the violence of her loss as though it were a fresh wound.

'I'm so happy to see you, sweetheart,' I said. 'I miss you. I miss you so much.'

She shook her head as she watched me, her soft, blank expression dissipating into something sad.

'What's wrong, Cora?' I wanted desperately to reach out and touch her, but I was scared she would evaporate between my fingers like smoke.

'Tell me, baby – what's wrong?'

I sensed fear in her as she shook her head slowly from left to right.

'*No?*' I asked, desperate to understand her silent message. 'What do you mean, no?' But she said nothing. 'Speak to me, darling,' I implored. 'Why have you come?'

Her eyes – those beautiful baby blues – grew as dark as they were wide. Though plenty more time had passed without her than we'd had together, I knew her inside out. A ball of fear swept through me. *She's trying to tell me something.*

My lower intestines squeezed in panic.

'Talk to me, Cora, please... Oh please, Cora,' I begged, 'just say... *something.*'

Her head continued shaking from left to right, violently now. My heart felt sharp-edged in my throat, the agony of being so close but unable to touch her, to feel her skin and bones against my fingertips. I reached my hands out towards her. But the more I stretched, the further away she became, as though falling backward, her body disappearing.

'*No, Mummy, no!*'

And then she started to scream.

ONE
CHRISTINE

I wake with a start, my heart pounding against my ribs. Something has wrenched me from my sleep. Was it the low, almost inaudible hum of voices coming from downstairs? I can't be sure as I rub my gritty eyes open, but it sounded like someone was crying. Maybe Con has left the bloody telly on again. I've told him so many times not to do that. *We're not made of money, you know!*

I wriggle out of Ed's warm embrace and stretch over to grab my phone from the bedside table. My warm skin meets the icy chill as I pull the duvet back and suck cold air in through my teeth. It's March, but it's still *freezing*; the type of cold that burrows right through your flesh and deep into your bones like a parasite looking for a host. It's 6.01 a.m. I groan, momentarily forgetting about the noises downstairs.

She'd come to me in my dream for the first time in years...

'Ed, *Ed...*'

I quickly slot back into bed and wrap my arms around Ed's bulk with a shiver and a fleeting sense of gratitude – we're lucky we still have a roof over our heads, *just about*.

I can feel the dull thud of Ed's strong heartbeat against the palm of my hand, the heat radiating from him as I spoon in behind him.

Temperatures have plummeted these past few nights, yet having Ed as my bed partner for the past twenty-nine years (give or take) really has been more efficient than any electric blanket.

I hear the familiar creak of the living-room door downstairs and then an animated female voice before it closes again.

'Has he got a girl down there?' I breathe the question into Ed's ear, not yet fully roused from sleep, the remnants of my unsettling dream still swirling around my mind. What was it Cora had been trying to tell me? Whatever it was, I have a terrible feeling about it.

It's too cold to get up, even though I know I must. 'I hope they're not having a set-to...'

'Mmm... what time is it?' Ed murmurs, half asleep as he grips my hand and pulls it tighter to his chest.

'Time to get up,' I reply, contemplating whether to tell him about my dream. I don't want the day to start off on a melancholy note, and I know that if I mentioned anything to do with 'premonitions' or 'bad omens' he'll tell me off. *Don't start with all that old nonsense again, Tee.*

'It's six o'clock,' I say, reluctantly releasing myself from his grip. 'I have to go to work.'

'But it's Sunday,' he whines, rolling over to face me, his eyes shut.

'Yeah, I know... and I still have to go to work.'

He exhales, the whisper of his breath meeting the cold air like cigarette smoke. I really need to put the heating on.

'Today? Really?'

'Yes. Really.' I sit up, swinging my legs out from underneath the warm duvet. The cold air stings my skin. 'I'll make us a cup of tea.'

'You're telepathic, do you know that?' he murmurs. 'And

why do you have to work *today*?' he asks, still refusing to open his eyes. 'I don't like you working for those people anyway... but Sundays? That's *our* time, Tee.'

'Because we need the money, *honey*,' I say dryly. 'Con starts training at the academy soon, and he needs things – *we* need things – and then there's Mum... Sunnyside's invoice is overdue again. That reminds me – did you speak to the bank?'

'Mmm...' he says, '*I* need things... things only you can give me.'

I smile with my back still to him, though I can tell he senses it. 'Well, have you?'

'Have I what?'

I roll my eyes. 'Spoken to the bank?'

'I will, first thing tomorrow. I promise. Come back to bed – give the old man a *special* cuddle...'

'No time for that,' I say, flopping back down into bed and snuggling in against him once more anyway. He's just too toasty, and his embrace feels reassuring,

'Why don't you call those Levinsons and tell them you can't make it today? Say you're sick, that you've got an upset stomach or something. No one argues with the squits.'

I laugh softly. His breath is warm and sweet-smelling as I turn to face him, placing my lips gently on his for a moment.

'No can do I'm afraid.' It's my turn to sigh. 'I told Mrs Levinson I'd be round at 7.30 to help. They had another "soiree" last night for all their fancy friends, and then I said I'd go up to Sunnyside and see Mum later...'

Ed groans. 'I hope she's paying you double. Up their own backsides that lot, not to mention corrupt.'

I laugh, though I don't disagree with him.

'They're all right,' I say. 'They're just rich. Helen's OK I suppose...'

I'm reminded of the letter then, the one I found a couple of weeks ago, hidden – or at least it had appeared to be – inside a book in the Levinsons' library. I'd been dusting, and it had fallen out from between the pages of my favourite ever book, *Gone with the Wind*. Instinctively, I unfolded the piece of paper:

> *I can't go on like this anymore. The pain torments me on a daily basis. Please release me. Please forgive me. I know I don't deserve to live.*

I instantly recognised Helen's florid and cursive handwriting from the endless to-do lists she always left for me when I came to clean her enormous six-bedroomed gated mansion house. I didn't know what to make of it exactly. They weren't particularly happy words, that was for sure. I knew they had clearly not been for my eyes, so I'd put the note back where I'd found it and thought little more of it. It was none of my business. I had enough problems of my own.

'And the daughter's quite sweet, although I hear her arguing with Helen *a lot*. She's always crying. I think she's a bit highly strung.'

'Spoiled you mean,' Ed sniffs, stretching before he settles back into the covers.

'Suppose it would be difficult not to be with all their money. I—'

The noises from downstairs reach my ears again. Someone is shrieking.

'He *has* got someone down there, hasn't he?' I say, wrapping my dressing gown around me with purpose. 'I thought he had training today?'

'He does,' Ed replies through a protracted yawn, finally opening his eyes. 'I think he's with a girl...'

I think my light bristle might go undetected, but Ed senses it of course.

'He's eighteen years old, Tee, and with a bit of luck he's

about to embark on a career as a pro footballer... better get used to groupies, eh?'

I roll my eyes. 'I don't want to stop him living his life, but you know girls are a distraction...'

'Don't I just,' he says, slipping his hand into my dressing gown and placing it on one of my breasts. I let it rest there for a second before finally standing.

'Yeah, well, this our home, *his* home. It's not a bloody knocking shop, and—' The voices downstairs are growing increasingly loud. Someone, the female, is wailing – the unmistakable high-pitched sound of distress. Ed hears it this time too, and he raises an eyebrow. 'I'd better go down and see what's going on.'

I slide my feet into my fluffy slippers and schlep down the stairs, listening at the living-room door for a second before knocking and opening it more or less at the same time. It is my house after all.

'Morning... Oh!' I'm not sure what, or who, I was expecting to see, but it definitely isn't *her*.

'Hello, Paris,' I say, unable to disguise the surprise in my voice. 'What are *you* doing here?' Paris is Helen Levinson's seventeen-year-old daughter. I've been working for her parents the past few months as a cleaner, or 'housekeeper' as Ed prefers me to call it. He hates me cleaning, thinks it's beneath me. He doesn't like me working full stop, and not least for the Levinsons. He believes it's a man's job to provide for his family; he's old-fashioned like that. But I don't mind the graft, and it gives me a bit of independence too. Moreover, it helps with the bills, and we've got plenty of those.

I turn and gasp at the anguish on my Conor's face, my hand rising to my mouth too late to stifle it.

'Oh God, Con, what's happened?' A rush of adrenalin hits me then, alerting me that I need to pee – urgently. I glance over at the telly in the background, at the red ticker tape that's running across the screen – 'Local man found beaten to death under railway bridge' – and I catch the images of police vehicles, of flashing blue lights in my peripheral vision.

'Turn that down!' I say, suddenly a bit cross. It's six in the bloody morning. What with the telly blaring and Paris's wailing, I'm worried they'll wake the whole street up.

I snatch up the remote and hit the mute button, then look over at Paris again. She's sitting on the small green Habitat velvet sofa that had once been my pride and joy but now, some ten years on, has admittedly started to look like it's seen better days. She's wearing what appears to be one of my old dressing gowns and is sobbing uncontrollably, her face in her hands. I stare at her for a moment, panic and confusion fighting for space among the myriad questions that are currently rushing me all at once.

I wasn't aware that Conor even *knew* Paris Levinson. He's certainly never mentioned it to me before. Are they an item? Why is she wearing one of my tatty old dressing gowns? I swing round, trying to temper the hysteria that's beginning to swell inside me, causing my heartbeat to accelerate. *Something's happened.* I glance over at Con again, my pulse throbbing in my ears. He's pacing the room, and that's when I notice blood on his T-shirt; spots and splashes of unmistakable claret.

'Con! Con? Are you hurt? What's happened?' I seize him by the forearms, scanning him for any visible physical injury. 'Can someone just tell me what's going on...? My eyes dart between them both. 'Paris? Does your mum know you're here...?'

But her head is still in her hands, and she doesn't look up.

'Has there been some kind of accident...?'

I can feel my son's arms vibrating in my grip as he looks at me in a way I've never seen before.

'Mum...' His voice cracks as he takes the remote and unmutes the TV, nodding towards it.

'... twenty-four-year-old identified as local man Mathew Reynolds was discovered by a passer-by at around 3.30 a.m. this morning. Reynolds, an unemployed father-to-be whose girlfriend is due to give birth to their first child imminently, appeared to have been beaten to death near Renton's nightclub in...'

I glance back at Conor, confused, though the name Reynolds rings a distant bell in my mind.

'Do you know him, Con...?'

He looks on the verge of tears, and I reach for his arm again, turning to Paris. It's only then, as she briefly removes her hands from her face to wipe the mucus dripping from her nose, that I see the burgundy stains on her hands; the green-and-yellow bruises on her wrists...

'What the...? Paris, love, are you OK?' She doesn't look up as she starts to cry even louder. Clearly *something* has happened, something awful. But no one is talking, and it's six in the bloody morning, and it's freezing, and I have to work, and Con has training, and I haven't got time for this crap, and...

Finally, he speaks.

'He's dead, Mum.'

'Who? Who's dead? This... this Reynolds fella you mean?' I flick a finger in the direction of the TV. 'Him? Is he a friend of yours or something?'

Con shakes his head as he rakes his hands through his thick hair, dragging his fingers down his cheeks before linking them on top of his head.

'And... what's that got to do with you, with us?' I hear the urgency in my own voice. 'Were you... were you there or something? Were you at the nightclub?' I glance over at Paris again. 'The pair of you?'

Con knows I won't be best pleased to learn that he's been out clubbing the night before he's due to attend training. He needs to stay on top of his game and impress the coaches if he really wants to excel at the academy and secure a Premier League place for his future, and staying out all night partying isn't exactly conducive to that.

'I've got to tell her, Paris,' he says, looking over at her apologetically.

'Tell me what?' My gaze darts between them, my guts twisting so tightly that I'm forced to place a hand on my belly. 'For God's sake, Con, you're scaring the crap out of me...'

'Sit down, Mum.' His tone is doing nothing to assuage my burgeoning panic.

'Why? No. I can't sit down; I've got things to do. I've got to go to work... at your mum's house, Paris.' I nod in her direction. 'And I've got to go and see your nan later, and...'

'He's dead,' he says again, his voice breaking with emotion as he comes towards me and places both his hands on my shoulders. At six foot exactly, Con towers over my five-foot-three stature. 'I'm sorry, Mum.'

My earlier confusion turns into acute terror as I see the look on my boy's handsome young face.

'I think we killed him.'

TWO

DAN

'It's a particularly nasty one, DCI Riley, and I don't just mean the weather.' Dr Victoria Leyton, my favourite forensic pathologist on account of her direct approach and somewhat maverick brilliance, pulls the mask down from her lips, her warm breath meeting with the wet freezing air as she raises an eyebrow.

It's a bitterly cold and windy March morning, and the rain is coming down in fine, unrelenting sheets; the type that renders an umbrella utterly ineffectual. I pull my coat a little tighter around me.

'I think I should warn you,' Vic says with a sombre expression, 'it ain't pretty.'

Despite the incidentals of when our paths do cross, i.e. whenever there's a dead body in unexplained circumstances, I'm genuinely pleased to see Vic, even if it did mean dragging me out of my warm bed at this unholy hour.

'Don't wake the kids up,' my wife, Fiona, instructed me from her semi-comatose state as I tried silently to dress myself in the dark. 'Or else there'll be another murder to deal with.'

'It's been a while, Vic,' I say, resisting the urge to embrace her.

She shoots me a wry smile. 'You have your sweater on inside out,' she says, pointing to my neck.

I glance down at myself; spot the label on the front. 'Didn't want to wake the wife and kids,' I say, shrugging off my embarrassment.

'Ever thoughtful, Detective Riley... Anyway, you're going to want to see this.'

I'm pretty certain I *don't*. I'll never get used to seeing dead bodies. Unlike Vic here, who practically lives with them, perhaps even lives *for* them.

'What a dismal place to end up,' I note as I glance around at the depressing location – a disused railway bridge that runs parallel to a shoddy footpath. Adjacent to it is a small, dirty brown river, wasteland essentially. It's a popular place with homeless people, prostitutes and drug addicts, on account of the shelter provided by the arches.

I spot an old, rusting shopping basket in the shallow water, the red plastic handles illuminated by the harshness of SOCOs' spotlights. To the left of me, there's a discarded plimsole and an abandoned sleeping bag surrounded by empty plastic sandwich containers and crushed tins of strong larger, the miserable remnants of some poor soul's al fresco dinner by the looks of it.

I'm a little late to the party, as it were, and the area is already crawling with forensics. The body has been tented off, which isn't a good sign either. Ostensibly, I suspect this is to protect the victim's identity from the ghoulish, prying eyes – and lenses – of the press and public, but it might also suggest that whoever abandoned him here probably hasn't left him looking his best.

I sigh, take in a deep lungful of freezing, damp air and brace myself.

'Gov! Gov!'

I instantly recognise the voice from behind me – DS Lucy Davis. It's a relief to see my 'work wife', my stalwart second in command, striding towards me with purpose. I note that she's holding two coffee cups. *Got to love Davis.*

DC Parker, the newest and most eager to please member of my homicide squad, is trotting closely behind her. He looks a little flustered, his mop of dark messy hair sticking to his face in the rain. I've quickly learned not to underestimate Parker's hapless demeanour though. He's as sharp as cut glass behind that carefully (de)constructed façade and has fast become a vital member of my team.

'Flat white, boss.'

I accept the soggy cup gratefully; take a sip of the tepid contents. *It's the thought that counts.*

'We think his name's Mathew Reynolds, gov,' Davis says. 'A local twenty-four-year-old male.'

'You *think?*'

'He had ID on him. He's a known drug dealer, pretty low-level stuff, plus he's had a few pulls for historical misdemeanours, domestic violence and resisting arrest... He lives on East Street, on the estate there.' She pauses. 'So, what do you reckon then, gov – drug deal gone wrong perhaps?'

'Could be.' I nod, keeping an open mind.

'Looks as though he may have been at the local club last night, doing a bit of business maybe...?'

I'm familiar with Renton's, a nightclub just round the corner from here, for all the wrong reasons, but they will have CCTV footage from last night, both inside the property and out. 'What about street-cam locations?'

'One on the railway bridge, boss,' Parker pipes up, 'and one just on the other side of the arches that leads to the footpath by the river.'

'But none here,' I say quietly to myself as I stare over at the tent. 'A blind spot. Convenient.'

I'm still muttering to myself as I step into the PPE suit. 'Right then, let's do this.'

'Don't say I didn't warn you,' Vic says as she pulls back the tent flap and I step inside.

I stop dead in my tracks, momentarily paralysed.

'Your silence speaks volumes,' Vic says sagely as I crouch down beside the body.

I look down at the man's face, or what remains of it because his features are no longer distinguishable. There's bone and cartilage where his nose once was, and his mouth is gaping open, exposing his teeth, some of which are missing. His face has been caved in, *obliterated*.

Unsurprisingly, there's a considerable amount of blood. The thin blue sports coat he's wearing – which I note seems a little too thin given how cold it's been – is soaked almost black with it. I note wounds to his hands too, cuts so deep you can see bone and bubbles of exposed subcutaneous yellow fat. I exhale loudly. Vic was right – this is as ugly as it gets.

'How long has he been here?'

'Not long. A couple of hours maybe, three at most. Minimal rigour mortis,' she says succinctly, 'though I suspect that the temperature has staved off the onset somewhat. He was still warm to the touch when the lady found him apparently.'

I check my watch. 'So, TOD around one–one thirtyish?'

Vic cocks her head, pausing thoughtfully. She likes to be precise. 'Yes, I'd say so.'

She crouches down next to me.

'What could've done this to his face?' I think of his mother in this moment because everyone has one. Assuming she's still in the picture, she won't be able to identify her son, even if we were to allow her to try, which we wouldn't. No mother should ever have to see their son like this.

'At first I thought he'd been beaten to death, kicked and stamped on essentially,' Vic surmises in her matter-of-fact tone. 'There are at least two visible sets of footprints on the ground next to him, and it would explain how his nasal bones were shattered. The ground was probably still wet, not yet frozen over when the imprints were made, so I suppose we can be thankful for that at least,' she says.

'At first?' I glance at her. 'You said "at first"?'

'Hmm, yes... well, as you can see, he's received considerable wounds to his face – and some particularly egregious defence wounds to both hands. He put up something of a fight, only I doubt he stood much of a chance. He didn't appear to be armed. This was a frenzied, extremely vicious attack, Dan.'

Tell me something I don't know.

'A cursory look at him would suggest that he choked due to his oesophagus becoming punctured and filling up with blood – asphyxiation essentially.' Vic pauses. 'Only with slightly closer inspection of the body, I noticed a small puncture wound on the left side of his neck, barely visible because of all the blood and the immediate injuries to his face.'

'A puncture wound? From a knife you mean?'

'A knife or sharp object of some sort, yes. The position of the body would indicate that he was on the ground at the time, no doubt trying to defend himself when the fatal injury came.'

I stare down at the body, curled up in a foetal position like he's somehow come full circle, exiting life in the same way he entered it.

'So, it could be more likely that he bled to death from the puncture wound,' Vic adds after a moment. 'It severed his left carotid artery, though I should imagine he'd already been incapacitated before then.'

'How long would it have taken – for him to bleed out?' I try to imagine the scene, piecing together this man's final diabolical moments as his life ebbed away.

'Well,' Vic says, seemingly glad of the opportunity to educate me, 'your cardiac output is around five litres per minute, and roughly twenty per cent of that goes to your carotids on either side of the neck.' She presses a gloved finger onto her skin in demonstration. 'Ten per cent each way, so at a flow of around five hundred millilitres per minute, his entire blood supply would've emptied in approximately ten minutes, give or take. Perhaps quicker if he was already unconscious.'

'And was he unconscious?' I ask, hopeful. The thought of what this man must've endured, knowing he only had a matter of minutes left before the life drained from him, causes the hairs on my arms to stand to attention. Who could cause such catastrophic damage to another human being? And why?

'Difficult to say,' she muses, continuing to examine the body. 'Given the beating it looks like he's taken, the probability is high. It's possible,' she adds softly, sensing my upset. 'Likely even.'

Parker suddenly enters through the tent flap and stops short as soon as he spots the body. He cups his mouth with a hand as he takes half a step back. I think this is Parker's first time up close and personal with a cadaver since joining my homicide team, and the poor man's turned as white as his shirt. Talk about a baptism of fire. He hands me something in a ziplock bag, his eyes widening.

'We found this, gov,' he manages to say through his fingers.

I look at the contents – a broken beer bottle, smashed at the neck, leaving an exposed, sharp jagged edge. It's covered with blood – this poor man's most likely.

'Thanks, Parker.' I nod at him as I take it. 'Why don't you go and get a drink of water?' I place a hand on his shoulder for a brief second. The first time is always the worst – and this, as Vic rightly pointed out, is a particularly nasty one. Poor Parker won't forget it in a hurry; he won't forget it at all.

'Would this do it?' I hold the bag up to Vic, and she takes it from me, inspects it.

She nods. 'But I'll have more accuracy once we get him on the table.'

I'm blowing a little myself as I exit the tent, my heart rate rising in tandem with my anger and dismay.

'Prep the team for a briefing ASAP, Lucy,' I instruct Davis. 'Let's collate all CCTV from the nightclub; see if we can get a sighting of him – who he was with, what he was doing, timelines... We'll need names of potential witnesses who may have been at the club last night, names of his associates...'

'Assuming he was actually *at* the nightclub,' Davis adds.

'He was there,' I say. 'Small-time dealers and clubs go hand in hand.'

'We'll need to inform his next of kin, appoint a liaison officer...'

'Yes, gov. I'll send someone over there now.'

'Send Parker,' I say, pushing back the regret of having to delegate such an unenviable task to my most likeable protégée.

'So, what are you thinking, DCI Riley?' Vic asks me as I return inside the tent.

'A drug deal gone wrong perhaps? A rival gang killing? It's rife round here with postcode wars and all of that. Plus the level of violence used would correlate.'

The unmistakable scent of death reaches my nostrils once again, and I'm suddenly grateful there was no time for breakfast.

'Whoever did this to him certainly wanted to make sure he wouldn't get up again.' *Or look in the mirror*, I think as I bend down next to the bloodied corpse once more. My empty stomach lurches as I ask myself again what type of person would, *could*, do such a brutal thing to another human being? Drugs and violence are statutory bedfellows – one rarely exists without the other – and these types of criminals are well known for their savagery when it comes to protecting their income and reputation. Most of those who've made it to the top of the chain haven't got there through their bountiful virtue and morals. They're ruthless individuals, the kind who wouldn't think twice about slaughtering their firstborn rather than lose money or face – quite literally in this case.

Maybe this *was* a retaliation killing and the perps wanted to send out a clear message to their rivals. It would be a fair assumption, and yet something tells me that it wasn't. This was complete overkill, *blind rage*. And it appears there's been evidence left at the scene, footprints, a possible weapon covered in blood, which would suggest that whoever did this wasn't forensically clued up – it wasn't a professional job.

'Maybe he had a fight in the club,' Vic surmises. 'And it spilled outside... Maybe there was a few of them.'

'Perhaps,' I say, my voice a non-committal whisper.

'Who did this to you, buddy?' I address what's left of this young man's face as I take one final look at him. Something catches my eye then, partially hidden just behind his head, and I pick it up with a gloved hand. It's a piece of broken pink plastic, round and hard to touch. I stare at it for a moment before placing it in a ziplock bag.

'Whoever did this to him wanted to annihilate him. This wasn't a business deal gone wrong,' I conclude.

'So you think it was personal?' Vic asks as she begins zipping him up in a body bag.

'Well, Ms Leyton,' I say, finally standing, 'it certainly is now.'

THREE
CHRISTINE

'Killed...? Killed who? What are you talking about, Con?'

I blink back at him crossly in stunned confusion; place my hands on his shoulders as much to steady myself as anything. I'm dizzy with panic. The room has started to spin, and his voice is dipping in and out of audibility.

I heard what Con said, but I can't process it. It's as if my mind has erected a firewall around my brain so that his words don't penetrate. *He's not serious. It's a mistake. He's winding me up.* My heart begins to pulse loudly in my ears as adrenalin spikes through me.

I know my son. Conor wouldn't joke about something as serious as this. I know every inch of that boy intrinsically. I'm familiar with every nuance, every tiny expression and micro mannerism he makes, and currently his whole demeanour, his body language, is screaming at me that whatever *this* is, it's bad. *Really bad.*

I try to focus, only I can't hold a single thought in my head for more than a nanosecond before it evaporates, and my vision has started to soften around the edges. *This must be what blind panic feels like.*

'Ed! *Eddddd!*' I attempt to project my voice, but it comes out as an uneven warble. I poke my head around the door; clear my restricted throat. 'Ed! Ed! You'd better get down here... *now!*'

I hear the thud of my husband in our room above as he jumps out of bed, no doubt startled by the distress in my voice, then his heavy footsteps as he hastily descends the stairs: *boom, boom, boom.*

'Jesus, Tee, where's the fire?' he says as he bursts into the living room. His hair is sticking up, and he's pulling a T-shirt over his head to cover his chest, which is admittedly still well-defined for a man of his advancing years. 'What's with all the shouting?'

He stops dead for a second, the look of irritation on his face dissipating into something else: *confusion. Concern.* He glances over at Paris. She's still on the sofa, her face buried into her hands as she sobs uncontrollably.

'S'all right, Tee,' Ed says, immediately taking control. I can see by his expression that he knows this is serious. It's like a terrible dark cloud has descended over us. 'Whatever's happened, let's all just stay calm, OK?'

My husband is good in a crisis. He's exactly the sort of person you want around when the proverbial hits the fan. Ed takes a measured approach to problems, and he doesn't do histrionics. *If you're not part of the solution,* he says, *then you're part of the problem.*

'What's happened, son? Did you get into a fight or something?' He nods at Con's bloodstained T-shirt as he approaches him, placing his hands on his shoulders and giving him the once-over, exactly as I did.

'Oh, Dad... you gotta help us!' Conor's face crumples as he collapses into his father's chest. 'We've messed up – we've seriously messed up – and now we're in big trouble. *Serious trouble!*'

I hover next to them, adrenalin coursing through me. 'He's... he's saying they've *killed* someone, Ed.'

'What? Killed who? What you on about, killed someone?' Ed looks at me incomprehensibly, almost irritably, like I've just told him something he knows could never possibly be true.

'This... this bloke on the telly, some young fella, outside some nightclub or something. I... I can't get any sense out of him. I don't know what's happened—' My voice finally breaks then. I'm desperately trying to hold it together, but tears are imminent – I can feel them pushing against the backs of my eyes. 'He's scaring the hell out of me. I don't know what he's saying...'

I do though. I know *exactly* what my son is saying. I just don't want to believe it. *I can't.*

'Who's she?' Ed asks a little sharply, nodding back in the direction of the sofa. I can forgive his lack of manners given the situation.

'It's Paris – Paris Levinson... the Levinsons' daughter.'

He shoots me a puzzled look. 'What's *she* doing here?'

I raise my hands and eyes simultaneously. 'I don't know...' I'm whispering though I'm not entirely sure why. 'I don't know what's going on!'

'He's dead.' Conor starts wailing again. 'He's dead, Dad! *Dead!*'

'Who's dead? What, this fella you mean?' Ed nods at the TV screen, at the muted headlines still flashing across it.

'We killed him.' Conor is dragging his hands down his face again. 'We *murdered* him.'

'What do you mean you bloody *murdered* him? Don't talk daft, Conor.'

To the untrained ear, it might sound as if Ed is getting cross, but I know the subtle difference. It isn't anger he's feeling; *it's panic.*

'Stop being a prat. What are you taking about *murdered*

someone?' He glances over at Paris again. 'What's he talking about, love?'

But she sobs harder into her hands and doesn't even look up.

'I was just trying to protect her, Dad. He... he tried to... I didn't... We never meant to... It was an accident, Dad. It was just a fucking accident.'

My son rarely swears – well, not in front of me anyway. Ed says it's disrespectful, but it only serves to compound my fears that this isn't some sort of wind-up, a twisted joke, a terrible mistake... even though it *has* to be.

'Oh my God.' I'm whispering the words underneath my breath on repeat. '*Oh my God, oh my God, oh my God.*' I feel nauseous, like I'm about to vomit all over the clean carpet.

'All right, Con; it's all right. Let's sit down, eh? Sort this out.' Ed's voice is level and calm as he puts an arm around our boy. 'Tee, put the kettle on, will you?' He throws me a backward glance as I continue to dance on the spot.

'Ed, he's just told us he's *killed* someone for Christ's sake!' I'm shrieking again; my voice is taut and high-pitched. I don't want to make tea. I just want someone to tell me this isn't real.

'Let's just get the kettle on and then we'll see what's what,' he replies gently.

'But, Ed...'

'Tea, Tee... Panicking isn't going to help.'

Neither is a bloody cup of tea, but reluctantly I do as I'm told and force my jittering body into our small galley kitchen. My hands are vibrating as I throw teabags into mismatching cups on autopilot, splashing boiling water onto the work surface as I hastily pour it into the chipped mugs.

It'll be OK, I tell myself on a loop. Con's got it wrong. He hasn't murdered anyone. He *can't* have done. That boy hasn't got a bad bone in him. He used to bring home baby birds who'd fallen out of the nest when he was little – would beg me to save them and would be heartbroken when I couldn't. 'It's just sometimes nature's way, darling,' I would try and comfort him as I buried their tiny paper-thin bodies in the back garden next to the rhubarb patch, placing a makeshift cross made of two lolly sticks tied together on top.

Thinking on it, my Con's never even had a proper fight in his life – a few minor scrapes here and there as a schoolboy perhaps, but nothing major, *nothing like this*. He's been such a good boy, never really caused us a day's worry. Not that this has ever stopped me from worrying about him. As well as it being in his nature not to cause trouble, I think Con has always tried hard to be a model son in a bid to make up for his sister's loss, which sometimes makes me feel guilty.

I glance at the clock on the wall. It's 6.25 a.m. *Shit.* I'm supposed to be at work soon. Helen Levinson is expecting me. What am I going to say to her? And then it dawns on me. *The police.* Oh God, if what Con's saying is true, then they'll come, won't they? They'll come, and they'll take him away!

A fresh wave of panic ensues, swiftly accompanied by a terrible sense of déjà vu. I've been here before, you see...

I've no idea how Paris takes her tea, and I'm not inclined to ask given the situation, so I haphazardly spoon two sugars into the cup and briefly stir it before hurrying back to the living room. I hand the mugs out with shaking fingers, my stomach lurching.

'I don't want any tea, Mum!' Conor snaps, his face a screwed-up ball of anguish.

'Drink it,' Ed commands him, though his tone remains as it was before, calm and measured. 'Sit down, Tee,' he says to me, and again I do as I'm told, taking a seat on the sofa next to Paris.

I'm glad when she takes the mug from me in her small hands. Hands, I note once more, that appear to have dried, congealed blood on them – and fingernails that are bitten down to the quick. I can't help thinking that's odd, and I don't just mean the blood. Helen Levinson embodies the word 'immaculate' – she's salon perfect every time I see her. Perhaps I'd be too if I had her money. Yet I've never seen Paris look anything other than a little scruffy. Always hiding herself away in baggy clothes that conceal her lovely figure. She's a very pretty girl, even with the make-up free, casual look she chooses to go with. The total antithesis of her well-put-together mother, though now I'm wondering if that might be the whole point.

I get the sense that Paris doesn't like Helen much. I often hear them arguing when I'm at the house, hushed exchanges that have, on occasion, left Paris in tears. I stay out of all that though – nothing to do with me.

Instinctively, I place a hand on her knee; try to offer some modicum of comfort. Paris is only seventeen, still a baby. She had a birthday recently, a few weeks back now. I remember because there were huge arches of foil balloons delivered to the house that morning and a bespoke cake in the shape of a Chanel handbag. I'd had a little peek at it in the box – couldn't help myself. The attention to detail was breathtaking; it must've taken ages to make. I suppose I was even more impressed when I saw that she'd been gifted the real version by her parents, a timeless classic, costing, as Helen had been keen to tell me, 'the best part of ten grand'. A drop in the ocean to the likes of the Levinsons, I imagine.

'It's OK, sweetheart,' I somehow manage to say to her, willing my hands to stop shaking. 'Drink this. It'll be OK. We'll sort this out, don't worry...'

She rocks back and forth slightly as she wraps her hands around the boiling-hot mug without even flinching. Her face is wet with tears and mucus, and I think to get her a tissue, so she can clean herself up, but Conor suddenly speaks.

'We're going to go to prison, aren't we?'

FOUR
CONOR

His whole body feels like it's on fire. Every muscle aches liked he's run a marathon; fear and adrenalin are reaching corners of him he never knew existed before and detonating like bombs inside him.

This is so frickin' bad. He rakes his hands through his hair as he turns in circles, the reality of what he's done – what it means – slowly beginning to chip through his disbelief. He's *killed* someone.

There can be no glittering premiership football career for him now, can there? He can kiss goodbye to all the years of hard graft he's put in and all the sacrifices he's made – weekends and evenings hanging with his mates and chatting up girls – to focus on his future instead. After this, he can forget the moments of glory as he scores a hat trick, or the lucrative endorsements and five-figure weekly pay cheques that he's fantasised about using to buy his folks a big house with. That's all disappearing like a magic trick right before his eyes. Now he's going to go prison for the rest of his life.

His brain still feels muddled by the alcohol and the pill

Paris gave him last night. That, coupled with the shock, is preventing him from forming a straight thought in his head. Maybe the drugs had tricked him into thinking he hadn't hit the bloke as hard as he had. *As she had.*

How is he going to tell his parents that he was off his face, drunk and high? He's never taken drugs before in his life, not even a puff on a spliff, not before last night. Drugs were for mugs – he understood that before he set his sights on a pro footballing career.

He can see the look of fear and despair on his parents' faces. The atmosphere in the room is so brittle it could snap at any minute. Oh God, what has he done? What have *they* done? He wants so much to be able to undo it all, to go back just a few hours and erase that brief moment of madness, do something different, *walk away*. If only he'd listened to his intuition, then he might be cuddled up in bed with Paris's warm, naked body next to his right now instead of standing here, shaking with shock and fear, his world imploding as his distraught parents look on.

But he didn't, and now what was done couldn't be undone.

His dad is demanding that he tell him everything from the beginning, only his thoughts are all tangled like a set of old Christmas tree lights. He can't seem to remember anything in order. He can't seem to remember much at all.

He *does* remember that his first instinct was to run though, *just run*. Not that he wanted to admit this, especially not to his dad. Hardly the actions of a hero, right?

'Let's go, Paris… c'mon!' He'd seen the expression of terror on her pretty face, a hybrid mix of shock, confusion *and rage* as he grabbed her by her bicep and began tugging her away. Only he'd lost his footing on the wet ground in his haste, hadn't he, bringing the pair of them down onto their knees in the slippery mud?

'*Shit.*'

He quickly scrabbled to his feet, hoisting her up in the process.

'Are you OK?' He attempted to check on her as they ran down the man-made footpath, a trail that had been stamped out by a million footsteps before them. 'What did he say to you? What just happened, Paris?'

One minute they'd been kissing, pressed up against the wall of the railway arch, arms entangled round each other, her tongue warm as it met his own in the freezing air. And then the next thing...

'Come back to mine,' he said. 'Stay over – my folks won't mind.' Though he wasn't entirely sure of this. His mum generally didn't like him having girlfriends overnight unless it was squared with the girl's parents first.

She giggled softly into his mouth; huddled in so tight to him that he'd felt her small body pinching the very heat from his own. She hadn't answered his question initially, and he wondered if maybe he'd come on a bit strong, made her feel uncomfortable, which in turn caused him to feel the same way.

The thought that she might still be a virgin crossed his mind again in that moment. He'd sensed a nervousness in her – something was holding her back and he certainly didn't want to put any pressure on her, especially if it was to be her first time. He wasn't – *isn't* – a monster.

'I have to get back,' she said, lowering her dark brown eyes apologetically. 'You know my dad doesn't like me staying out all night.'

'When you gonna tell him?' he asked her. 'About us I mean?'

'Us?' She beamed at him then, and he could tell she was pleased with his use of the word. 'Soon. I promise. It's just... you know what dads are like...'

Paris's dad, Bryan Levinson, was a big-shot local MP. He

was *somebody*. And he was filthy stinking rich. Not that you'd know it, looking at Paris. That was partly the reason why she intrigued him. She was different to all the other designer dollies that hung around the training ground with their hair, lash and nail extensions, kitted out in head-to-toe designer logos, looking to bag themselves a footballer and ultimately WAG status.

'I need to pee,' he said as he released her from his tight embrace and waggled the bottle he was holding at her. 'It's the beer.'

He could hear her giggling as he walked a little way up the bank, searching for a secluded spot to do his business, only there wasn't one. He was forced to walk a little further up past the arches before spotting some shrubs and was mid-flow when he heard the commotion, the sound of raised voices.

'*What the...?*'

Zipping himself up before he was quite ready, he quickly made his way back down to the arches where he'd left her.

A sense of foreboding crashed right through his chest as soon as he saw the man with Paris. They appeared to be having some sort of heated exchange. This didn't look good.

'Oi! *Oi!*' he'd shouted over to them automatically, causing them both to swing round. 'What's going on?'

He remembers thinking, as he almost slipped down the wet bank in his haste to get to them, how he really didn't need this right now. Only moments ago they'd been kissing and giggling, both of them drunk and high.

He thought he recognised the bloke from the club as he drew closer, was sure he'd seen him milling around inside earlier looking a bit shifty, though he'd never met him before that night. Now though, with hindsight, he's wondering if he might have seen him around and about after all. He had a bit of a ratty-looking face, small eyes that were set back in his skull and a thin pointy nose.

'What you doing, mate? Leave her alone!' The beer bottle

dropped from his hand as his fight-or-flight mode kicked in. The man momentarily stopped as he approached; gave him the once-over before smirking.

'Who's this then, eh? Does lover boy here know what your lot get up to, eh? Does he? Shall I tell him, Paris?'

'Take your hands off her!'

He'd felt compelled to defend her. From the moment they'd met, he'd sensed a certain vulnerability about her that made him feel protective towards her. It was as if she somehow needed looking after.

Rat Face whispered something in Paris's ear, and almost immediately she became hysterical, struggling to squirm her way out of his grip. There was nothing for it. He had to do *something*.

The initial shove was largely a reactionary one, and it did the trick.

Rat Face stumbled backward, releasing Paris from his grip. But the next thing he knew, he was stumbling backward himself as a fist connected with his cheekbone.

Paris started screaming. 'Don't touch him! Leave him alone!'

At that moment, he'd been struck by the idea that maybe she somehow knew this man. He'd called her by her name, hadn't he?

Chaos ensued. Too much to be able to relate it all in any kind of order to his parents anyway. His memory feels sketchy, like parts of it have been erased, though he recalls getting up off the floor, a sliver of anger breaking through to the surface as he attempted to steady himself.

Paris was crying hysterically, but her tone had changed. The edge of her voice was sharper now, harder. '... that *piece of shit*...'

He thinks Rat Face was on the ground at this point, murmuring incoherently as he appeared to drift in and out of consciousness. He remembers seeing a little blood splatter on his mouth and feeling shocked by it. He'd never hit anyone before in his life, not like that anyway.

'Does Daddy know you're out gallivanting, putting it about with lover boy here?' he snarled up at her from the floor. 'Shall I tell him, Paris, let him know that you're...'

He hadn't caught the last part, but whatever he'd said had really set her off. *That's when she'd really lost it.*

Paris had always struck him as being a shy person, or maybe quiet was a more accurate description. She'd never so much as raised her voice since he'd known her and had certainly never shown any propensity towards anger or violence. But in that moment, he witnessed a completely different side to her.

'Not so cocky now, are you, eh? You evil scumbag!' Spittle flew from her mouth, and the veins popped in her neck. Now Rat Face was curled up in a ball on the ground, his hands covering his face in a bid to protect himself from the blows she was raining down upon him. He could see Paris's chest heaving with the exertion, with the effort she was putting in, kicking and stamping. At one point, he thinks she stopped, mid-assault, before turning to face him expectantly.

He hadn't wanted her to think that he was scared. He'd look like a right pussy in front of her if he didn't join in though. And so, in a bid to save face, against his better judgement, he'd tentatively stuck the boot in a few times himself before quickly coming to his senses.

Rat Face was groaning on the ground. Clearly he'd had enough. Only Paris showed no signs of letting up, baring her teeth in what looked like sheer hatred.

'Paris... Paris, stop! STOP!' He tried to pull her away, but she resisted, like she'd slipped into some kind of trance. 'Leave it... leave him, Paris... Stop! You're going to kill him!' The words fell from his mouth before he had time to think about them. But they seemed to do the trick because she suddenly stopped dead in her tracks.

They both stood for a few seconds, paralysed, the sound of their laboured breathing amplified in the freezing darkness as they stared down at the body on the ground.

And then they started to run.

FIVE

CHRISTINE

I watch Ed as he paces the room, his bare feet leaving imprints on our dated old pile carpet.

I can feel the walls closing in on me as I hear the words coming from Conor's mouth, the room shrinking with each syllable as the air rapidly disappears around me.

Not my son, not my boy. He's all I have left.

I don't really drink alcohol, maybe a glass or two of something at Christmas or on special occasions, but right now, that bottle of bourbon I know is in the kitchen cupboard behind the cereal boxes is whispering my name. Ed thinks it's hidden, but nothing's hidden from me in this house.

'It was self-defence, right?' I blurt the words out.

Ed briefly glances over at me, though he doesn't stop pacing. His brow is fixed in a deep furrow.

'He was just doing what anyone – what any man – would do.' My voice is desperate and shrill. 'This... this... Reynolds bloke. He was harassing you, wasn't he, Paris?' I turn to her for confirmation, but she doesn't look up. She's barely made a sound, save for the sobbing, and hasn't offered up much in the way of explanation. Con has done all the talking instead.

Something about this dynamic doesn't quite sit right with me, but I put it down to the shock. It affects people in different ways. Like when the doctor told me they'd done all they could for our daughter Cora, but that she'd died from septicaemia, a complication arising from bacterial meningitis. I'd only brought her in with a high temperature a few hours earlier. She'd been a little restless the night before, and I'd given her some Calpol to try and help settle her, but then I'd noticed a smattering of red dots on her tiny tummy, like sprinkles of burned sugar, and thought it best to bring her in.

Before that terrible night, Cora had never been sick in her painfully short little life. She was a strong, happy, healthy baby and had been since birth. I was worried of course, like any mother with a feverish baby would be, but not overly. It took less than twenty-four hours from when I'd noticed her temperature was a little high to her life ending. *So yeah, I know all about shock.*

'He... he had his hands on her... and... and... Con just pushed him off!' I address the room like I'm already standing in the dock before a judge and jury. '*He* threw the first punch!' I say with conviction. 'You would never have hit him otherwise, would you, Con?' I'm animated now, failing miserably to hold back the hysteria that's rising up and threatening to explode from every orifice. *Police... trials... barristers... prison... the stigma of being a convicted killer...* It's like machine-gun fire and I've nowhere to duck for cover. 'It was an accident, just a tragic accident...' Tears are streaking my cheeks now, the salt raw on my sensitive skin.

'It's second-degree murder, Tee,' Ed replies flatly. 'Manslaughter with a sympathetic jury. Even with a clean record, he'll still be looking at prison time.'

'NO!' I stand then; I'm not sure how. 'No, not prison... he's *not* going to prison. Oh, Ed, please... *please.*' I look at him to fix this, and yet as much as I plead with him, as much as I want him to be able to, I know deep down not even Ed can get our boy out of this.

Conor comes to me then, and I squeeze him so tightly it's a wonder he doesn't pass out. I bury my head into his neck. He smells faintly of last night's aftershave and fear.

'Oh, Con, what have you done...?'

'I'm sorry, Mum. I'm so sorry.'

'We'll just tell them the truth,' I splutter. 'You've never been in trouble in your life, never set a foot wrong! They'll see that, won't they?' I try and swallow back the bitter reality burning a hole in the back of my throat.

Ed looks over at me. 'Tell who the truth?'

'The police!' I'm shrieking now, losing control. 'We'll call them, and we'll tell them what happened, and they'll understand, and—'

'No one's calling the police,' Ed states coolly. 'What do you think they'll say? "Oh, no worries about the dead bloke down at the railway arches, Mrs Carter; your Conor's been a good boy all his life. Just don't do it again, eh, son?"' He shakes his head. 'Jesus, Tee.'

I reach for my phone with shaking fingers. 'Well, we'll just have to *make* them understand, won't we? Paris will explain everything – she saw what happened, didn't you, love?'

Finally Paris looks up, her young face a melted mess of tears. 'This... this is all my fault. It was me – *I* killed him... I'm the one who should go to prison.'

Con releases himself from my arms and goes to her on the sofa; puts an arm around her. I watch as she collapses sideways into him. It's the first time she's spoken since I opened the living-room door to this nightmare, and I can't shake the feeling that something's amiss – that there's something neither of them are telling us.

'No one's going to prison, OK?' Ed says. 'I need to speak to your mum, Con, in private.' He looks at me; nods in the direction of the kitchen. 'You two sit tight. Stay calm. We're going to sort this out, OK? OK, Con?'

Con manages a thin smile for his dad. His pale face is so young and handsome that I can barely look at him as I follow Ed into the kitchen. It's like a knife through me.

Closing the door behind me – and out of Conor's sight – I quickly feel myself unravel.

I start tapping on my phone.

'What the hell are you doing?' Ed snatches it clean out of my hands, causing me to emit a little gasp.

'I was going to google it, Ed, try and find out what the press are saying about this Reynolds bloke, about the incident... I—'

'Are you *mad*, woman? What if the police check your phone history? What will you say when they ask you why you were googling a murdered stranger's name at six in the bloody morning?'

It's actually 6.45 a.m. now, but I daren't correct him. And why would the police want *my* phone anyway?

'We'll go with him, to the police station,' I say in hushed tones. 'We'll tell them what happened, tell them everything that Con's just told us. We'll be there with him the whole time. They'll be lenient on him, won't they, if he comes clean and cooperates? This... this Mathew Reynolds, whoever he is... he started it! *He* was the aggressor. It was self-defence.'

'And what are we going to pay a good defence lawyer with, Tee, chocolate buttons?'

'We'll sell the house.'

'And live where?'

'Somewhere else.'

'What about your mum?'

I frantically begin pulling at my bottom lip, finding a small piece of loose skin and picking at it relentlessly with the tips of my fingers until it begins to bleed. Ed silently takes hold of my wrist to stop me.

'He must've hit his head when he fell. How could he just *die* like that, Ed? Why did he have to go and *die*?'

My entire body is vibrating as Ed pulls me into him. Ordinarily, this would be all it would take to calm me down, being in my husband's powerful embrace, my safe place, where I feel protected. That fact it doesn't this time only forces my anguish to the next level.

'I can't lose my boy,' I sob into Ed's chest as he grips me tightly. He still smells of sleep. 'We've already lost one child; we can't lose another. What are we going to do?'

Suddenly I feel cross; can feel the heat of my anger warming my cheeks as we stand, embracing in the cold kitchen. I still haven't switched the heating on.

Haven't we had enough heartache in our family? We're not bad people – what have we done to deserve this?

Again, I think of telling Ed about my dream last night, and again I think better of it. *If you're not part of the solution, then you're part of the problem.*

'I... I can't bear the thought of him being locked up, Ed. He's not cut out for prison. It'll be the end of him – *the end of us*. You of all people know what happens in those places, a good-looking boy like that...' I shudder, a sob catching in my throat. 'You know how talented he is, what kind of a future he's looking at. He could be a star, the next Jack Grealish or David Beckham! He's worked so hard for this. *We've* worked hard so that he doesn't have to go through life scrimping and saving and going without like we've had to. That'll all be gone forever if he's convicted.'

The room has started spinning again, the green-and-pink colour scheme blending to create a dirty brown dishwater mix.

'Come on, Tee, come on now, shhh.' Ed grips me by my shoulders; shakes me gently. 'It's OK... Look, I'm going to sort it, right? I'll sort this...'

'How?' I want to believe him more than I've ever wanted to

believe anything in my life. 'We *have* to talk to the police. Tell them what's happened and how. It was self-defence, Ed. Any judge in the land will agree, won't they?'

He still has me in his tight grip. 'When have I ever let you down, eh?'

I open my mouth to speak, but he beats me to it.

'Except for that one time, Tee. And I learned my lesson, didn't I? Never stepped out of line ever again.'

Before Mum's mind started going AWOL, she used to say to me, *Life will teach you the lessons you need to learn, Christine. And if you don't learn them the first time, it'll keep on teaching you.* Ed's right though. After his release from prison, he'd vowed to go straight, promised me that he wanted to live a decent life and make an honest living, and he'd been good on his word.

'It's going to be OK.' He starts rubbing the back of my head in a bid to soothe me. However, it seems to have the opposite effect.

'Stop saying that!' I pull back from him sharply. 'It's *not* going to be OK. Our son has just told us he's *killed* someone! We can't just erase that fact like it didn't happen, can we – carry on as if everything's normal?'

Ed takes hold of my shoulders again; looks into my eyes intensely. 'Actually, Tee,' he says, nodding, 'that's *exactly* what we're going to do.'

SIX
DAN

Ah, the unblinking witness that is CCTV. You've got to love it. Unless you're a shoplifter or a murderer perhaps. But from my side of the fence, it can be pure gold.

'There's a lot to go through, boss,' DC Mitchell says, adding brightly, 'but I think we may have come up trumps early doors!'

Tenacious, that's the adjective I'd use to describe Mitchell. If it takes her ten minutes or ten years, she'll keep going until she hits the jackpot. It's this kind of dogged determination that makes her an exemplary team player. That and an unrivalled attention to detail. There's no polite way to phrase it – or at least perhaps none as accurate – she has eyes like a shithouse rat.

'So,' I say with a frisson, 'what you got?'

'We took the DVR from both inside and outside Renton's, plus footage from the public street cameras, and—'

My phone suddenly beeps. It's Fiona. A sliver of unease trickles into my empty stomach – I still haven't managed breakfast, those gruesome images of Mathew Reynolds's mutilated face not yet softened in my memory – because my wife doesn't often text me. I open it gingerly.

Have you noticed anything different about Jude lately?

Our son, Jude, is nine months now and a proper little dude he is too, 'full of beans and sunbeams' as I say. He's a smiler, perhaps even more than Juno, my Pip, was at his age. I don't even need to pull faces to get a giggle out of him. He breaks into a chuckle as soon as look at me. It amuses Fiona no end.

No. Why?

I quickly reply, slip my phone back into my pocket and return my attention back to Mitchell.
'And?'
'*Annnd,*' she continues, 'we pick our man up inside the club on a few occasions...'
She runs the footage, and we see Mathew Reynolds come into view. From the intelligence we already have on Reynolds, it's fair to say that the way he operated in life may well have contributed to how he met his end. Find out how someone lived and usually you'll find out how they died. Reynolds, by all accounts, was hardly what you might call a model citizen. His rap sheet includes a lengthy list of previous arrests going back to his early, and seemingly troubled, youth.

Before he met his untimely end at the grand age of just twenty-four, he'd racked up no less than eleven arrests, one resulting in a conviction for dealing a class B substance, low level, category three, which saw him slapped with a three-month community order and a £600 fine. It was hardly a deterrent though because he was arrested for possession on no fewer than four further occasions that same year, each time falling just short of intent to supply, which may suggest he wasn't quite as stupid as he appeared.

Even more of an insight into Reynolds's arguably unsavoury character is the tug he received some months previously for an alleged assault against his girlfriend, a young lady by the name of Alana Watkins. He'd been nicked after it was alleged he hit her with a cylinder of nitrous oxide, otherwise known on the streets as Smart Whip. It never got to trial though. Perhaps unsurprisingly, Alana retracted her statement soon after, and the pair obviously continued with some kind of relationship because as it stands, Alana is currently days away from giving birth to their firstborn child, a child that will now grow up to be fatherless.

Admittedly, it would be forgivable to surmise that this may well be a good thing, but two wrongs never make a right, and I'm not convinced *anyone* deserves to be murdered in such a brutal way as Reynolds was. Not even low-level drug thugs who hit their girlfriends. Who knows though? Maybe becoming a father for the first time would have changed the course of Mathew Reynolds's life, taken him down a different path, brought out the best in him and given him an incentive to eschew his old ways. Now, regrettably, he'll never get the chance to find out.

My eyes lock on the screen, and I watch Reynolds standing by the bar, one arm against it as he checks his phone. He appears to be alone. He also appears a little shifty as he surveys the sea of dancing bodies around him, like he might be waiting for someone?

'He's picked up again throughout the night, twice more in fact,' Mitchell states. 'He makes a call at 11.27 – look,' she says, running the footage forward, 'here.'

I lean in towards the screen as she zooms in on the image, which is, I'm happy to note, exceptionally sharp, quality-wise. Judging by Reynolds's facial expressions – his eyebrows are fixed in a frown, and his left arm is gesticulating wildly at one point – the conversation appears to be an animated one.

'Looks like a burner phone,' I say.

'Standard drug dealer accessory,' Mitchell agrees.

There was no phone on Reynolds's person when we found him though, burner or otherwise, and so far the fingertip search uniform are currently undertaking of the immediate area hasn't uncovered it. We'll need to call the divers in, get them to drag that dirty river. Something of an unenviable task I should imagine, not least in these temperatures. Of course, the perpetrator could've taken it with them, disposed of it in another location, though they left his ID behind, which is something of a head scratcher.

I'd initially assumed that whoever had inflicted such grotesque injuries on Reynolds's face may have done so in a bid to conceal his identity, thus making it harder for us to name him, but that didn't make sense given that they'd left photo identification on the body. Then again, no murder makes sense in my opinion.

The next image from the footage is the one that really piques my attention though. It shows Reynolds perched on a sofa. He appears on edge, staring out towards the crowd intently. At one point, he seems to be craning his neck.

A bolt of adrenalin spikes through me. 'He's... he's looking for someone... he's *watching* someone.' I point at the screen.

Mitchell grins, her eyebrows raised. 'That's not the best part though, gov...'

Now she's really teasing me.

'No? Can we get another angle on this, towards the crowd?'

She runs the tape on some more. 'Watch this.'

The camera angle switches direction towards the partygoers, though Reynolds is still in frame, left of screen. My eyes scan the mixed crowd of young, attractive bodies bobbing up and down to the beat of the music, arms in the air as they leave the constraints of the working week behind them.

'OK? So what am I looking at?'

It's tricky to pinpoint who Reynolds might be watching out

for – too many faces in the crowd for one thing. But this is why Mitchell is on CCTV. Those rat eyes...

'These two here, gov.'

She zooms in on a young couple. They're standing to the far right of the frame, a young man and a woman – well, girl really. I watch them as they dance together, the young man perhaps slightly awkward as he throws a few shapes. At one point, he grabs the girl by her waist and lifts her up off her feet. They're laughing, intermittently kissing and chatting into each other's ears. They appear to only have eyes for each other, and I find myself inadvertently smiling. Lord knows I can't remember the last time *I* went dancing. Thankfully, I suspect it was long before social media ever exploded, and therefore there's no supporting evidence.

'And what's special about these two then, eh?' I ask, aware of Mitchell's penchant for building up a little suspense before the big reveal. But I let her have her moment – so far it looks as if she's earned it.

'Watch,' she says, rolling the image on a little further to show the couple making their way through the crowd towards the exit. The camera captures them in the entrance to the club, the female collecting her coat, a big puffer that the disinterested cloakroom attendant hands her.

'There!' Mitchell almost rises from her seat with the momentum. 'Look who's behind them.'

Only the top of his head is in frame at first, the rest of him only briefly captured as he appears to follow them outside.

'Reynolds.'

This proves nothing of course. It could simply be coincidence that he left the club at the same time as this young couple.

Mitchell clearly senses my anti-climax though because she adds, 'It doesn't end there, boss. Baylis has been going through the street-cam footage. And she picked the same pair up again, walking in the direction of the railway arches, towards the crime scene, up along the footpath, heading north.'

Oh, now this is *really* beginning to sound interesting.

'What time is this?' I ask, engrossed, watching the couple as they make their way towards the railway bridge. They're holding hands, swinging their arms together, almost childlike. They appear happy, unbothered by anything, maybe a little drunk perhaps.

'Not long after midnight – 12.06 according to the time-stamp.' She swings round in her chair and looks up at me, the grin still fixed on her face. 'And would you believe it... here he is *again*, Reynolds, walking in the *same* direction towards the railway arches.' She smiles triumphantly. 'The camera picks him up a couple of minutes behind them.'

It's impossible to know for certain if Reynolds's actions are deliberate and that he's following the couple, although I detect a sense of purpose in his stride and something about his furtive body language which would certainly suggest so. So who are they? And why is he interested in them? Were they associates of his? Was he planning to rob them maybe? Judging by the footage, initially, the couple appear unaware of his presence, but as Mitchell rolls the tape on, something catches my attention – the girl. At one point, she glances behind her, as though checking for something. *Or someone.* Reynolds isn't in frame at this point, so I can't be sure if it's him she's turning back to look at, though I suspect it might be, but when she does it again – glances over her shoulder some moments later – I get a slight chill, which I take as a good indicator that my assumptions are most likely correct.

'The arches lead down towards the other side of town, right?'

Mitchell nods efficiently. 'You have to walk up the bank from the old river though because a few metres further ahead is a dead end. Scaling the bank will take you up onto the pavement, on Brockenhurst Way, the long road that leads out of town.'

I inhale as I stare at the screen. 'So it's hardly a shortcut then? I wonder why they took this route?'

'Maybe they went that way so that they could have a bit of... you know, *privacy*.' Mitchell raises her eyebrows almost comedically. 'It's a notorious "beauty spot" after all, gov.'

'We need an ID on that couple, Mitchell,' I say. 'Even if there's no connection, they could be potential important witnesses.'

'Conor Carter and Paris Levinson you mean?' Davis, who I hadn't noticed standing behind me until now, suddenly pipes up.

I slowly turn to face her and see the small self-satisfied smile she's wearing turn into a full-on grin.

'He has a membership card for the club,' she starts to explain. 'All members get free entry and ten per cent off the bar bill, entrance to the VIP area... and the cards are swiped on entry, capturing all the member's details... time and date of entry, name, DOB, *address*.'

'I don't want to belong to any club that would accept me as a member,' I quote, elated.

She blinks blankly at me.

'Groucho Marx?' I offer. 'Oh, never mind.'

'And the girl,' she continues, 'well, Renton's have a cloakroom policy whereby whoever checks in their coat has to write their name down in a register... something to do with people stealing each other's tickets and taking expensive coats that don't belong to them... so, cross-referencing the time she collected her jacket from the cloakroom with the timestamp on the cam footage and... her name's there, in black ink – Paris *Levinson.*'

The name Levinson rings a bell somewhere, though I'm not

sure if it's an alarm just yet. Hang on... Levinson, isn't that the surname of a local MP?

'Neither of them have any form, gov,' Davis tells me. 'Though Conor Carter's dad, Edward Carter, does...'

'OK...?'

'Historic,' she muses, 'some twenty-odd years ago. He got an eight stretch for his part in an armed robbery where a security guard was shot and killed. He did four. They tried to do him for joint enterprise at the time, but in the end he went down for aggravated burglary. He was the getaway driver, never entered the premises apparently, claimed to have no idea the gang was armed.'

'Interesting... And the girl?'

'She's the seventeen-year-old daughter of a local MP, boss. Bryan Levinson, founder of Levinson Communications, though he sold the business some years ago to pursue a career in politics. Made him a *very* rich man in the process. He's highly respected locally and extremely well connected, a pretty powerful man by all accounts. He even acted as a public relations specialist and advisor to the Met at one point back in the mid-nineties.'

I was right. *Levinson*. Of course.

'You mentioned something about an address?'

The sound of the heavy rain battering against the window almost drowns out my voice.

Davis nods. 'Conor Carter, yes... He's registered at number 25 Albert Road, gov.'

'You can drive,' I say, handing her my car keys. 'Oh, and, Davis...'

'Yes, gov?'

'Bring an umbrella.'

SEVEN

CHRISTINE

'You're not serious?' I rapidly blink at Ed, only I can tell by his facial expression that he is *deadly serious*. I wipe my nose with the sleeve of my dressing gown; glance over at the kitchen cupboard that holds the bourbon. The seductive whisper from earlier has now become an ear-splitting scream.

Ed seizes my face with both hands and fixes me with his gaze. 'I want you to listen to me, Tee, OK, just listen. I'm not going to let our boy go to prison – that's *not* happening. So you can relax.'

Relax? He's got to be kidding me!

He glances over at Mum's old clock on the wall. *It's never been a minute out in twenty-odd years, that thing.* I hear her voice in my head for a moment and feel the sting of her absence. I wish she was here. She would know what to do.

'You're due to be at the Levinsons' in a what, half an hour?'

I nod, unsure where he's going with this.

'And Con's got training. So that's what's going to happen,' he says succinctly. 'You'll go to work as planned, and Con will show up for training like he's supposed to.'

I stare at him, incredulous. He doesn't realise what he's saying. He's talking like a madman.

'But the *police*. Ed...' I continue to blink at him through blurry eyes. 'We *have* to report this – you know we do! We can't pretend it didn't happen; we can't... we can't cover it up. No one gets away with... *murder*, you know that! You watch all them programmes on the telly like I do.' I stare up at him. 'We have to do the right thing. We have to report it to the police.'

But he isn't listening. He's started to pace again, deep in thought.

'Here's what we're going to do. You're going to take Conor's clothes – and Paris's. And then you're going to get rid of them.'

'Get rid of them?' I can't believe I'm hearing this, that I'm even entertaining it, and yet...

'Hide them,' he continues. 'Dump them somewhere no one will find them. Now, today, as soon as possible. Then we're going to find similar clothes to match what they were both wearing last night.'

Ed clocks my expression. 'The cops might want to take their clothes away for forensic examination down the line, Tee. If they were caught on CCTV at some point during the night – which I'm pretty certain they will have been – and they become suspects, then they'll come for those items. We get rid of the clobber and replace it with replicas, and when, or if, the cops ask for them, we'll give them those items instead.'

'But where would I hide the clothes so that they won't be found?' I find myself asking.

'You'll think of somewhere,' he responds quickly. 'We'll say we heard them both come in around 1 a.m. That they woke us up but they were fine, nothing amiss, nothing unusual, and then we all went to bed.'

'But you said yourself they might've been captured on CCTV, Ed. How can you be sure they weren't picked up around the scene, at the time of the... accident?' I can't bring myself to say the M word again.

'They'll have cameras inside and outside the club premises, but I'm pretty certain there aren't any cameras down by the railway arches, where Con says the fight happened.'

'*Pretty* certain?'

'It's wasteland – nothing there except for prossies, druggies and rough sleepers.'

'How would you know?' I pull my chin into my chest.

Ed rolls his eyes. ''Cause I just do. Everyone knows what it's like up there.'

'Well, I don't, and... and no... no, Ed, we can't.' I'm shaking my head. 'We can't do this – it's wrong, it's immoral... it's a crazy idea, and...'

'Tee. *Tee.*' He grasps my shoulders, his nose almost touching my own as he pulls me in close. '*Listen to me.* We get rid of the clothes. We tell the old bill that we think – *that we know* – we heard the kids come in around 1 a.m., OK?'

I open my mouth to speak, but my thoughts are like a thousand-piece jigsaw all loose in my head.

'We'll brief the kids on what to say to the cops, get their stories straight, and ours.' Ed continues pacing, tapping a finger on his lips as he verbalises his stream of consciousness. Just watching him is exhausting. 'We'll plead ignorance, say they were unwitting witnesses and didn't even realise until they watched the news... In fact, yeah! Maybe you're right – maybe we should go to the police *first*, pre-empt them, tell them that the kids *were* at the crime scene, that they'd *seen* Reynolds but didn't come into contact with him, didn't think anything of it at the time... That way, any forensics they might find at the scene – DNA, footprints, fibres or whatever – can be explained. We'll make out that we're helping them with their enquiries, that we've nothing to hide and are happy to assist in any way we can...'

'Lie you mean?'

'What other choice do we have?' Ed throws his hands up at the ceiling. 'Do you want to turn our son over to the police? And before you say it,' he says, watching as I once again open my mouth to speak, 'they'll not go easy on him, be lenient or whatever it is you think. He's a Carter for one thing,' he adds with a splash of bitterness. 'The justice system doesn't exist for the likes of us. Look at what they did to me.' He stabs his chest with a pointed finger. 'They tried to have me up for murder when I wasn't aware anyone had even been murdered, not at first anyway. I was only asked to drive the car! I thought I was helping a mate out...'

I'm still shaking my head as I raise an eyebrow at him.

'OK, so I knew it was *something* dodgy; it was Billy Noye's job after all, but when that slippery bastard asked you to do something, you did it, no questions asked.' Ed's animated now – no doubt this whole nightmare has triggered him. It certainly has me.

He stops pacing for a second. The kitchen really isn't big enough to expunge all his nervous energy, and in truth, it's starting to get on my frazzled nerves.

'But we *can't* lie, Ed.' My voice is a nasal whine. 'This man, he's dead. *Dead*. And whoever he is, he's someone's son, someone's brother, a father-to-be apparently. What about *his* mother? What about *his* family? They have a right to know what happened, don't they? We would want to know the truth if the shoe were on the other foot – you know we would!'

Ed places his palms down on the work surface, looks down at the fake wooden flooring and exhales loudly. I notice a piece of the lino has come loose at one corner and has begun to peel away.

'The *truth*, Tee? The truth only depends on who you believe, doesn't it? It's all about perception. And what about *our* family? If Con gets done for this, then his life is finished, over, kaput. He'll be tarnished forever, and—'

'But *you* did, Ed – you came back from it, didn't you?' I remind him. 'You made a mistake, a bad choice when you were young *and stupid*. But you haven't let it define you; haven't let it ruin your life, have you?'

'Haven't I?' He gives a little derisive snort as he turns towards me. 'Look at us, Tee. Look at the state of this floor.' He kicks the peeling lino with his bare toes. 'Look at this house – everything's falling apart, old and on its last knockings.'

'We do OK,' I sniff, mildly affronted. This house and everything in it may be old, but it's *our* house, and I keep it immaculate. You could eat your dinner off this kitchen floor.

'The window-cleaning business just about pays the bills. There's nothing left for anything extra, and you have to scrub some stuck-up bitch's house for a living to make sure your mum's cared for, which makes me feel like a failure...' He rakes his hands through his hair, just like Con did earlier. 'We can barely make ends meet. If I'd never been stupid enough to get involved in all that business years ago, then who knows what I would've gone on to achieve? No one wants to employ a failed armed robber... Shit sticks!'

'You were the getaway driver,' I say weakly. 'You weren't the one holding the gun, the one who used it on that poor man who lost his life. You never even knew they were armed! You only did it for us, for me and Cora, for a bit of extra money and—'

'And look what happened. I was behind the iron door when our Cora passed... didn't even get to hold her, to be there for her, or for you. Never even got to say goodbye...'

I break down at the mention of her name, big fat tears leaking down my cheeks as I start to sob into the sleeve of my dressing gown.

'I've never forgiven myself for that, Tee, never.' He takes me in his arms once more. 'I swore to you when I got out that I'd never let you down ever again.'

'I know you did,' I splutter into his chest.

'Well, I'm not about to start now. We'll get our Conor out of this mess somehow, sweetheart, OK?'

'He won't be able to live with it,' I sob quietly. 'I know that boy inside out. He has a conscience. It'll mess up his head. It'll mess up mine too...'

Ed snorts. 'Not as much as a stint inside will, trust me. And I know the Reynolds family of old. They're all wrong 'uns, Tee. Thieves and drug dealers and scroungers – rats, the lot of them.'

'Even if that's true, it doesn't make it right, does it?' I can't hide the incredulity in my voice. 'Doesn't mean it's OK to mur — accidentally kill someone and say nothing? And what about Paris in there? What about *her*? You've seen her – the poor girl looks absolutely traumatised.' I don't, at this stage, voice the nagging misgivings I have about Paris's demeanour because I can't put my finger on them. I suspect that maybe she – maybe both of them – aren't telling us the whole story, that they're holding something back, but whatever it is, it could hardly be any worse. Could it?

'Her parents will know something's wrong. And what if she can't hold it in? What if she tells them everything that's happened? This is the Levinsons we're talking about here... He's an MP for Christ's sake, a politician, a—'

'Corrupt, no-good liar himself!' Ed interjects. 'Come on, Tee – like you said, he's a politician. You can tell when he's lying because his lips move... Do you honestly think he's going to want a scandal like this on his doorstep? Highly respected member of the community with a murderer for a daughter? The press will annihilate him. His opponents will destroy him. My bet is that the Levinsons will want it kept as quiet as we do.'

I didn't want it kept quiet though; I wanted it not to have happened in the first place, and even Ed couldn't fix that.

'You don't know that!' I shriek. 'What if they decide to go to the police and say it was all our Con's fault, minimise Paris's part in it, or eliminate it altogether and let him take the rap for it? What if they grass us up and say we tried to coerce them into staying silent? We can't go up against the likes of the Levinsons. They've got more money and clout than you or I will ever see in this lifetime.'

I instantly regret my choice of words. Ever the optimist, Ed likes to believe that we're only one number away from winning the lottery, one year away from his business going stratospheric, one season away from our Conor getting picked for a premiership side...

'We'll ask her to keep quiet,' he says with a shrug. 'She'll not want to bring the family name into disre— whatever it's called.'

'Disrepute,' I offer miserably.

'You see?' He touches my nose with his finger. 'This is why I married you... You've always been good with words.'

'Not when it comes to police interrogation I haven't,' I shoot back.

There's a moment's pause as we stand together, embracing in the kitchen. I suppose, blessed with perfect hindsight, that somewhere in that moment I knew, deep down, what I was agreeing to, even if I hadn't yet verbalised it. I wasn't thinking with my head. It was my heart that was screaming out in pain and protest. It was my heart that was prepared to say or do anything to protect our son and keep him out of harm, *out of prison*. It was a mother's unconditional and desperate love. Yet, as Ed searched my eyes with his own, I knew that neither of us could've possibly predicted just where making such a decision would take us, how it would change everything. And what I would become as a result.

'We'll be obstructing a police investigation.' I rub my cheek against his soft skin in a bid to self soothe. 'Accessories to murder... We'll be guilty of harbouring a criminal, perverting the course of justice, call it what you will... We *will* get caught, Ed, and we'll go down with him, all of us. Then who'd look after Mum? Who'd look after the house? Who'd—'

A sob catches in my tight throat.

'We *won't* get caught. I promise you. I'll make sure of it somehow, Tee.'

I believed him. I wanted so much to believe him.

'I'm a terrible liar,' I tell him. 'Two things always float to the surface: rubbish and the truth. We can't take that kind of risk – you know we can't!'

He laughs a little then, and for a fleeting moment, it's like balm to my broken soul.

'No risk, no story, Tee. And you'll just have to act.' He strokes my hair softly; tucks a piece behind my ear. 'It shouldn't be too difficult – you've been married to me long enough after all.'

'It's not funny, Ed!' I snort softly. But that's Ed for you – he finds the funny in everything.

'They'll never believe us,' I say after a moment. 'The police – they'll see straight through us and know that we're covering for him. They'll try and break us down, break the kids down... *They'll know*, Ed, c'mon.'

He kisses my forehead as I drop my face onto his chest again, wishing, praying I could open my eyes and wake up to this all being just some hideous nightmare.

'It won't matter if they don't believe us. It's all just a game, a battle of wits. If they haven't got the evidence to prove it, then they can suspect whatever they like. Without enough hard evidence, it'll be circumstantial, our word against theirs. And it won't be enough to go to trial, let alone get a conviction. We'll just have to hold our nerve, OK?'

I knew it was wrong. I knew that everything about what Ed was suggesting was morally and ethically wrong on so many levels, but there was something unspoken between us, an unwavering shared sense of purposeful instinct to protect our son that seemed to bypass any rational judgement. In that moment, it almost seemed justifiable because the alternative was just too distressing to contemplate.

I meet my husband's eyes. I've always felt like I'm standing in the sunshine every time Ed looks at me.

'We're going to get through this, Tee,' he says with such conviction that it's difficult not to believe him. 'You, me and Conor. Just do as I say, and it'll be OK.' He looks into my eyes; searches them for uncertainties. '*OK, Tee?*'

And then the doorbell rings.

EIGHT

CHRISTINE

We stare at each other, silent but for the ringing in our ears, the proverbial rabbits in headlights.

Ed nods. 'I'll go.'

'No!' I lunge at him; pull him back from the door. 'What if it's the police? What will we say to them?'

The shrill scream of the bell ringing for a second time startles me, and I cover my mouth with my hand as my adrenalin spikes.

'Let's get them both upstairs,' Ed hisses, springing into action. 'The pair of them, quick.'

We burst into the living room, and he turns to Conor. 'Go on upstairs, both of you.' He shoos them from the room. 'And don't come down unless I come and get you, OK?'

I can barely breathe through the stiff girdle of panic that's wrapped itself around my upper chest cavity as I watch my Con take Paris's hand and scurry from the room.

'It's not them.' Ed is breathless as he peers through the living-room blinds. 'It's not the cops.'

Relief floods through me, warm and comforting like a bath, though it's painfully fleeting.

'Who the hell is it then?' I whisper as I move towards the front door next to him. I hear low voices coming from behind it.

'Let *me* do all the talking and just agree with everything I say, OK?' It's a man's voice. 'I said, *OK?*'

'Yes, of course.' The thin female voice sounds faintly familiar as I reach across Ed and pull the door open.

Then I take a step backward; watch as the expression on her face mirrors my own surprise back to me. It's Helen Levinson and her husband, Bryan – Paris's parents. Oddly, it suddenly strikes me that this is the first time I've ever actually seen them together in all the months that I've been working for them.

'Christi— *Christine?*' Helen's eyes widen in shock, like she momentarily hadn't been able to place me but now that she has, she's as perplexed as I am as to why she's here, *on my doorstep*. How do they even know where we live? I've never told Helen my address; have never needed to. I'm one of many employed to work for the Levinsons via an agency, Continental Cleaners, and I'm fairly certain they wouldn't give out my personal details without my permission. Perhaps Paris called them, though that seems unlikely as she was still crying on the sofa before we shooed them upstairs and hasn't been near her phone as far as I've seen.

In the few months I've been cleaning the Levinsons' huge house – one of them at least – Helen has barely acknowledged me unless it's to hand me one of her lengthy to-do lists. Though not unpleasant as such, generally she doesn't seem to engage with staff unless necessary. That's always suited me just fine – I've only ever wanted to get the job done, get paid, and get out of there.

I blink at her, slightly shrouded by her husband's imposing bulk, her hair freshly blow-dried, dressed in an expensive-looking lounge suit and a black coat with what appears to be real fur around the hood.

'H-Helen! *Bryan!*' I swallow back my unease as they stare

back at me, one of their expensive cars glinting in the background behind them, conspicuous among the other average vehicles that line our street. I give Ed a nervous sideways glance. 'Please come in.'

Bryan strides through the door first with purpose – or perhaps entitlement is more accurate. Helen, almost subservient, follows behind. Something about the dynamic between them strikes me as strange, like opposing magnets rubbing each other the wrong way. I catch the look on Bryan's face as he steps straight into our living room, which incidentally is roughly the same size as Helen's walk-in closet and *definitely* smaller than her kitchen. I know it shouldn't matter, given the gravity of the situation, but suddenly I feel self-conscious about my home, how small and modest and shabby it is comparatively. I can tell what they're thinking. *Do people really live like this?*

'What a... *lovely* home you have, Christine!' Helen speaks first as she surveys my humble but spotlessly clean abode. She glances around the lounge almost in childlike awe, like she's visiting Disneyland for the first time or something. I can't tell if she's being condescending or genuine. 'Very cosy... very inviting, and so... *immaculate!*'

Bryan glares at her with displeasure, but his expression instantly softens when he catches me noticing.

'Mum!'

Paris comes rushing down the stairs as soon as she hears her mother, still wearing my old dressing gown, her face a frightful mess of tears and snot. Conor is right behind her.

'Paris! Whatever's happened?'

Helen stares at her daughter in horror, frozen like a statue, but she doesn't go to her.

'Shall we sit down?' I sound more serious than I intend to, but I'm in a state of shock myself. 'I didn't even realise you knew where we lived, Helen? Did you call your parents, Paris?' I turn to her, and she glances up at her father.

'Actually, no.' Bryan steps forward then and puts his hand out to shake mine, like he's meeting me for the first time. Come to think of it, perhaps he actually is, formally at least. Bryan would probably pass by most of his employees if he ever saw one of us on the street. Despite his carefully cultivated 'man of the people' image, I sense he secretly views fraternising with the staff as beneath him.

'It's me, Christine,' I say. 'I work for you. In fact, I was due to come to your house today, only...'

'*Only* we seem to have run into a bit of a problem.' His voice cuts through my shaky response. 'Helen, Bryan...' He strides towards them with purpose, his hand outstretched. 'Ed... Ed Carter. Pleased to meet you both.'

Helen steps forward first but is beaten to it by Bryan.

'*This* is your husband?' She turns to me with a look on her face that I can't quite translate, but it's gone as quickly as it appears. 'I was just saying what a lovely home you have, wasn't I, Christine?'

'Thank you,' Ed replies graciously. 'Too small to keep secrets in' – he chuckles jovially – 'but it's ours. Obviously you already know my wife, Christine,' Ed says before I can respond, placing his hand lightly, reassuringly, around my waist. 'And this is our son, Conor.'

Helen glances over at him and moves to stand by Paris. My poor Con looks pale and frightened, and I desperately want to go to him, but I'm paralysed. For a moment, no one speaks or moves.

'Bryan Levinson. It's a pleasure to meet you too, Carter. We apologise for coming here unannounced like this, but we've been looking for our daughter... Paris, darling...' Bryan places a hand on her shoulder. 'Are you OK?'

I think I see Paris recoil from him slightly in my peripheral vision though I could've imagined it.

'Where have you been? We've been worried sick.' He looks

up a little sharply. 'Would someone mind telling me just what's happened?' I hear the tightness in his voice. 'Why our daughter is here, in your house?'

It's a perfectly reasonable question, even though they haven't answered my own yet as to how they *knew* she was here in the first place. Did they have a tracker on Paris's phone? It's the only logical explanation I can think of right now.

'I think,' Ed says sagely, 'that we'd better sit down.' He gestures towards the sofa; begins to explain to them how we were woken a short while earlier by their daughter and our son, about the altercation that took place last night that had tragically seen a young man – a man named Mathew Reynolds – accidentally lose his life.

Helen watches Ed intensely, silently scanning him with her small dark eyes as he speaks.

'Jesus Christ!' Bryan's gruff tone slices through my conscious thoughts like a machete. He's giving a much more convincing display of shock and horror and disbelief than Helen. 'You... you stupid, *stupid* girl!' He turns to Paris, unable, for a brief moment, to disguise his anger. 'Do you even realise what you've done? Do you realise what this means, for all of us?'

Paris starts to cry then, and Conor places a protective arm around her. The gesture alone tells me that he thinks a lot of her.

'It was my fault,' Con suddenly says. 'He... he was harassing her, and—'

'Let's all just stay calm, OK?' Ed interjects firmly but gently, with just the right balance between the two. 'It was an accident, OK? No one meant for him to die. We need to sort this out – decide what's best to do.' His hand is still resting gently on my waist, and I notice Helen's eyes are drawn to it.

I know what's best for us to do. What's best is that we tell the police the truth, but instead I say, 'I'll make us some tea,' and I stand suddenly, the momentum causing my thin dressing gown to open slightly and expose a flash of my upper thigh. Embarrassed, I wrap it tighter around me.

'I'll help you.' Helen follows me into my tiny galley kitchen – three's a squeeze and there's no dishwasher – and once again I'm conscious of the divide between us.

'Oh God, Helen, I'm so sorry about this...' I turn to her, on the verge of tears, apologising as I flip the switch on the plastic kettle, my hands visibly shaking. 'It's all been such a terrible shock... I didn't even know Paris and Conor knew each other until this morning, let alone were dating, did you?'

She shakes her head softly. 'No... I had no idea, I...'

'It's... it's just awful,' I splutter. 'How could something like this have happened? My Con would never even hurt a fly...' Helen watches me, almost fascinated, as I haphazardly throw teabags into a mismatched collection of chipped and stained mugs. 'What do you think we should do?'

'I think we should let the men sort it out,' she says after a moment's pause. 'Your husband looks like... a very capable man.'

'My Ed? Yes, well, he is.' I clutch my chest lightly. 'I suppose I'm lucky, in that respect.'

'You've been married long?'

The small-talk question surprises me a touch, given what she's just heard has happened.

'You could say that!' I somehow manage a small smile. 'I've known him practically my whole life.'

'Oh? Childhood sweethearts? How *perfect*.'

'We met at primary school,' I find myself saying, 'started dating each other when I was just thirteen, married at eighteen. Like I said, I've known him – I've loved him – more or less all my life.'

'You have a beautiful home, Christine,' she says, watching me a little strangely.

'Thank you,' I say, convinced she's simply being polite. 'It was— well, it still is my mum's house actually. It's tiny, as you can see, but it's ours, and we love it. Lucky to have it.'

She's awkwardly close to me.

'And your mother? Is she still with us?'

I exhale heavily; start stirring the tea. 'Sort of.'

'Sort of?'

'She lives in a care home now. She has... dementia. In fact' – I glance behind her at the clock on the wall. It's 7.38 a.m. – 'I'm due to see her later today – was planning to head up after I'd finished my session at your place.'

'I'm sorry,' Helen says, dropping her head to one side. 'That must be hard on you. I didn't know.'

'Oh, please, don't worry.' I attempt to smile, but my facial muscles feel locked. 'Why would you? I work for you; we're not friends—' I stop myself. 'Sorry, I didn't mean that to sound how it did...'

'It's fine.' Helen waves a hand. 'Perhaps we can *become* friends? Looks as though we might need to after this...' She smiles at me warmly – makes it sound easy. She really doesn't seem too distressed by this whole tragic event, the fact that our respective offspring have committed the ultimate sin and killed someone. Maybe it simply hasn't hit her yet.

'Helen...' I meet her eyes, which now I think of it appear a touch glazed, though it's still early. 'I... I think Ed wants to try and cover it up, this... this *accident*.' My voice drops down to a whisper. 'He doesn't... *we* don't want our boy to go to prison. He... he's everything we have – he's *all* we have, aside from each other – and he's a talented football player, and he has such a bright future ahead of him, and—' I bite my lip, bury my head into my hands and start to cry. 'Oh God, this is awful... it's *so* awful. I don't want him to go to prison, and yet I know I can't be part of such a terrible lie either.'

Helen places a comforting arm around my shoulder. I know

I shouldn't have said anything, but I just can't hold it in any longer, and I wanted to sound her out, to get her take on it.

'Try not to panic,' she says reassuringly. 'Bryan knows people, important people... We'll just have to stick together.'

'Really?' I can't believe how calm and together she seems. 'I'm worried that we'll all go to hell if we try and cover this up, or prison, or both! Your husband's an MP for God's sake, and I'm a terrible liar...'

Helen squeezes my shoulder. 'I think,' she says, her tone friendly, 'that you should come back to the house with me. Do your cleaning session just as planned, and then go and see your mum. Whatever happens, I'll be here to support you, Christine. We can support each other, OK?'

I sniff back my tears, mildly embarrassed by my emotional display. She glances down at my robe. It's not silk, but it looks like it, and she lightly touches the edge of it with the tips of her fingers. Then she adjusts it like a wife would straighten her husband's tie. I feel my awkwardness return, though maybe she's simply being nice. This is as much as she's ever spoken to me in all the months I've worked for her. I suppose I've automatically, subconsciously always thought that the Levinsons are somehow above us because of all the money they have. It's hard not to feel inferior against such exorbitant wealth.

'What about the police?' My voice drops down a notch. 'What will we say—'

Just then, the doorbell rings, and Helen quickly peers through the kitchen door. A rush of adrenalin explodes inside my solar plexus as I catch a glimpse of a blue flashing light from the window.

'Looks like we're about to find out.'

NINE

DAN

'Nice car, all things considered,' I say to Davis as we pull up at 25 Albert Road, surveying the shiny Bentley that's parked outside the address. I say 'all things considered' not in a judgemental way, but this is a notoriously run-down estate. The row of tiny two-up, two-down Victorian workers' cottages have stood here since 1881, and in brutal honesty some of them look like it too. Number 25 stands out as it's clear that the occupants take pride in its appearance. Arguably, it's the best-kept house on the street.

'Run a plate check on the Bentley's reg, will you, Davis?' I say. 'See who it belongs to. Looks like the Carters may have important visitors.'

'Gov.' She nods, pulling out her phone.

Ed Carter, an ex-con, runs a small window-cleaning business, which, while I'm sure it keeps the wolf from the door, is hardly big league – or Bentley league for that matter.

'Well, well,' Davis remarks a few minutes later as she kills the call.

'Don't tell me,' I pre-empt her. 'Bryan Levinson.'

'You're psychic, gov.' She raises a sardonic eyebrow. 'So,

what do you think the Levinsons are doing here, at the Carters' humble residence, at 7.45 a.m. on a Sunday morning? Bit early for a social call, isn't it?'

But before I can answer her, my phone rings.

'Riley?'

It's Superintendent Gwendoline Archer, my immediate boss. And I'm pretty sure I know what the purpose of the call is going to be. Maybe Davis is right and I *am* psychic.

'Ma'am?'

'Where are you?' she demands.

'Outside number 25 Albert Road, hopefully just about to speak to the Carters. We need eyes on the young couple we identified from the CCTV footage last night, Conor Carter and Paris Le—'

'Levinson,' she interjects, 'yes, well, that's what I'm calling about.'

I thought so.

'You are aware, I'm sure, of who the girl's father is?'

'Yes, ma'am. She's Bryan Levinson's daughter, the MP.'

'Exactly.' She clears her throat and, I imagine, bristles slightly. 'Which is why I want – *why I'm asking* – you to proceed with caution, Dan.'

Uh-oh, she's using my first name. This doesn't bode well.

'As you know, Bryan Levinson is a prominent individual,' she continues measuredly. 'He's a... respectable man, does a lot of great charity work and... and he's an associate of Commissioner Lennard – in fact they're friends.'

Davis is watching me – Archer is on loudspeaker – and she's raising her eyebrows at me comedically. I pull a face at her, silently mouthing the word, 'Stop.'

'OK.' I draw the word out. 'So?'

'So don't go in there like a bull in a china shop, Riley. Speak to the Carters first, get the jimmy on them before you pay the Levinsons a visit, and when you do, just make sure you're on your best behaviour. The commissioner doesn't want any unnecessary upset – or attention.'

'But I thought all publicity is good publicity, ma'am? And no, of course not. We'll save the *unnecessary upset* for Mathew Reynolds's family, shall we?'

She audibly exhales. 'Don't get smart, Riley – it really doesn't become you. These kids, they're not suspects, so don't treat them as such. Mitchell tells me they're simply potential witnesses who may or may not have encountered our victim last night.'

'That's right, ma'am,' I say, adding, 'currently, at least,' as much to annoy her as anything.

'Well, the commissioner is keeping a close eye, just be mindful of that. He's going to put in a call to Bryan Levinson; thinks it best we speak to the girl with him present... He wants to set something up at the station and—'

'No need, ma'am.'

'What?'

'The Levinsons are already here, at the Carters' address.'

There's a moment's silence on the line. I know what Archer's thinking though because I'm thinking it too. Despite our brittle exchanges and innate ability to rub each other up the wrong way, Archer hasn't reached the lofty position she has by being naïve – or stupid.

'Why would the Levinsons be at Conor Carter's house?'

'I'll let you know as soon as we find out, ma'am,' I say, hanging up before she can say any more.

I don't know much about Bryan Levinson other than that he likes to portray himself as a 'man of the people'. His constituency is largely made up of ordinary, everyday hard-working folk like the Carters, his manifesto based upon understanding the 'average working man and woman's needs and struggles'. But even I, with my admittedly limited understanding and interest in politics, can see that while he may be championing the 'everyday folk', he most certainly isn't one of them.

Davis rings the bell. I think I hear movement inside the house, footsteps on stairs, and I detect a hum of low voices. We wait for a moment before Davis presses it again then pokes her head around the window.

'Here we go, gov... someone's coming.'

Eventually, the door swings open, and a man who looks to be in his early forties opens it. He's wearing a pair of grey joggers and a fitted white T-shirt that accentuates his well-built arms, standard Sunday attire for your 'everyday folk'.

'Mr Carter? Ed Carter?'

'Yes. I'm Ed Carter,' he replies pleasantly, yet I detect a hint of caution. 'And you are?'

'Detective Chief Inspector Riley – Dan Riley. And this is DS Lucy Davis.' We flash our respective badges. 'Would it be OK if we come in?'

TEN

DAN

I could be wrong, but I'm getting the sense that Mr Carter here isn't as completely shocked to see us as he'd have us believe.

The first thing I notice upon entering the property is just how clean it is. It smells fresh, like newly washed laundry. I recognise Bryan Levinson immediately. He's often in the local news, his face plastered all over charity events and campaigns. With his natty expensive suits, light tan and white teeth, I've always thought that there's a slight whiff of game show host about him.

The woman standing in the doorway must be his wife, Helen Levinson, a face I also vaguely recognise from various press appearances. Well presented in a demure yet expensive-looking leisure suit, her hair immaculately styled, she's the perfect accessory to her charismatic husband, and yet something in her expression right now tells me all might not be well.

'This is my wife, Christine,' Carter says as another woman – smaller, younger, attractive, wearing a silky robe – appears from the doorway. I notice that her hands are very lightly shaking.

'Hello,' she says quickly.

'And these are our friends, Bryan and Helen Levinson,' Ed Carter says.

Friends? Don't get me wrong, it's not that I don't believe him; it just comes across as somewhat unlikely is all. The Carters and the Levinsons are clearly from very different worlds.

'Detective Chief Inspector.' Bryan Levinson stands and shakes my hand firmly as he addresses me. His presence is overpowering, much like the aftershave he's wearing. 'I think I may know your boss, Superintendent Gwendoline Archer, and Commissioner Lennard is a good pal of mine. Great to meet you. You guys do one hell of a fantastic job – I want you to know that.'

'Thank you,' I reply. 'It's a pleasure.' A second or two of slightly awkward silence ensues.

'Can I offer you both a cup of tea – or coffee? It's so cold outside today...' Christine Carter pipes up.

'Thanks, Mrs Carter,' Davis says. 'Tea would be nice.'

She nods and hurries off into the kitchen.

I cut to the chase, addressing Ed Carter.

'We're here because, regrettably, the body of a young man was discovered down by the railway arches in the early hours of this morning, and we have reason to believe that your respective son and daughter attended the same club last night as the deceased. Is it possible to speak with them? Are they here?'

'Yes.' Carter nods. 'They're upstairs, in bed, sleeping. They had a bit of a late night, didn't get in until oneish. Woke me and Tee up, crashing and banging about.' He chuckles lightly as he gives a little eye roll. 'Teenagers.'

'I'll go and wake them, shall I?' Helen Levinson suddenly speaks, and I clock the sharp look her husband gives her.

'No bother, Helen. I'll...' Ed Carter makes to move.

'It's really no bother, Ed,' she quickly interjects. I notice that she softly pronounces her Rs more like Ws. 'You stay here with the policeman. I'll go and check if they're awake...' She's already halfway up the stairs.

'I hope we aren't ruining your plans this morning,' I say, remembering Archer's warning. 'This shouldn't take long. Just some standard questions and then we'll leave you people to enjoy your day.'

'Yes, well, we came to pick Paris up, then we're heading off to church,' Levinson says affably. 'Aren't we, Helen?' he adds as she re-enters the room moments later.

'What's that, darling? Yes, oh yes! We came to pick up Christine; she works for us you see, as one of our clean— our domestic employees.' She smiles brightly at Ed Carter.

Bryan Levinson has just told us they're here to pick up their daughter on their way to church. *So which is it?*

'Is that how you became friends?' Davis addresses Helen airily. 'Through Mrs Carter working for you?'

'Yes, that's right,' Bryan Levinson answers for her. 'That's how our Paris and Connell met too.'

Did he just say *Connell*?

'Ah, look, here they are now. Paris, Connell, this is Detective Inspector Dan Riley. He's just popped by to speak to you both about a body that's been found down by the railway arches. Some poor young soul's been found beaten to death, and the detective here thinks you may have been at the same nightclub as him last night.'

Funny, but I don't recall mentioning *how* Reynolds had died – that he was beaten to death – although Bryan Levinson could've already watched the news, I guess.

'Hello.' I nod at the young couple as they enter the living room, eyes wide and looking a little dishevelled. I introduce myself and Davis. 'Thank you for speaking to us. We're sorry to have woken you up.'

'It's no bother, is it, Con?' Ed Carter prompts his son. 'Had to get out of his pit anyway, didn't you? He's got training this morning.' He turns to me proudly. 'He's a talented player, this one. Got trials coming up for Crystal Park no less, Premier League! You a football fan, Dan?'

I have no problem with Ed Carter addressing me informally – it's my name after all – only there's something in his inflection... an edge to it that unsettles me. Frankly, this whole situation is beginning to unsettle me.

I hold my hands up. 'I confess, I don't really get the chance to watch much sport, not in my line of work. Though I enjoyed playing football as a boy.' It's a white lie. In fact, I hated playing football as a child. I was left footed *and* flat footed, and my particularly disagreeable PE teacher, Mr Blundell, used to call me 'Donkey Daniel', but I want to put Conor Carter at ease, find some common ground.

'Conor,' I address him gently, 'were you and Paris at Renton's nightclub last night?' I glance at Paris, who's sitting on the green sofa next to her father. Her body language is rigid, and she's staring at the floor, almost as if she's in a trance.

'Yeah, we were at Renton's.' He runs a hand through his thick mop of dark hair.

'Can you tell us what time you arrived at the club and what time you left?' Davis pulls out a notebook. I can feel the tension in the room rising like heat. It's almost as palpable as Levinson's aftershave.

'Um... well... I dunno,' he says. 'S'pose we got there around nineish maybe?'

'OK. And when you were inside the club, did you see anyone you know, meet up with friends, speak to anyone in particular?'

Conor Carter briefly glances over at his father.

'It's all right, Con,' Ed Carter says. 'You're not in any trouble... Just answer the policeman's questions as best you can.'

He turns to me then. 'She's underage you see,' he whispers,

nodding in Paris's direction. 'To be going into bars and clubs I mean.'

'We're not here to talk about that,' I assure him. 'We just need a few details. You see, we checked the CCTV footage from the club—'

'CCTV?' Bryan Levinson suddenly says. I suspect he's the type of man who prefers asking questions to answering them. He's a politician after all.

'That's right, sir,' I say, playing to his ego, which, again I suspect, is sizeable.

'No,' Conor replies. 'It was just me and Paris. We didn't speak to anyone else, except for maybe the staff...'

'Paris?' Davis turns to her for confirmation.

She wipes her nose with her sleeve. 'No, no one.'

I pause. 'And you left the club at what time, roughly?'

Conor glances at his dad again. 'Around midnight maybe?'

'And where did you go after that?'

'Home – back here.'

'Together?'

'Yeah.'

I look over at Paris, and she nods in agreement.

'What route did you take home?'

Levinson stands then. 'I'm sorry, er, Riley isn't it?'

I nod. 'That's right, sir. You can call me Dan.'

'Dan, OK, great. Brilliant. Yes. Can I ask why or how this is relevant to the body you found down by the arches? Do you think the kids may have seen him – come into contact with him? Perhaps it would be easier to do this down at the station. We could speak with Gwen...'

Gwen!

I pause again. 'No need, sir – not at this stage anyway.'

'Well, we did walk down by the arches, down by the abandoned railway bridge...' Conor offers.

'Would that be your usual route home?' Davis asks, pen poised.

'No... well, yeah... well, sort of...'

Now he looks a little spooked; his eyes begin darting between his parents and Paris. 'We went that way so that we could... you know, have a bit of a kiss. We were a bit... a bit drunk I s'pose.'

Davis nods her understanding.

'Did either of you see this man here?' I pass my phone to him – show him the image of Mathew Reynolds on it. 'Do either of you know him?'

Conor stares at the photo for a few moments though his expression remains static. 'No, I don't know him, but I saw him, yeah. We saw him last night, didn't we, Paris?' He shows her the phone. 'He walked past us, near the bridge under the arches. We were... we were kissing and drinking a beer... just chilling out... and, yeah, I think it was him.'

'That's great, Conor,' I say as he hands the phone back to me. 'What time was that, when he walked past you, do you remember?'

Conor puffs his cheeks out; shakes his head. 'I dunno. Gone midnight? Maybe ten, fifteen past – something like that?'

'Did he say anything to you? Speak to you, either of you? Did you see which direction he was headed, or if he was with anyone else, talking on his phone, anything?' I turn my attention to Paris once more. She's still looking down at her feet.

'No. Not that I remember, did he, Paris?'

She shakes her head; looks up nervously. 'No.'

'His name is Mathew Reynolds,' Davis says. 'He's a local twenty-four-year-old from the East Street estate.'

'Was,' Bryan Levinson corrects her. 'He *was* local.' He shakes his head. 'Terrible business, absolutely terrible... Such a young fellow as well. What a tragic waste of a life. And such a brutal death as well.' He tuts in quick succession. 'I should go and see his mother, offer my condolences and support.'

'I'm sure Mrs Reynolds would appreciate that, Mr Levinson,' I say, though inwardly I'm not entirely convinced. 'Mathew Reynolds was about to become a father. His girlfriend is due to give birth any day now.'

Christine Carter re-enters the room and emits a small gasp, placing both hands over her mouth to cover it.

'Oh no...' she says, obviously distressed. 'Oh no... How awful.'

I nod my agreement.

'So you'd never seen him before last night, and he didn't say anything to either of you as he passed you under the bridge, didn't turn to look back or acknowledge you in any way?'

'No, I've never seen him before until last night. And he walked straight past us – I remember 'cause we waited for him to go, so we could, you know... *carry on.*'

'Do you remember what he was wearing?' Davis asks.

'Umm... no, not really. I... we didn't take too much notice of him to be fair.'

'Yes, you were, busy,' I say, giving him a knowing smile. 'How about you, Paris? Can you remember anything about what he was wearing? His demeanour? Anything unusual about him?' Though as I say the words, I notice something unusual about *her*. Her hair – she's fiddling with it and has just tied it back off her face into a ponytail with an elasticated hair band. A pink one with a plastic bobble on it. Or what looks like half of one.

A jolt of adrenalin spikes inside me. I'm almost certain I found the other piece of it next to Reynolds's body, tucked away, just beneath his broken skull.

'A blue or black jacket or hoodie maybe, but... but I can't really remember any detail. I... I'd been drinking.' She glances at

Bryan Levinson again, and for the briefest moment, I'm sure I see a flicker of sheer terror flash across her pretty young face.

'And you didn't see anyone else there, down by the arches where you were, no one else at all.'

'No,' they say in unison.

I turn to Davis and give her a micro nod, signalling that it's time to wrap things up. I don't want us to outstay our welcome, not at this stage anyway.

I turn to Christine Carter. 'What time did the pair of them return home last night? Did you hear them come home?'

'Ummm... oh God...' She glances at her husband. 'I... er...' I can tell that she's holding her breath. Her pale face has flushed a little pink.

'It was around 1 a.m.,' Ed Carter interjects. 'Or thereabouts. I heard the front door go, heard them crashing about downstairs...'

'Yes!' Christine adds, her voice more animated now. 'It was definitely around that time because I remember thinking that I had to get up in a few hours to go to work.'

'Work?' I raise a sympathetic brow. 'On a Sunday?'

'Yes,' she says, dancing on the spot. 'Needs must and all that...'

'Well, I can certainly empathise,' I say as I stand. 'OK. That's about it then, for now. Thank you so much, all of you, for your time. You've been very helpful. We apologise for disturbing you this early on a Sunday morning. We'll be in touch if we need to speak to you again at any point.'

'Great to meet you, Riley.' Bryan Levinson stands up with an air of authority, the one in charge.

'I'm sorry we couldn't be of any more help,' Ed Carter cuts in. 'If the kids think of anything else, we'll be in touch.'

I thank him as I shake his hand once more.

'I'll leave you my card.' I hand it directly to Christine

Carter. 'It has my personal number on it. Don't hesitate to use it should you need to.'

She glances at it briefly; is still holding it between her fingers as Ed Carter closes the door behind us.

'So...' Davis is watching me expectantly, like an excited schoolgirl, as we walk back to the car. 'What do you think, gov?'

'I think, Davis,' I say, 'that they're lying.'

'Which one?'

'All of them.'

'About what?'

I turn the key in the ignition and glance sideways at her. 'Everything.'

ELEVEN

CHRISTINE

I knew as I made the familiar journey to Sunnyside care home that there was no coming back from this. It already felt too late. A line had been crossed, and it couldn't be uncrossed. We'd lied to the police. *I'd* lied to the police. Only it hadn't been my intention to. There had been no time for any proper discussion before they'd turned up unannounced on our doorstep. I felt as if I had no option but to follow my husband's narrative. I couldn't betray my own family, the two people I love most in the world. So, in spite of the guilt that was swelling and rising like dough in my stomach, I could see no other option but to fully commit myself to the lie.

'They know we're lying!' I gripped on to Ed the moment he'd shut the door behind the police. 'They could tell, especially that whatshisface... Detective Riley.'

Detective Riley had been apologetic about turning up impromptu so early on a Sunday morning and, mercifully, had kept the visit short. But the haste in which they'd suddenly appeared had meant there had been little or no time to arrange our ducks in any order, to get our story straight, to get a story at all.

I marvelled at Ed's ability to keep so calm and collected in front of the police. I felt like the weakest link. I couldn't stop shaking. My body's natural reaction to stress and trauma had betrayed me, made me feel exposed, like there was a giant great speech bubble above my head that read: 'We're lying! We're guilty! Arrest us!'

The tension in our tiny living room had snapped like an elastic band once the detectives had left. I exhaled loudly; I hadn't realised I'd been more or less holding my breath the whole time they'd been there.

'Just leave everything to me, Carter, OK.' Bryan Levinson had stood with an authoritative air. 'We'll do exactly as we've agreed. I'll be in touch.'

Ed later told me that Bryan Levinson had said that this Commissioner Lennard bigwig 'pal' of his 'owed him a favour or two', alluding to the fact that should anything come to light forensically, then he might be able to 'make it disappear'.

'That sounds like a line from a bad gangster film, Ed.' I looked at him, unconvinced. 'The police don't cover up a serious crime just because they're "mates" with someone... *do they?*'

'I told you them Levinsons are as bent as a nine-bob note,' Ed said derisively once Helen and Bryan had finally left our house, taking a worryingly pale-looking Paris with them. Oddly, I hadn't wanted her to go; had almost suggested that she should stay here, with us, but thought better of it at the last moment. Helen had wanted me to leave with them too, continue our day as planned. Only I'd needed some time to gather myself first and I'd desperately needed to speak to Ed.

'That Detective Riley, he didn't strike me as someone who's easily fooled.' I started to pace the room, taking up where Ed had left off, matching his footstep marks with my own. 'I'm convinced he knew something was amiss. And did you see the way Paris looked when her parents turned up? Something's not right, Ed!' I started picking at my lip. 'I'm worried that if push comes to shove, the Levinsons will sell our Conor down the river soon as look at him to save themselves.'

'Stop doing that, Tee... with your lip.' He gently moved my fingers away from my mouth. 'And that's why you're not going to tell them – tell anyone – where you're going to hide those clothes,' he replied. 'It'll be leverage if we ever need it.'

Now, I glance sideways at the holdall on the passenger seat of my Fiat 500 that contains my son's and Paris's bloodstained clothes – evidence in a murder inquiry. It's only now that I'm alone and have the space to think, to assess everything properly, that more questions start firing at me, putting me under siege.

How had the Levinsons known that Paris was at our house? Paris said she hadn't called them when I asked her, and I believed her. The poor girl could barely speak she was in so much shock. And yet there they suddenly were, large as life on our doorstep.

It hadn't escaped my notice either how Paris had visibly flinched from Bryan Levinson when he'd gone to comfort her – from both her parents in fact. I couldn't seem to get that image out of my head. It bothered me. It wasn't just fear that I'd sensed from her; it was something else, more along the lines of... *repulsion*.

And why had Con not told us he and Paris were an item in the first place? He'd never hidden girlfriends from us before. I didn't understand it. Any of it.

In truth though, it's Helen I can't stop thinking about. She'd just been so... *friendly*, so helpful and supportive, kind even. And, in direct contrast to me, cool as a gin and tonic on a hot summer's day throughout the police visit, almost blasé, like it was no biggie that her daughter was partly responsible for the death of a man and could potentially go down for it. Perhaps that's what being married to a wealthy MP affords you: protection from the authorities and the confidence not to care. She'd seemed far more interested in how long Ed and I had been married!

I try not to think then about the outstanding £6K debt we need to find to pay for mum's care. And if we can't meet the £5K a month that it costs to keep her at Sunnyside going forward, then we'll have no choice but to sell the house so that we can. And that sends me tailspinning into a black hole of despair, on top of everything else.

'Why don't you take one of my cars when you go to visit your mum today, Christine?' Helen offered earlier, once I'd finished cleaning her house. Though I say finished, the fact was I could barely lift the mop and bucket my mind was such an aching mess. For once though, the usually fastidious Helen had turned a blind eye.

'You can use the Merc – take her for a drive out somewhere in style.' Helen followed me around the room as I vacuumed on autopilot, my hands still shaking. 'It would be no trouble. It might even help you forget about things for a few hours?'

Quite how Helen could think that my driving around in a fancy car would make me forget that my son was basically a murderer and that we'd just lied to the police only proved what different worlds we occupied – and what different people we were. Or perhaps she was simply thinking along the same lines as I had been and was worried that *we* might go to the police before they could and tell them everything, put the lion's share of the blame onto Paris, and therefore was trying to keep me sweet. I suppose the Levinsons had just as much, if not more, to lose than we did.

'Oh no, really, it's OK,' I said, perhaps a little too readily. 'But thanks anyway, Helen. I really do appreciate the offer.'

She looked right at me then, almost through me somehow. Maybe it was because I was so on edge, but it caused my skin to prickle.

Parking my Fiat 500 in haste, I rush through the double

doors of Sunnyside's building, clutching the bulky holdall, which, now I think of it, looks somewhat conspicuous. *What the hell am I doing?*

'Christine! Hi!' Joy, one of Mum's carers, greets me with a warm smile. 'We were expecting you a little earlier today.' Her expression drops suddenly. 'Is everything OK?'

Great! It's written all over my face! I may as well be carrying a bloody neon placard.

'I'm fine, Joy, just tired.' I attempt to sound as casual as possible, only nothing ever truly sounds genuine when you're not being sincere. 'How's Mum been?'

'Well, put it this way – there's been some... *challenging* moments.' She smiles at me apologetically. 'Come on...' She takes my arm. 'She's been waiting patiently to see you.'

I know that Joy has said this for my benefit because the truth is Mum barely recognises me these days. And if she does, then it's only in painfully short-lived bursts. Dementia is a degenerative disease, and its name certainly suits it.

I clutch the holdall tightly as I enter Mum's room. It's nice, I suppose; clean, if a little sparse. But it's not her home, our house, where she should be, with us.

'Hello, Cynthia!' Joy booms as we enter. 'Look who's here to see you! I said she'd come, didn't I?'

Joy turns to me. 'She was getting in a right tizzy. Thought something bad had happened, didn't you, Cynthia?' She widens her eyes at me a touch. 'But look! She's here now, and she's brought you some things!' She glances down at the holdall. 'That'll cheer you up, won't it, my love?'

'She's been eating my biscuits, this one,' Mum says, narrowing her eyes at Joy. 'Been stealing my custard creams she has... there were five left in that packet yesterday, and she's had the lot! Look at her – no wonder she's the size of a house!' She starts snorting, 'Oink-oink!'

'Mum!' I swing round and clasp my mouth with my hand as I flush red. 'I'm so sorry, Joy. I...'

'It's OK, it's OK. Don't worry, love,' she says kindly, leaning in towards me and whispering, 'For the record, I prefer a Jammie Dodger myself. *Maaaaybe*,' Joy addresses Mum slowly, 'Christine here has brought you a new packet of biscuits, eh?'

Her eyes briefly hover over the holdall again. She cocks her head. 'You really don't look yourself today.'

I genuinely like Joy, but I wish she hadn't said that. I'm seconds away from coming apart.

'I'll leave you to it, eh?' she says gently as she retreats from the room.

I go over to Mum's bed, a bed she seems utterly resigned to now, like a coffin with blankets.

'Hello, Mum. How are you?' I kiss the top of her head. She smells like Nina Ricci's L'Air du Temps. It's always been her signature scent, ever since I can remember. Even when she's not wearing it, she still smells of it somehow, as if it's become part of who she is. Was.

'Can't hide nothing from that lot.' She leans towards me; taps the side of her temple with a finger. 'Trying to make me think I'm not the full pound note. Greedy, fat—'

'Mum! *Please.*' I can barely stand this at the best of times *but not today*.

Mum was always a polite and eloquent woman before her mind was ravaged by this awful disease, and the idea of her speaking to anyone in such a way would've been utterly abhorrent to her. It's a sad, stark reminder that while she still *looks* like my mum, she's no longer the mum I'd always known.

'What you doing here?' She looks at me suddenly, like she's seeing me for the first time. 'Why aren't you at school?'

'I left school a long time ago, Mum. I go to work now.'

She blinks at me, and I see the confusion behind her watery grey eyes. I exhale as I take her small, soft hand in my own.

What I wouldn't give for her to hold me again, to tell me everything will be OK like she has my whole life.

'Ed sends his love, Mum, and... and Conor too!'

'Ed? Who's Ed? Is Ed dead?' She chuckles then. Sometimes I think she does it on purpose.

'You know who Ed is,' I tell her resignedly. 'He's my husband. We've been together since I was thirteen – over thirty years ago now. You know this. You love Ed.'

'Oh yes, the criminal!' She snorts like a pig, something she never used to do. 'That useless, good-for-nothing idiot? Bring you down with him he will, that one!' She kisses her teeth. 'You could've done so much better for yourself, just like your sister, but you wouldn't listen.'

'I don't have a sister, Mum. I'm an only child, remember?' I'm at breaking point.

She stares at me. 'What's with the face? You look like you've lost a shilling and found a penny!' She starts to laugh again. 'Has something happened, Christine?'

For a second, she sounds just like she used to. She very briefly slips back into being my lovely mum again, only I know it's just a trick.

'Are you ill, sweetheart?' She taps the top of my hand with her free one.

'What's that, Mum?' I wipe my eyes; begin searching the room for somewhere to stash these bloody clothes.

I knew it was wrong, and I felt disgusted with myself, but the thought of hiding the items in Mum's room had come to me on the journey over. For some reason, I thought they might be safe there, for a while at least, and in truth I just couldn't think of anywhere else.

The small bedside cabinet would be too obvious; the old wooden wardrobe perhaps more so. *Think, Christine, c'mon...* The mattress! It's the only other option. I'll have to put the clothes under it and hide the trainers in the wardrobe, beneath the spare blankets. There's a chance one of the carers could find them though, when they change her bed sheets, something I know they do regularly. It costs £5K a month to keep my poor mum here with round-the-clock care and yet the people who do all the real caring probably don't even see half of that between them.

I take the clothing from the bag and begin stuffing it underneath the mattress, sliding it as far towards the middle as I can reach, silently praying that they won't be discovered.

'Just checking the bedclothes, Mum,' I say. 'It's freezing out, and I want to make sure you're warm enough.'

Could I hate myself any more than I do right in this moment? I don't think so.

'Got to run, Joy!' I call out to her as I make my hasty exit, still clutching the now empty holdall. 'I'll see you the day after tomorrow.'

There's a collection of large waste disposal units round the back of Sunnyside's premises. Choosing the green one in the middle, I look around me before I flip the lid open and throw the holdall in. I turn to leave; hesitate. Maybe I should've buried it deeper among the waste. *Shit.* I go back and randomly throw some rubbish over it. Was that enough? I throw more. Close the lid.

Hyperventilating, I start to make my way back towards my car, contemplating how I'm definitely going to hell, when I see her. She's leaning up against it, smiling at me and waving.

Helen.

TWELVE

DAN

It's been a deliberate move on my part not to publicly release the exact details of how Mathew Reynolds met his gruesome end. A strong sixth sense is telling me to sit on this information, at least for now. I want to wait and see what, if anything, comes back from forensics first. And I need more background info on Reynolds's life, to find out what he was up to and, most importantly, who might've wanted him dead – because someone sure as hell did.

I suppose I've been expecting something of an exhaustive list of potential suspects, given his sketchy background, but as it turns out, I may have been a touch presumptive. Because while it's no secret that Reynolds wasn't about to win any prizes for being a Good Samaritan, he didn't appear to have any real obvious enemies either, or at least none that would want to carve up his face and stab him in the neck until his life ebbed away.

'He doesn't have any outstanding debts either,' Davis informs me, 'or none that we've found. In fact, he was up to date with all his bills, judging by the bank statements we've got. His last large transaction was for a pram for the baby, purchased the day before yesterday at Babyworld.' She sighs. 'Interestingly though, a few months back it was a different story and he was very much in the red. That only seems to have changed in recent weeks. He had a very healthy bank balance when he died, gov – a little shy of twenty grand in fact.'

'Twenty grand?' I give a little whistle. 'Who says crime doesn't pay, eh, Davis? So do we know where it's come from? Is it legit?'

'Cash deposits largely, gov – untraceable provenance probably. Maybe Reynolds was more of a prolific dealer than we thought.'

I'm not convinced. From the intel we already have, he was only distributing small amounts of weed and coke and pills right up until his death, selling to locals on the estate primarily, and while I'm sure there was no lack of customers, he had to have been shifting far higher quantities of drugs than that to have reached the figures reflected in his bank account in such a short space of time. So where had this influx of cash suddenly come from? What had he got himself involved in?

We head over to Reynolds's house to speak to his mum and his heavily pregnant girlfriend, Alana, to see if they can throw some light on his recent business dealings.

'Valerie Reynolds?'

The diminutive woman who answers the door in a tatty dressing gown gives me a disdainful once-over. Her thin face looks pale, and her eyes, set far back in her skull, are bloodshot from crying. I see a brand-new fancy-looking pushchair parked in the small hallway, incongruous against the shabby decor, and my heart drops into my stomach.

'I'm DCI Dan Riley, and this is DS Lucy Davis...'

'Took their time, didn't they, eh?' she mutters, clearly unimpressed. 'Sending in the big guns... I s'pose you'd better come in, for all the good it'll do.'

It's no less of a welcome than I'd expected. This is East

Street estate after all, a notoriously run-down council project that houses some of the area's most impoverished families, ergo crime is a way of life here, a survival tool. As you can imagine, the police aren't exactly welcomed with bunting and cake.

'Do you know who done it yet? Who killed my Matty? And why can't I see him? Why won't you lot let me see him so I can say goodbye properly?' Valerie lights up a rolled cigarette from an ashtray on the plastic kitchen table, inhales deeply then launches into a tirade. 'Your lot won't give two shits about finding my son's murderer. He's just another drug-dealing lowlife to you, one less of 'em on the streets, eh? Only you didn't know him, did ya?'

'You're right, Valerie,' I say gently, 'we didn't know Mathew, which is why we're here. I realise this is an incredibly difficult time, and the shock must be terrible, the worst kind any mother, any parent, could have, and we're so sorry, Valerie. I can call you that, can't I? But I promise you, we're here to help.'

Her demeanour softens slightly then, her shoulders sagging like all the fight's suddenly gone out of her.

'I can't believe he's gone,' she sniffs, the veins in her neck protruding through her thin skin. 'He was only here yesterday, right at this table! Gabbling on about the baby, about all the stuff they'd been buying for it. He was due to be a dad, you know, any day now...' Her voice cracks at the edges as it trails off. 'I know he wasn't always a saint, but I'm telling you' – she wipes the tears from her eyes, but they keep replenishing, and she gives up; lets them slide down her sunken cheeks – 'he was absolutely chuffed at the thought of becoming a dad. He'd really got his act together these past couple of weeks. Stopped all that drinking and drugging nonsense... He wanted to be a good dad, not like the useless absent bastard his own was.' A sob catches in her throat. 'It would've been the making of him, and now, now I'm having to bury him, my own son, twenty-four years old! Dear God, help me...'

I pull up a chair and sit opposite her. 'Listen, Valerie, I understand how you feel about the police. And I understand why,' I say, meeting her eyes. 'But I want you to know, from the horse's mouth if you like, that while Mathew may not have been perfect, he didn't deserve to die like he did. He didn't deserve to die at all. I give you my word that I will do all I can in my power to find out who did this to your son and bring them to justice.'

'Justice? Ha!' She blows thick blue smoke through her nostrils. 'That don't exist for the likes of us. Trust me, if you'd grown up on this estate, then you'd have done what you could to survive, just like my Matty did.'

There's never going to be a good time to inform Valerie of the extent of the injuries her son suffered in his final moments, but she has a right to know, and it's my job to tell her. I slide my hand across the plastic table to meet hers and take a breath. I've been in the business of imparting dreadful, often unspeakable, details to the loved ones of victims for a long time now, and trust me when I say it never gets any easier. Each time is like the first all over all again.

Valerie looks down at my hand upon hers mistrustfully. 'What?' she says. 'What is it?'

'Mathew was beaten very badly about the face and stabbed in the neck with a sharp object, a broken bottle perhaps. He died as a result of the blood loss from a wound that severed his carotid artery. It would've been quick,' I say, largely to protect her feelings, 'and he was probably already unconscious when the fatal injury was inflicted. So, mercifully, it's unlikely he suffered for long.'

She blinks at me. 'Who... who would do that to him? What kind of animal...?'

Conor Carter and Paris Levinson come into my head then, an image of them savagely attacking Mathew Reynolds with their hands and feet, stabbing him with the beer bottle found at the scene, watching as the life drained from him. It seems unfathomable to believe that such an attractive young couple could or would be capable of committing such a violent crime, and yet I can't shake the idea that they're both involved in this somehow.

'Mathew – Matty – was he involved in something he shouldn't have been? We know he was a small-time dealer around the estate, and I'm not worried about that, Valerie, but I *am* worried about who he might've been mixing with. Can you shed any light on anything – anything at all that you think might be useful to us? Any names of associates, people he hung out with, any enemies he might've had, someone he could've upset, or owed money to... *anything?*'

Davis is making tea in the small kitchenette, heaping spoonfuls of sugar into cups, no doubt to help the medicine go down.

'Listen, Detective... Ronson...'

'Riley,' I gently correct her. 'But please, call me Dan.'

She meets my eyes with her own. They're so raw from crying that they've practically disappeared into her skull.

'I stopped knowing what that boy got up to when he was twelve years old. He never had a dad, or a decent father figure,' she says bitterly. 'And I had two more to worry about, to feed and clothe and take care of. I was always working, always away from the house. I couldn't keep tabs on him; I didn't have the luxury of being able to, so he just had to get on with it.'

She lights another roll-up; begins to suck on it. 'When you live on East Street that's what you do – you get on with it.' She snorts. 'The papers will say that he was dragged up, that he was a lowlife. But them people, them ones who judge, who look down their snooty noses, they ain't got a clue what it's like, what you have to do round here to get by. Matty weren't doing nothing that a hundred others weren't and aren't doing on this estate. He was no different. He got himself into a bit of bother here and there, lost his temper a few times, but it don't make him an evil monster, and it don't make me a terrible mother. I loved him, and I did me best with him, like I did with the rest of them.'

I nod; let her get it off her chest. The more she offloads, the more likely it is she'll tell us something that could prove useful.

'No one's blaming you,' I try to reassure her, but sadly, I suspect that she's probably right. 'Matty had almost twenty thousand pounds in his bank account when he died. Do you know anything about that? How he might've got hold of that kind of money?'

Her small, sunken red eyes suddenly double in size. 'Twenty grand? You're kidding me? *Twenty grand?* No! I've no idea. I had no idea he had that sort of money! If I had, I would've tapped him up for a piece of it, trust me.' She gestures around at the pokey, messy apartment with its old, mismatching furniture and shabby carpet.

'We're going to need to search the apartment, Valerie. Any laptops, phones, anything like that of his on the premises?'

'Do what you like,' she says, defeated. 'But I ain't seen no phones or laptops. He always had his phone with him. Was never off the damn thing.'

'And Alana? Is she here? Can we speak to her?'

Valerie stands then, wipes her face with her hands and attempts to compose herself. From the information we have, she's in her mid-forties, and yet looking at her now, you'd think she was a ninety-year-old woman.

'You ain't upsetting her any more than she already is,' she says, her harsh tone returning. 'I'm surprised the shock of all this hasn't sent her into labour already. She's only nineteen – nineteen and about to have a baby, the father in the morgue! It ain't right!'

The door opens, a very heavily pregnant young woman behind it, her protruding belly almost filling the entire frame.

'His phone's not here,' she says flatly. 'I dunno where it is. And he ain't used a laptop in his life.'

'Alana?' I turn to her. 'I'm Detec—'

'Yeah, I know who you are.'

Her young face looks puffy from crying, and my heart drops for the second time in quick succession. She looks terrified, though whether that's because she's about to give birth having just found out her partner has been murdered or because she knows something, I have no idea. Maybe it's both. I need to proceed with caution. I'd rather not have to deliver a baby on the kitchen floor. It's been a hell of a day already as it is.

'You can search the gaff,' she says, 'but you won't find nothing. Matty only ever did business on his phone.'

A phone we still haven't found.

'We had a row,' she says, her gaze dropping to the floor, 'before he left last night. The last thing I said to him was "piss off".' She starts to cry then, and Davis goes to her.

'Come on – let's sit you down, eh?'

She doesn't object as she waddles towards us with Davis's help. The poor girl can barely walk.

'We're so sorry, Alana,' I say. In situations like this, 'sorry' just doesn't feel enough, but right now it's all I've got.

She lets out a loud exhale as she gingerly lowers herself into the chair. 'He's kicking like mad today.' She rubs her swollen belly. 'I think he's trying to escape.'

'You're having a boy?'

'Pfft!' Valerie snorts. 'No flies on you is there, Ronson?'

I don't bother correcting her this time.

Alana nods. 'Matt junior – that's what I'm calling him, after his dad.'

I reach for her hand; take it in my own. 'Please, Alana, if there's anything... anything at all you can remember, or if there's something you know that can help us find out who did this to Mathew...'

'What were you arguing about, Alana?' Davis asks. 'Last night, you and Matty? You said you had a row...'

She sniffs loudly. 'I didn't want him to go out. I'm two days over my due date, and this little fella' – she continues rubbing her stomach – 'he could come at any minute, and I wanted Matty to be here, with me, with us. But he said he had something he had to do, something important.'

'Did he say what? Did he tell you who he was meeting or where he was going?'

She shakes her head. 'He told me not to worry about nothing, that we had enough money now to buy Matt junior some decent stuff, said we could get whatever we wanted, the best.' She looks up at us. 'I asked him how we could suddenly afford it, where the money had come from.'

'And?' Davis prompts her.

'And he just tapped his nose with his finger. He told me all I needed to know was that we were going to be rich, that he'd sorted it, that he'd been doing some business, that he'd... what did he call it? Tapped into a new revenue stream, whatever that means...'

I glance over at Davis. 'But he didn't tell you what this new "revenue stream" was? Do you think he meant drugs?'

Alana shrugs. 'He said that if he played his cards right, then he could jib the dealing, knock it on the head and that soon we'd have enough money to get our own place. Somewhere nice, away from this shithole.'

She blows her nose so hard and loud that I'm worried her waters will break right on the spot.

'I didn't believe him at first; Matty's always been a bit of a bullshitter, but he's not a bad man. He's no saint' – she shrugs – 'but I can't think of anyone who'd want to kill him.' She pauses for a moment; winces slightly as she rubs her belly. It's making me nervous as hell.

'Maybe you should talk to *Katya*.' She sneers the name as if it upsets her.

'Katya?'

'Yeah, that's who he got the phone call from.'

'Phone call?'

She rolls her eyes. 'He got a phone call last night, right before he went out. I saw her name come up on his phone.'

'And do you know who she is, this Katya?'

'Yeah,' she says. 'Well, I don't know her personally. But I know *what she does*.' A look of contempt crosses her puffy features.

'What does she do, Alana?'

'Sells herself,' she says as she glances over at Valerie. 'She's a prostitute.'

THIRTEEN
ED

He inwardly sighs as he hears the doorbell ring for the third time this morning. They've never been so bloody popular! Surely the police weren't back so soon? Ed curses under his breath. He's really gone and done it now, hasn't he – blatantly lying to their faces and giving them false information to cover for his son? Now they really are up the creek without a paddle.

Upon the benefit of reflection, Ed Carter realises that the decision not to come clean to the cops had been more of an instinctive than consciously thought through one. He's aware of the gravity of the situation though, and the potential outcome if Conor is implicated in the killing of this Reynolds. He's been there himself after all, albeit some years ago now. In fact, the more he ponders on it, the more this whole horrible mess feels like history repeating itself, a miserable fait accompli somehow, like his own historic ill-advised actions have been passed down to his son through his DNA.

There had been no time to properly consider the pros and, ironically, the cons of what to do before the cops had come calling. All Ed could consider in that moment was his family's safety and protection, and he'd been prepared to do or say anything to ensure both things without time for any real rational contemplation. Plus, Bryan Levinson's arm hadn't needed much, or indeed any, twisting, just as he'd called it. A man of his wealth and status wasn't going to want such a scandal, albeit for different reasons.

Tee had wanted to tell the police the truth from the off of course, a truth he knows deep down is by far the right box to tick because she's a good person, a woman of integrity and morals. Tee is honest and fair and decent, and in truth so is he. Only she doesn't know what it's *really* like being in prison, caged like an animal twenty-three hours out of every twenty-four. She doesn't know how it feels to be told when to eat, shit and sleep. Or that the latter is something you largely learn to live without much of when you're behind the door, the anguished screams of a thousand men's despair preventing you from getting a moment's uninterrupted rest, or how you're dehumanised until you no longer recognise the distorted image staring back at you from the broken plastic mirror.

His beloved Christine knows nothing of the constant state of fight or flight, always one eye open as your body floods itself with cortisol, the omnipresent threat of violence following you like a dark shadow. She's never witnessed someone having boiling sugar-water thrown into their face, their agony etched onto your memory like a tattoo. She hasn't been privy to the beatings and the power plays, the unwanted sexual advances, or the relentless wail of the alarm, alerting staff that yet another inmate has been found mutilated, burned, broken or hanged in his cell. And he wasn't about to tell her.

Ed has always tried to make those four years he was incarcerated sound as if he breezed through them with a degree of aplomb. He's shielded her from as much of the truth as he can, not least when the truly worst thing that could've ever happened to them did and they lost their beautiful baby daughter. The tragedy changed them, left them with a gaping, raw hole that could never be filled, one that had only softened ever so slightly around the sharp edges when they'd been blessed with their boy some years later. Consumed by guilt and convinced that somehow the gods had seen fit to punish them for his unwitting crimes by taking his daughter, the moment he'd witnessed his son enter the world, Ed vowed that nothing bad would ever happen to this child. He'd make sure of it. Even if it killed him.

Ed peers through the crack in the venetian blinds with a small groan escaping from his lips.

Bloody hell, what is *she* doing here?

His heart drops in his chest as he swings open the front door, still dressed in the clothes he'd been wearing earlier that morning. He's been so consumed by his thoughts that he hasn't even had time to take a shower yet.

'Helen?'

'Ed, I'm *so* sorry to just turn up unannounced like this – *again*,' she apologises, a touch out of breath as she edges closer towards him. 'Do you mind if I come in?'

He pauses for a second, briefly glancing behind her as if it's some kind of trick.

'Um... yeah, of course,' he says, even though she's already halfway through the door. 'Is everything OK, Helen? Is Tee OK? Is she still at yours? Are *you* OK?' A wave of concern crashes into him as she steps into the living room. 'How do you think it went with the police earlier?' he says with some immediacy now that they're alone. 'Tee reckons they saw straight through us. That Riley fella... the DCI – there was something about him, something I can't quite put my finger on... What did you reckon? Do you think they bought it?'

He glances at her expectantly, genuinely interested in her take on it. Had he come across as sincere? He really isn't sure and desperately needs feedback.

'Er, well... I don't know, Ed. It was all such a dreadful shock.

I still can't believe any of this has happened. I didn't even know Paris and Conor were dating until this morning!'

'Join the club!' he shoots back. 'Tee had no idea either. Our Con has never kept anyone a secret from us – no idea why he felt the need to this time.'

Helen nods. 'Well, I suppose Bryan is a bit... protective,' she says with a thin smile, 'and she's still so young after all.' She places a hand lightly on his left bicep; lets her fingers rest there for a few seconds longer than Ed feels entirely comfortable with. Clearly, she's attempting to reassure him, and he appreciates her efforts though he can't shake off the feeling of unease that seems to be insidiously creeping in around him.

'Try not to worry. We'll just have to hold our nerve for now. And stick to our story, stick *together*. I mean, nothing's actually happened yet, has it? They're only potential witnesses at this stage.'

'Yeah, you're right.' He puffs out his cheeks a little and takes a step backward, forcing her to drop her hand from his arm. 'Only we don't know what they might have in the way of forensics yet, do we? At best we've got a couple of days to think about how we're going to handle it when they do, but we need to be prepared for every eventuality, best- and worst-case scenario.'

He rakes a hand through his hair; exhales. 'Look, I know this all sounds mad, sounds like we don't have a conscience about this lad, this Mathew Reynolds being, you know, *dead*. But those kids wouldn't have meant to hurt anyone. It was just a terrible accident, not some premeditated act of violence. We're not bad people.'

She's watching him intensely, nodding in what appears to be agreement, her eyes searching his, though for what exactly he isn't quite sure.

'We feel for his mum, for his family.' Ed hears his own protestation, like he's trying to justify it to himself as much as to her. 'You see, our Con, he's our everything, and, well, how can we turn him over to the police, our own flesh and blood, our only boy—?'

'What did you do with the clothes?' she suddenly interrupts him. 'Have you got rid of them yet?'

He pauses for a second; questions why she's asking. In fact, he's still wondering why she's here at all. She's yet to explain the purpose of her visit.

'Don't worry about the clothes. I told your husband we'd sort it.' He doesn't, of course, mention the fact that he also told Tee not to tell the Levinsons where she was planning on hiding the clothes. Despite Helen's current display of what appears to be concern, he just doesn't trust them – either of them.

'Jesus, it's been one hell of a morning, hasn't it?' He snorts softly with resignation; runs his hands through his hair yet again, a nervous gesture he's only just become aware of. He feels exhausted already and it's not even midday.

Helen lunges forward suddenly and puts her arms around him, momentarily touching his shoulder with her face. He waits for a few seconds that feel more like minutes, his arms hanging down by his sides, frozen to the spot, before lightly touching the tops of her arms with his hands, gently edging himself out of her embrace. He doesn't want to be rude, especially since she appears to be openly offering him her support.

'Try not to worry, Ed,' she says. 'Gosh, that's a pretty ridiculous thing to say, isn't it? *"Try not to worry."*' She does a goofy, bad impersonation of herself, her cheeks flushing pink as she giggles softly.

Well, this is getting weirder by the second.

'Sorry, Helen,' he says after another moment's pause, wishing that he'd never opened his eyes this morning, 'where's my manners? Do you want a cup of tea?' It was all he could think of saying in that moment, aside from asking her to leave, which is what he really would prefer her to do.

Her eyes light up. 'Thank you, Ed. Tea would be lovely.'

She follows him into the kitchen, though he was hoping that she wouldn't. He should've asked her to sit down first before offering her something to drink.

'What time does Tee finish her shift at yours? Was she OK when you left her?' He's genuinely concerned as he rinses out the stained, chipped mugs. 'Like she hasn't got enough to worry about, and now this!'

'Actually, I sent her off early to visit her mum. She wasn't really in any fit state to be working given this morning's revelations.' Her tone is empathetic as she cocks her head to one side, though she appears perfectly at ease. 'Is Conor here?'

He can feel her watching him as he pours milk into the mugs. He isn't sure why, but it's unsettling. And Ed Carter doesn't really do nervous.

'No.' He turns to look at her. 'He's gone training, like he always does on Sundays, though God knows how he's bearing up, poor fuc—' He checks himself, remembers she's a guest in his house, and who she is. 'But he's a Carter, a survivor. We'll get him through this somehow. And we agreed, didn't we, that we'd all carry on as normal with our plans for the day, nothing different, nothing that could raise any suspicion from the police? That's what we said, wasn't it?'

He hears the edge of desperation in his words and berates himself. He doesn't want to sound like he's begging.

'Yes, yes, absolutely, we did,' she agrees, smiling emphatically.

He has to hand it to her: all things considered, she appears to be taking this in her stride. He assumed that given her money and marital status that she'd be a real spoiled diva, demanding and histrionic even. Seems he was wrong.

'Um... so, Helen...' He pours boiling water into the two mugs. 'Aside from the obvious, was there another reason you came over? Something I can help you with?'

She's watching him again as he stirs the contents of the cups and removes the teabags. He wishes she'd stop it – it's making him feel self-conscious.

'My earring,' she says. 'A diamond earring. I think I may have lost it here, this morning, in your house.'

He hands her the steaming-hot mug.

'I realise it's not that important,' she quickly adds, 'but they were a present you see, an anniversary gift from Bryan. He'll be terribly upset if I've lost one.'

'Oh, really? And you think you may have lost it here somewhere?'

'I've checked my car – it's not there. So I can only think I must've lost it here. Would you mind looking for me? I know it's probably the last thing you want to be worrying about all told, but like I say, they were a gift from Bryan...'

'A pretty expensive gift I imagine.' He raises an eyebrow and smiles simultaneously. No doubt one of those earrings alone could cover their outstanding care-home fees, maybe even with change left over. It doesn't seem right somehow, that the Levinsons are so exorbitantly rich that they can afford to lose diamond earrings without too much of a song and dance, and yet he's heard stuff over the years that Bryan Levinson is a bigger crook than he himself ever was. It was just rumours, mind, and he wasn't especially one for gossip.

'Perhaps it fell out somewhere in the living room, while we – while you – were talking to the police?' she offers, adding, 'You handled them so well by the way. I was very impressed by your ability to stay so calm, so... together. A lesser man would've simply crumpled.'

He doesn't want to tell her he's had considerable practice dealing with the boys in blue. She doesn't need to know any of that.

'I did my best,' he says, unsure of how to play it. 'Anyway, I'll have a look for it now.'

'Would you mind? I'd be so grateful. It looks like this one.' She tucks a piece of her hair behind her ear, inviting him to inspect the perfect platinum round-cut cluster earring, forcing him to move closer to her. He can smell her perfume now, strong and floral.

'Course,' he says, 'no problem.'

She follows him through to the lounge but then seems to think better of it.

'Actually, would you mind if I used your bathroom?' she says quickly as he begins upending the cushions on the old sofa. Like him, it's seen better days and looks a bit tired round the edges. He'd give anything to buy his Tee a nice new one. He's sick of them always just about scraping by.

'Up the stairs, straight in front of you – you can't exactly miss it.'

He starts searching for the earring down the side of the sofa, using the torch on his phone for guidance. Satisfied it hasn't slipped behind the cushions, Ed replaces them and drops to his hands and knees; begins searching underneath. A few solid minutes pass before he realises that she's behind him, watching him silently scrabble around on the floor.

'Any luck?' she asks.

Ed shakes his head, a little exerted. For reasons he can't explain, he again wishes she would leave, even though she's been nothing but friendly and polite.

'I'm sorry, Helen – nothing I'm afraid. Listen, I'll ask Tee to have a thorough look when she gets back from Sunnyside. If it's here, Tee will find it. She's good at finding things.'

'Sunnyside? Is that the name of the care home where her mother is? The one down by Wickham Drive?'

'The run-down-looking one with the tired sign outside that may as well say "God's Waiting Room" you mean?' He sounds sardonic and wishes he hadn't given away such candid insights to his thoughts. The less the Levinsons – and people in general, for that matter – know about your business, the less they can control you. 'Did she mention it then?'

Helen nods slowly, sympathetically. 'She told me about it, the dementia. Must be awful...'

'Yeah it is. Tee was very close to her mum – still is I suppose, or the memory of her at least. She was a lovely woman, Cynthia, before that disease got a grip on her. Now she doesn't even recognise her own daughter; doesn't know what day of the week it is mostly.' He's doing it again – can't seem to help himself. It's like she's drawing it all out of him.

'Must be a terrible struggle for you all, and these care homes, they're not exactly cheap...'

'Ha! Tell me about it!' he says, suddenly animated. 'Five grand a month, *a month*, just to give her the basics.'

'That must be a huge pressure on you.'

'It is – a *real* pressure on me... on us. We had to remortgage the house to pay for last year's fees and we're still six grand in debt over it. God only knows how we'll manage this year. It's daylight robbery if you ask me, these greedy swines getting rich on the back of other people's misery and—' He suddenly stops himself short. 'Sorry, here's me banging on... Anyway, I'll keep my eyes out for the earring. I'm sure Tee will too when she's home, and we'll let you know if it turns up. In the meantime, we do as we agreed and carry on as normal, whatever that bloody well means.'

FOURTEEN
CHRISTINE

'I was just driving past when I saw your car parked outside,' Helen explains with a look of concern on her perfectly put together face. 'I thought I would stop to check on you, make sure you're OK? You seemed so distressed when you were at my house earlier.'

For a moment, I think she must've followed me here, to Sunnyside. I wonder if she's keeping tabs on me in case I – in case *we* – go to the police. My paranoia has gone stratospheric.

'I just want to let you know that I'm here for you, Christine,' she says sagely. 'That we're in this together, all of us. You don't need to feel alone, to struggle with your conscience, because I know I'm really struggling with mine. I could do with a friend, someone to talk to.' She rakes her hand through her hair, something I've never seen her do before. 'After all, it's been one hell of a day, hasn't it?'

I nod; realise I'm holding my breath again.

'Maybe we can go for a drink together?' she suggests with a light shrug. 'I know I could do with one.'

I could kill for a large gin and tonic, but the 'together' part doesn't appeal. It isn't even personal as such, I just desperately want to get home and be with my family. They need me. *We need each other.* Because as Helen rightly said, it's been one hell of a day.

'I would, Helen, and thanks for asking, but I must get home. I need to make sure my boys are OK. I've been going out of my mind ever since this morning. Look at me,' I say, holding my hand out. 'I can't stop shaking. I can't stop thinking about everything, that none of it seems real. And I can't stop thinking about... you know, *him.*' I've dropped my voice down to a hushed whisper, suddenly aware that someone from the care home could be listening in on our conversation. My paranoia really is starting to make me edgy.

It strikes me then that perhaps Helen has seen me dispose of the bag that contained the clothes in the rubbish bin, and I feel a hot rush of panic. Ed explicitly instructed me to make sure the Levinsons wouldn't know where I'd hidden them. 'Another time maybe?' I say hurriedly.

'Of course.' She smiles, yet I sense her disappointment and a sliver of guilt runs through me. She's my employer, and for that reason alone I don't want to upset her.

'Actually, Christine, I was wondering if you could use some extra cleaning shifts at my house? I realise it must be a huge financial strain on you to pay for your mother's care, both you and Ed, so if it helps in any way...'

She says his name with an odd familiarity, like we really are old friends. She isn't wrong though. I *could* use the extra shifts.

'That's really good of you, Helen, thanks,' I reply, stepping past her to get to my car.

'Well, I'll keep you updated.' She flashes me a friendly smile as I unlock the door. 'In case, you know, the police turn up or anything...'

. . .

I swing by Continental Cleaners on my way home to drop off my time sheet and run into another employee, Linda, who I've worked with on and off in the past.

'I haven't seen you in ages, Christine!' she says as we briefly embrace.

I like Lin – she's one of us, a local girl. Her husband left her some years ago with three young kids, and she's nothing if not a grafter. I've always enjoyed the shifts we work together – her banter always makes the time pass quicker.

'How are you?' I ask, doing my best to sound normal even though I feel utterly transparent, like she'll be able to read every terrible thought in my head. 'How are the kids?'

'Oh, you know, same crap, different day. Where have you been lately anyway? I haven't seen you since we were on the leisure centre job together. I thought you might've won the lottery or something.'

'Chance would be a fine thing.' I roll my eyes, feeling painfully self-conscious. 'I was put on another gig, at the Levinsons' house.'

Her eyebrows rise. 'Oh, *them*,' she says cryptically. 'How's that working out for you?'

She really doesn't want to know.

'Yeah, good, fine... a job's a job, and we've all got bills to pay – you know how it is.'

'Don't I just! I did a few stints for the Levinsons a while back. Beautiful house they've got, or one of them at least, lucky so-and-sos. Not that I'd want to be in her shoes mind...'

'Helen's shoes you mean?'

'Yeah, funny kettle of fish she is. Bit tapped. You must've heard the rumours?'

I'm desperate to get home, back to Ed and Con, but the conversation has started to intrigue me.

'What rumours?'

Linda's eyes light up. 'Some of the other girls reckon there's all sorts going on in that house...'

'All sorts?'

'Yeah... him, the husband, that MP fella she's married to... apparently they, or he, liked to throw these wild parties. They used to see a conveyor belt of men and women coming in and out...'

I blink at her, taken aback. 'I know they like to throw parties, but I've never seen anything like that,' I say truthfully.

'Yeah, well, you know what these politicians are like... think they can get away with murder.'

My stomach lurches. She really has no idea just how close to the truth she is.

'Kerry Jones says that the wife, Helen, is jacked up on pills round the clock and that the marriage is a sham, that she only stays for the money, not that I'd blame her if she did. I'd probably do the same!' Her sharp laugh cuts straight through me. 'Apparently' – her voice drops an octave as she leans in closer – 'there's a secret room in the house or something.'

'A *what?*' I feel a slight chill pass through me and wrap my coat around me a little tighter.

'Yeah, well, I suppose this has come from Jonesey. She loves a gossip that one, but she swears they're up to all sorts down there – that's it's a pleasure room.'

I laugh nervously. 'You're having me on!'

'I suppose when you're that rich you can do whatever you like.' She shrugs. 'Must be nice...' Her voice trails off. 'Anyway, good to see you, Chris. Love to Ed and Conor too,' she says with a backward wave.

'She was just standing there, next to my car, right there, outside Sunnyside. How the hell did she even know where Mum's care home is? I know I never told her.'

I roll in closer towards Ed when we finally make it into bed. It's felt like the longest day I've ever known. I feared it might never end and I'd be trapped in this purgatory forever. Which reminds me, I've still not mentioned my dream about Cora to Ed, and yet somehow now, given what's happened, it seems more poignant than ever.

'Actually,' Ed says, stroking my outer thigh gently with the tips of his fingers, 'I think that might've been my fault.'

'Oh?'

'Well she turned up earlier...'

'Helen turned up? What, here, at the house you mean?' I sit up and face him.

'I haven't had the chance to tell you, what with everything else that's been going on.'

And by everything else, he means Conor. Con is naturally effervescent, my little ray of sunshine. Only I could tell as I put my arms around him when he returned from training that he was doing his best not to fold – we all were.

It hit me like a bag of bricks as I held him in my arms that Mathew Reynolds's mother will never get to hug *her* son again, to breathe in the scent of him through her nostrils, and that my boy is the reason. It still hasn't sunk in properly; it really hasn't sunk in at all. I've been running on adrenalin, my mind moving at 90 mph all day, but now the true horror of what happened, and what we did, has made me feel so mentally drained I could sleep on a washing line.

'Are you sure there's nothing you're not telling us, Con.' I asked him the question again simply because my instincts were telling me to. 'Why did you not tell us you and Paris were in a relationship?'

Ed had exhaled. 'Give it a rest, eh, Tee? We've been through it all as many times as we can today. We should all get some sleep, see the back of today. We're going to need our wits about us going forward.'

'Has there been any more from the police?' Con asked his dad anxiously. 'Have they been round again, said anything?'

'No, nothing, nothing at all, son. Let's hope that'll be the end of it all, eh?'

Con stared at Ed. 'The end of it? Dad, I *killed* someone last night. I didn't mean to, but I did. And it's all over the news today. Wherever I turn, I see his face, right there in front of me, whenever I close my eyes... I can't stop reliving it, can't stop it from playing loops in my head. Me punching him as Paris—' He stopped himself.

'As Paris what, sweetheart?' I prompted him gently, conscious of his fragility.

'Nothing.' He shook his head; turned away from me. 'I just don't know how I'm going to live with it, that's all.'

My earlier fears of Con not giving us the full story levelled up a notch. Now I knew he was hiding something.

'Let's just get an early night,' Ed said, his gaze moving between us. 'We'll all feel better with a decent night's rest behind us.'

Only I couldn't let it go.

'Did Paris do something?' I looked at Con. 'Did she say something? Did she goad him? Did she instigate it? Is that what really happened?'

His reticence spoke volumes, but Ed refused to let me push it, and I had no more fight left in me.

'She turned up out of the blue,' Ed continues now as I flop back down onto the bed and snuggle into him again, wishing he could somehow absorb me through his skin like osmosis so I won't have to feel the way I'm feeling now. 'Said she'd lost an earring and thought that maybe it was in the house. She wanted me to look for it.'

'Oh...' The sense of unease I've been carrying around with me all day spikes a little. 'What time did she come?'

'She said you'd gone to visit your mum; said she was concerned about you so had let you go early.'

'She didn't mention that she was here at the house.' I glance at him, perplexed. 'So was it here, the earring? Did she find it?'

'No. I had a quick look, but funnily enough, Tee, finding Helen Levinson's bloody earring wasn't high on my list of priorities today. If she's stupid enough to lose a diamond earring, then that's her lookout. She'll get it on the insurance if it doesn't turn up.'

My mind begins to race. Why hadn't Helen mentioned this to me, that she'd been to my house and talked to Ed? Even considering everything, it felt odd and intrusive somehow.

'She was very friendly though,' Ed continues.

'Friendly?'

'Hmm.' He nods, closing his eyes. 'Yeah, it was a bit...' He pauses.

'A bit what?'

'I dunno... weird.'

'Weird in what way?'

He sighs. 'Oh, I dunno. I get the impression that she's maybe a bit lonely or something. She was perfectly nice, kind even, not that I'd trust any of that lot as far as I could throw them, but the fact is they're on board with us and so it'll pay to keep them onside, if you know what I mean? Anyway, forget the Levinsons for now. Let's get some rest, sweetheart – it's been one hell of a day.'

I snort gently. 'Funny, that's just what Helen said... those exact words.'

Ed yawns loudly.

'I think maybe she saw me dispose of the holdall, the one I took to Mum's with the clothes in.' I bite my lip silently, concerned about his potential reaction. He'd been adamant that I was to hide them carefully, covertly. 'Although I can't be certain,' I quickly add.

'Did she say something then? Did she ask about the clothes?'

'No. She just invited me to go for a drink with her and then suggested I take on more shifts at her place to help with Mum's bills. Which reminds me: we have to talk to the bank tomorrow. I can't keep avoiding the staff at Sunnyside. It's embarrassing, and I can tell it's awkward for Joy to keep mentioning the overdue invoices.'

'Well, maybe you *should* go for a drink with Helen? I mean, show some solidarity. It might even look good to the police, add weight to the ridiculous notion that we could in fact be genuine friends.'

'Hmm,' I say, unconvinced.

'And I promise I'll call the bank tomorrow, Tee, OK? Try not to worry about everything. One thing at a time, OK? I'll sell the van if I have to, to pay this month's fees off... We'll manage somehow... When have I ever let you down, eh? Aside from that one stupid mistake?'

I grip his body a little tighter. I feel like crying again.

'Two you mean,' I correct him with a small smile that he can't see.

'Two? Oh hang on. Not the...'

'The lost weekend at CoCo's in Shoreditch, July 2007. Hmmm, yes, that's right...'

Ed snorts a little gentle laughter with closed eyes. 'Jesus, Tee, that was eighteen-odd years ago. You're like an elephant, you are! Never bloody forgets!'

'How could I forget, Ed? We'd not long lost our baby girl, remember? We were both still in the thick of grief for Cora.'

I sigh softly in response, feeling the sting of the pain I was in at the time – that we both were.

'I still don't know what really happened that night,' I tease him, trying to steer the conversation away from that terrible period in our lives.

'You *do* know what happened that night: nothing. I went into town with the lads, got drunk and woke up on the couch at one of Billy Noye's girl's houses top and tailing with that big hairy lump Darren Paige. The *only* person I slept with that night was another bloke!'

We both start to laugh then. I remember being beside myself at the time, not knowing where Ed was, why he hadn't come home and thinking the worst. It was the only time in our entire lives together where he'd ever stayed out all night without calling.

'I didn't speak to you for a week afterwards if I remember rightly.'

'Yeah, I do. It was the best seven days of my life.'

'Oi!' I poke his ribs with a finger and he pulls me tighter to him.

'You know I've never even looked at another woman since the day we met.' He kisses the top of my aching head, but the brief moment of respite gradually dissipates as my mind returns, kicking and screaming into the present.

'I ran into Linda at Continental on my way home – you know, Linda Samson, who I used to work with?' I can tell Ed is drifting off now by the slowing of his heartbeat against my ear. 'She said something odd about the Levinsons, something about them throwing wild parties... that there's supposedly some kind of secret room in their house.'

'Well, you never know what goes on behind closed doors, Tee,' Ed says with his eyes closed. 'I wouldn't put anything past that lot. Anyway, it's probably just you girls gossiping. Have you ever seen any secret room since you've been working there?'

'No.'

'Well then, there you go. Let's not worry about idle gossip, eh? Focus on keeping our boy out of the clutches of the old bill.'

He's right, I know, and yet as I close my eyes in what I know is a futile attempt at sleep, that note I found in the library of the

Levinsons' house comes into my head, the one written in Helen's florid handwriting that said something about her not wanting to go on like this, pleading to be released from some sort of purgatory. In that very moment, I knew exactly how she felt.

FIFTEEN
DAN

'I've never heard of no one called Katya, boss, honest. Dunno who you're talking about.'

She blows cigarette smoke forcibly from her thin, dry lips as she picks at a scab on her face with chipped red-polished fingernails.

I've been on the go for seventeen hours straight. While my body is screaming out for sleep, my mind has other plans, namely locating a sex worker by the name of Katya. Davis and I are back near the crime scene in the freezing drizzle, exhausted, cold, hungry and no further along as to who did this to Mathew Reynolds – or why.

The bright yellow police tape protecting the crime scene hurts my tired eyes as it flaps in the biting wind, and I feel a stab of empathy as I watch the small team of wetsuited police divers embarking on the unenviable task of dragging the dirty riverbed in a bid to locate Reynolds's missing phone, one I'm convinced will reveal at least some of the answers to the puzzles in front of us. We need that phone, and we need it fast.

'The team has put in the request to the service provider, gov, see if it throws up any call logs, messages or tracking, but it all depends if the device was using GPS,' Davis told me on the way here. 'You know these burner phones are harder to trace.'

I sighed.

'We *do* know it was purchased just a few weeks ago though,' Davis added by way of recompense, 'beginning of December at a shop on the local high street. The team is going to send someone down there as soon as it opens in the morning, see if they have any records, CCTV, or if anyone remembers selling it to him.'

Now, a gust of icy wind forces me to put my hands in my pockets as I shake off my feelings of despondency before they can get a grip on me. I can't stop thinking about the conversation at the Carters' address this morning. It's bugging me. It wasn't so much *what* was said; it was more *how* it was said and, perhaps pertinently, how it left me feeling. My intuition has been pulling at me like a toddler at his mother's skirt. Something about that whole scene just didn't sit right with me: the Levinsons both being there at the Carters' house at that time in the morning; the fact their claim to being 'friends' had felt contrived and disingenuous, not to mention unlikely; the discrepancy between Helen and Bryan Levinson as to the reasons why they were at the Carters' in the first place; and, perhaps most of all, Christine Carter's demeanour. She hadn't been able to make eye contact with me once. I *knew* they were lying, all of them. I just didn't know exactly what about yet.

Our lines of enquiry have taken us down a route that strongly suggests Mathew Reynolds was involved in something he shouldn't have been, and I don't just mean a few class A drugs. It's clear he stumbled into something that was even more lucrative – and certainly more dangerous, as it turned out – hence his healthy bank balance when he died. Alana's claim that Reynolds had received a call from someone called Katya and had gone to meet her the night he was murdered could be vital – only unsurprisingly, no one it seems felt like talking, at least not to us.

'Listen, Honey' – I look up at the woman whose name I'm fairly certain wasn't given to her at birth – 'this isn't about grassing on anyone. We only want to talk to Katya at this stage. You're absolutely sure you don't know who she is or where we can find her? We know you're a regular down at the arches – we've seen you here before. You know everyone...' I try to appeal to her ego, make her feel valuable, because frankly she could be.

She looks back at me, frozen solid beneath a lightly padded old coat with tatty fake fur around the hood. It breaks my heart to see such a young woman out here in this weather, at this time of night, touting for business, selling the only commodity she has to feed what is clearly a raging habit. I have a daughter of my own, a daughter I could never imagine standing before me like this girl is now, sick and addicted, scruffy and emaciated, looking twice her real age as she sells herself to strangers. Not even the police presence, or the fact that there could be a vicious killer at large, has prevented her from returning to this miserable spot. Seeing her now, it's difficult to imagine that she was once no doubt an innocent little girl, just like my Juno.

'I promise you, boss, honestly,' she says again in a strong South London accent, 'if I knew this Katya, I'd tell ya. I mean, they shanked him up good, ol' Matt Reynolds. Had his head bashed in, or so they're saying on the news. If I knew sumfink, I'd tell ya, I swear down, boss. I mean, there could be some nutter out there...'

'Exactly,' I say, encouraging her, although she doesn't know the half of it. We haven't yet released the information about the fatal stab wound. 'And it's not safe for you to be out here alone.'

She shrugs; looks down at the old trainers she's wearing.

'Maybe you should call it a night tonight, eh? Go home – it's freezing.'

'Go home? To what?' she says quietly.

I don't know Honey's full story, and the sad truth is that I don't have the time or means to find out, but I'm pretty sure it's a tragic one, and one I've regrettably heard before – many times before.

'How well did you know Mathew, Honey?' Davis asks. 'When was the last time you saw him?'

'Nah, we weren't close or anyfink.' Her nose is running, and she sniffs loudly. I take a tissue from my coat pocket. 'He came down here sometimes,' she says, wiping it, 'but recently I see him a lot more.'

'You bought drugs from him?'

'Sometimes.' She shrugs, discarding the used tissue on the ground. 'Only his gear weren't the best. Some of the other girls didn't like him because he'd never give you nufink on tick, always demanded cash... and his drugs were a bit shit anyway. But he started coming more and more lately, or maybe I just was about more while he was here, I dunno. Anyway, he liked the fresh, pretty, young ones.'

'Girls you mean?' My antenna twitches. 'Did Mathew pay the girls for sex? Was he a client?'

Suddenly she glances around her nervously. 'No... I...'

'What do you mean, he liked the pretty, young ones?'

'Well, I saw 'em, didn't I? One of the girls who was new to the game, small, scruffy-looking little thing but very pretty, didn't know her name but I suddenly started seeing her about a lot on the patch. I saw 'em talking one night when Reynolds came down to the arches – saw her go off with him somewhere in his car.'

My adrenalin spikes.

'Next time I saw her she had a new hairdo and clothes, a fancy designer handbag and a fresh pair of trainers.'

'And you never spoke to her, never asked her where she'd been or how she got these items?'

'I figured she'd just got lucky with a new client. Some of the regulars have favourites.' She gives a one-shouldered shrug. 'Some even buy you gifts, a packet of fags here and there, but not many, and not fancy designer gifts like what she had. Most of them just want to...' She pauses. 'Anyway, and then I see her again a week or so later – this time she had a mate with her, another young-looking girl, like really young, a teenager basically... Again, I saw 'em chatting to Matt Reynolds before they went off somewhere with him. Never seen 'em since. That was last week.'

Davis shoots me a look that tells me what she's thinking – my wife often does the same, albeit for different reasons. I guess it's what comes with knowing someone so well.

'A penny for them, gov,' Davis asks as we walk back to the car in silence.

I have to go home, take a quick shower and change my clothes, maybe even eat something before Fiona and the kids forget what I look like. Plus I need to ask Fiona what she meant by the cryptic text she sent me this morning about our Jude. It's been playing on my mind all day, along with everything else.

'Maybe he was recruiting them for something – or someone,' I say, 'the girls... It would explain how Reynolds suddenly found himself with that much money in the bank, wouldn't it?'

'So you think he switched trades, from dealer to pimp?'

'It's possible. Get on to missing persons – see if any teenage girls have been reported missing recently.'

Davis looks thoughtful as she digests the idea. 'Yes, gov... but the girls on this patch...' She cocks her head to the side. 'I mean, you've seen them, proper down-and-outs, bad skin and dirty clothes, selling sex for less than the price of a decent coffee to get their next hit. Who would he have been recruiting them for?'

Her phone rings before I can answer, and I let my mind wander as she takes the call, try to figure out how to find the elusive Katya. We only have a name at this point; Alana claims she's never met her and couldn't even give us a description.

'Do you want the good news or the good news, gov?' Davis turns to me, a little breathless, as she kills the call.

'Both.' I already like the sound of this.

'Forensics have come back. There's a job lot of DNA – footprints and fingerprints on the bottle, and that piece of plastic you found underneath the body. They've detected no less than four different sets! The blood belongs to the deceased. Two of the sets are unknown, but the other...'

'There's a match?' I can feel my battery recharging as I put my thoughts of sleep and sustenance on the back-burner.

'Not exactly, boss. They ran it through the system, and initially it came back with nothing, so Mitchell requested a familial DNA test, and guess what?' She doesn't give me time to answer. 'We got a hit!' Her face is lit up. 'And you're not going to believe who it belongs to...'

'Ed Carter?'

She blinks at me, open-mouthed. '*How* did you know that, gov?'

'I'm psychic, Lucy, remember?' I say, jubilant, as I swing the car around.

SIXTEEN

DAN

'I need a search warrant, ma'am.' I'd burst into my boss's office, surprised to see her still here this late in the day.

Superintendent Gwendoline Archer, affectionately known throughout the nick as 'Cupid', has been silently staring at the information I put in front of her for the past five minutes, though it's felt more like fifteen. 'There's enough there to warrant a warrant,' I add – no pun intended – as I practically dance on the spot, desperate to chivvy her along. 'I think we should bring them in – the boy *and* the girl.'

'Let's not jump the gun, Riley,' she says without looking up from her desk. 'From everything I've read here, there isn't enough to make any arrests... at least not yet.'

I can feel my patience fraying. I need sleep, and sustenance, and the feeling of my wife's warm skin next to mine. Yet something is telling me I'm still some way off from making that a reality this side of midnight.

'Come on, ma'am,' I press her. 'This places both Conor Carter and, I suspect, Paris Levinson, at the scene of the crime. If we can get hold of the clothes and shoes they were wearing, then we can fast-track them through forensics. There's an unidentifiable fourth set of DNA too, which would suggest a third perpetrator, or an accomplice perhaps.'

'Such as?' She closes the lid of her laptop and shuffles the papers on her desk until they're perfectly in alignment. She places her pen precisely next to them. Only then, when everything is symmetrical, does she do me the honour of looking up. 'Have you any thoughts on who this "third" accomplice might be if we're going off the premise that Conor Carter and Paris Levinson are our perpetrators? There was no one else on that CCTV footage, was there?'

'No, ma'am. And I can't answer that yet,' I reluctantly admit. 'But at the very least we need to identify the other two sets of DNA. I'm almost certain one of them will match Paris Levinson's.'

'Perhaps it will, but it still doesn't *prove* anything,' she says, monotone. 'Except for the fact that they were where they said they were. Both Carter and the Levinson girl have admitted to being at the scene of the crime not long before the offence took place, and that they'd seen Reynolds as he passed by them. We would expect to find their DNA at the scene.'

I quietly exhale. Customarily, Archer is inclined to want to try and wrap things up fast, no room for procrastination. She likes things done quickly and succinctly – and by the book. Yet I get the distinct impression that she's stalling somehow, like she's trying to talk me out of going after who I believe could very well be responsible for Mathew Reynolds's death. And I've a horrible sinking sensation in my stomach as to why.

'I agree, ma'am, we would expect to find their DNA at the scene, though not necessarily on the body.' I point to the papers on her desk. 'A body, incidentally, underneath which I found what I believe to be part of Paris Levinson's hair toggle. And the autopsy shows that someone left a partial imprint on Reynolds's face as they repeatedly stamped on it. If we can get hold of the footwear, then we can compare— We have to act fast, ma'am.' I can hear the urgency in my own voice. 'Because I also suspect that the parents are lying, that they're covering up for their kids and—'

'You *suspect*, Riley?'

I've already primed the team to get ready to pay a surprise visit to the Carters and the Levinsons respectively. I want to catch them off guard before they get the chance to dispose of any potential evidence, if they haven't already done so. I need that warrant.

'It's my job to suspect, ma'am – you know that,' I mutter irritably. She throws me a sharp glance, detecting it, and I press my palms against the edge of her polished wooden desk, as much to keep myself upright as anything. I'm flagging fast.

She's silent for a moment.

'You do realise who – and what – we're dealing with here, don't you, Dan?' Her voice is softer now, almost apologetic.

'Yes, ma'am – two suspected murderers and a possible third accomplice.'

She snorts; shakes her perfectly styled head. There's not a single hair out of place, despite the late hour. 'You know exactly what I'm talking about!' she fires back. 'And your facetious tone isn't helpful. I'd like to remind you of—'

'And I'd like to remind *you*, ma'am, that a young man is dead, murdered in a savage attack that left him with some of the most egregious injuries I've ever seen in my career! We can't afford to sit on this, whoever the suspects are. We have an obligation to Mathew Reynolds – and to his family. His girlfriend is about to give birth to a son he'll never get to meet. His mother, Valerie Reynolds, has no faith in us – she believes the justice system doesn't serve the likes of her. And I'd like to prove her wrong.'

'The likes of her? Criminals and thieves and drug dealers you mean?'

Her words hit me like a punch in the throat, and I take a

step back from her. I can't quite believe what I'm hearing. Like I say, Archer has always been by the book. Get the job done no matter what. As caustic and prickly as she can often be, I've never doubted her integrity. Until now.

'So you're saying that because Reynolds was a drug dealer, then his murder is less important than someone with a clean record? If he'd never set a foot wrong in his life, then we'd be having a different conversation?'

She picks up her pen then; begins clicking the top of it.

'No, Riley,' she says after a moment, her tone measured yet irritated. 'That's *not* what I'm saying.'

Well, she could've fooled me. And I'm not easily fooled.

'What I'm saying is that this is a *sensitive* case.'

'All murder cases are sensitive,' I fire back. 'This is because Paris Levinson is the daughter of a prominent MP, isn't it? An MP who's "pals" with the commissioner...'

'I think we need to – we *have* to – proceed with caution is all I'm saying at this stage.'

Which very much sounds to me that it means exactly that.

I blink at her, unable, I'm sure, to hide the incredulity on my face. 'Jesus, ma'am. I know money talks, but it can't buy you out of a murder charge. You know that!'

'Shut the door, Riley,' she sighs, nodding at it. 'Please.'

I reluctantly do as she asks.

She addresses me with gravitas the moment it's closed. 'Listen to me – I need you to understand my position here.'

I open my mouth to speak, but she holds a finger up to stop me.

'Commissioner Lennard has requested that I oversee everything meticulously in this case. He made me promise to consult with him at every stage of our enquiry before we act on anything. Bryan Levinson is a good man, an altruistic man. Over the years, he's done much for those in the community who're less off, endless charity work and fundraising for extremely worthy causes. He's friends with the prime minister for goodness' sake, and he's a huge advocate of the police, of us and the work we do and—'

'All the more reason he'll want us to find the perpetrators of this horrible crime then.' I can't hold back any longer. 'These people that Bryan Levinson claims to be a man of, these "less off" everyday folk he supposedly cares so much about, will quite rightly want to see Mathew Reynolds's killers brought to justice.'

She fixes me with a strange expression, one I'm not sure I can accurately read. 'Yes, but not if it's his bloody daughter who's committed the crime.'

And there it is, just as I suspected. I stare at her in silence for a moment.

'What are you saying, ma'am? That we should cover this up?'

'No! No, that's not what I'm saying. Don't twist my words.' She looks up at me; exhales loudly. 'Look, Dan, you're a decorated officer, the best detective on homicide, that's not in dispute, even if...'

'Even if what, ma'am?'

'Even if your... *methods* can be somewhat unorthodox at times. But I'm warning you on this: you need to tread very carefully, very carefully indeed. Bryan Levinson is a powerful man with serious connections. He won't take too kindly to having his life infiltrated. This is his precious daughter we're talking about here, his only child, not to mention his untarnished reputation. So unless we have hard evidence...'

'What about Valerie Reynolds?' My voice sounds pitchy in protest. 'What about *her* child? Her *brutally murdered* child? And I'll get the evidence, ma'am. Look at the forensic report in front of you! Carter's DNA is all over it, and so, I'm sure, is Paris Levinson's. We *have* to bring them both in for questioning at the very least – you know that!'

'OK... *OK*,' she acquiesces. 'But I'm warning you, Dan, you do what you always do and go charging ahead, firing both barrels, and it'll be the end of your illustrious career.'

'So be it,' I say, defiant. 'I'll blow the whistle. It'll be the end of the commissioner's career as well my own then, won't it? *And yours.*'

She discards her pen onto her desk in protest. 'No one is saying we should cover anything up. And you don't yet know for certain his daughter is guilty of anything! Just go in with a soft approach, if you can manage that! If you're convinced that Paris Levinson is involved in this murder, then I want rock-solid evidence of it before we make any formal arrests. Right now, all we have is circumstantial and one of your bloody hunches. These forensic findings may well place her at the scene, but it isn't a smoking gun, and you know that! Besides, what could the possible motive be for Paris Levinson to randomly murder a small-time drug dealer that she's never even met?'

The fact that Archer doesn't even mention Conor Carter just proves to me what – or who – is truly important here.

'Maybe she *has* met him before. What if she *does* know him?' I say, considering this idea properly for the first time. 'I spoke to a sex worker earlier who claims Reynolds was seen hanging around the arches more frequently of late. He was seen talking to a few of the girls, and then they went off with him somewhere...' I'm thinking aloud. 'He had over £20K in his bank account when he died, so I think it's safe to say that he was up to something, and potentially that something could've got him killed.'

'I'm sure he was,' Archer replies. 'But how does that involve Paris Levinson?'

'I don't know... yet. But I'm convinced that both the Carter boy and Paris aren't giving me the full story of what happened last night.'

'And your intuition is telling you that they killed him?' Her tone is borderline mocking.

I meet her steel grey eyes. 'Maybe, possibly, yes.'

'Well, which is it? And what's the motive? Why would two young people with no history of violence or criminal behaviour between them suddenly decide to beat a random stranger to death?'

She's put me on the spot, knowing full well I haven't fully established this part of the equation yet.

'An attempted robbery gone wrong? Maybe Reynolds attacked them first and they defended themselves?'

'By stamping on his face until he was unrecognisable then stabbing him in the neck? There were two of them, and he wasn't even armed. Does that sound like self-defence, let alone the behaviour of two teenagers without a shred of historic violence between them? And even if that were the case, then why didn't they just come clean and tell it like it was? You said yourself this was personal, that whoever did this to Reynolds wanted to annihilate him, to destroy him. It's far more likely that he found himself on the wrong side of the wrong people; drug dealers, pimps, someone from that murky underworld he was on the periphery of.'

When she puts it like that, it's difficult not to agree with her, and yet I *know* there's more to this than meets the eye, something more complex and sinister. I sense it so strongly, like it's siting here right next to me.

'Sleep on it,' she says dismissively. 'We'll bring them in tomorrow, talk to them then, OK?'

I don't move as she opens her laptop again and starts reading something on it, signalling that my time is up. 'Go home, Riley,' she says after a moment. 'Go home to your wife and kids.'

'Yes, ma'am,' I say tightly, though I have no intention of doing so. At least not yet.

And she knows it.

SEVENTEEN
CHRISTINE

I wake the next day from a fitful night's sleep with a feeling of dread in the pit of my stomach. The space next to me is empty. Ed must've set off for work already. I check the time on my phone. It's gone 9 a.m., later than I would normally wake, but then again, nothing is normal right now. I rub my temples with a thumb and forefinger. My head is a swirling mass of pressurised thoughts. I feel like my skull could crack at any moment.

Ed's instruction that I continue to go about my daily business sounds much easier in theory than it is in practice. Something fundamental had shifted, and I know that things were never going to be the same again.

'They could be watching us, Tee. The feds might be keeping tabs on us,' he warned me. Well, if that wasn't enough to send my burgeoning paranoia off the chart, I wasn't sure what was. It felt like I was starring in a surreal remake of *The Truman show*.

I'm relieved to see that Con's sleeping when I go and check on him. Thankfully, he doesn't have training on Mondays; Mondays are rest days. I watch the gentle rise and fall of the covers as he sleeps, and a crushing sense of remorse squeezes in my chest. Even if we get away with this, even if Conor is never held accountable for this terrible accident, how will he, *we*, ever come to terms with what's happened? This kind of secret isn't the kind you can easily carry. Guilt is the gift that keeps on giving. What if I'd brought Cora to the hospital sooner? Why hadn't I checked her tiny body earlier when I'd first detected the fever? Guilt is a cancer that grows within you. It's a torturous, bottomless black hole, breaking you down bit by bit until it consumes you and then spits you out again. Is this the future for my boy, for all of us?

I take a deep breath. I've got to be strong for my family if we've a shred of hope of getting through this. Only with this resolve comes an image of Mathew Reynolds's broken and bloodied face flashing up in my mind. The press are calling it a 'savage' attack; they're saying that he was left 'unrecognisable'. They must be sensationalising it for clickbait. How could his injuries have been so severe with one punch? It doesn't make any sense. Unless, of course, Paris was the one who inflicted the damage? It's the only other possible explanation. And yet as I entertain all of this before I've even made myself a cup of tea, it just seems so... *inconceivable*. Paris can't weigh much more than 100 lbs tops. She doesn't look physically capable of inflicting such damage on anyone, not least a grown man. But as my old nan used to say, looks can be deceptive. I'm sure I've read somewhere how a mother once singlehandedly lifted a car that her daughter had become trapped beneath, that she'd displayed superhuman strength in a bid to free her child from a life-threatening situation. Had Paris done something similar? And if she had, what could have prompted her to do so? Why hadn't she spoken out? Why hadn't Conor?

These thoughts are still gnawing at me as I arrive at the Levinsons' house, a rattling bag of anxiety, to begin my cleaning shift.

'Christine!' Helen greets me with a flourish, like I really am an old friend, opening the front door before I even have the chance to ring the buzzer. Usually, it's her regular housekeeper Carmelita's job to do that. Carmelita is Filipino and barely speaks much English, as far as I know. In fact, she hardly speaks at all. I don't think I've had more than a nod of recognition from her all the months I've worked here. Not that I care. I'm not here to make conversation, or friends, though I have the sinking sensation that Helen may have other ideas this morning.

'I'm *so* glad you're here,' she gushes, linking her arm through mine conspiratorially. 'Come – I need your advice on something.'

'Oh?' I listen to the click-clack of her Chanel sliders against the highly polished marble floor as she takes me through the long hallway that leads into the sprawling kitchen. It has wall-to-wall bifolding doors that open out onto the landscaped garden with lush grass and pristinely pruned box trees, the stuff of my dreams. Helen looks fresh-faced and appears energetic and upbeat, dressed in a cashmere jumper and matching soft palazzo pants, her styled hair hanging in freshly blow-dried waves around her shoulders. As she begins rearranging the huge white hydrangeas in a vase on the shiny granite island, I'm reminded of Linda's words about Helen being 'jacked up on pills round the clock'. Seeing her now, it doesn't seem so implausible.

My heart drops as she pulls up one of the modern chrome kitchen stools and gestures for me to sit. I don't even want to be here. It was a wrench to leave Con home alone. I know he's in a bad place and needs my support, only I don't have much in the way of choice. If I don't work, I don't get paid, and I *need* to get paid. Ed has promised me he'll speak to the bank today. I don't know what we'll do if they refuse to help. We'll be forced to sell up, and then we'll be homeless. I glance around Helen's enormous kitchen and try not to think about how the combined cost of her state-of-the-art appliances alone could probably cover a good six months of Mum's care-home fees.

'We're going up to the Brighton beach house for a few days soon – you know, to get away from it all!' She rolls her eyes a little, like the fact our respective offspring have beaten a man to death and we've lied to the police is little more than an inconvenience to her. I desperately want to talk to her about the things that are being said in the press, about Paris and the police, and yet I sense it's the last thing she wants to discuss in this moment.

'It's our wedding anniversary, and I think Bryan's invited one of his friends and his new wife, Cindy – who is terribly glamorous – to join us, so I wondered if you might help me choose some outfits to take with me?' She blinks at me, adding, 'It's always good to get another woman's opinion, don't you think?'

The last thing I feel like doing is acting as Helen's unpaid personal stylist. I'm stunned by her laissez-faire attitude. Here she is, planning which designer outfits to take on a luxury weekend break to her clifftop holiday home in Brighton, while I'm a wire wool ball of vibrating panic, wondering how I'm going to keep my home and my only remaining child out of prison as well as live with my nagging conscience corroding away my soul on top of it.

I can't stop thinking about Mathew Reynolds's girlfriend having just given birth to their first child. I'd heard it on the news this morning: a boy! What should've been a joyous occasion has been completely overshadowed by his father's horrible untimely death. That little boy will grow up never having known him. And this is on top of the agony I know Reynolds's mother is currently going through. You see, it changes you when you lose a child. Something in you ceases to be as you were before it happened; part of you is gone forever and can never be replaced. It becomes an eternal pain that you somehow must learn to live with. And even after all these years, I'm still learning.

All I want to do is clean Helen's house and get home as fast as I can, although admittedly, I can't help feeling intrigued about this alleged 'secret room' that Lin mentioned in our conversation. I've been cleaning this house for months now and I've never seen anything that would remotely suggest such a room even existed. It's probably all a load of nonsense.

'I'd be happy to,' I lie, attempting to sound apologetic, 'only I have to get back to Conor once I've finished up here. He's home alone today, you see, and I'm so worried about him – he's really struggling with all of this, as you can imagine.' I fleetingly meet her wide eyes. 'And how's Paris bearing up? Is she here, at home? Maybe I could speak to her and—'

'No!' she says quickly, her voice a little pitchy. 'She's... she's sleeping right now. Probably best not to disturb her. I think she's still in shock.' She wrinkles her nose. 'Look, it won't take long, and I'd be ever so grateful.'

I have no clue why Helen would even think of asking me to help her with her packing. The only clothes she's ever seen me in are my black leggings and Continental Cleaners tabard – and the old housecoat I was wearing yesterday morning when they turned up on our doorstep unannounced. Then I remember Ed's advice about keeping her 'onside'. Plus, she's giving me a few extra shifts to help out with the care-home fees, so I feel as if I can't afford to say no. Literally.

'OK then,' I agree with a weak smile.

'Fabulous!' She claps her hands together as I get up and make my way towards the utility room to collect my cleaning products. The sooner I finish my work, the sooner I can leave.

'Oh, let's not worry about that today,' she says, taking the mop from my hand. 'Let Carmelita do it. Carmel!'

She appears almost instantly in the doorway, like she's been waiting behind it all this time.

'Carmel, I need you to take care of the cleaning chores today, OK? Christine here is going to help me with something more pressing.'

Carmelita throws me a stony sideways glance before giving a tight nod.

'Oh, and can you bring up a bottle of the usual on ice – two glasses!'

'But, Helen...' I pause, uncertain.

'Don't worry, Christine – you'll still be paid your hourly rate. In fact, I've decided to double it.' She flashes me a grin. 'You help me, I help you. We help each other.'

I follow her up the huge winding staircase. Now I'm convinced that she's on something – no one could be this happy and relaxed given our situation. I glance behind me to see Carmelita watching us from the bottom of the stairs and force myself to give her a small smile that she doesn't return.

'It'll be cold by the coast, not least because the house is so high up on the cliffs.' Helen begins randomly pulling things from the padded hangers in her large walk-in closet room, throwing them down onto the bed. 'I'll probably need some sweaters and maybe a long-sleeved dress for evenings, even though the entire patio area is heated...'

It occurs to me for the first time since I've been working at the Levinsons' as I look around the room that there is nothing here of Bryan's – no clothes, or a watch, or even a bottle of aftershave; not one thing to suggest that he shares it with his wife whatsoever.

'I don't know much about Cindy.' Helen is talking quickly. 'I've only met her once, briefly, at their wedding in Cannes last year, but she's extremely young and trendy, and I don't want to look like an old frump next to her... Ohh, what about this?' She holds up a soft-looking knitted gown that wouldn't look out of place on a runway, though perhaps might on Helen's broad frame. 'It's last season's Balenciaga, but it's a classic... What do you think, Christine – should it go in the case?'

The situation feels so surreal that I want to scream.

'Yes... It's... it's lovely,' I say. 'Actually, I meant to ask, did you find your earring? Ed mentioned you'd stopped by the house yesterday while I was visiting Mum. He said you thought you may have lost it there.'

She swings round to face me. 'Ah, yes, I thought I may have mislaid it at your house yesterday morning, but as it turns out, I'd left it in the en suite after all.' She taps her forehead with her fingers. 'Ed kindly had a look for it for me though.' She smiles through glassy eyes. 'Do you know, it's ever so odd, but I swear I've met Ed somewhere before. As soon as I saw him yesterday, I just had this sensation that I knew him from somewhere.'

'My Ed? Really?' I was pretty sure that Ed had never met Helen in person. Why would he have? He knew who she was of course because of her husband – everybody did – but I was certain they'd never crossed paths until yesterday. I shrug. 'Maybe he just has one of those faces.'

'Yes.' She watches me a little strangely. 'I think perhaps he does.' It may be my imagination, but I'm sure her voice is beginning to slur around the edges. 'I meant to mention it to you, but it must've slipped my mind, what with all the drama going on.'

Well, that's one word for it I suppose.

'Helen, listen, I really think we ought to talk about what's happened with Con and—'

'What about this?' She holds up a tweed skirt suit with the unmistakable double CC logo on the lapel. 'No?' She pulls a face before throwing it like a rag onto the floor. 'Too austere. I don't want it to look like she's sitting next to her old aunt.'

It's clear that Helen doesn't appear to be in any mood to discuss our predicament, and yet I'm bursting at the seams. I need answers. I'll have to try another tactic.

I spot a vibrant red dress set apart from all the others on one of the rails and point to it. 'What about that one?'

'The red?' She snatches it from the hanger. 'This old thing you mean?' She holds it in her hands; stares at it. 'Well, perhaps I would if I was two stone lighter and ten years younger.' She sighs. 'Gosh, this dress brings back some memories...'

I suspect she's about to share them with me, but then there's a knock on the door, and Carmelita enters with an ice bucket containing a bottle of Krug.

'Just leave it there, Carmel, thank you,' Helen says without looking up.

I can feel Carmelita's stony eyes on me as she enters the room. Carmelita is a long-standing live-in employee of the Levinsons and probably thinks I'm trying to step on her toes toadying up to the mistress of the house, though she couldn't be further off the mark. I have no desire to take first place in Helen Levinson's affections. Truth is, I find her behaviour a little odd, and I just want to go home. I give Carmelita another small smile, but she looks straight through me.

'Isn't it a little early in the day?' I say, forgetting myself for a moment. I don't want to appear judgemental. Not least because Helen's being so nice by offering me more shifts *and* doubling my hourly rate, plus I still can't be sure she didn't see me dispose of the holdall at Sunnyside yesterday. I must keep on her good side. 'I mean, I'm driving,' I quickly add. 'It's probably best I don't, and—'

'Oh, don't be such a stick-in-the-mud, Christine!' she scoffs loudly. 'A little glass of bubbly won't hurt, will it?' She shoves the large crystal flute into my hand; takes one for herself. 'What shall we drink to?'

I want to say something along the lines of 'keeping our children out of prison', only I don't think it's what she wants to hear.

'Your wedding anniversary?' I suggest feebly.

'Oh that, yes.' Her voice flattens as she taps my glass with her own. I watch with barely concealed incredulity as she almost throws the whole thing back in one, still clutching the red dress.

'Do you know, I wore this dress the night Paris was conceived.' Her eyes suddenly glaze over as if she's mentally rewound to the exact moment in her mind. 'Almost eighteen years ago now – can you believe it?' She begins to inspect the dress. 'What a night that was,' she says, reminiscing. 'That night changed the course of my life forever. It changed *everything*.'

'Yes, well, motherhood does that to you, doesn't it?' I say, wondering if she's picking up on my burgeoning discomfort.

She stops then and turns to me with a sage expression that instantly unsettles me.

'Christine,' she says, meeting my eyes, 'can I tell you a secret?'

EIGHTEEN
CHRISTINE

I don't want to hear Helen's secret. I have no desire to be entrusted with it, and I certainly don't want the burden of it. I have enough secrets right now, and one more might break me completely.

'I want to tell you about this dress,' she says, pressing it up against her body. She's right – it looks at least two sizes too small for her now.

'I was tiny back then,' she says ruefully, 'young and beautiful and... *hopeful*. The designer is Hervé Léger... all the rage at the time,' she continues. 'All the supermodels wore them – not that I ever looked like one of those, although *he* thought I did...' Her voice dissipates into a melancholic whisper.

I take another cursory sip of the champagne she's just poured me. By 'he' I assume she means Bryan.

'Were you in Paris at the time?' I desperately want to steer the conversation round to our situation, only I'm sensing that Helen is somewhat fragile – or perhaps off her head – and that I need to pick my moment carefully. 'Is that why you named her Paris, after the city she was conceived in?'

She starts laughing; sloshes some of her champagne down

the cashmere she's wearing. 'Good God no! Though that would've been terribly romantic. Actually, it was Bryan's idea to call her Paris. I always wanted to call her Cora.'

I almost drop my champagne flute, gasping as a little of the amber liquid splashes onto my skin. '*Cora?*' My adrenalin spikes painfully hard and fast. I have never mentioned my dead baby daughter's name to Helen, have never mentioned her at all. Up until yesterday, the extent of our conversation had never gone beyond basic pleasantries and my work chores. It had to be a horrible coincidence, didn't it?

'Yes,' she explains. 'I've always loved that name... Anyway' – her voice hardens – '*Bryan* wasn't having any of it, so Paris it was. She was conceived on an impromptu night out, at a nightclub in London.'

I blink at her, taken aback. Does she mean Paris was actually conceived *inside* the club, or is she simply referring to the night she went to one?

'I think it might even still be there today. CoCo's... though it's probably called something else now.'

My adrenalin peaks again, this time so harshly that my ears begin to burn as blood furiously pumps through me. CoCo's is the name of the club Ed went to during his infamous 'lost weekend' all those years ago. Oddly, we were just talking about it last night! My sense of unease is multiplying like a virus. CoCo's was the club du jour back then – everyone who was anyone went there at some time or another. It had to be just a weird coincidence, didn't it? Another one.

'This dress got me in all sorts of trouble,' she continues with a wry smile. 'Looks a bit tired and dated now though, like me I suppose!' She laughs so loudly that it startles me. This encounter is growing stranger by the second.

'Well, Bryan clearly liked it,' I say, attempting some form of humour. I haven't eaten a solitary morsel since yesterday morning – my appetite always abandons me when I'm stressed

– and the small amount of alcohol has gone straight to my head, loosened my lips.

She pulls a face as she pours herself another glass of Krug. 'Bryan...' she snorts. 'I was never *his* type,' she says, with more than a hint of bitterness. 'I was never pretty enough, never slim enough, never... *young* enough.'

She places such emphasis on the word that it makes me look up at her.

'Anyway, to us,' she says as she tips more bubbles into my glass. Perhaps Ed's right and Helen really is just lonely and desperate for a friend. I gingerly take another small sip before making an excuse to use the en-suite bathroom, where I tip the remainder of it down the sink. I've got to drive home yet feel as if I can't refuse her hospitality.

'How was your mum when you saw her yesterday?' Helen calls out to me from behind the bathroom door.

I'm still reeling from the revelation that she wanted Paris to be given the same name as my dead daughter – something she couldn't possibly have known, unless of course Conor told Paris and Paris told Helen, which seems unlikely. Surely Helen would've said something if she had? I make a mental note to ask Con if he's ever mentioned his sister to Paris.

'Must be horrid to see her like that, not knowing where or who she is, unable to recognise her own daughter?'

'Yes,' I croak, 'it is.' Ordinarily, I'd be glad of the opportunity to talk about Mum, but now my mind can't focus properly. And how does Helen know that Mum struggles to recognise me anyway? I've never discussed the extent of her dementia with her or her symptoms. She's probably just assumed.

'They're nice though aren't they, the carers – they look after her well?'

It sounds like a statement rather than a question, as though she's somehow familiar with the staff at Sunnyside. Jesus, my paranoia is sending me left. I run the tap, pretend to wash my hands as I look in the mirror and tell myself it's all just a weird coincidence. It's probably the drink and the pills talking. I'm no doctor, but I'm pretty sure you shouldn't mix the two together. She's clearly a bit all over the place, and I feel a little guilty suddenly, like I've judged her too harshly. Maybe Helen really *is* struggling with everything that's happened and this is her way of coping. Besides, I get the distinct impression that the Levinsons' marriage isn't quite as rosy as they like to publicly portray. I'm convinced they must have separate bedrooms, and her barbed asides about her husband certainly suggest so. Perhaps that note I found in the library was a cry for help in an unhappy marriage? It did sound pretty desperate.

'Yes, they're lovely.' I rejoin her in the bedroom. 'I couldn't ask for a nicer set of people to be taking care of her. I suppose, though, I wish I was able to do it myself. So, tell me,' I say, mildly intrigued, 'which wedding anniversary will you and Bryan be celebrating this weekend? How many years have you been married?' I feel a slight sense of triumph that so far I seem to have distracted Helen from telling me this secret of hers that I don't want to be privy to. I have a bad feeling about it.

'Twenty-fifth,' she says flatly. 'Twenty-five whole years of my life...'

Regret suddenly fills the room, cloying like cheap perfume.

'A quarter of a century,' she adds with a wry snort. 'Time flies when you're having fun, doesn't it, Christine?'

'Silver,' I say, 'your silver wedding anniversary. Ed and I celebrated that not so long ago ourselves. He bought me a charm for my bracelet, a little elephant. He's always telling me I'm like one. You know, that I never forget anything.'

'Bryan isn't Paris's biological father.'

My triumph vanishes.

'He couldn't have children,' she says flatly. 'We tried and tried for years to no avail, and eventually he agreed to get himself checked out.' She goes over to the large tallboy and opens a drawer, takes out a packet of slim, white-tipped cigarettes and lights one. I've never seen Helen smoke before now. 'You want one?'

I shake my head, mute through shock.

She sighs, throwing them back into the draw. 'I was desperate for a child,' she continues, blowing smoke forcibly from her lips. 'But they said his sperm count was extremely low, and that the ones he was producing had low mobility, that they were sluggish and lazy, swimming around in circles... can you imagine?' She laughs bitterly. 'Telling someone like Bryan that he's firing blanks?'

'Oh,' I say, in the absence of knowing exactly how to reply. 'I'm sorry.'

'Anyway, we tried IVF, maybe four, five times,' she continues. 'Only that didn't work either,' she sighs, 'like it wasn't meant to be somehow, *or at least not between us.*' She pours herself another glass of champagne and does the same for me before I can prevent her. I realise that I'm gripping the glass tightly with my fingers as I pretend to take as sip. 'So I took matters into my own hands.'

My knees are jiggling now – my fight-or-flight mode has kicked in, and it's all I can do to stop myself running from the room.

'And so, one night, I decided to go into town with the sole purpose of having a one-night stand and getting pregnant.' She drains her champagne glass and instantly refills it again. I place my hand over the top of my own and hope my face doesn't betray my shock. To look at her, Helen Levinson is the *last* person I would've had down for this kind of behaviour. She's the embodiment of an upper-class MP's wife, one who promotes family values and Christian morality, an upstanding member of the community, the sort of person you couldn't ever imagine having sex, *with anyone*. I have no idea why she's even telling me this.

'So that's what happened.' She shrugs. 'I went to CoCo's nightclub wearing this dress.' She holds it in her hand like a trophy. 'I made sure it was the right time in my cycle, and I had thrilling, spontaneous and passionate sex with a handsome stranger in the bathroom of the club. That's how Paris was conceived.' She imparts this information like she's telling me the weather forecast, matter-of-fact and emotionless.

I open my mouth to say something, but nothing comes out. I'm genuinely lost for words.

'Did... does Bryan know?' I eventually ask.

'Not for a long time he didn't, no.' Her eyes have glazed over now, the alcohol and pills I think she must be on taking full effect. 'But he found out eventually *of course.*' Her expression clouds over, like a darkness befalling her. 'And I've paid for it ever since. *We both have.*' She whispers the last part so it's barely audible.

'And what about the... the man... the man you... Paris's real father. Does *he* know?' I really don't want to know any of this, and yet I find myself compelled to ask.

She looks up at me then. I could be mistaken, but I'm sure I see the faintest smile cross her lips.

'No,' she says. 'He was married. Or at least he told me he was. He was bereaved at the time if I remember rightly, grieving for... hmm, I can't quite remember now. He was drunk I think – he was on a stag do – but so was I. I doubt he can even recall it. I barely can myself.'

'Bereaved?'

Her words hit me like a truck at 100 mph. I clutch my chest, my heart pounding against it like it's trying to make a break for freedom. *CoCo's nightclub... a bereaved stranger... on a stag do...* Cora had only been gone around six months or so when Ed's infamous 'lost weekend' took place. Both of us were barely functioning at the time, still in the vortex of our collective grief for our baby girl. Only I know she can't possibly be talking about

Ed. That would be insane. It's all just a bizarre and horribly surreal coincidence. I push the ridiculous thought away, but it bounces right back to me.

'When was this, Helen?'

'Hmm?' she says, distracted as she continues to rifle through her clothes rail. 'Oh, when it happened you mean? The summer of 2007 – July twelfth to be exact,' she adds. 'Funny, I can't remember much about him, what he looked like or even his name,' she says, biting her bottom lip, 'yet I can recall the exact date quite clearly. I've always been good with them – dates I mean, not one-night stands.' She chuckles.

'Does Paris know?'

'No!' she answers quickly. 'And please, she mustn't. She really can't find out, especially now, given everything. I think it would be too much for her to deal with.'

I nod. 'Of course. I won't say anything.'

She looks directly at me, her eyes narrowing a touch.

'I promise you,' I add, quickly, placing my glass onto the bedside table before it slips from my shaking fingers. 'Your secret's safe with me.'

NINETEEN
CHRISTINE

I'd rather rip out my own eyeballs than stay at the Levinsons' house a second longer. The need to extricate myself has started to feel like a matter of life and death.

In a bid to make my excuses, I lie and tell Helen that Sunnyside has messaged, asking me to go over there urgently.

'I hope it's nothing serious!' she says, like our situation isn't serious enough already. 'Let me know if there's anything I can do to help.'

She could stop acting weird for a start, I think as I run down the spiral stairs like a child with a pound in her pocket for the ice-cream van. I stop short as I reach the bottom. Carmelita is standing there, staring up at me with those cold, steely eyes of hers.

'And what are *you* looking at?' I mutter underneath my breath as I brush past her and out of the front door. I'm beyond caring at this point. I just want to leave.

I turn the key in the ignition with shaking hands. In less than forty-eight hours, I've discovered that my only son has committed an unspeakable act that's left a man dead, I've committed perjury and now I'm being forced to entertain the idea that my husband has potentially cheated on me with Helen Levinson, *of all people*.

It only occurs to me then, as I switch the wiper blades on – it's started to rain heavily, almost poetically somehow – that in the tiniest 'if' that Ed impregnating Helen Levinson in a toilet cubicle is even remotely true, Conor and Paris would then be half-brother and sister, related by blood. They could've unknowingly committed incest – in all likelihood probably already had!

I'm overcome by a wave of nausea as I grip the steering wheel. For a moment, I think I might genuinely have to pull over and empty my guts out all over the ground. My mind is spinning like a top.

I cling to the 'bizarre coincidence' theory like a kid on a rollercoaster as I begin the drive home. Ed would *never* have cheated on me, least of all with Helen flipping Levinson, however much younger and slimmer and prettier she might've been at the time! He was only saying just last night how he'd never even *looked* at another woman that way in all the years I've known him, and I believed him. Now I'm wondering whether I might have been a touch naïve.

In the three decades we've been together, Ed has never once given me cause to be jealous, or suspicious, or mistrustful about another woman, *about anything*, perhaps with the exception of my classmate Sally Jones, who sent him a Valentine's card when he was fourteen. Incidentally, something I still tease him about to this day. If Ed had cheated on me, I like to think I would've known somehow, that I'd have sensed it. We don't have secrets from each other, which ironically is perhaps one of the secrets to our largely happy and long union. The secret to a good marriage is not having secrets! Along with Helen's claim to have wanted to give Paris the same name as our dead daughter, it *has* to be some kind of twisted, freak coincidence. She had to be talking about another bereaved stranger she met that night of 12 July.

Is there such a thing as too much of a coincidence?

I switch the car heater on in a bid to warm up. My bones feel cold to the marrow. All this is somehow happening because I broke my moral code, I feel sure of it. The fact that I'm concealing the truth about something so dreadful has sent instant karma calling and has set off this chain of events. A Pandora's box has been opened, and I can't close it again.

'Bullshit,' I say angrily to myself as I try to regulate my breathing, taking deep breaths in through my nose and out through my mouth. 'It's all bloody bullshit and—' I see the blue lights in my rear-view mirror then, and a bolt of panic shoots through me.

'*Shiiiit.*'

The police are behind me, sirens flashing!

I hold my breath as I slow down, waiting for them to pass. When they don't, I pull over, giving them room to overtake. I'm still holding my breath as I check the rear-view mirror again and see that they've pulled up on the side of the road behind me.

'*Oh my God!*' What do they want? Is this something to do with Conor? Are they going to arrest me?

I curse repeatedly under my breath and watch as two uniformed officers – a male and a female – exit the car and begin making their way towards me. Briefly, I entertain the idea of putting my foot down on the accelerator and taking off, but I'm completely paralysed by fear, and it's a mad idea anyway. Was I speeding without realising it? Maybe they've been following me, keeping tabs on me like Ed said might happen. My paranoia spikes out of control as I open the window, allowing the rain, which is coming down in heavy sheets now, to splatter into the car and onto my leggings.

When Ed was in prison and ergo had a lot of time on his hands, he read up on the law and educated himself on all aspects of police procedure. As a result, he's become something of an aficionado. His words return to me now.

They don't need a reason to stop you. If you ever do get stopped, Tee, don't offer any information as to why you think they might've pulled you over, and don't answer any of their questions. You could incriminate yourself without even realising. They're tricky bastards them lot – they'll try and trip you up.

I'm practising deep breathing as one of the officers – the male – approaches the window.

'Hello there,' he greets me with an affable smile. He seems friendly enough. 'Would you mind stepping out of the car please?'

'Sure,' I reply, though I'm not sure if I'm physically capable. My feet feel like they've been welded to the foot pedals.

'Is everything OK?' I ask cautiously as I step unsteadily from my car, pulling my hood over my head to protect myself from the downpour. Ed didn't mention if it was OK for me to be the one asking the questions, but I feel compelled to say *something*.

The female officer is speaking into her radio a little distance behind us. I imagine she's probably checking the car registration.

'Where are you headed?' he asks.

Ed told me never to answer their questions, and yet it seems so counterintuitive not to. I haven't done anything wrong. Or, at least, not that they know of, unless they actually do and they're here to put the cuffs on me.

'I was going home,' I say, pointlessly motioning in the direction I was driving. 'I'm on my way back from work.' I'm suddenly grateful for the rain and chilly wind – I'm vibrating with stress, and it's helping to disguise it.

'Can I see some identification please – your driver's licence?'

He looks so young, the officer, I think as I begin rifling

around my handbag for my purse, no more than a few years older than my Conor at a guess and a similar sort of age to Mathew Reynolds. Conor flashes up in my head then, and I visualise my son kicking and stamping on Reynolds's face as he lies helpless on the ground, his arms bunched together like a shield as he attempts to protect himself.

'Are you OK?' the officer says, looking at me, his brow lightly furrowing in concern.

'What? Sorry? Yes... yes, I'm fine... Ah, here it is.' I shakily pass him my licence.

'Thank you... Mrs Carter?' he says, glancing at it before handing it to his colleague. 'Do you have any idea why we pulled you over?'

'No,' I reply genuinely.

'We have reason to believe that you may be driving under the influence of alcohol,' he says with that affable tone that seems somewhat incongruous to the situation.

'But I haven't been drinking!' I respond defensively. 'Well, just a few sips of champagne, but not even a glass!' My voice sounds a little squeaky with protest.

'Celebrating something?' he asks.

'No, I... my employer... well, she's more my friend actually,' I quickly think to add. 'We toasted her wedding anniversary as I was helping her pack for a weekend away, but like I say, no more than a glass, maybe half a glass, even less than that probably, and...' I'm talking too much and too quickly, my nerves jangling like a wind chime in a hurricane.

It strikes me then what he said about having 'reason to believe' that I'm under the influence of alcohol.

'Was I driving erratically?' I ask him. I suppose it's possible given the state of my nerves and the myriad thoughts in my head distracting me, yet I'm pretty sure I hadn't been, and I definitely know I wasn't speeding. I've always been careful behind the wheel.

The young officer eyes me a little cautiously. 'We've been informed that you may be intoxicated, that you'd consumed alcohol before getting into your vehicle – someone telephoned in. We need you to take a breath test.'

I stare at him in disbelief. 'Sorry? *Informed*? Telephoned by who?' My head is spinning so fast it feels like it might detach from my neck and roll away. 'How?'

He produces a small device with a white plastic pipe at the top. 'If you can just blow into this for me please.'

I don't want to argue with him. I know I'm not over the limit, though I would have been if I'd actually drunk all the champagne Helen kept pouring me. Thank God I'd had the sense to tip it down the sink.

'No need to be nervous. Just take a deep breath, place your lips round the pipe, and blow a strong and steady breath until you hear the long beep stop, OK?'

'OK,' I say. Only I'm not OK. Right now, I'd need a passport to get back to OK. Someone has tried to stitch me up, get me done for drink-driving!

Carmelita. Those steely eyes flash inside my head. It has to be her who tipped off the police. She was giving me daggers all morning, like I'd somehow done something to offend her. She must've called them, forewarned them that I'd been drinking champagne and would be driving home. Perhaps her spoken English is better than I thought.

A ball of anger sweeps through me, warming my skin in the rain. How could she do this to me? *Why?* It was Helen who'd asked me to help with her packing – who'd suggested that Carmelita do my cleaning shift and offered to double my hourly rate. It had all been at Helen's behest. I hadn't wanted or asked for any special treatment. I'd just wanted to go home.

I took a deep breath and blew as hard as I could into the device until the beep stopped before handing it back to the youthful-looking officer.

He nods, turns to his colleague and after a moment shakes his head. I glance over at her; could swear she looks a touch disappointed. 'It's a reading of 0.01.' He smiles at me. 'You're all clear.'

Calm. I must try and stay calm, I tell myself over and over again as I somehow make it home on autopilot. But my heart is beating so fast it's like I'm having an out-of-body experience by the time I pull up to my house. Like I'm standing on the edge of myself looking in, and I can hardly bear to watch.

I know I have to say something to Ed about Helen's confession, but I mustn't go in hard. I can't accuse him of anything, not least because I simply refuse to believe that any of it could ever be true. Yet the more I mull it over, such a coincidence just seems just so... *unlikely*. What are the chances of *two* handsome, bereaved strangers being in the same nightclub, on a stag do, around the same time, eighteen years ago? *If* Helen really *is* talking about Ed, then it occurs to me that maybe *he* told her about Cora, and that gave Helen the idea of using the same name for her own daughter, who was conceived that very night, *in a toilet cubicle*.

At the time of Ed's 'lost weekend', things were, understandably, a little fractious between us. We were both in the darkest depths of grief for our darling daughter, Ed consumed by guilt and remorse at being inside when she was cruelly ripped from our loving arms, and me, despairing, angry and in denial among myriad other things. But we never once truly blamed or turned on each other. No one could've foreseen what was going to happen to our Cora. If anything, losing our precious girl eventually made our bond even stronger.

I'll just have to calmly talk to him about it; look him in the eyes, and then I'll know in an instant.

Ed's van is parked outside, which tells me he's home. I turn my key in the lock, my fingers vibrating.

'Ah, you're home,' he says, stating the obvious as I burst through the front door. 'How's my—' He takes one look at me. 'What's happened? What's wrong?'

'Did you shag Helen Levinson in a nightclub toilet in 2007, you cheating bastard?' I shriek at him.

So much for staying calm.

TWENTY

CHRISTINE

'Have you been on the funny fags?'

Ed pulls his chin into his neck; stares at me in a mix of confused horror. 'What the hell are you on about, *shagging Helen Levinson in a toilet*? Christ, Tee, have you completely lost the plot?'

My burst of anger fizzles out like a faulty firework as I drop down onto the sofa and bury my head into my hands. A giant wave of mental and physical exhaustion has just crashed into me, taking me clean out.

'Tee?' Ed's voice is heavy with concern as he sits down next to me, and I collapse sideways into him. I want to cry, to release some of the tension, tight like a drum, trapped inside my chest. 'You're shaking... Talk to me, Tee. What's happened?'

I genuinely don't know where to start but finally manage to find my voice. 'Where's Con?'

'He's upstairs, Paris is with him. Wha—'

I bolt upright. 'No! Oh no, Ed, you'll have to go up there. You... you'll have to ask her to leave.'

'What? Why? Calm down. It's fine. They're both fine. Stop panicking. There hasn't been any word from the old bill yet. So let's just keep doing what we're doing. Be prepared and cross each hurdle when we come to it, eh?'

His eyes are fixed on mine, searching them.

'I've... I've just been stopped by the police. They pulled me over. I thought they were going to arrest me!' Even my voice doesn't sound quite like my own.

'*What?*' He grips me by my arms. 'Why? When? Are you OK?'

'It's... it's just been the weirdest day,' I stammer, still struggling to regulate my breathing. 'Helen Levinson has suddenly decided I'm her new best friend and is going to double my shifts *and* give me extra cash on top!'

He side-eyes me. '*OK?*' He draws the word out. 'And that's bad news *how* exactly? And what did you mean when you came in? You called me a *cheating bastard*, Tee? What did the police say?'

His questions are coming as quickly and as randomly out of sync as my own thoughts.

'I think she's on drugs.'

'Who's on drugs?' He shakes me gently. 'You're not making any sense!'

'Helen – Helen bloody Levinson!' My voice is pitchy now. 'When I saw her today she seemed a bit...'

'A bit what?'

'I don't know! High, off her head I suppose. Spaced out, not quite there.' I look up at him; drop my voice to a whisper. 'She told me Bryan isn't Paris's biological father.'

Ed pulls back from me a little. 'You're joking! Why would she tell you that?'

'I don't know! And does it look like I'm laughing? She just came out with it all... that Bryan couldn't have kids and IVF failed and all of this, and so she met a stranger in a nightclub, had sex with him in a toilet cubicle and deliberately got herself pregnant.'

I almost burst out laughing as I say it; it sounds so... absurd – not least when you think of who Helen Levinson is – but I'm mindful that Paris is upstairs and don't want her to hear.

Ed's face is a *real* picture now. '*Helen Levinson,*' he says. 'This is the same Helen Levinson we're talking about here? The one you work for who's married to MP Bryan Big Balls...'

'That's not even the half of it. It gets weirder and even more bizarre and—' I stop myself; take a slow, deep breath to try and steady my heart. I'll have a stroke at this rate. 'She claims that this stranger she met, this man whose name she can't remember, was a recently bereaved, married man who was at the club that night on a stag do.'

I'm watching Ed's expression carefully for clues, but so far all I can detect is shock and slightly amused disbelief.

'Well, well, she's a dark horse, isn't she?' He half chuckles. 'It's always the ones you least expect, eh? I'd never have had her down as that type.'

'What type?'

'The type who shags a stranger in a toilet to get herself up the duff!'

'CoCo's,' I say.

He shakes his head. 'CoCo's? The nightclub you mean?'

'The same club *you* went to eighteen years ago for Billy Noye's shag— sorry, *stag* do! Eighteen years ago, Ed. Twelfth of July 2007, Helen said. She remembered the exact bloody date!'

He's still staring at me blankly.

'*July* 2007. That's when *you* were there! I remember! We were only talking about it last night! I mean... it's a bit of a coincidence, isn't it?' It sounds like I'm being accusatory now, which is exactly what I didn't want. Only I'm not sure there's any other way it *can* sound. 'A "handsome", "married" and "*bereaved*" stranger Helen said, and...'

I'm reminded now of the comment she made about Ed looking familiar to her when she met him yesterday. I brushed it off at the time – had forgotten about it until now. 'How many handsome, married, bereaved strangers could there have been in that same venue around the same time?'

Ed starts to laugh then; his face is cracking open.

'It's not bloody funny!' I say, trying not to smile myself. 'It's freaking me out! It would make Conor and Paris' – I pull a face – 'you know, *related*,' I whisper. 'Half-brother and sister!'

'I can't believe I'm hearing this!' He stands up then, his jaw widening in sync with his eyes. 'You don't actually think – *believe* – that I had sex with Helen Levinson in a nightclub toilet eighteen years ago and that *I'm* Paris Levinson's biological father? Are you sure you're not the one on pills, Tee? Come on! Seriously!'

'Yeah but the *same* nightclub, Ed, on the *same* day in the *same* month of the *same* year, a recently bereaved, handsome married man on a stag do...? Even you have to admit, that's more than a few coincidences right there!'

'Jesus, Tee!' He runs his hand through his hair, which tells me he's getting a bit stressed. 'How could you think... I mean, *Helen Levinson* for God's sake!'

'She was younger and slimmer and prettier back then, or so she says,' I add. 'You said you were drunk, that you and the boys got paralytic. Maybe you don't remember!'

'Don't flipping remember!' He's turning in circles now, his hands linked above his head. 'I think I'd remember cheating on my wife in a nightclub toilet for Christ's sake! And I was grieving for Cora at the time! We both were! You can't *really* think...'

I love it whenever Ed says our daughter's name aloud. It's like she's still here somehow. A flutter of sadness suddenly dances through me and settles in my empty stomach. None of this would be happening if Cora was still alive, I'm sure. We'd be different people, Ed and I, living a different life perhaps instead of this one. I thought things couldn't get worse than yesterday, yet today has already superseded it. Moreover, I can't seem to quieten an inner voice that's telling me it's going to get even worse.

'Look, if Helen Levinson *was* at CoCo's nightclub eighteen years ago, then she never saw me there, Tee.' Ed sits back down next to me on the sofa. 'I've never met the woman in person before until yesterday, let alone given her one in a toilet cubicle. That's just bloody ridiculous, and frankly, the thought of it's given me the ick!' He's a little animated now, maybe a touch angry even. 'If she happened to meet a bereaved stranger one night and used him as a sperm donor – and I can't believe I'm having to say this – but I swear on our baby girl's grave, it was someone else, not me.'

Ed has never once sworn on Cora's grave in all the years she's been gone. For that reason alone, I know he's telling the truth. Not that I ever really doubted it.

'Something weird is going on,' I say.

'No shit! You didn't – you *don't* – actually think it was me, do you?'

'No,' I say, feeling guilty, 'that's just it – I don't believe it for a second. But I can't understand it either. *And* she told me she wanted to give Paris the name Cora originally but that Bryan wouldn't let her.' I look up at Ed. '*Cora!* I mean, it's not a totally uncommon name, but it's not particularly common either. I've never mentioned Cora's name to Helen before, unless Con told Paris and she told her? It just seems like a horrible coincidence, all of it... and—' I hit a wall then, burst into tears, exploded like a balloon.

Ed looks at me in horror – I rarely cry – and immediately pulls me to him; wraps his arms around me.

'We shouldn't have done this,' I splutter into his warm chest. He smells of sweat and washing powder. 'We should've just told the truth from the off. Bad things are going to happen now. I can sense it. We're going to be punished one way or another!' I pause. 'Cora, she came to me in my sleep – she tried to warn me, like an omen. She's trying to warn me, Ed...'

'Bad things? Warn you about what? Come on – calm down. You need to take a deep breath—'

'I was breathalysed by the police just now on the way home from the Levinsons',' I interrupt him. 'They told me that someone had tipped them off that I'd been drinking alcohol.'

'What the...? *Who*? They told you that, the police...?'

'Yes! They said someone had "informed" them that I was intoxicated before getting behind the wheel!' I'm starting to shriek again. 'I think maybe it was Carmelita.'

Ed is staring at me like I'm talking in Mandarin.

'She's the Levinsons' live-in housekeeper.'

'And why would she do something that?'

'I... I don't know.' I wipe my nose with the sleeve of my coat; start picking at my lip. 'I think she's jealous maybe? Perhaps she thinks I'm after her job or something?'

'Even so, that's just downright malicious.' He pulls my hand away from my mouth.

'I know. I don't know; it doesn't make sense. Oh God, Ed, I was terrified. I thought they'd come for me, the police. I thought they were going to put cuffs on me, arrest me! Thank God I tipped that champagne down the sink, otherwise...' I actually physically shudder to think. 'I don't think I can go on with this. I...' I'm holding my breath as he grips me tightly. 'I think we should contact that Detective Riley and tell him the truth.'

'Shhh... come on now. It's OK, it's OK... Calm yourself down. You've had a bit of a shock, that's all, but it's going to be OK – it's over now.'

But just as he says it, the doorbell goes.

TWENTY-ONE
DAN

The next day, I'm still so pent-up about Archer – and the fact I haven't had a chance to speak to Fiona about her concerns over Jude because she is taking Juno to swimming lessons first thing – that Davis drives me down to the service station and buys me a consolatory cheese-and-tomato sandwich.

'Why don't you pop home for a bit, gov?' she says, handing me the plastic wrapper. 'See Fiona and the kids – they'll be back by now, won't they? I can oversee the team and work on tracking down Katya, and then maybe we'll get the go-ahead to speak to the Carters again later.'

'And the Levinsons,' I add sharply. 'Bloody hell, now *you* sound just like Archer!'

She gives me a look.

'Sorry,' I apologise, shaking my head. 'But we've got more than enough to bring both the kids in for questioning. We leave it any longer and any of that golden evidence... poof! It'll disappear faster than a ferret up a trouser leg. Both you and I know it. Stalling those search warrants will give them time to get their ducks in a row. That's how they're going to let them get away with it!'

'Who's "they", boss?'

'Whoever Bryan bloody Levinson has got in his back pocket at the top, the commissioner...' Anger prickles at my skin again.

'Well, it's never what you know, is it?'

'I guess that depends on what it is you know exactly, Davis. And right now I want to *know* everything there is about Bryan Levinson. And his wife. The whole Levinson family. Get the team on it – put Mitchell in charge. I don't trust any of them. And I hate to say it, but Valerie Reynolds is right – seems there is no justice for "the likes" of her.'

I'm ranting as I open the sandwich wrapper and stare at the unappetising flimsy bread and cheese that looks as plastic as the container it comes in. 'We need to get hold of the clothes Conor Carter and Paris Levinson were wearing on Saturday night. I want their devices, and we need forensics in there doing their job. He who has nothing to hide hides nothing, so if that's the case, then they'll hand them over willingly, won't they?'

'Well, they don't dispute they were there at the crime scene, gov,' Davis says, 'and they claim to have seen Reynolds pass by them around the time that correlated with the CCTV footage. Plus, it definitely looked as if Reynolds could have been following them from what we saw on the CCTV, but equally, he could just have been headed in the same direction, unrelated, the law of averages, simply coincidence. We can't *prove* otherwise right now.'

'No such thing as coincidence in murder,' I whisper quietly to myself.

'Conor Carter's DNA is all over that bottle. So is someone else's, yet to be identified. Paris Levinson's probably...'

'Or this third unidentified person's,' I say. It feels as if the more Davis speaks, the further I drift from where I want to be. And I'm not even sure where that is yet.

'Ed and Christine Carter both confirmed that they heard the pair get in around 1 a.m. Time wise, it would be cutting it extremely fine, boss, and they would almost certainly have been covered in blood – soaked in it probably. It would have to have been a lively clean-up job. As yet we have no links, no connections between either of them to Reynolds in any way, no obvious motive to kill him, not least so brutally, unless one of them is a violent psychopath.'

'Or both of them are,' I reply. 'And it's all entirely possible. Moreover, it only works if you believe the alibi the Carters have given – that they did get in around 1 a.m.'

She exhales. 'So you *really* think Conor Carter and Paris Levinson viciously killed Reynolds – for no obvious reason – and the families know this and they're covering for them?'

'Yes, Davis, that's exactly what I think. *I think*.'

She exhales again. 'OK. So *why* did they kill him? This was no accidental death. You saw the body, gov...'

This is the part I'm struggling with most – what kept me awake long into the night, among everything else. I can't see either Conor Carter or Paris Levinson acting particularly violently, even in self-defence. They're just kids. But *something* happened. Something that's forced them to lie to the police. I'm sure of it.

'If Reynolds had attacked them, let's say, tried to rob them or whatever... why would they have used that level of violence against him? Bit much in the way of self-defence for someone outnumbered who wasn't even armed, don't you think, gov?'

She's right. But stranger things have, can and do happen – all the time in fact.

'Maybe he *was* armed and they disarmed him. Maybe they were drunk or high or both and just got carried away in the moment – once they started, they couldn't stop?'

In the same way that misery likes company, violence often self-perpetuates and can spin out of control fast. Maybe they're a pair of serial killers in the making, a modern-day Bonnie and Clyde, or part of a secret murder pact perhaps, or members of a cult. As outlandish as it sounds, any or none of it could be true, but unless we get those warrants and dig deeper into their respective lives, then we won't know one way or another.

'So where do you think this Katya fits into it, boss – the sex worker Reynolds was going out to meet that night who we can't find? What about the £20K in his usually empty bank account and the young girls' services he was allegedly procuring in the run-up to his murder? He was definitely involved in something murky, gov.'

'Maybe they're related somehow,' I say, drifting deeper into my own thoughts.

'What do you mean?'

'Hmm? I don't know. Something. Nothing.' I turn to look at her. 'Do us a favour, Lucy.' I give her my best pleading eyes. 'Drive me home, will you?' I place the plastic container in front of her like a prize. 'There's a cheese-and-tomato sandwich in it for you.'

It was always going to be a pit-stop visit. I couldn't rest knowing that with each passing second, a vital piece of evidence was potentially being hidden or destroyed thanks to someone high up on the inside stalling the investigation.

Davis is right though. There are no obvious links between Reynolds and the Carter boy or the Levinson girl, at least not yet. So maybe those links just aren't so 'obvious' and we need to dig a little deeper to find them. I leave her in charge to follow up the leads, primarily focussing on trying to locate Katya while I take a short detour home.

Fiona's text about her concerns over Jude has got me worried and I'm struggling to give anything else my full attention until I speak to her.

'Pop-Pop!' Juno, my almost four year-old daughter, bounds towards me as I walk through the front door. It feels warm and inviting, the smell of something fragrant and delicious cooking in the kitchen hitting my nostrils and awakening my saliva glands. *Home.*

'Pip!' I swoop her up and give her neck a good sniff as I twirl her around in my arms. She smells like I imagine a cherub to. 'How's my best girl, huh? What mischief have you been up to? Whose heart have you broken today, eh? Pip tell Pop-Pop all about it.'

'Heyyyyyy!' Fiona spies me from where she's standing in the kitchen, cooking something on the hob. 'What are you doing home?' She looks pleased at least.

Juno rushes off, probably to get something she wants to show me, and I plant a kiss on Fiona's lips. 'That smells *goooood.*'

'Jesus, Dan.' She gives me the once-over. 'You look like crap. Did you get any sleep last night?'

'No really, please, Fi, tell me what you actually think.'

'So, you going to tell me about it then?' She sounds interested, which isn't surprising given that it's her nature as a journalist to be inquisitive, aka nosey.

'Where's the little dude?' I'm desperate to see my nine-month-old son, Jude, and give him a good sniff too.

'He's napping,' she says, continuing to stir the contents of the pot.

'I'm going to pop in and say hi. Don't worry – I won't wake him up,' I say. 'Then we can catch up; have lunch together.'

'I think Jude might be deaf,' she says suddenly, randomly, as she continues to stir.

'Pardon?'

'That's not even funny, Dan.' She shoots me an unimpressed look.

'I wasn't joking.'

'I'm being serious.'

'You think our son's deaf?'

'Yes!' she says. 'You're not hard of hearing yourself, are you?'

'More like selective.' I wink at her. 'What makes you say that?' I feel the tiniest trickle of nervousness begin to slither into my bloodstream. 'He's not deaf, Fi,' I say before she can answer. 'He seems alert and bright and—'

'He's not startled by loud sounds,' she interrupts, 'like yesterday, he was in his high chair and some pots and pans came clattering out of the cupboard as I opened it. It scared the crap out of me – the sudden loud noise – but he didn't even flinch. He just started laughing... and... and... when I say his name, when I call out to him, he doesn't turn his head towards me – he only turns if he sees me... and I've been trying to get him to say "mama" or "dada", but he just doesn't seem to be responding in the way I think he should be, not like Juno did, and—'

'I've never seen anything that's caused me any alarm or concerns...' I say gently, placing my hands on her shoulders.

'Yes, but you're never here, Dan,' she says, without a hint of malice.

It stings like a slap, but I can't really disagree with her.

'He's a boy is all it likely is,' I try to reassure her, and myself, incidentally. 'We take our time reaching those milestones that you girls seem to race through.'

She hesitates; nods. 'Maybe you're right... Oh I don't know... I'm overthinking it perhaps.'

I wrap my arms around her waist from behind. Stoop to rest my head on her shoulder briefly.

'So' – she goes back to stirring the pot – 'the body by the arches, Mathew Reynolds, the lad from the estate?'

'Viciously beaten unrecognisable then stabbed in the neck. But we haven't yet released that last bit of information, so keep it to yourself for now.'

'Was it drugs related?'

'Possibly. A young couple down by the arches saw him just

before he was attacked. They were all at Renton's nightclub, not together, but from the CCTV it looked as if Reynolds could've been following them. He could also just as well have been innocently walking in the same direction... Anyway, we found a familial DNA match via blood on the suspected murder weapon.'

'Oh! Exciting!'

'Conor Carter. Seems like a nice boy as well, from a decent family, although the dad's got previous, hence the DNA match.'

'And what about the girl?'

'That's where it gets a bit tricky...'

She stops stirring; glances at me. 'The girl is Paris Levinson, daughter of—'

'Bryan Levinson, the MP?'

She pulls a face. The wife is a hive of information sometimes thanks to her being in a similar profession to mine – minus all the red tape and corruption it seems anyway. When she's not on maternity leave, she's one of the chief investigative reporters on the *Gazette*. And she's bloody good at her job.

'Why the face?'

'Rumours,' she says. 'Been circulating for years...'

'Such as?'

'Corruption in business, backhanders to the council, dubious sexual activities, the usual...'

'Define dubious sexual activities.'

She raises her eyebrows. 'In our case? Any.'

'And a comedian as well!'

She giggles. 'Oh, I don't know, Dan... He's an MP – there're always rumours about MPs. It goes with the territory. They're often started by the opposition and can be quite an effective method in discrediting someone and—'

'And what rumours, Fi?'

'Well, there were a few historic rumblings about him using

prostitutes some years back, but we never got anything solid – it was mainly hearsay and gossip, certainly nothing publishable.'

'But did you believe it?'

'I never worked on the story; it was before my time, but it's hardly original is it: MP uses prostitute? Anyway, even if it was true, he'd probably have got the story killed. Bryan Levinson is an extremely rich and powerful man – he has a lot of very important people in his pocket, and no one really wants to upset him. He can afford to make things go away, like the NDA he got someone to sign a while back. Money talks, Dan – you know that.'

'A non-disclosure agreement? So he paid someone off to silence them?' She has my fullest attention now.

'It's standard stuff for these rich celebrities and those in power. We get hold of a potential scandal and they'll just shut it down with pound notes and threats of legal action. It's common procedure – happens all the time.'

'So did he pay off an escort to keep her mouth shut then, was that it?'

'Oh no, it wasn't him; it wasn't even actually anything to do with Bryan Levinson himself. It was his wife, Helen.'

'His *wife?*'

My phone rings. 'Davis?'

'Christine Carter was stopped by uniform a short while ago, boss, on suspicion of drink-driving.'

'Really?'

'Yes, on her way home from the Levinsons' house. They breathalysed her...'

'And?'

'And she was clear. But the interesting part is that someone put a 999 call in twenty minutes before she was stopped, giving Christine Carter's name and registration number, claiming that she'd been drinking alcohol and was driving her vehicle.'

'What?' My mind suddenly zigzags off in all directions. 'Do we know who?'

'No. But I've requested the audio.'

'Who would want to get her into trouble like that?'

'No idea, gov.'

Screw the warrant. I'll drop in on the Carters, use this new information as an in.

'I've got some new info, and I want you to focus in on Helen Levinson,' I say. 'See if anything comes up.'

'Yes, gov.'

I hang up. I don't want to involve Davis in my unauthorised plans just yet – I don't want to get her into trouble.

'Listen, Fi, I...'

She turns to me with a resigned look that she's doing her best to disguise. 'Don't worry,' she says, with the gentlest raise of her eyebrow, one hand still stirring the pot. 'I'll save some for you.'

TWENTY-TWO

DAN

I make my way over to Albert Road, to the Carters' address, no better off than I was a couple of hours ago, except for the brief morale boost of seeing Fiona and the kids for all of ten minutes. I'm wondering if I was too dismissive of my wife's concerns about Jude. I hadn't meant to sound glib, but there isn't anything going on with our son. I feel sure I'd have picked up on it if there was...

Helen Levinson. I steer my mind back to the present. Fiona was about to tell me something about a non-disclosure agreement but then Jude stirred and I had to head off without finding out what it was. My phone rings.

'Lucy.'

'Sorry to disturb you again, gov, but I— Where are you? I can hear traffic.'

'In the car, on my way to... the supermarket,' I lie. But only to protect her, so it doesn't count.

'OK, well, you're going to *love* this.'

'You know how much I appreciate a bit of romance,' I say dryly. 'Talk dirty to me.'

'Well, I focused on Helen Levinson like you asked, and something pretty surprising has come up, gov.'

'Go on,' I say as casually as I can. If she detects that I'm overly intrigued, she'll only torture me.

'She had a non-molestation order put out on her a few years back.'

I almost go through a red light; have to slam the brakes on. I take a breath. That's not what I was expecting her to say.

'Are you *sure*? We're talking about the same Helen Levinson here?'

Years in this job have taught me that it's prudent, perhaps even wise, to never judge a book by its cover, and yet it's entirely instinctive and we all do it subconsciously. Actually, occasionally you really *can* judge a book by its cover, and it does exactly what you thought it said on the tin, but it often pays to reserve your judgement. The devil always comes with a smile on his face after all, as the old man used to say, God rest his soul. Maybe we're all programmed to make initial judgements on each other as part of our survival instinct. But I know first-hand that criminals come in all shapes and sizes. Just because Helen Levinson *looks* like a slightly dumpy, privileged, unassuming middle-aged woman doesn't mean she isn't capable of committing a crime.

'Uh-huh, absolutely sure, gov. A twelve-month order was granted to a man called Aaron Young, some six years ago in Croydon Crown Court.'

'Interesting. We got an address?'

'Yep. I'll send it over. Do you want to pay him a visit?'

I do, but right now I need to swing by the Carters', and I don't want Davis to know about that.

'See if you can track him down,' I tell her.

'I'll do my best, boss.'

. . .

'Mr Carter? Ed, isn't it?'

He greets me with an affable smile and a nod, and yet I sense that inwardly he's not exactly overjoyed to see me. 'Is it OK if I come in?'

'Of course. You like making a surprise appearance, don't you, Detective Riley?' he says as he opens the door to let me in.

Christine Carter leaps up from the sofa as soon as she sees me.

'Hello,' she says, quickly wiping her eyes, but I can see she's been crying. Her mascara has run.

'Are you OK, Christine?' She looks traumatised.

'Would you like a drink? A cup of tea or something?' Ed says, though he hasn't moved from the front door.

'It's Dan, please, and no, thank you. I won't keep you long.'

I turn to his wife. 'I heard that you were stopped by a patrol car and breathalysed. I just wanted to check everything is OK?'

Her eyes dart straight to her husband. 'Yes... I... they stopped me on my way back from the Levin— from Helen's. I was... I was helping her choose outfits to take on a weekend away.'

'Well, if she's anything like my wife, she'll probably need to take another suitcase, just in case.' I smile at my own lame attempt at humour, though her expression is frozen solid. 'Only someone put in an anonymous 999 call to us alleging that you were driving while intoxicated. Have you any idea who might've done that, Christine, and why?'

She glances at Ed again; opens her mouth to speak. 'Just some disagreement at work. I... I...'

'Listen, um, Detective Riley, Dan,' Ed interjects. 'I'm not sure why you're here asking my wife about this? With the greatest respect, it's not really anything for you to worry about, is it? You're a homicide fella...'

'Is Conor here?' I ask.

'He is. *Why?*' Ed Carter's tone suddenly has an edge to it, and I remind myself not to go in too hard.

'Would it be OK to speak to him? We'd really like him to come down to the station and give an official statement if that's convenient?'

'Oh? Really?' There's a wobble in Christine's voice. 'Why would he need to do that?'

'It's all right, Tee.' Ed touches his wife's arm. 'Look, Dan, it's been a pretty shi— difficult couple of days. Tee's mum isn't well, you see, and then getting stopped by your lot... we're all a bit shook.' He pauses. 'I'm sure Conor would be more than happy to come down to the station and give a statement tomorrow – anything he can do to help with your enquiries – but he's resting right now; yesterday really took it out of him, and he needs to be a hundred per cent for football training. Perhaps he can come down after he's done tomorrow?'

I look around the small living room; glance at the photos on the wall behind Ed Carter. There's one of Ed and Christine holding a baby, a newborn by the looks of it. A younger Christine is gazing lovingly down into the baby's face while a boyish-looking Ed is gazing lovingly at her. It's a beautiful photograph, a perfect moment captured in time. You can almost feel the joy coming from it. Next to it is another photograph where again they're holding a newborn. The dynamic is the same, with Christine looking down at the baby and Ed gazing at his wife. Only this time there's an unmistakable tear tracking Christine's face. It's still a beautiful, intimate photo, but I sense something is missing.

I point to it. 'Was this taken the day Conor was born?'

'Yes, that's right,' Ed answers even though I directed the question at Christine.

'And this one?'

There's a moment's pause.

'That was our first child, Cora, our daughter,' she answers quietly.

'Yes, we lost her to meningitis, twenty years ago now,' Ed cuts in. 'I'm sorry, Detective Riley. But like I say, it's been a trying couple of days and—'

'I'm sorry.' I continue to address Christine Carter. 'I can't imagine the pain of that, of losing a child.'

'Yes,' she says, 'it's a despair that can't be described, Detective.' Which is in fact probably the best and most succinct way I've ever heard someone describe it.

'As a father of young children myself...' I shake my head. 'No parent should ever have to bury a child. It's just... *wrong*. It upsets the natural order of things. That's why my heart goes out to Valerie Reynolds right now.'

I'm sure I hear an intake of breath as Christine's gaze drops to the floor.

'Yes,' she says, visibly swallowing, 'my heart goes out to her too.'

She looks on the verge of tears again.

'As parents, we'd do anything for our kids, wouldn't we?' I say, without taking my eyes from the photo on the wall. 'Even die for them?' Ed still hasn't moved from the front door. 'Before I ever had kids, I thought that was something parents just said, you know? I didn't fully understand at the time that it is in fact true and that you *would* literally sacrifice yourself rather than see your child come to harm. I know I would die for my own children, *and* lie for them too if necessary, probably. Anything to protect them. But, you see, a man is dead...'

Christine's legs are jiggling manically.

'Course you would,' Ed says. 'Any parent would. Well, most normal ones anyway.'

'Losing a child in *any* circumstances is a terrible, heart-breaking, tragic event – though clearly I don't need to tell either of you that.' I keep my voice soft. 'But when your child is *murdered*, their face literally battered unrecognisable *and then* stabbed in the neck, that really is—'

'*Stabbed?*' Christine suddenly looks up. 'You never mentioned anything about him being stabbed.' Her eyes dart from mine to Ed's and back.

'Yes, a single stab wound from a broken bottle. It cut clean through his carotid artery. He bled to death, relatively slowly in fact, probably took about ten minutes, maybe less given his other injuries and the blood loss and—'

'Oh please, stop!' Christine puts her hands over her ears. 'I... I can't bear to hear it.'

The air in the room feels suddenly thicker, like you could choke on it. I think I've probably said enough.

'I'm sorry. I didn't mean to upset you, Christine. Look.' I study each of them; read the respective concern on their faces – which Ed Carter is managing to disguise much more efficiently than his wife. 'I understand what Conor means to you. It's evident how much you love him and that you want the best for him, but if there's anything either of you want to talk to me about, want to tell me...' I scan their faces again. 'I just want to help. It's not too late, and—'

'And he'll come to the station tomorrow to give you that statement,' Ed chimes in. 'I'll bring him myself.'

He opens the front door, and I can almost feel him mentally pushing me through it.

'It's Conor's DNA on that bottle,' I say to Ed quietly as I make my leave, although technically this is still unconfirmed. 'We'll need his clothes – the clothes he was wearing on Saturday night – and his shoes. It's standard procedure at this stage of the enquiry. Look, Ed' – I'm careful to keep my tone as friendly as possible – 'clearly you're a hard-working man who's dedicated to his family, and I applaud that, I really do, but I don't need to tell you how this works. It won't work out well if you—'

'He already told us he had a beer bottle with him that night and that he chucked it.' Ed shrugs. 'Of course it has his DNA on it – you'd expect it to be there.'

'Yes, absolutely.' I nod profusely. 'But your son and his girlfriend were the last people to see Mathew Reynolds alive—'

'Aside from the killer you mean?' he quickly interjects.

I smile. I can't help liking Ed Carter.

'Christine.' I nod at her, frozen like a statue on the sofa, her gaze locked on the floor. 'Sorry to drop in unannounced again.'

'Um, sorry, hang on,' Ed stops me. 'How do you even know it's Conor's DNA on that bottle? He's never been in trouble with the police before – his DNA isn't on any database.'

'No, Ed,' I say. 'You're right. *But yours is.*'

TWENTY-THREE
CONOR

'I swear to you, Mum.' He grips her by the forearms; looks into her eyes. 'Mum, I promise you that we didn't stab him. We didn't stab anyone!' he tries to reassure her, but she's not listening – she's losing it.

'In the neck! Severing his what's-it-called artery... the main one! That's what he said, that Detective Riley. Oh my God! Conor, please... *please tell me you didn't.*'

Her eyes are bulging. He's never seen her look like this before – a bit mental – and it scares him. Surely his own mum can't believe he's capable of doing that? Surely he isn't capable of doing that? If only he could remember properly!

'I was drinking a beer when we left the club... I dropped it when I was having a pee, up by the arches, and I heard Paris...' he tries to explain as he glances over to where she's sitting on the sofa, fear written all over her face. She has such a pretty face. He just wants all this to go away so that he can look at it. He never for a moment envisaged something like this happening in the story he hoped to write with her. And now his mum and dad have lied and implicated themselves too in a bid to protect him. It's all such a clusterfuck. He can only hope that

Paris's powerful dad might intervene somehow and save their sorry arses. Then they'll just have to take it one day at a time, find a way to live with the guilt of what they've done.

That afternoon, while his parents were at work, he and Paris had made love for the first time. He supposes, given the circumstances, that this might be considered inappropriate. A man is dead after all – and by all accounts they are responsible for that. Yet as dreadful as it all is, he has to admit that he doesn't exactly *feel* like a killer. Not that he knows what one is supposed to feel like because he's never killed anyone before – it's just something, an inherent knowledge deep inside of him.

'Are you sure you want this, Paris?' he asked her earlier between deep, lingering kisses as they snuggled into each other, semi-naked underneath the covers to keep warm. He didn't want her to feel like he was pushing her into anything, yet their shared predicament had undeniably brought them closer together and seemed to place a sense of urgency upon them – or on him at least.

Her skin felt like cashmere as he gently touched it, mindful that this might be her first time with a man – and maybe his own with a woman for a while to come – though he couldn't bring himself to entertain that idea for too long because it scared the hell out of him.

'We don't have to if you don't want to,' he said. 'I can wait until you're ready, until you feel like you can trust me.'

He didn't really know where those words came from. He'd never spoken to a girl that way before. It was different with her though. He *felt* different, couldn't really explain it, didn't understand it, though he kind of liked it. The disparity between the situation and his amorous feelings wasn't lost on him though. How could he feel so alive and turned on and filled with anticipation when he'd played a part in the death of that innocent man? Was he some sort of sociopath?

'I do trust you, Conor,' she breathed into his ear. 'You're the only person I can trust – maybe the only person I've ever really trusted,' she added with a soft sigh.

'What, not even your friends, your parents...?' He looked down at her flawless skin; noticed the faintest smattering of freckles across the bridge of her nose for the first time.

Paris never really talked about her friends much, which left him wondering if she had many – or any in fact. It was a little strange he supposed – most girls he knew came mob handed with their annoying mates – but then there was something mysterious about Paris Levinson, something different and alluring. He sensed a sadness in her too, only he couldn't quite work out where that came from either, though he heavily suspected it might have something to do with her parents. She practically flinched whenever they were mentioned.

He hoped once they'd been intimate together, she'd open up and tell him. He sensed she needed some sort of help.

'Are you OK, Paris?' Once they finished, he looked down at her in his arms and was shocked to see tears streaking her cheeks. It wasn't quite the reaction he was used to, or had hoped for, and for a moment, he wasn't sure what to do or say. Was she already regretting what she'd done? Was this because of what had happened to Reynolds and she was feeling guilty? He was feeling guilty too, but he'd wanted her so badly. 'Why are you crying?'

He took hold of her arm then; began to stroke it. She had tiny wrists, dainty like a bird's, and...

'How did you get that bruise? Looks nasty.'

She jerked her arm away. And that's when he saw the other one, on her other arm, in the same place, as though someone had violently gripped her. A trickle of unease slithered into his stomach.

'Must've been from the other night...' She settled back down onto his chest, her soft hair spilling onto his torso.

But he didn't think so. Those bruises looked much older;

green and yellow, not fresh. He wanted to probe her further about them, only he could feel the tension in her small body as it rested on his and he didn't want to ruin the moment. Besides, they were both a bit sleepy...

The commotion downstairs, namely his mother's shrieking, woke him with a start sometime later.

'When you heard Paris *what*, Con?' His mum is looking squarely at him, her eyes wide in demand. He glances over at Paris again on the sofa behind her. 'Tell me the bloody truth, Conor!'

'When... when I heard Paris being harassed by Reynolds and ran down to see what was going on. I dropped the bottle. I swear I never picked it up again, Mum...' He looks over to his dad for some kind of support, but he's staring silently out of the window. 'Don't you believe me?'

A jolt of panic runs through him as the reality of what he's learning hits him. How can Mathew Reynolds have been *stabbed*? That's not possible. He knows *he* didn't stab him, did he? But admittedly the memory of that night is clearer in parts than it is in others, like a half-remembered dream that's out of sequence, the detail diluted. But if *he* didn't stab Reynolds, then... His eye is drawn back to where she's sitting. *No.* That's just a *mental* thought.

Only it probably isn't *that* mental a thought. He witnessed the change in her that night, didn't he? How she just switched up like that? He saw that twisted look of hatred on her face as she repeatedly stamped on Reynolds with her expensive trainers until he had to physically pull her away. Did she pick up the bottle and stick it in his neck when he wasn't looking? He doesn't think so, but he can't swear on it either.

He stares at her intensely as she looks down at her feet, then at his parents – one paused like a statue looking out of the window, the other pacing around the room manically in the background. Is Paris capable of stabbing someone to death? Is he falling in love with a violent murderer? Man, that would just be his luck.

'Have you ever spoken to Paris about your sister, Con?' His mum is in his face asking questions again, though this one blindsides him.

'Have I what...? Cora? Yeah, I told her about Cora. Why?'

Christine immediately turns to Paris. 'Did you ever tell your mum about her? Did you ever mention Cora by name to your mum – to Helen?'

Paris looks anxious in the spotlight, and he feels bad for her. His mum can be quite formidable when the situation warrants it.

'What is this, Mum?' he interjects. 'You're interrogating her!'

'Interrogating? Have you heard this, Ed?' She turns to his dad, only he's still deep in thought, staring out the window. 'Interrogating? You'll know what interrogation is when you get down that cop shop, Conor, trust me! I just want to know if Paris has ever mentioned your sister to her mum by name.'

'What's Cora got to do with anything?' He's confused. He just wants to wake up and for all of this to be over and Mathew Reynolds to be alive and well. He'll never complain about anything ever again, never set a foot wrong, never tell another lie. He'll even play National League if he has to...

'Did you, Paris?' she continues to push her.

'No!' She shakes her head. 'No, I've never mentioned Cora by name to my mum. I've never mentioned her at all.' Her eyes and voice lower simultaneously as she whispers under her breath, adding, 'I wouldn't tell that bitch anything.'

Christine hasn't heard her though. She's too busy going nuts.

'Tee, come on... really?' his dad, finally coming out of his trance, chimes in at last.

He blinks at his parents. He doesn't know what Cora has to

do with any of this, or why his mum's asking Paris if she's ever mentioned his dead sister to her mother. All he knows is that he's almost certainly going to go to jail now for stabbing someone he feels almost certain he didn't stab.

'I think you'd better take Paris home now, Con,' his mum says flatly.

They drive back to Paris's in his mum's Fiat 500, silent for most of the journey. His head is vibrating with all the questions he wants to ask her, and yet he doesn't know how to put them to her without making it sound like he's accusing her of something.

'I never stabbed him,' he eventually says. 'I dropped that bottle, and I never saw it again. At least, I think that's what happened. Can you remember, Paris?'

More than anything, he wants her to know that she's not alone, that they're in this shit together. That even if she *did* stab Reynolds, he isn't going to abandon her. But he doesn't want to go down for it either, for something he didn't do.

'Could the detective have got something like that wrong?'

She continues to look ahead in silence as he sporadically glances sideways at her, waiting for a response.

'I don't want to go to prison.' He can't stop his fear from breaking the surface. 'I can't get my head around what we did, about what happened... Paris, I need you to talk to me about that night.' He takes his eyes off the road for a second longer than could be deemed safe. 'It felt... it felt like you knew him somehow, Reynolds. He – he said something about telling me what "your lot get up to", or words to the effect, and he knew your name and... and... the anger, Paris – I saw it and... what did he mean by "what your lot get up to"? How did he know your name? Please, I need you to talk to me. I'm going mad here, and—'

'And it was a mistake,' she says flatly. 'Today I mean, you and me.'

'What?' Her words feel like a knife in his chest, and he hits the brakes, pulling over to a stop. 'What do you mean, *a mistake?*'

'It wasn't my first time today, Conor,' she says, still staring blankly ahead. She can't even look at him.

'OK?' he says, his heart banging hard against his ribs. 'Well... that's OK.'

He reaches out to touch her, but she shies away from him, and something sinks inside him.

'It wasn't my second, third, fourth or fifth time either.' She's getting a little animated now, tearing up. 'You... you don't understand,' she says. Her voice is a barely audible whisper. 'I'm damaged goods, Conor. Look at what happens to anyone who comes near me. *Near my family*. They destroy people. You need to stay away.'

It starts to rain suddenly – drops like pennies hitting the roof of the Fiat – and for a moment, they say nothing, just listen to it.

'How did you get those bruises, Paris?' he asks her again. 'Paris...?'

But she won't look at him.

'Has this got something to do with your parents? And why would you even say that about yourself? You're not damaged goods – you're beautiful.' He reaches out to touch her again, and his fingers briefly connect with her skin before she pulls her arm away. 'Why don't you just tell me what's going on?' He doesn't know why this is so important to him right now.

He has to go into a police station tomorrow and lie to within an inch of his life because if he doesn't, then he'll almost certainly be going to prison, with his parents close behind him. Only now he thinks about it all, he didn't actually *ask* them to lie for him. He hadn't even *wanted* them to. It just sort of *happened*. And now he isn't even sure what he's lying about anymore! There's a certain irony in the fact his parents made the decision to lie after spending his entire life bringing him up to tell the truth.

He can't help thinking about the summers he'll never get to spend with Paris now if he's locked up. Not to mention the trips to Ibiza with his mates and his glittering career on the pitch. Why is he worrying about all of this when someone has lost their life because of him?

The inner turmoil between self-preservation and his conscience is a pendulum swinging inside of him. Is there something wrong with him? He honestly doesn't know. What he *does* know is that Paris is keeping secrets from him and, despite everything, he has an overwhelming desire to protect her, even though he's unsure exactly what from.

TWENTY-FOUR

CHRISTINE

It feels as if life has completely turned against me as I make off for the Levinsons' the following morning, like it's somehow chasing me down. By the time I got to bed last night, I felt like I'd become a completely different person to the one I'd been up until two days ago.

'You'll have to go over to Sunnyside tomorrow,' Ed said as we lay in bed next to each other. Clearly, he couldn't sleep either. 'You'll have to take those clothes from wherever you stashed them and destroy them.'

'Underneath the mattress on Mum's bed,' I said quietly.

'You put them under your mum's mattress? Jesus, Tee, that's the first bloody place the cops will look!'

'And the shoes are in her wardrobe, buried under some blankets,' I quickly added, swallowing back the shame I felt. 'There was nowhere else! I didn't know what else to do with them.'

'OK, OK.' He rolled onto his side, facing me. 'So you go over to Sunnyside tomorrow, you visit your mum and get them back, and then you get rid of them.'

'Get rid of them *where*? How?'

'I don't know.'

'Well, neither do I!' I shrieked back at him. 'I'm not an expert at this kind of thing!'

'Look, I'm thinking, all right?' he said. Only something told me it was a bit late for that. In truth, all of this was happening because we *weren't* thinking. At least not with our heads. 'Bury them in a skip maybe, throw them in a river or down a drain, burn them in a—'

'A charity shop,' I say. 'I'll take them to a launderette, wash them and then I'll give them to a charity shop, one that's out of town.'

He pulled me closer into him so that our noses were touching. 'See, we'll get through this together, what with my looks and your brains...'

'It's not even remotely funny, Ed,' I replied, but I was unable to feel cross with him. Ed always sees the funny in everything. I think it's a coping mechanism. 'It's a bloody screwed-up mess is what it is.'

He didn't argue with me.

'I just can't stop thinking about the Reynolds family, about his poor mother, and his girlfriend who's literally just given birth to his child! I can't reconcile it all in my head. I was so close to just blurting it all out in front of Detective Riley. It's like a tick inside me, one I can't control...'

'I know, I know.' He stroked my face with the back of his fingers. 'But you're going to have to. We can't think about Reynolds or his family – not right now. We have to focus on protecting our Conor, on getting him out of this mess and—'

'But we're not those kind of people,' I said.

'What kind of people?'

'We can't just cover up a *murder*, not even for...' Only I couldn't finish the sentence because I knew that's exactly what we were already doing. It was like an instinct overriding my common sense somehow, a lioness protecting her last and only cub. But at what cost? I knew in my heart that none of this was going to end well. How could it? It was insanity. But hope really is the last thing ever lost, and I was clinging on to it like driftwood in open sea. Maybe Ed was right and we just had to be brave, push the guilt and the fear away and focus on doing whatever we could to keep hold of our son. Beyond that, I didn't know.

So, the plan was for me to go to the Levinsons', do a double shift then head off to Sunnyside. I was to do nothing different.

'They could be watching us, Tee, the Feds,' Ed said before I left, doing nothing to assuage the shadow of my ever-present paranoia.

I thought of him then, Detective Riley, who – again – had turned up on our doorstep unannounced and apologetic, about the way he'd expressed what appeared to be genuine remorse about the loss of our Cora, and said how, as a parent himself, he'd do anything for his children, even die for them. *Lie for them too* – that's what he'd said.

I sensed that the purpose of his visit was to give us the opportunity to come clean, to do the right thing and explain everything, maybe even offer us his support and understanding in the process. Or was I being naïve, and it was simply a trap to get us to confess and incriminate our son in Reynolds's murder? I knew we weren't doing the *right* thing by lying, not morally anyway, but it was about context in that moment. The fear of losing my son, the only child I had left, to prison, for him to carry the stigma of being a convicted killer throughout his life and the need to protect him against it was just so unbelievably strong that it was practically a foregone conclusion. I also knew it was selfish deep down. And stupid.

I wasn't even sure whether to believe Detective Riley when he dropped the bombshell about Reynolds being stabbed in the neck. That information hadn't been released publicly – I hadn't seen or heard anything reported in the news about it, and I knew unequivocally that my Con would never, *could* never do something like that. Killing someone accidentally in self-defence is one thing, but sticking a broken bottle in the neck of an unarmed man while he's lying injured on the ground is quite another. But if it *was* true, then that could only really leave one other culprit responsible, couldn't it?

'You need to keep your eyes open – check you're not being followed. If you think you're being followed, then you turn round and come straight home again, OK?'

'Jesus, Ed... *followed*?' I replied, wondering if that was what my life was now – forever looking over my shoulder, the police on one side, my gnawing conscience on the other.

The amber light has been flashing on my dash since yesterday. I need petrol. I won't have enough juice to get from Helen's to see Mum otherwise. I pull into the nearest service station, put ten pounds in the tank, pay quickly and I'm almost to the car when I see her. If I'd just been a few seconds earlier...

'Chris! Christine!' She's walking towards me diagonally across the forecourt – Linda, my old cleaning pal from work who I hadn't seen in ages until the other day. Only here she is again, large as life. I can't help feeling that my life suddenly seems to have become one horrible string of coincidences. My heart drops like a stone, and that's even before I see who she's with.

I recognised her the moment I saw her face on the telly, in truth. She's got a stall down the market that sells cheap household products. I've bought furniture polish and bin bags from her before. She lives on the estate; I've seen her around and about over time, like you do everyone I suppose, though I don't know her personally. A bomb feels like it's detonated inside my belly. It's his mum... it's *Mathew Reynolds's mother*! And she's only with the girl, a pretty young girl who's pushing one of those fancy prams that cost as much as a small car. I try to open my car door, but I can't move. It's like I'm wearing concrete boots.

'All right, love!' Linda approaches me with a look of pleasant surprise as she wraps her chunky knitted coat around her to keep out the icy chill. We're in the depths of a particularly brutal cold snap, and yet I have to loosen the scarf around my neck I'm that hot with stress. 'You're like a bus, you are – don't see you for ages and then two of you turn up at once!'

My laughter sounds strained, even to my own ears.

'You OK, Chris?' She dips her head; looks at me. 'You feeling all right?'

My face must be betraying me. I really am the weakest link. I attempt to pull myself together.

'Yeah, yeah. It's nothing... I'm fine. Time of the month,' I say with an eye roll. 'Had to stop off and get some painkillers.'

'This is my neighbour Val,' she says, 'and this is Alana and her newborn... they're just out on their first ever walk! She only had him yesterday, didn't you, darlin'? We needed the fresh air.'

Her *neighbour* Val?

'Ahh, that's... that's lovely.' I don't know what I'm saying – the words just come. 'Only a day old, eh? You youngsters recover so quickly these days, don't you? Look at you, up and about already!' I smile in Alana's general direction, but I can't make direct eye contact with her. I know they're going to ask me to look at the baby. I can feel it coming.

'Come and say hello to him,' Linda says on cue as she nods into the pram encouragingly. 'Gorgeous ain'tcha? Hello, little Matty junior. Yes... oooh yes, you're a beautiful boy...' she coos. 'He's called Matty after his daddy – that's right, isn't it, Alana?'

'After Matty, yeah,' she says, staring vacantly ahead.

I think she may be on something. Or maybe she's just exhausted after losing her partner and giving birth within days of each other. I want to go to her, hold her in my arms and comfort the poor girl; drop to my knees and tell her how sorry I am that this has happened, that it was all just a dreadful accident, a terrible mistake, and that now she's a mother herself, she'll understand why I've had to do this, won't she? It strikes me then that Alana must be around the same age my Cora would've been today; that this could be my daughter in front of me, my own grandchild, and... I start to feel dizzy; grip on to the door handle of the Fiat. I've hardly slept or eaten in two days.

'Carved him up they did, my boy.' Valerie turns to me. 'Sickening, ain't it? Police are doing nufink of course. He were a piece of scum to them, weren't he? A lowlife, one less on the streets... but he was *my* boy.' She starts wailing. 'He was my baby.'

'Sorry, love,' Linda apologises to me. 'I s'pose you've heard the terrible news – what's happened to her son, to Matty?'

I nod, blinking furiously in a bid not to pass out.

'Yes, I... I did hear. It's... well, it's awful, really bad... worse than bad in fact, and—'

'What kind of world are we living in now, eh?' Valerie Reynolds is still talking to no one in particular, shaking her head. 'Where people do that to another human being? They're bloody animals is what they are, not human!' She's staring straight at me again now with hooded, watery grey eyes, only I can't bear to look at her. 'I couldn't even see him, you know – they wouldn't let me identify his body, my own son! He was battered unrecognisable...' She's wailing hard now, and Linda moves to comfort her. 'Those savages... If I ever find out who done it to my boy, I'll do 'em meself – burn their bleeding houses down I will. Monsters... evil monsters...'

"S'all right, Val... all right, love...' Linda gives me an apologetic look as she begins to steer her away. 'Nice to see you again, Chris,' she says over her shoulder, mouthing, 'Sorry,' as she goes.

I ring the bell at the Levinsons' wondering what I'll say if Carmelita opens the door, how I'll react. Maybe I won't say anything at all and I'll just knock her clean out with one punch instead. Not that I'm a violent person; I've never hit anyone in my whole life, but it would be no less than she deserves, and I'm not myself right now, not thinking straight. Anger prickles my skin as I think of her bringing the champagne up to Helen's room yesterday, the daggers she gave me at the bottom of the stairs as I was leaving. She wanted to have me arrested, done for drink-driving, leave me with a criminal record and a ban that would inevitably affect my livelihood.

I'm somewhat relived when Doreen, another of the Levinsons' regular housekeepers, opens the door.

'You're late,' she says flatly. 'But she's not in anyway, so you're in luck.'

Yeah, luck is my middle name right now.

'Where has she gone?'

'How should I know?' Doreen is already shuffling back down the hallway. 'Spending money somewhere probably.' She gives me a wry backward glance. 'That or the shrink's.'

Is she serious? I didn't know Helen was seeing a shrink. But then again, I don't know much about Helen Levinson at all, as it turns out.

'Is Paris here?' I know she's hiding something, and I'd really like to talk to her, try and get to the truth of what really happened that night.

'Haven't see her,' Doreen says, shrugging without turning to look back at me. Though to be fair it is pretty easy to disappear in this house – it's that big.

'I'll get cracking then,' I say to myself as she disappears into the kitchen.

Having finished the downstairs bathrooms, I make my way up the winding staircase, lugging the vacuum cleaner with me. I'm out of breath by the time I approach the third floor. That's when I see her standing there at the top of the stairs, her arms folded across her chest, fixing me with that steely gaze.

Carmelita.

TWENTY-FIVE
CHRISTINE

I freeze.

My earlier thought of socking her one right in the chops disappears rapidly as she stares down at me, unblinking, with those cold eyes. Carmelita is slight, built like an adolescent child, and yet I feel a gust of ice-cold fear as I tentatively approach her like she's ten feet tall.

'Hello, Carmelita,' I say tightly, waiting for her to move out of the way so that I can get past. Only she doesn't. She stays still as a statue, watching me intensely.

'I don't suppose you were expecting to see me today thanks to that stunt you pulled yesterday, shopping me to the police?' I can hear the slight wobble in my inflection as my resolve instantly begins to lose momentum.

Nothing. Her face remains blank, expressionless like a robot.

'Well, sorry to disappoint you,' I push myself, 'but you got it wrong. I wasn't over the limit.'

She continues to stare at me silently, unnervingly.

'How could you do that? *Why* would you do that? As if I

haven't got enough on my plate right now, what with my mum and—' I stop myself short; can feel my cheeks burn with the blood that's risen to them. As if she gives a toss about my problems! 'Look' – I soften my tone slightly – 'if you think I'm after your job or something, then I assure you, I'm not. All I want to do is do my *own* job and then get on with taking care of my *own* family, so if you don't mind, I'd like to get past...'

I blink back at her, irritated that she has nothing to say to me, nothing by way of explanation or apology, and that she's just standing there, staring at me like she's battery-operated.

'What's the matter, Carmelita – cat got your tongue?'

She finally moves then, affording me room to place the heavy vacuum cleaner on the floor next to her. It's a relief – it was beginning to make my arm ache.

I watch as she slides past me and slowly makes her way down the stairs, stopping briefly to glance back at me over her shoulder.

'Come,' she says, beckoning me with a small finger.

I pause for a moment, drop the vacuum head and follow her, albeit with some trepidation.

This could be a trap, and yet I get the impression she wants to show me something and am compelled to follow her. I stay a safe couple of paces behind her though as she moves through the house, down to the second floor, then the first. I have no idea where she's taking me, or why, yet still I blindly follow her through one of the drawing rooms that leads into the library. The Levinsons' house is huge, far too big for one person to clean, so my allocated areas include the six bathrooms – three en suites – plus the main living area, bedroom and the library. It's my favourite room in the whole house thanks to its magnificent, vaulted glass ceiling and custom-built floor-to-ceiling shelves filled with hundreds, maybe even thousands of books, none of which I've ever seen Helen so much as glance at.

'Why have you brought me here?' I ask her. I'm so light with adrenalin that I feel I might take flight.

She doesn't speak as she begins rearranging the magnificent bouquet of flowers in the crystal vase.

'Carmelita?' I feel impatient, confused, *annoyed*. 'Can you say something please? Why are we here? What's going on? Have I done something to upset you?' Suddenly I feel fear, like this *is* a trap and something terrible is about to happen to me.

'I'm going to call Helen.' I pull my phone out of my pocket, but Carmelita swipes it clean from my hand with all the stealth and speed of a seasoned ninja.

'What the... what are you *doing*?' I gasp. 'Give me my phone back! What the *hell* is this?'

And then, in a flash, she's gone, leaving me standing there, momentarily stunned. My phone! I run after her, only... the door doesn't open when I turn it. I try again. *Oh my God. It's locked.* She's locked me in!

I bang on the door. 'Carmelita! Carmelita, open the door! I'm locked in. *Carmelita!*' I slam my fists against it. OK, now I'm *really* panicking. 'Carmelita! Helen! *Helllllen!*' The library is on the ground floor, the furthest room from the kitchen, and it's soundproofed. There's a bespoke neon sign above the door that reads, 'In silence we find solace,' and I stare at it as I continue to scream out and start to look around for other means of escape. There's no phone in here, no laptop. It's just books, rugs, tables, lamps and a reading desk. There's no window either, just the glass vaulted ceiling that the sunlight streams through. Today though, as I look up, the sky is ominous, black like a bruise.

Why has Carmelita done this to me? Why has she led me here and locked me in? Is she out of her mind? First she tries to get me in trouble with the police and now she's imprisoned me! This is a crime – it's got to be, hasn't it? She could be arrested for this! Everything is so messed up and confusing, like I'm flip-flopping between reality and madness. It's a struggle to keep a mental grip.

I'm sure she's brought me down here for a reason though, to show me something. I sense it somehow. But what?

I start practising some deep breathing, placing my hand on my chest to try and regulate myself. I have to keep calm, focus on getting out of this room. Then I'll go straight over to Sunnyside and get the clothes. I *have* to get out of here so I can get those clothes!

With my heartbeat steadying, I begin to look along the walls at the myriad books, the different colours all somehow complimenting each other, like someone has really given their display some considerable thought. And then I see it – *Gone with the Wind*! It's there, on the shelf right in front of me, the red cracked spine and faded gold lettering like a beacon! I'm staggered that my eye has found it so quickly among the thousands of others. Is this yet another coincidence, or did Carmelita position me in such a way that I couldn't help but see it?

I pluck it from the shelf. Open it. There's no air in the room and yet the letter it contains seems to flutter to the floor as if the wind has taken it. I pick it up. It's the note – the one containing Helen's desperate words. I place it in my tabard pocket, close the book and make to replace it on the shelf. But then something else catches my eye – there, at the back of the shelf where the book was.

I push my face up closer; squint. I can't quite see what it is, but it's definitely *something*. I strain my eyes, tip my head left to right. It... it looks like... *a keyhole*, a brass lock of some sort. Yes! I see it! *Oh my God...*

I begin to pull the surrounding books off the shelf in haste, but then I realise... if it's a lock, then that means there must be a key to open it. I pick up *Gone with the Wind*; turn it so it opens like a fan. I shake it and... it's there, hidden in a cut-out section of the book, *a key*. I hold it between my thumb and forefinger and just stare at it before I frantically start throwing more books behind me until there's a whole pile of them stacked up. I take a step back and survey my handiwork.

There's a door.

TWENTY-SIX
CHRISTINE

I put the key in the lock, my palms sweating as I feel it give. I pause for a moment, listening to my own laboured breathing in the still silence. Common sense tells me I'd be better off not knowing what's behind this door, and yet I can't stop myself from opening it.

It dawns on me then that this must be what Carmelita intended me to find – the door to a secret room, the reason she's brought me down here and locked me in. I have no idea why though. What's any of it got to do with me?

A clicking sound causes me to jump as I gingerly step inside. Strip lighting whirs into life, illuminating the darkness around me, and I automatically duck for cover, placing a shaking hand over my mouth.

The first thing I see as my vision comes into focus is a group of leather banquettes, three or four of them around the room, all with what looks like a dancer's pole and a small, raised area next to them. On one side of the room there's a large purple velvet chaise longue, with a strange-looking chair in front of it, like one of those antique dentist's ones from Victorian times with straps and various contraptions attached to it that look like they might cause pain.

What in the hell is this?

Everywhere I turn, I see my own distorted reflection staring back at me in the mirrors that line the walls and ceiling. I can't escape how dreadful I look, almost ghoulish in this light, *in this room*. On the other side of the wall, I see a series of restraints, what looks like pairs of hand and leg cuffs attached to the exposed brickwork, and there's a long metal chain hanging from the ceiling with some kind of device next to it, a hoist perhaps? *Oh God*. I recoil.

A giant TV screen sits on the furthest wall of the room next to a row of chairs, a small makeshift cinema almost. I don't even want to imagine what sort of films are played here...

I move to the other side of the room like a ghost; spot a black leather book on one of the low tables. There's what appears to be remnants of white powder on the glass, cocaine maybe. Compelled, I pick the book up; flick through it. It contains a list of names, mostly men's names, some with girls' names next to or adjacent to them, and dates and times... a visitors' book? There's a pile of instant photos randomly scattered next to it, small Polaroid pictures of very young-looking women in varying states of undress draped over notably older men. In one of the photos, a scantily-clad girl appears to be in restraints. She looks vacant, and her eyes appear glazed over. I drop them back onto the table.

Is this the room Lin told me about – the secret 'pleasure room' Jonesey had mentioned that I'd laughed off as ridiculous gossip? It had to be. Only I sense no pleasure coming from this place whatsoever. A chill runs through me. As horrified as I am by what I'm seeing, part of me still thinks that maybe this isn't really any of my business. So the Levinsons are into a bit of weird kinky stuff. Maybe they really *do* swing and throw sex parties. Is it anything to do with me? Why make it my problem when I have enough of my own already? Only I'm suddenly hit by a frankly terrifying thought: have I been locked down here for a reason? Am I going to be forced into becoming a secret sex slave for them? *Oh my God!*

I run from the room, frantically locking it behind me. Hyperventilating, I start replacing the books on the shelf until they're all back in position. Then I put the key inside the hidden compartment of *Gone with the Wind* and shove it back where I found it. I stand for a moment, vibrating, my lungs heaving with exertion and adrenalin, my head aching to the point of explosion.

I glance at the clock on the wall. It's coming on for 1.30 p.m. *Oh no.* A small whimper escapes from me. I *have* to get out of here. I need to get over to Mum's. Only that crazy Carmelita has my phone and she's locked me in. I can't even call Ed!

I rush to the door again, push hard on the handle and... it swings opens immediately. I fall through it onto my knees with the momentum – and, incidentally, onto my phone, which seems to have been left on the floor just outside the door. I snatch it up and try to make a call to Ed, but my sweaty, shaking fingers keep slipping on the keypad. *Shit.* It'll wait. I have to get out of here right now, get over to Sunnyside and get those damned clothes.

I'm almost at the front door when I hear Doreen call out to me.

'Oi! Christine! Where do you think you're off to? You haven't finished all your rooms yet.'

'Family emergency,' I shout back over my shoulder as I slam the front door behind me.

I don't care if she's heard me.

TWENTY-SEVEN
CHRISTINE

'Hi, Joy.' I'm a hot sweaty mess as I practically crash through the double doors of Sunnyside. It's bitterly cold outside, yet I'm overheating with stress, my shirt sticking to my skin beneath my coat. I need a glass of water. *I need a stiff gin and tonic.* 'I'll just go straight through to her, shall I?'

'You don't look so great,' Joy says, cocking her head to the side as she surveys me with a look of concern. She really does put the care into 'care home'.

'I hope you're not going down with something. There's a lot of it about at the moment,' she says, nodding sagely.

'I'm fine,' I lie. I'm literally seconds away from passing out with stress. 'Just a bit tired... long shift, you know?'

Her eyes twinkle in sympathy, and for a brief second, I feel like collapsing into her large bosom, telling her everything and begging her to make it all stop.

'Don't I just. Listen, Christine' – her tone switches – 'I've got something to tell you.'

My stomach lurches. I know what she's going to say. 'Look, Joy, this outstanding invoice—'

'Actually, that's what I wanted to speak to you about. I—'

'I know, I know. It's late – *really* late,' I interject, 'and I'm *so* sorry you have to keep asking about it; it's just that we need a little more time to get the funds together. Ed's speaking to the bank today, trying to work something out. We'll have the money soon, I promise. We're doing all we can. If the company can just hold on for a few—'

'Oh!' she says, taking half a step back from the desk, her smile suddenly widening, though it's already broad. 'You don't know?'

'Know what?' I really like Joy, but my patience is starting to unravel along with my nerves.

'It's been settled already. Today, this morning. So now you don't have to fret anymore!'

I blink at her. No, Ed is going to see the bank today. He called them yesterday, as promised, but they advised him to come in to discuss our options; had arranged an appointment for today. He would've called me if he'd managed to get the money from them. I've misheard her.

'Sorry, you said it's been *settled*?'

She nods, her grin still fixed. 'All of it!' She beams. 'And the next three months' fees – twenty-one grand in total.'

I feel lightheaded all of a sudden. 'Sorry, what? *What?*'

Now Joy looks as confused as I feel. 'I thought you already knew. I assumed Ed had paid it and...'

I'm shaking my head. 'Ed paid it? Ed's settled the debt *and* paid the next three months' fees?'

'I... don't know.' She starts tapping something into the computer. 'It just says "amount settled".' She brings her face closer to the screen. 'It was paid over the phone, by bank transfer – a gift apparently, or so it says here, on the reference.'

'Gift? A gift from who?'

Joy shrugs. 'It doesn't say. Maybe Ed wanted to surprise you?'

I can't stop shaking my head. I can't stop shaking full stop.

'Anyway, whoever it is, you should thank your lucky stars for them!'

I'm too stunned to speak. Life as I've always known it has completely ceased to exist. I want to feel relieved, overjoyed even. But somehow, I just can't. Ed knows I can't take any more surprises right now, not even good ones. Something doesn't feel right.

'I... I'll be back,' I stammer. 'I have to check on Mum.'

I burst through Mum's door, startling her. She's sitting up in bed, watching an old black-and-white film with the sound down.

'Sorry, Mum, I didn't mean to scare you!'

I need to calm down, try to stop shaking, but the more I try, the more I become aware I'm doing it and that seems to make it worse. I go over to her; briefly kiss the top of her head. Her hair smells like L'Air du Temps. What I wouldn't do for a hug from my mum, as she used to be.

'Who's that then?' she says without taking her eyes from the TV screen.

I inhale; prepare myself for the ritual I go through most days with her now. 'It's me, Mum – it's Christine, your daughter. Are you OK? How have you been? Did you sleep well?'

'Are you Sonia?'

'Insomnia?'

'Not insomnia! Cloth ears!' She starts to laugh, though it's more of a cackle now, nothing like my mum's soft, gentle laugh used to be. 'Son-i-a!'

'Who's Sonia?' I haven't heard her mention that name before.

'The girl who was here yesterday... the new one.'

I let go of Mum's hand and walk over to the wardrobe; start looking through it. 'What girl?' I don't know anything about any new carers. Joy always introduces them to me first before they meet Mum. 'Are you sure she's a carer and not another resident?'

'That was always your problem, Christine.' She casts me a mild look of disdain. 'You just never listened, did you? Not like your sister.'

'I don't have a sister, Mum. I'm an only child, remember? You know that. You only gave birth once, to me.'

She goes back to watching the silent telly.

Blood swooshes in my ears as I bend down to search beneath the blankets for the trainers I left there.

I pull at them, separate them, my fingers beginning to get frantic. I drag them out onto the floor and start shaking them, dread engulfing me with each passing second. They're not here! Conor's and Paris's trainers... I try to stand up, but it feels as if I've been winded by a heavy object.

'Mum... *Mum*.' I turn to her slowly, my voice low with gravitas. 'Have you moved the things I put in the wardrobe the other day? Do you remember where you put them? Did you put them somewhere else?' I try and fight back the sheer panic forcing its way into every crevice of my body. 'Mum, *please*...'

'I don't know what you're talking about. Where's Joy? Did you bring my magazines and biscuits?'

I'm shaking on the spot as I hand her the plastic bag.

'Fig rolls and custard creams... and I brought your magazines and a TV guide, OK? Now, can you remember where the shoes are... the ones I put in the wardrobe?'

I'm reminded of the clothes then. *The clothes!*

'I just need to check something underneath your bed, Mum – your mattress, OK? Can you go and sit in the chair for me?'

I breathe a sigh of relief when she does what I ask without any resistance. Then I drop to my knees, lift up the mattress and peer underneath.

No. *Noooo*. This can't be happening! There's nothing there!

Refusing to believe it, I run my hands over the divan, like I can't trust my own eyes. Panic rings in my ears as I tip the mattress up on its side. *The clothes are gone.* It's all gone.

I'm going to be sick.

'That Sonia took them to be washed,' Mum pipes up from the chair without looking away from the telly.

'What Sonia? This new carer you mean, from yesterday? Did she come in here? Did she take anything from your room?' I can't hide the urgency in my voice.

'You see! You really *don't* listen, do you, Christine? I *told* you. Sonia came yesterday and took it *allllll* away.' She sing-songs the last part.

I'll have to try and find this new member of staff, this Sonia, ask her what in the hell she's done with the clothes and why she even took them in the first place and then... *Oh God.* My stomach is churning like an ice-cream machine. I'm definitely going to be sick.

'What did she look like, Mum – this new girl, Sonia? Was she Black, white, tall, small? What colour hair has she got? Has she been in to see you today?' I'm trying to keep the terror from my voice and failing miserably.

Ed must've taken Conor to the police station by now to give the statement he'd promised Detective Riley. I'm trying not to think about it, but it feels like an axe waiting to fall. I'm livid with myself. One job – I had *one job* and I couldn't even do that properly. I messed it up royally. This could be the deciding factor, the difference between looking at my son from across the dinner table or from behind a plastic screen.

'She gave me some sweets.'

'Who, Sonia did?'

Mum begins to shuffle back to her bed now that I've replaced the mattress. I look down at it; see the large, dark yellow urine stains and feel a stab of utter despair in my solar plexus. I feel like I'm being punished somehow, that we all are.

'No,' she says crossly, 'it wasn't *Sonia* who gave them to me. Fruit pastilles. And there was a red one! The reds were always your favourite.'

I gather up my things. Oh God, I need those clothes! Ed'll go mad! He'll pretend he's not angry with me, but he will be, and I'll feel even more wretched.

'So who was it then? Who gave you the sweets?' I'm not really listening to her now as I fold the blankets and start placing them back into the wardrobe, fighting off despair.

'I told you – it was Sonia! Are you going deaf? Your dad went deaf in the end, you know. Though I always thought it was more like selective hearing...' She chuckles as I collapse onto the bed in despair, my head dropped in my hands. For the love of God, I have no idea what's going on. I need to try and find this Sonia, whoever she bloody is, and see if I can get those clothes back.

I kiss Mum's head swiftly before fleeing the room.

'Joy! Joy!' I call out as I rush up to the reception desk.

She looks up, startled. 'You OK, love? Is your mum OK?'

'Sonia,' I say, breathless with adrenalin. 'The new girl... Mum says she took some things from her room yesterday, stuff that needed washing... Do you know where she is, what she might've done with them?' I'm on the verge of tears, of complete collapse. I can feel the white walls in the reception area start to close in on me. Am I having a panic attack?

'Christine, love.' Joy hurries around the reception desk and places a concerned arm on my back as I lean forward, trying to get some blood pumping to my head. 'Are you sure everything's OK?'

'S-Sonia,' I croak. 'There was a carer called Sonia in Mum's room yesterday...'

'There was just me, Bonnie, Sylvie and Shannice on duty yesterday. I don't know who you mean, love,' she says, fixing me with a worried expression and shaking her head. 'There's no one called Sonia that works here.'

TWENTY-EIGHT

DAN

'Aaron? Aaron Young?'

'Yeah? Who's asking?'

The man who answers the door to the average but tidy-looking ground-floor apartment – tall, well-built, dark skin, late thirties, braided hair, dressed in joggers and a soft oversized hoodie – blinks back at me with the slightest hint of suspicion.

I flash him my credentials. 'I'm Detective Chief Inspector Dan Riley, and this is my colleague, DS Lucy Davis. Is now a good time to talk?'

'I hate it when people say that,' he says, his warm breath meeting the freezing air like cigarette smoke as he takes half a cautious step backward. 'Usually means something bad.'

I know what he means as I wrap my heavy wool coat around me. It's warm, but not waterproof, and it's really coming down heavy out here now. 'Um, would you mind? Could we come in and speak to you, if it's convenient?'

He hesitates for a second but then stands back to let us in.

The apartment is tastefully done out inside, modern, clean, like some money's been thrown at it. 'You live here alone?'

'Nope.' He shakes his head. 'With my wife, Lisa. She's at

work. She's a nurse down at the hospital, St Cat's.' He turns to me after a brief pause. 'This is about *her*, isn't it?'

'Your wife?'

He sucks in a breath, drags his hands down his face and suddenly looks distressed. 'No. I mean *her*.'

'Who?'

'Has something happened?' he asks.

'Like what, Aaron?'

He shrugs and shakes his head simultaneously. 'You're the ones on my doorstep – you tell me!'

I'll cut straight to it then.

'Aaron, you took out a non-molestation order against someone called Helen Levinson, back in 2019. It was granted on May fourth—'

'They'll sue me if I talk,' he interrupts quickly.

'Aaron, we're investigating a murder.'

I shouldn't have said that – our visit today is purely to get background on Helen Levinson in light of what our intel threw up and is, as yet, unrelated to the case. Arguably, we shouldn't be here at all.

'Has she killed someone?' His eyes dart between mine and Davis's. 'She's killed someone, hasn't she?'

It's an interesting first reaction.

'Why would you say that, Aaron?' Davis cocks her head. 'Why would you think Helen had killed someone?'

'Because the woman's mad, that's why,' he says flatly.

'Can you tell us about her?' I ask. 'Why you had to take out the non-molestation order against her? Look, nothing you say to us will go any further – this is purely confidential, I assure you. We just need some information that potentially could help us with our enquiries.'

It isn't obvious what the connection between them is – or was. One is a youngish, attractive, mixed-race man who clearly frequents the gym and probably grew up on the local estate judging by the accent he's trying his best to hide, and the other is a short, white, slightly overweight middle-aged woman who's married to a multi-millionaire businessman and MP.

'I was working at her house, the London place. She was having her garden landscaped. Summer 2019. It was a beautiful summer that year – it was the year me and Lisa got married...' He pauses for a moment, reflectively. 'Turned out to be both the best *and* the worst summer of my life. Ironic, eh?'

'Why was that?'

He blows air loudly through his lips. 'Because that woman made my life hell, that's why. Mine and Lee's. We almost didn't go through with the wedding because of her craziness.' He looks slightly agitated. 'She's touched.' He taps the side of his temple.

'Can you tell us how it started?'

He sighs heavily again. 'I didn't mind her at first, Helen. She was friendly and that, pleasant, more than some clients anyway. We struck up a bit of conversation one day while I was shifting bags of cement through the garden, and she made some comment, something like, "That looks heavy," and I says, "Yeah, it is," and she says, "Burdens are for shoulders strong enough to carry them." And I says to her, "That's a quote from *Gone with the Wind*, that is." And it stopped her dead in her tracks. She couldn't believe it, couldn't believe someone like me would know something like that. A bit of unconscious bias I reckon.' He sniffs a little derisively. 'And I told her I'd always been interested in English Literature since I was a kid, and that I was studying to be a teacher – that I was just doing this job for the bread because I was saving up to marry my girl.' He looks up at us. 'And that's when it started.'

He has our full attention now.

'When the job finished and we left, I thought nothing more of it, or her, but then she randomly turns up at my apartment unannounced one day, and she wants to give me this copy of *Gone with the Wind*, some first-edition shit, worth some serious money. She said she wanted me to have it as a wedding present. I don't know how she found out where I lived...' He shrugs; continues. 'Anyway, I didn't want to accept the book, but she insisted over and over that I take it, wouldn't take no for an answer.'

He pauses again; rubs his temples. I can tell this isn't easy for him.

'So then she starts coming round unannounced more and more, just turning up on our doorstep, day or night, even if Lee was in... The text messages began then too, hundreds of them, the quotes and the poems and the confessions of her love for me, her' – he lowers his eyes – ' her *sexual attraction* to me... how she felt there was some sort of spark between us, and that it was written in the stars and all that malarkey...'

He looks a touch embarrassed as Davis shoots me a look of surprise.

'Yeah, my thoughts exactly,' he says. 'You wouldn't think to look at her, would you? I just thought she was some older woman with a crush, you know, some privileged housewife after a bit of rough?' He lowers his eyes again. 'We laughed about it at first, me and Lee, but it quickly stopped being funny.' His voice drops an octave. 'The calls and texts were getting out of hand and, well, things got even weirder...'

'Weirder?'

'Yeah, like she knew stuff about us... stuff she couldn't possibly have known.'

'Like what?' Davis has started taking notes.

'Like one time she knew which restaurant we were going to be at for my birthday, and she showed up there – was sitting at the table right next to us. She claimed it was a coincidence, but I mean, of all the restaurants in London on that particular night? And then when Lee' – he sucks in a deep breath – 'Lee had a miscarriage, a couple of months before the wedding – we weren't trying or anything; it just sort of happened, and then...

and then it stopped happening – somehow Helen knew about it, and she sent flowers to the apartment with a card offering her condolences, saying it was God's way, natural selection and all that. Really freaked us out it did!'

'OK... and?'

He shakes his head. 'And I told her I was getting married, and that I was sorry... it was awkward, you know, because I didn't actually dislike the woman as such, not in the beginning anyway. I felt sorry for her really.'

'Why was that?' I ask.

'I dunno. She seemed lonely in that big old house... I always got a bad vibe from it, can't explain it... and I never once saw her with her husband. Must've seen him come and go a few times, but I never saw them together the whole five or six months we were working there, nor the girl... the daughter, Paris. Yeah, she was always hiding away in her room as well, always arguing with Helen. It wasn't a happy house...' He shakes his head.

'So anyway, I blocked her in the end – had to. She was blowing up my phone, sitting outside the flat in one of her fancy cars all hours of the day and night... She was watching us, watching me, watching Lee. So I spoke to Helen. I told her politely but firmly that I wasn't interested, that I was getting married and that I was flattered and stuff, but that I was in love with my fiancée. We'd booked the wedding venue and everything; there was only a few weeks to go, but we hadn't paid off the rest of what we owed, and I was scratching around for the bread to sort it. And then when Lee finally goes to see the planner at the hotel venue to settle the difference, he tells her that the outstanding bill's already been paid and that our package has been upgraded to the top one, the super platinum all-singing, all-dancing one, another £10K on top of the £12K it was already going to set us back. I mean, what the fu— *what the hell?*' He throws his hands up in the air. '*Helen* had paid it. She'd settled the bill, ordered in crates of Cristal and even booked a live singer. It was *mental*. We didn't... we couldn't wrap our heads around it.

'I told the venue to reimburse her and go back to our original bronze package – which they weren't too happy about understandably. Then the text messages started up again, this time from a different number, sometimes up to fifty a day telling me how I shouldn't marry Lisa, that I was making a terrible mistake, that God had killed our baby because it wasn't meant to be, that me and her were destined to be together instead, that she'd felt it between us the moment I'd recognised that quote from *Gone with the Wind*. It made me wish I'd never listened in English class, trust me...' He laughs dryly.

'She told me she could give me absolutely everything I ever wanted. She said she'd buy me a house, buy *my parents* a house, that I'd never want for anything ever again in life if I left Lee to be with her. She said she wanted to help me with my career, that she'd get me a teaching job, pay for my training... I'll admit,' he says, sheepish, 'I was getting scared around this point, like, proper scared. It was like it was real in her head, this connection she thought she'd found with me that didn't exist. And even though I wanted it to stop, I didn't want to be out-and-out horrible to her or go to the police because she seemed, I dunno, vulnerable somehow, but it was seriously interfering with my life, my relationship, and it was... a bit, well, *embarrassing* I suppose.'

He looks far away for a moment. 'When she discovered we'd refused to accept her "generosity", she came to see me, and that's when she calmly told me that she was going to go to the police and tell them that I'd stolen a valuable copy of *Gone with the Wind* from her library while I'd been working at her house, and that her husband knew everyone and I'd be locked up, charged with theft unless I cancelled my wedding and went with her to her beach house for the weekend.'

I can feel my eyes widening as he speaks. Is he serious? He

certainly looks it. Not much shocks me in this game, but I'll admit I'm genuinely taken aback. 'She started *blackmailing* you?'

'Yeah.' He shakes his head. 'Mad, innit? And I believed her as well. I mean, she's married to a millionaire politician, someone rich and powerful, and I was worried for a bit, really worried. I thought that if I involved the cops, then I'd come out worse. I mean look at me and then look at her – who were your lot going to back?'

He rolls his eyes, and I feel annoyed and ashamed that his assumption is probably correct.

'I had to do *something* though. So I took out a non-molestation order. There was more than enough evidence – reams of messages going back months, voicemails... and the judge granted us one in her absence.'

'So that was the end of it?' Davis says. 'She left you alone after that?'

'Look, we suffered for months because of Helen Levinson. So when the reporters got wind of the order, they showed up offering us money for our story and we agreed.' He looks down at the floor. 'I had a wedding to pay off... and I suppose I felt like she owed me something for making my life, and Lee's, a misery. I don't think she would've stopped unless she'd been stopped. Trust me, the woman was obsessed. At one point, Lee was even threatening to cancel the wedding and book another venue. She was sure Helen was going to turn up on the day and spoil it... and I was worried she might too. But luckily, Bryan Levinson stepped in before any of that could happen.'

'Stepped in?' Davis is scrawling notes so quickly I'm surprise the pen isn't smoking.

'He offered us a life-changing amount of money not to speak to the press, not to speak to anyone, made us sign an NDA and threatened to sue the newspaper if they printed anything. He said if we didn't agree, then he'd tell the police that we were trying to extort him by making up lies about his wife and that we had some kind of political agenda, a vendetta against him. I remember he said to us, "You won't come out of this well." So we took the money, signed the agreement and then buried it.'

I nod. 'I see.'

'It was the kind of money you couldn't say no to,' he continues to explain, clearly feeling the need to, 'not people like us anyway. And Bryan Levinson promised that we'd never hear from Helen again. And we didn't – haven't – and trust me, we're all the better for it.' He glances at Davis then me. 'Don't tell me you wouldn't have done the same thing?'

'You asked if Helen had killed anyone, Aaron. Do you really think she's capable of that – of causing someone physical harm? Do you think she's dangerous?'

He raises his eyes then; looks a touch awkward. 'Look, man, I don't like admitting it – I mean, you've seen her, right? She's hardly a femme fatale, is she? Not to look at anyway. Got more of a librarian vibe about her, like she wouldn't hurt a fly. But *she scared me*,' he says. 'That time she told me she'd go to the police if I didn't agree to go to the beach house in Brighton? It all felt premeditated somehow, like she'd given it some real planning. She was deadly serious – I saw it in her eyes. She'd definitely have gone through with it. I don't know what would've happened if I'd given in to her blackmail... Jeez, I feel violated all over again just thinking about it, but to answer your question, Detective, do I think Helen Levinson is dangerous? Do I think she's capable of murder?' He fixes me with his gaze. 'Put it this way: I'm really glad I didn't stick around to find out.'

TWENTY-NINE

DAN

I don't know what, if anything, Helen Levinson's historic, and fairly serious, stalking episode against Aaron Young has to do with Mathew Reynolds's murder, yet my intuition tells me that it's *something*. 'Maybe we should go and see Helen Levinson, talk to her.' I'm thinking aloud, still a touch shocked by what Aaron's just told us.

'I'm sure Archer would love that, gov,' Davis remarks. 'Anyway, this stalking business happened six years ago now... all it really proves is that the Levinsons are in the privileged position of being able to afford to pay off their mistakes.' She snorts. 'Imagine if we could all do that, eh, boss?'

'Well, you'd be broke for starters.'

'Funny, gov.' She pulls a face at me. 'When they pension you off early, you should think about doing stand-up for a living.'

'Would you buy a ticket to see me, Lucy? Mates' rates?'

She laughs. 'Look, Helen Levinson had an infatuation with her gardener, maybe went a bit bunny boiler on him when he rebuffed her. Maybe she was having a mental health crisis at the time and it's all behind her now.'

'Maybe... though she seemed quite dedicated to her cause, if what Aaron Young says is all true. I mean, it's something of an insight into her character, wouldn't you say?'

'OK, gov, what is it?' Davis cocks her head to the side. 'Do you think Helen Levinson could be dangerous – that she has something to do with Reynolds's murder?'

I stare out of the windscreen. The rain is battering against the glass, and all I can see are nebulous shapes and shades of grey, like the insides of my brain staring back at me.

I sigh. 'Fiona told me about all these historic rumours...'

'Rumours?'

'About Bryan Levinson's less-than-savoury activities over the years, corruption in business, links with prostitutes... Speaking of which, any luck locating Katya yet?' I'd left the team in charge of this particular job while I'd spent the day digging into the Levinsons, or, more specifically, Helen Levinson.

'Nothing, boss. No one's even heard of her it seems.'

'Or no one's talking.'

'Either way, we're no closer to finding her, if she even exists at all.'

I suspect Katya does exist though. And I also suspect she was the one recruiting girls for Reynolds, and that he was the one procuring them for someone else. Was that someone else Bryan Levinson?

'It's going to be tricky getting at the Levinsons though, isn't it, what with him being top of the commissioner's Christmas card list? You've seen how jumpy Archer is about this already.'

Haven't I just.

'Put a tail on her,' I say. 'Get Parker and Mitchell on it, and keep it on the down-low for now.'

'You want Helen Levinson followed, gov?' Davis's voice drops to a whisper, even though it's only the two of us in the car.

'Where she goes, who she goes with...' I glance at her. 'I don't trust her, Lucy. I don't trust any of them.'

'OK, gov,' she says with a roll of her eyes. 'But it's your funeral if Archer finds out.'

I start the engine; turn to Davis. *'Frankly, my dear, I don't give a damn.'*

'Conor.'

He stands as I enter the room; shakes my hand cordially. He's dressed casually in a dark navy Nike tracksuit and box-fresh-looking trainers.

'Thanks for coming in – we really appreciate you taking the time out.'

He smiles, sits back down in the chair opposite and swings one leg over the other as he folds his arms across his chest. He appears calm, relaxed, a touch red in the cheeks still from being out on the pitch in the freezing temperatures. Only I've been in this job a long time now, and how people present and how they really feel beneath those appearances can be very deceptive. And all those little nuances that give you away – visibly swallowing, folding your arms, tapping you toes, all of which Conor Carter is currently doing right now – these are signs of anxiety, of stress, and while they're not proof of any wrongdoing, those minute gestures are often revealing.

'Conor, I need you to talk me through the events as they happened last Saturday evening, the night you and Paris attended Renton's nightclub; the night Mathew Reynolds was attacked and killed.'

He nods.

'You said you think you left the nightclub, you and Paris, around midnight?'

'That's right, yeah, midnight or thereabouts.'

'We checked that on the CCTV we took from the club and

you're right: you and Paris collected your coats at 11.58, and you left the premises at 12.01.'

'CCTV?'

His body language has altered again, and I can see he's breathing from the upper thorax, suggesting he may have been hit by an influx of cortisol. Yep, he's definitely stressed, although to be fair to him, he's doing a pretty good job of disguising it. I'm quietly impressed.

He's still nodding as I press play on the laptop and spin it round so that he can see the screen.

'We see you and Paris walking towards the railway bridge at 12.06. Can you identify yourself?'

'Yes,' he says, pointing at the screen, 'that's me, and that's Paris next to me.'

'And this man here?' I pause the image; zoom in closely. 'Do you recognise him?'

He's still nodding. 'Well, I do now. Now I know that's Mathew Reynolds, but I didn't at the time.' He looks up at me. 'I barely recall seeing him pass by us – didn't take much notice of him.'

'Do you remember seeing him inside the club?'

'No, though now I know he was there, I can't quite be sure, like my mind's playing tricks on me. We were both a bit drunk, me and Paris...' He pauses. 'We'd taken a pill, some MDMA. I didn't want to tell you in front of my parents.' He lowers his eyes. 'They'll go completely mental if they find out. I swear I've never taken any drugs in my life before that night,' he says, adding, 'I wish I never had. It was a stupid idea.' He shakes his head; exhales heavily. 'You're not going to tell them, are you – my mum and dad? I mean, I'm eighteen, right? I'm an adult.'

He's right, he is an adult, and he'd be tried as one too. Though I find it interesting that he seems more concerned about the drugs than staring down a ten-stretch for murder.

'Where did you get them from, Conor – the pills?'

'Does it matter?' he asks nervously.

'Maybe.' I shrug. 'Did you get them from Mathew Reynolds?'

'No!' He shakes his head vehemently. 'Definitely not. I told you I never saw him inside the club, never spoke to him.'

'And he never spoke to you? He never stopped when he walked past you both, never called out to you, never approached you or tried to engage with you in any way?'

'No.' He gives a one-shoulder shrug.

'And what about Paris? Did he try and speak to her? Did he engage with her or try to? Does – sorry, *did* – Paris know the victim, Conor? Was she familiar with Mathew Reynolds?'

'No.' He breaks eye contact. 'I dunno. You'd have to ask her that yourself, but not that I know of, not that she told me.'

He starts fiddling with the neck of his T-shirt. 'Can I have a drink of water please?'

'Of course.' I nod at the plastic bottles on the table, and he takes one; opens it.

'How long have you known Paris?' I notice that his eyes sparkle a touch at the mention of her. I get the sense he's quite fond of her.

'A few months – not that long.'

'How did you meet?'

'My mum works for her mum. She cleans her house. They're also friends,' he adds quickly. 'I sometimes drop her off at work, and that's when I first saw Paris. And then she came down to see me at training one day, and we got chatting...'

'Ah yes, you're at the academy, aren't you? Doing well by all accounts. You're a talented player so I'm told, got a good career ahead of you, not to mention a lucrative one if you're picked up by a premiership side.'

'With a bit of luck.' He smiles; seems happy to be able to change the subject. He's a good-looking, polite young man. I sense he has a caring nature. I also sense he's lying through his teeth and that this is all well rehearsed.

'I'm sure luck has little to do with it and it's everything to do with hard work, dedication and determination.' I pause for a good moment. 'Conor, why would your DNA be on the weapon that was used to kill Mathew Reynolds?'

'The bottle you mean?' He looks up.

'How did you know it was a bottle, Conor?'

He looks spooked again. 'My... my dad said. He said you told him my DNA was on the beer bottle that someone stabbed him with. I took it with me, from the club – I was drinking it when we left, or I still had it in my hand anyway. I'd sneaked it out inside my coat. Then we went down to the arches, and I needed to take a pee, and I finished it, chucked it on the ground,' he explains. 'I never touched it again, never saw it. But that's why my DNA was on it – it was my beer.'

I nod; smile. 'And you're happy to give us samples today so we can confirm that's definitely your DNA on that bottle?'

'Yes, of course. Whatever you need.'

He's been well coached, I'll give him that.

'You get on well with your parents, don't you, Conor?' I fix him with my eyes.

'Yeah.' He nods. 'We're a tight family – always have been.'

'They've invested a lot into you, haven't they – a lot of time and money to help you achieve your dreams? You must be very special to them for them to have sacrificed so much, especially after losing your sister so young. I was sorry to hear that by the way.'

He shrugs. 'Yeah, thanks, though obviously I never knew her. Though it feels sometimes like she's watching over me, you know? Looking out for me.'

I pause. 'I can see why your mum and dad would be even more devoted to their only remaining child.'

I see what I think might be a flicker of sadness in his eyes, and I feel a stab of empathy for him. I can see the fear behind them too. He's not giving me the whole story, and we both know it.

'You do know that withholding or disposing of evidence in a murder inquiry is perverting the course of justice, Conor? It can carry a five-year sentence. Your dad... you know about his past?'

'His record you mean? Yeah, course I do. We don't have secrets in our house – my dad always says it isn't big enough for them.'

I smile; lean closer across the table towards him. 'He must've told you what it's like in prison?'

'Well put it this way: it's definitely not top of my bucket list...'

'How do you think your mum would fare, in a place like that, Conor? In prison I mean?'

'My *mum*?' He pulls his chin into his chest; looks at me in horror. 'Why would *she* be in prison?'

I look at him directly then, man to man, and silently implore him. I don't want Conor Carter to ruin his life; I don't want his parents to ruin theirs either. They're a nice, decent, ordinary hard-working family, and something like this would shatter them.

'Conor.' I address him with some gravitas; meet his eyes. 'Tell me what happened that night, what *really* happened. Did Reynolds attack you first? Was it a drug deal gone wrong? Did he try to rob you, take Paris's handbag? Did you get into a fight? Did he pick up the bottle and you disarmed him in self-defence, didn't mean for it to happen, you panicked, ran... Did it go down like that? Was this all just a terrible accident?'

He's attempting to maintain his coolness, but his knee is violently jerking up and down underneath the table. I'm fairly certain that if I shouted, 'Run,' right now, he'd bolt from the room.

'Or was it Paris?' He's shaking his head now. 'Did Paris attack Reynolds? Was *she* the one who picked up that bottle?'

'No one picked up any bottle,' he says eventually, his voice tight with stress. 'We never saw Mathew Reynolds again after he walked past us. And I didn't know who he was at the time. I absolutely swear. We never spoke to or engaged in any way with him. We walked home. That was it. That's what happened. I could never stab anyone. I don't like violence, not off the pitch anyway,' he says with a small smile.

I believe him, the bit about him not liking violence. But the rest of it?

I hold his eye for a moment and then let out a heavy sigh. 'OK, Conor,' I say. 'Are you sure there's absolutely nothing else you want to tell me, nothing about that night, something you remember, anything at all, because now would be a good time.' I lean in towards him across the table. 'I want to help. If something happened and you just can't face it... I can – I *will* – help you, you and Paris, I promise you. It's not too late...'

He looks up at me then, poised to speak, and I hold my breath.

'I think Paris is being abused by her parents.'

THIRTY

ED

He's pacing the room, chewing on his thumbnail as he strides back and forth.

How long has it been? He checks the clock. Shouldn't they have been done with him by now, the police? He glances at his phone; wills it to ring. It's all going to be OK, he reassures himself. They went through everything thoroughly before he left, what questions he's likely to be asked and the responses he should give.

'Comply with everything, OK, son?' Ed instructed him. 'You have nothing to hide, remember, so you hide nothing.' Though he knew this wasn't strictly true, or in fact true at all. 'You say nothing.' He gripped his boy by his shoulders, triggered by his own encounter with the law all those years ago, remembering the horror of it all like it happened yesterday. 'Look into my eyes, Conor, and repeat it all back to me one more time...'

As confident as Ed is that his son will keep his cool and that he won't fold under questioning, he can't prevent the voices from his subconscious leaking through. What if this is all a trick and they've got him down to the station only to arrest him?

What if the cops have more evidence than they've let on? He glances up at the clock again. Damn thing hasn't moved.

Ed exhales loudly, linking his hands above his head as he turns in circles on the living-room carpet. He stares down at it. It's immaculate, not a speck of dirt to be seen. Tee has always wanted to take the carpets up and get the floorboards underneath sanded and varnished. He promised her that when they had a spare bit of cash that he'd hire the machine and do it himself. *A spare bit of cash!* Such a thing doesn't exist in their world right now – or for the foreseeable if he's honest. Cynthia's care-home fees are crippling them financially, and now the bank has turned him down for a second remortgage, despite him practically getting down on his hands and knees and begging them. They don't care if you go under. They don't care if you lose your house and have to put your mum into some state-run 'care' home. All the money those greedy banks make from hard-working people like himself, yet when *you* need help... it's all take and no bloody give.

Ed runs his hands down his face and groans. He doesn't know how he's going to break the news to Tee. They'll probably lose the house. It feels like their lives are in free fall and he somehow needs to stop them from going under. He's Ed Carter. He promised never to let Tee down again, and he's nothing if he's not a man of his word. Whatever happens, he'll just have to see it through to the bitter end.

At least Tee will have collected the clothes from Sunnyside by now and disposed of them. Aside from the fact that he knows he's actively coerced his wife – the love of his life and mother of his children – into perverting the course of justice, this is one less thing to worry about at least. When the police inevitably – no doubt imminently – come to search the house, they'll find nothing.

Ed swallows down another mouthful of guilt. It's all *his* fault Conor was identified. It was *his* DNA on the national database that resulted in a familial match. That's the thing about making the kind of mistake he made all those years ago – it finds new ways to haunt you. Ed regrets his brief and naïve brush with criminality bitterly of course, has atoned for it by losing his liberty and his daughter in the process, and he's never again put a foot out of place. Yet still it doesn't seem enough in the way of penance. As much as he's tried to convince himself otherwise, you can never truly get away from a mistake like that, nor the ripple effect it creates. You're branded for life, no such thing as a clean slate and—

The doorbell rings, startling him.

Shit. Ed freezes. *Who's that?* Is Tee home already? Maybe she forgot her key. *Or maybe it's the cops.*

Ed dips his head as he opens the venetian blind a crack and squints through it. He knows he should feel a sense of relief when he sees who's standing on the doorstep, but he doesn't. *Bloody hell.* What in God's name did *she* want – *again*?

He sucks in a deep breath and composes himself before opening the door.

'Helen!'

'Ed!'

She smiles at him, a bit coquettishly he thinks. Instantly, he feels uneasy.

'Would it be OK if I come in?' She has a large holdall at her feet, like she's here to stay for the weekend. Maybe she's got some news about the police?

He steps back and ushers her inside, taking a quick look up and down the houses opposite to see if anyone's watching them. 'Have you heard something, Helen? Has there been an update?'

'It's very cold out today,' she says, removing her fancy designer silk scarf, sliding it from her neck and unbuttoning her thin coat with a little shiver, 'but it's lovely and warm in here, very *cosy...*'

Blimey, he thinks, as she turns round to face him. She looks different. It's the clothes. She's wearing a tight – a bit too tight – low-cut black dress, her chest spilling out over the top of it, and she's got red lipstick on.

'You going somewhere, Helen?' he asks, trying not to stare.

'Why do you ask that?' she says, slowly raising an eyebrow at him.

Is it him or is she being just a tiny bit... *flirtatious*? He isn't sure, can't call it. But whatever it is, he wishes she'd stop.

'Well, you look...' Immediately, he realises that it sounds as if he's about to say she looks *nice*, so now if he doesn't, she might feel offended. 'You look... *smart*.' Her expression drops slightly. 'Like you're off out somewhere important.'

'*This* is important,' she says, fixing him with her gaze.

'Conor is down at the station now,' he tells her. 'I talked him through everything; he knows what he's got to say, word for word... so don't worry. He's a Carter – he won't let us down. I suppose they'll be speaking to Paris too, won't they, the police? Have they been in touch yet?'

She's silently walking towards him now with a strange look on her face, discarding her handbag onto the sofa without breaking eye contact with him.

'I... I'm sorry, Helen.' Ed swallows dryly as he backs away from her, the scent of her perfume lingering in his nostrils. He could swear it's the same perfume Tee wears, something sweet and feminine.

'This house isn't big enough to keep secrets in, is it, Ed?'

He forces an awkward smile. 'Well, I often say that myself.'

'Do you know' – her chest is rising and falling as she swishes her hair back from her face, which has gone a pink colour that clashes with her lipstick – 'it was the first thing I thought as I walked into your house the day I met you, those *exact* words. And then you said them right after I'd thought them!' She blows air through her nostrils. 'Incredible, like you'd *actually* read my mind.'

Read her mind? He has absolutely no idea where she's going with this, but he's got a terrible feeling about it.

'Well, it's a skill I wish I possessed, mind reading, but sadly it's not one for the résumé.' He tries to keep his tone light.

'The moment I walked into this room for the very first time, you mirrored my thoughts right back to me in words.' There's the tiniest hint of desperation in her voice as her head drops to the side. She fixes him with her gaze. 'Do you believe in instant connections, Ed? In invisible threads that bind people together?'

Is she drunk? She must be. Only she doesn't seem it – or smell of alcohol. But hang on... didn't Tee mention something about Helen seeming a bit off her head when she was round at the Levinsons' yesterday? Ed recalls yesterday's conversation – that Helen told Tee that Bryan wasn't Paris's biological father, and that she'd been conceived in CoCo's nightclub toilet with a stranger around the same time he'd been there, eighteen years ago. He'd been certain it was a coincidence; it *had* to be... only suddenly he's hit by a thought *so* diabolical it's enough to send his heart fluttering in his chest. Suddenly he feels hot.

'I've only ever had that feeling twice before in my life,' she continues, sighing. He really doesn't want to know about these occasions but suspects she's going to tell him anyway. 'Once that night with the stranger, and once with that charlatan, Aaron... and now, with you!'

With him? An adrenalin bomb detonates in his guts.

Helen's eyes are glazed over now, and her whole demeanour seems different somehow, strange and sort of detached.

'That's nice, Helen,' he says gently. He's going to have to play this very carefully. 'I'm glad we can all be friends throughout this difficult time.' It had sounded less ridiculous in his head.

There's a loaded pause.

'Um, not to be rude...' His voice is a little shaky as he speaks.

Jesus, man, get a grip – she's just a lonely middle-aged woman. 'But is there a reason you came by today? It's just that I've got a lot on and—'

'I want to show you something, Ed.' Her voice is low and slightly ominous.

OK, now he *really* doesn't like the sound of this.

'What's that then?' he asks as breezily as he can, though he can feel impending doom creeping in on him like a shadow.

She hands him her top-of-the-range iPhone, still smiling as she presses play on the screen.

The footage shows Tee walking up to the front entrance of Sunnyside and through the double doors. She's carrying a large holdall. You can tell it's quite heavy by the way she's holding it in the crook of her arm. Bless her, she's only small. Then it jumps to Tee coming back out of Sunnyside, still carrying the same – now obviously empty – holdall. She stops, turns to look around her furtively and then walks to the left behind the premises. Ed's heartbeat is in his ears as he watches her disposing of the bag in one of the large dumpsters. She walks away only to almost instantly return and throw rubbish on top of it. She does this twice more before finally closing the lid and walking away. She's always been thorough.

'What is this?' He turns to Helen perhaps a little too sharply, only he's *really* confused now. 'I don't understand? Why did you record Tee on your phone disposing of the—' His heart drops almost as simultaneously as the penny does. He can only pray, pray hard, that what he's thinking isn't what she's thinking.

'You say Christine has disposed of the clothes?' Helen asks. 'The clothes your son was wearing on Saturday, the night that he killed Mathew Reynolds, stabbed him to death with his beer bottle?'

'My Conor never stabbed anyone,' he says defensively. 'He's not capable of doing that. Anyway, it could just as easily have been your Paris who inflicted the fatal injury.' He takes a breath. He doesn't want to get into a confrontation with her, but he also doesn't like her tone. Ed is well aware that the loaded Levinsons hold most of the cards, and he certainly doesn't trust them. 'But, yes, Tee went to retrieve the clothes today and dispose of—'

'These clothes you mean?' She drops her gaze to the bag next to her, bends down and unzips it; shows him the contents. 'And don't think about trying to wrestle them from me, Ed, much as I think I might enjoy that.' She smiles lasciviously, and it sends a shiver of horror through him. 'You wouldn't want an assault charge against you, would you? Not on top of everything else.'

His heart is sprinting in his chest now.

'What is this, Helen? What are you saying?' Only he thinks he knows exactly what she's saying. The problem he's currently grappling with is believing it.

'Serious offence, perverting the course of justice, especially in the brutal, senseless murder of such a young man.' She shakes her head, almost in mockery.

'Is... is this some kind of joke? Look' – he holds his hands up – 'if you think we were going to double-cross you, or try to put the blame onto Paris and that's why you're doing this, then please, think again. We made an agreement to stick together, remember? All of us. I'm a man of my word.'

'I don't want to have to show this video to the police. I don't want to have to hand over Conor's bloodstained clothing to that nice, handsome Detective Inspector Riley.' Her nose wrinkles as she smiles.

A trickle of sweat prickles his skin as it slips down his spine. Ed doesn't want to admit it, but he's genuinely worried now.

'So what it is that you *do* want, Helen?' His throat makes a nasty clicking sound as he swallows dryly.

'Sit down, Ed' – her voice is a saccharine command – 'and I'll tell you.'

THIRTY-ONE
DAN

'Play it back, Harding.'

He rewinds the recording I requested of the anonymous 999 call received yesterday, informing us that Christine Carter was driving her vehicle while under the influence of alcohol.

'Yes, hell-o... hell-o. I am calling to let you know that there is a *laaaady*, and she get into her car drunk, and she drive off. She just left now...'

'OK. You're saying you've just seen someone get into their car while intoxicated, is that right?'

'Yes...'

'And who am I speaking to?' the dispatcher asks.

There's a pause on the line.

'She work for the Levinson family on Mulbourne Drive. She just left the house now.'

'Right, OK. And what is this lady's name please, the driver of the vehicle's name?'

'Her name is Christine Carter, and her registration number is GU11 8HC. She is in a white Fiat 500.'

Then the lines goes dead.

'And again.' I nod at Harding.

Davis appears behind me then, holding a cup of coffee.

'Listen to this.' I look over my shoulder at her. 'Tell me what you think.'

Harding hits play again, and we listen.

'Do you hear it?' I ask Davis.

She shakes her head. 'Hear what, gov?'

I suddenly think of Jude then, of my baby son, and Fiona's concerns about his hearing. It strikes me in this moment that if her fears are recognised and my son *is* deaf, then he will never be able to do what we're doing right now, listening out for a tiny nuance on a recording... I squash the thought down, taking with it the way it makes me feel.

'And again...' I nod.

'Yes, hell-o... hell-o. I am calling to let you know that there is a *laaaady*, and she get into her car drunk, and she drive off. She—'

I hit stop.

'There, when she says "drunk, and she drive off ", do you hear that slight impediment, on the R sound?'

The R sound is the most difficult letter of the alphabet to pronounce apparently, and while it's more of a common affliction among children, for some it continues into adulthood. Although it's only just detectable on the recording, I noticed that Helen Levinson pronounces her Rs with a soft and subtle W sound during our first meeting, though I had no cause to pay it any real attention at the time.

'That's Hel—'

'Helen Levinson?' Davis cuts in, blowing onto her hot coffee as she smirks.

I turn slowly towards her. She raises an eyebrow at me.

'It was traced back to the Levinson address, gov. Someone made the call from the house phone.'

'She's pretending to be someone else; she's putting on an Asian accent – a pretty bad one as well,' I note. 'Let's get a list of all the employees' names at the Levinsons' – sounds like she might have been impersonating one of them.'

Davis finally takes a tentative sip of her coffee. 'Why would Helen Levinson want to get Christine Carter in trouble? I thought they were supposed to be friends?'

That's the part I'm trying to work out, though my thoughts are beginning to slip quietly into a nagging suspicion. I have a horrible sensation in my stomach as I play the audio once more.

'Conor Carter told me he thinks that Paris may be being abused.'

Davis looks up sharply.

'By her parents,' I add.

She almost loses her grip on her cup.

'Did she confide in him?' Her eyes are wide in shock.

I shake my head. 'No. He just said he felt that something was going on in the Levinson house, that maybe Paris was being abused or mistreated somehow and that she has unexplained bruising on her arms.'

'So what makes him think it's the parents?'

'The way she acts around them, her reaction whenever their names are mentioned, so he says.' I meet her eye. 'He senses it.'

'And you sense that what he's sensing is correct?'

I pause. Shrug. 'Perhaps...'

'Maybe they're a bit dysfunctional, the Levinsons – what family isn't? But... *abusive?*'

'Ah, well' – I wave my finger at her – 'you see now that this concern has been raised, Davis, you realise that we're professionally obliged and duty-bound to investigate.'

'I was worried you were going to say that, boss. But you're wrong actually.' She's eyeing me cautiously. 'We have a duty of care to pass this information on to the *relevant authority* – in this case, child social services and—'

'There's something going on at the Levinsons', and something going on between the Levinsons and the Carters. It's all wrapped up in this murder somehow. I just need to find the devil.'

'The devil?'

'Details, Davis, the devil in the details.'

'What about the Katya line of enquiry?'

'We keep looking, keep asking, make a nuisance of ourselves until someone tells us something, even if it's just to get rid of us.'

She nods.

I chew on my thumb a little, my mind turning like a tumble dryer. 'How long on the fast track from forensics – the clothes?'

'Can't say exactly, gov. A day, maybe two?'

I exhale just as my phone rings.

'Mitchell?'

'Helen Levinson has just left the Carters' house, gov. She arrived about an hour ago, dressed up smart, like she was going somewhere. Ed Carter answered the door; she went inside and didn't come out again until a few minutes ago, looking quite pleased with herself I have to say.'

'Do you know if Christine's at home?'

'Don't think so. Her car isn't here.'

My interest is pricked. What was Helen Levinson doing all glammed up at the Carters' house, specifically with Ed Carter, alone? Were they plotting something together, planning to dispose of evidence, or was it something else?

I'm almost certain that the clothes we retained belonging to Conor Carter will come back negative from forensics. I doubt they're even the same items he was wearing the night of the murder and that they've disposed of them already, given us decoys instead. It's one of the oldest tricks in the book.

I need a search warrant, and I need to speak to Paris Levinson. Those clothes could be ashes already, blown halfway to Donegal by now. Without them and minus a confession, there's no way it'll get past the CPS, maybe not even to arrest. However, no results could be just as damning. Both Conor

Carter and Paris Levinson admit to being at the scene of the murder moments before Reynolds was attacked. They trod the same path as the victim, and they shed hair and skin and fibres, left fingerprints and footprints. We'd expect to be able to find a match from the crime scene to their clothes, even if there's none found on the body, but no results at all would suggest they've given us false evidence and are trying to cover up their involvement.

A bang on the office window causes me to spin round. It's Archer.

'Gov.' Davis gives me a warning look as I follow Archer into her office.

'You've got the go-ahead to interview Paris Levinson,' she begins.

'The go-ahead?' My brow creases. 'Did I need it?'

'Just don't start, Riley,' she snaps irritably. 'Tomorrow morning, you and Lucy Davis are going to the Levinson house, where you'll speak to Paris Levinson with her parents present, OK?'

I make to object to this, the Levinsons calling the shots, telling me where and when and how I can speak to a witness/suspect in a murder inquiry. Clearly they're of the mind that they're above the law.

Just how powerful *is* Bryan Levinson? Powerful enough to get away with murder? I'm really beginning to think so. But perhaps being there, with them all together in their house, could prove revealing. A wise old detective I knew once told me, 'Don't judge anyone until you've been inside their house.' And he was right.

'OK, ma'am.' I nod; smile.

She blinks at me, clearly waiting for a different kind of reaction. 'OK?'

I nod. 'OK.'

There's a long pause where she eyes me suspiciously.

'Find Katya,' she eventually says, her voice flat. 'Take yourself down a different path, Riley.'

'I'll follow the evidence, ma'am, wherever that takes me.'

'Nine a.m. at the Levinsons' house,' she replies, looking up from her laptop and giving me the once-over. 'Oh and, Riley... wear a decent suit, won't you?'

'Of course, ma'am.' I force a smile.

I'm already looking forward to it.

THIRTY-TWO

CHRISTINE

'Ed! Eddddd!' I explode through my front door, the keys slipping from my sweaty hands onto the carpet. I scrabble to scoop them up and call out to him, but there's no answer. 'Ed? Ed! Are you home?'

I run up the stairs and crash into the bedroom. Exhale. The relief at seeing him almost causes my bladder to collapse and prevents me from asking what he's doing lying down at this time of the day.

'Oh, Ed, you are *not* going to believe any of what I've got to tell you...' I let my handbag slide from my shoulder; almost fall with it onto the floor. 'I don't know where— how to begin. None of it makes any sense but... the clothes are *gone*.' I bite my bottom lip. 'I'm so sorry. I went to Sunnyside to get them and dispose of them like we agreed, and Mum, well, Mum was saying that someone called Sonia took them, but when I asked Joy, she said that no one of that name works there... *and* she told me that our outstanding debts have all been paid off! The six grand in arrears and the next three months' fees! Did you pay it, Ed? Did the bank come good? Joy said that someone had phoned in and paid it; called it a "gift"...' It's all coming out of me in what feels like one long string of unedited nonsense. 'And when I was at the Levinsons' house earlier, Carmelita... oh my God, she locked me in the library – *deliberately locked me in!*' I'm almost jumping up and down on the spot as I try and relay it all to him in a way that might start to make sense.

'She took my phone from me and... it was terrifying. And there was this room, a room behind the bookshelves, and... and... and I went inside, and oh God!' I gasp for air. 'There *is* some kind of secret room in that house, and I saw whips and chains and this horrible-looking chair thing... like some sort of torture device.' I shudder at the memory of it. 'I haven't a clue what's going on down there, but I got a *terrible* feeling about it, and Carmelita obviously wanted me to see it for a reason and... Ed? Why are you looking at me like that?'

I've been too busy purging myself of all the day's madness to fully register his expression until now. I freeze on the spot. 'What is it? What's happened?' I gasp; take half a step back. 'Is it Conor? Have they arrested him?' Fear ignites like a ball of fire inside me. 'Oh my God, they have, haven't they?' I cover my mouth with both hands.

'I need you to sit down.' Ed's voice is worryingly calm. *Too calm.*

'You're really scaring me.'

'Just sit down, Christine.'

He rarely calls me by my full name, and that alone is enough to send my anxiety stratospheric. I do as he asks though and perch on the edge of the bed, my knees jiggling as I rub them with my hands in a futile attempt at steadying them. I know that whatever my husband is about to say, I'm not going to want to hear it. I can feel the devastation on its way already.

'There's no easy way to tell you this.'

Here it comes. It's only then that I spot he's got a pen and a notepad in his hand.

I point to it. 'Why are you holding a—'

He violently shakes his head at me; brings his finger to his lips sharply as his eyes widen in a bid to silence me. It works. I blink at him, frozen.

'Yesterday,' he says in a low voice, 'when we were talking about Billy Noye's stag do...'

He visibly swallows, his Adam's apple moving up and down like a switch.

'The lost weekend?' A thin layer of unease settles onto my stomach like fresh snow. 'What about it?'

'Well...' He's fixing me with his eyes now, eyes I've looked into more times than could ever be calculated probably, and he's looking at me in a way I've never seen my Ed look at me before. 'I lied.'

I pull my chin into my chest. 'You... *lied*? Lied about what?' Only now I don't want him to answer me. Because then I'll know he really *has* lied to me, and my world is already falling apart as it is. 'Is Conor home yet? Have you heard anything from the police?' I try to change the subject.

'I lied to you, Tee,' he repeats. 'I'm sorry.'

I stare at him, paralysed by adrenalin and fear. No, Ed doesn't lie to me. Ed doesn't lie at all. *We don't have secrets in this house*, he always says. *It isn't big enough*.

'You know that stranger, the one Helen told you about that she met in a club back in 2007 – the bereaved stranger?'

I'm a statue as he speaks, hoping he's not about to say what I think he is.

I hear him take a breath as I hold my own until my face begins to burn.

'Well, that *was* me. Helen was right. I don't remember it well – the details I mean...' He's turned away from me now. 'But I cheated on you with Helen Levinson that night, all those years ago.'

I clutch my chest like I've been shot. For a moment, I don't say anything at all. I can only blink at him, as though he's an apparition.

'I'm so sorry,' he says as he starts scribbling something down on the notepad. 'It's as much of a surprise to me as it is to you.'

As much of a surprise! He's not serious, is he?

I try to speak but only a serious of short outward breaths come from me. Something isn't right here. *Everything isn't right.* This isn't Ed. This is not my husband in front of me telling me this. It doesn't sound like Ed; it doesn't even look like Ed.

'Please, Ed.' I can feel tears pricking the backs of my eyes. 'This is a joke, right? Because if it is, it really isn't funny. I mean it – not with our Con down the police station, not with everything else, and—'

'It's not a joke,' he interrupts me softly. His voice has always been able to soothe me, but right now it's like nails down a blackboard. 'We... Helen and I...' He looks so uncomfortable that I feel a stab of empathy for him – I can't help it.

Helen and I?

'We had some sort of... a sort of c-con... connection.' He struggles to release the word; almost has to spit it out of his mouth. 'I had a one-night stand with her back in July 2007, the night of Billy Noye's stag do in CoCo's,' he says quickly as he looks up at me finally. 'Paris *is* my daughter, Tee.'

THIRTY-THREE
CHRISTINE

'Bullshit!' I angrily square up to him, finally reaching my flashpoint, all my emotions crashing together at once. I'm studying his face, circling him, trying to size up if he's really telling me the truth or not. But why would Ed be lying about something like this, something so... *awful*. So it must be true, mustn't it? Only I just don't believe him. I know this man. I know him like I know myself, *and I smell bullshit*.

'So *now* you're saying that it *wasn't* all just some crazy coincidence, and that *you* and *Helen Levinson did* have sex in a toilet cubicle after randomly meeting in CoCo's one night, and that our son is now sleeping with his half-sister. Is this what you're telling me?'

Suddenly he holds up a piece of paper in front of me, puts his finger to his lips and gives me that wide-eyed look again, silently instructing me to be quiet.

Play along with it. I will explain.

Play along with what? My mind is clogged with confusion. 'Ed, I...'

He starts scribbling again.

She's listening in.

'I'm sorry, Tee, but that's what happened.' He quickly picks up the conversation but keeps pointing at the note. 'It was a mistake— no, I mean' – he winces; bangs his forehead as he quickly corrects himself – 'not a *mistake*. Just something I... I never intended to happen.'

I take the pen off him.

Who is listening in?

I hold his gaze as I slide the paper towards him, then bring it back, quickly adding:

Have you been drinking?

He slides it back to me; doesn't break my stare.

Helen Levinson!!! She's bugged our house. And no I haven't! FFS! PLEASE JUST <u>ACT</u>.

I nod silently. What else can I do? I have to trust him. I *do* trust him. But for the love of God, why would Helen Levinson have bugged our house – *and how?* There has to be some explanation for all of this.

I scribble a reply, gesturing silently to him.

What shall I say?

Get angry. Walk out.

For reasons I can't explain, I give him the thumbs up sign.

'Never intended it to happen! NEVER INTENDED IT TO HAPPEN!' I rear up at him, causing him to genuinely pull away from me in surprise and drop the pen. 'How could you have done that?' It hits me then, the pain I now know I would feel if Ed really ever were to betray me. I've just been given a tiny preview of it. And even though our son is at the police station, even though Helen Levinson is supposedly bugging our house and something strange and horrible and bizarre is happening, the relief of knowing I don't actually have to feel that pain for real causes me to burst into tears for real.

'Do you know what you've done? Do you realise what this means?' I'm investing in the role now, utilising all my acting skills, which as it happens amount to none. Overcome with emotion – no acting required – I start pummelling his chest with my fists. 'How could you do that? How could you lie to me about this for all these years?' *Do I sound convincing?*

We begin to tussle then, falling back onto the bed together as he holds me by my wrists. In this moment, I can honestly say that I've lost all sense of what's real and what isn't. Catching Ed's eyes as we roll around on the bed, I find myself wanting to switch from crying to bursting out with laughter. It's just such a surreal moment that I don't know how else to react.

Ed reaches for the pen again.

Meet me by the shed.

'Please Tee,' he says, holding the piece of paper up and widening his eyes at me. 'Can you ever forgive me?'

I'm waiting at the bottom of our small backyard as per Ed's instructions, dancing with anxiety by the shed and wishing I smoked. When I see him striding towards me, his arms are outstretched, and we collide, collapsing into each other.

I'm grateful for the warmth of his body against my rattling bones as he holds me tightly.

'I'm sorry...' He's panting with adrenalin. 'I'm so sorry I had to do that to you, Tee. But I couldn't tell you... Your reaction had to sound authentic. Oh God.' He's hyperventilating, and I place my hand on his arm; grip him.

'We're in trouble.' He looks up at me, his voice a low, deep whisper, as he struggles to breathe. '*Serious* trouble.'

'What do you mean? I already know we're in serious trouble.' Only I can tell by his voice that it's about to get worse, if that's even possible.

He takes a step back from me; places his hands on my shoulders. 'It's Helen. She's... she...'

'She's what, Ed?' I search his face. 'For God's sake, *just tell me?*' I can see he's on the verge of tears now – his eyes are all glassy – and my panic escapes in a small whine. Ed doesn't cry! Aside from a few tears of happiness on our wedding day and on the births of both our children, the only time I've ever seen him cry is when Cora passed away.

I gasp as a tear slips from his left eye, and I reach out and brush it away from his cheek. It has no business being there. Ed is my rock. If he crumbles, then what chance do I have? 'Please, Teddy, no...' I wrap my arms around his neck and wrestle back my own tears. I only ever call Ed 'Teddy' in moments of extremity – joy and happiness, or... *fear*.

Ed bends forward and places his hands onto his knees; drops his head as he begins to breathe deeply, in and out. I watch his warm breaths meet the freezing-cold air in a smoky coil.

'She's blackmailing us,' he says after a moment, standing up straight and wiping his face with his hands.

'*Blackmailing* us?'

'Shhh, keep your voice down!' he hisses at me. 'We don't know if she can still hear us.'

'Hear us?' I'm repeating him, parrot fashion.

'Look, Tee, Helen Levinson isn't the person we think she is...'

I see that his hand is shaking as it comes up to his mouth. I've never seen him look so frightened and it's terrifying me.

'She's... she's not right in the head. *She's sick, Tee – she's really sick.*' He starts taking short paces in front of me – two steps forward, turn, two steps back – and I watch him, mesmerised for a second. 'She bugged our bedroom... that's how she knew about the lost weekend, and how she knew Cora's name.' He drops his head. 'She's been listening in on our conversations.'

I blink at him; try to process what he's telling me.

'Our *bedroom*... when? How?' I start to feel the horror wrapping itself around me, squeezing my diaphragm.

'On Sunday, when she came round looking for that diamond earring I told you about, she used the bathroom... she must've slipped into our bedroom while I was downstairs looking for it.' He's shaking his head, as though trying to piece it all together in his mind. 'But do you know what the *really* scary part is?'

This part. This is the scariest part, seeing Ed like this, panicked, frightened, *vulnerable*.

'The really scary part is that she must've planned it all – in just a few hours, she must've come up with this crazy idea that...'

As absurd a thought as it is that Helen has bugged our bedroom, this explains how she appeared to know such detail about Ed's 'lost weekend', but it's the 'bereaved' part that's leaving the nastiest taste in my mouth; how she used Cora in the conversation she'd had with me in her bedroom, telling me how she'd wanted to call Paris by the same name – my darling dead daughter!

Anger suddenly bubbles up inside of me. How could she do

that? *What an evil...* And then it dawns on me that if Helen really *has* bugged our house, then she'll have heard us in bed together last night... *Oh God.* I clutch my stomach like I've been disembowelled. I feel physically sick. *Helen's been listening in to our private conversations; our most intimate moments together!*

It comes at me then, the violation, the horror and the disgust. I feel like I need a hot shower to get the stink off. '*Oh my God!*' I whisper the words on repeat. 'Why, Ed? Why would she do that? It doesn't make any sense.'

'It's all a game, Tee, some really warped, sick and twisted game.' He taps his temple with a shaky forefinger; starts chewing his fingers. 'I don't know... Oh, Jesus...' Now he's doing that thing he does where he starts dragging his hands down his face. 'Helen filmed you going into Sunnyside, with the clothes in that holdall. She recorded you coming out again with the empty bag, caught you disposing of it in the dumpsters behind the building. It's all there, on camera. And she has the clothes. Helen must've been Sonia. And I suspect it was her who settled our debt.'

I'm shaking my head at him, open-mouthed; my face is beginning to ache from holding a fixed, confused scowl.

'But why?' My own breath plumes around me in the cold. 'As insurance so that we won't talk to the police? We'd already agreed we wouldn't do that! We take those clothes to the cops and we all go down together, don't we? So why would she take them?'

Ed pulls his hoodie over his head then stuffs his hands into his pockets as he shuffles on the spot. It's a cold day, the air deathly still, like snow is imminent.

'You're not listening to me!' he says, suddenly agitated. 'The Levinsons have got the law on their side! He's got the whole of the bloody Met in his back pocket, for Christ's sake! We can't go to the police with any of this now, even if we wanted to. The

Levinsons will destroy us. And she probably paid off your mum's bill as a sweetener, some kind of compensation maybe, or so that she could claim *we* were blackmailing *her* more like and forced her to—'

'Blackmailing *her*?' I drop to my knees then; can't help myself. I can't take it anymore. 'I haven't a clue what's going on, Ed... Our Conor's at the police station, someone paid off Mum's debt, Carmelita locks me in the library where I discover this room, and... and now Helen's been spying on us, blackmailing us. I don't understand any of it. I... I...' I'm sobbing now; I don't care who hears me.

Ed crouches down next to me, places a hand on my back and starts rubbing it. 'Listen' – his voice is a whisper in my ear – 'if Helen goes to the police with that footage and the clothes, then we're all going to prison. Conor will be convicted of murder, and we'll do time for perverting the course of justice. Conor might get ten years, maybe more given the violence used, and we'll do two and a half each on a good day.'

'How did you find out that Helen bugged our house?' It strikes me suddenly that I haven't thought to ask this question until now.

'Because she came here again today.' His voice has dropped even lower with gravitas. 'She came to the house, and she showed me the footage on her phone.' He sucks in a deep breath. I can tell he's holding something back – not telling me everything. 'We're really in deep.' He visibly swallows as he rubs the sides of his head, I imagine, to relieve the tension that's building there. 'I don't know how to tell you...'

I let my own head fall forward. *What have we done?* I ask myself. How did we get here, hiding at the bottom of our garden, whispering to each other while our son is at the police station being interviewed about a murder? This time last week, I was watching soaps and wondering what to cook for dinner. All that's gone now though, isn't it, normalcy? Things are never going to be the same again, and the thought plunges me headlong into an abyss of grief.

'This isn't going to end well for us, is it?' I find myself quietly saying after a moment, though in truth it's less of a question than it is a statement. I knew it was the wrong decision to lie about something as terrible as this even as I was going along with it. Most of the mistakes we make in life only become mistakes in hindsight, but I can't say the same for this one. I knew I – *we* – were making a dreadful error in trying to cover this up; it was inherently wrong, and yet I went along with it anyway. I abandoned my integrity, my morals and my conscience, all the things that make me the person I am, or always thought I was. I chose wrong over right to save my son, and now we're in it up to our necks.

Our eyes are locked as I will Ed to respond to my question, to tell me something different, to reassure me, like he always does, that everything will be OK. When he doesn't, I feel crushed.

'If the Levinsons hold all the aces, then why is Helen blackmailing us?' I implore him, desperate for answers. 'Why would she need to? What could *we* possibly have that she could blackmail us over? *What does she want?*'

Ed stops pacing then; looks up.

'Me, Tee,' he says. 'She wants *me*.'

THIRTY-FOUR

CHRISTINE

There are no words to describe how I feel once Ed has told me everything. I stand in a stunned, horrified fog of disbelief, listening to my husband speak as he paces up and down; have to keep asking him to repeat himself in a bid to try and process what I'm hearing.

'She thinks we have some sort of spiritual connection,' he says, the incredulity thick in his raised pitch. 'And she said something about invisible threads and that I had read her mind, read her thoughts...'

'And what *were* her thoughts?' I'm dreading the answer, but I had to ask. I need to know what we're really up against.

'That our house wasn't big enough to keep secrets in, you know, that phrase I sometimes use?'

I blink at him, perplexed.

'Well, apparently I said it out loud right after she'd thought the exact same thing, and somehow this "coincidence", if it even was one, meant in her twisted mind that we're supposed to be together somehow, you know, destined, the two of us, me and her.' He's shaking his head.

'What does "be together" mean?' I glance at him nervously, my stomach so tight I'm almost bent double.

'Jesus, Tee, I don't know... and seriously, I really don't *want* to know. My mind's gone to all sorts of horrible places.'

But I know what it means, and so, I suspect, does Ed, only neither of us wants to say it out loud.

'She says I have to go to this beach house of theirs in Brighton tomorrow night. I'm to drive down there for dinner at 8 p.m.'

'The beach house? *Dinner?*' I'm agog. 'This... this is insane – *she's* insane! What does she think you're going to do, divorce me and run off with her?'

I wonder then if what Helen told me about Paris not being Bryan's biological child is even true. She's clearly unhinged. Maybe she really is on some kind of medication, or certainly should be, but now the bottom of the bottom's bottom's bottom seems to be falling out from beneath me yet again.

Ed is still pacing. 'She says if I'm not there, if I don't show up, then she's going to send that video of you, complete with the clothes she took from your mum's, to the police. She also said that if *we* go to the police about this – any of this – then she'll tell them that *we* are blackmailing *her* and trying to pin Reynolds's murder onto Paris, when really it's Conor who's responsible.' He almost runs out of breath he's talking so fast. 'She said she'll make sure that our son is convicted and sent to prison and that you'll go to jail for perverting the course of justice!' His voice has taken on a slightly manic tone now, like he's really starting to lose it.

'And what about you? What happens to you if Conor and I are in prison? Or is that the idea? She makes sure Conor and I go to prison and then she can have you to herself?' I'm struggling to believe I'm even having this conversation, that these words are my own. I think of Mum suddenly then. Who would take care of her if we all went to prison? Oh God! She'd end up in a state-run hellhole, confused and alone, with no one to visit her, her family all gone, her home repossessed, everything destroyed! I started to hyperventilate, small despairing noises I've never made before escaping my lips.

'I dread to think what would happen to me, Tee. In all honesty, I think I'd prefer a stint behind the door than being forced into becoming Helen Levinson's bitch!' He visibly shudders, and I feel our combined despair hanging heavy in the air around us.

'What are we going to do, Ed?' I say after a moment. We're damned either way.

'Maybe *I* could talk to her?' I suggest. 'Maybe she might listen to me, another woman; maybe she just needs someone to talk to, to confide in... She's clearly not well in the head!' The speed at which my mind is racing is mentally exhausting me. 'Who do we turn to? We can't go to the police! What about Bryan Levinson? Surely he isn't complicit in any of this, is he? Can't we talk to him – tell him his wife's gone mad?'

Ed shakes his head. 'Same rules apply. If either of us speaks to Bryan, then she's pressing send on that video. In fact, she was adamant that Bryan can't know about any of this.'

'She can't do this!' I shriek. 'It's... it's... *twisted!*' I start picking my top lip as I turn in circles. 'Do you think she's genuinely serious, that she's actually going to go through with this, really?'

Ed's grave expression needs no translation.

I drop my arms by my sides with a smack.

'So she wants you to meet her at the Brighton beach house for dinner at 8 p.m. tomorrow?'

He nods.

'And then what?' I throw my hands up to the sky. Only we both know what the "then what" refers to.

'I don't know. I can't... I can't think about it.'

'But you have to. *We* have to! God knows what she has in

mind!' Spittle flies from my lips. I'm balancing on the edge, about to tip over it. 'I saw that room, Ed... the secret room in the Levinsons' house with handcuffs and restraints... I think they must throw sex parties down there, be into S&M and all of that kinky stuff. What if she tries to—'

'Leave it out, Tee, *please.*' Ed's face has started to pale in the low afternoon light that's creeping in around us. 'Look, as far as I can see, we don't have much choice, do we? If I don't turn up, then she's going to the cops.'

'Is she though?' My voice is a desperate whisper. 'Do you *really* believe that she'll go to the police, blame everything on Con and have me arrested if you don't show up and be her gigolo for the night?'

Ed looks up at me; pulls a face. 'Do you want to chance it and find out?' His gaze drops back to his feet. 'You didn't see her – or hear her.' He shakes his head. 'The woman's unstable. God only knows what she's capable of! I don't think we can afford to take the risk.'

'But what if she's *dangerous*?' Anyone looking at Helen Levinson would struggle with the idea of her being violent in any way, but then again, I wouldn't have ever believed she was a fantasist capable of blackmailing someone into being with her either. It's a deeply disturbing thought – the idea of my Ed and Helen Levinson together – and I have to try hard not to allow my imagination to start painting such horrible vivid pictures for me.

'I'll just have to turn up.' Ed's voice is laced with resignation. 'Maybe I'll have dinner with her, try and talk her round, compliment her a bit, make her feel... oh I don't know, whatever it is she's hoping to feel, and that'll be enough to get her to stop all this nonsense?'

Only we both know it's wishful thinking. Helen Levinson has set her sights on my husband, and she's going to use my son to make sure she gets what she wants.

None of us sleep that night, despite the indescribable relief I felt when Conor walked back through the front door, still a free man, for now anyway. Ed and I decided not to tell him anything, not yet, not unless – or until – we had to. We just needed to find a way to sort this mess out somehow, and despite the sick feeling of dread in my chest, eventually I acquiesced. What choice did we have? Ed was to do as Helen asked and drive down to the Brighton beach house tomorrow night, where he would try and get her to see reason.

Ed really can talk the talk when he needs to, but the feeling of unease I have isn't chartable. I feel violated, like my home and family have been contaminated. Lying silently next to Ed, it feels as if Helen is in the room with us. Ed eventually found and removed the recording device she hid in the lampshade above our bed, but my paranoia is still spinning out of control. I won't be satisfied until we scour the entire house from top to bottom in case she planted more.

By the time I wake the next morning, my fear has morphed slightly into something steering dangerously close to anger. How *dare* Helen Levinson do this to me and my family! How dare she violate us all, blackmail us, threatened to destroy us! I'm not going to let her do it! I have to do something, think of something. *Think, Christine, think!*

And as I'm driving to see Mum, it comes to me.

THIRTY-FIVE

CHRISTINE

I'm sure I recognise the black saloon as I pull up a little way down from the Levinsons' London residence, having raced there instead of heading to Mum's. I think it belongs to Detective Riley. *Shit.* He's here, standing at the front door – I can see him and his female colleague going inside the house. I hang back; wait for them to close the door behind them.

The Levinsons' have CCTV and cameras all around their property of course – it's a gated millionaire's mansion – but I know how to avoid them; I know where they are. I dip and duck between them as I run up on the inside, stealthy, like an intruder, and down the side of the house. There's a gate at the bottom that will take me round the back. I can get in that way. I punch in the security code, hear the click as it gives and I slip through it, my chest heaving with adrenalin. Smoothing out my tabard, I take a deep breath.

I surreptitiously peer through the glass and see that the downstairs kitchen area is empty. Relieved, I slide open one of the bifolding doors and quickly slip through it. I'm dressed in my cleaning uniform, so even if one of the other girls does see me, they won't be surprised. I think I hear voices as I walk through to the hallway, towards the stairs. Yes, coming from the living room, the front one to the left. Bryan Levinson is speaking. I can't hear what he's saying exactly, but I detect that unmistakable self-important tone of his.

Quickly, I take the wide staircase and run down it, heading towards the library. No one has seen me so far. The door creaks loudly as I open it, causing me to wince, but I immediately set about trying to locate *Gone with the Wind* on the shelves. I need to be in and out as fast as I can if I'm not to get caught. After spotting it, I take the hidden key from inside it then start pulling all the surrounding books away until the door comes into view, only it's not exactly light work. I have to keep wiping the sweat from my forehead onto my sleeve before I finally turn the key and step inside.

The black leather visitors' book is visible on the table, exactly where it was when I last saw it. The photographs are scattered next to it. Relief ripples through me. I hurry to it, open it, take my phone out and begin to screenshot the pages that contain names and dates and times written in black ink. I do the same with each photograph, wincing as I am forced to look through them again, at the blank, vacant expressions on the young women's faces while various, and vaguely familiar-looking, older men paw at them, grinning lasciviously. I'm pretty certain I've seen Bryan with one of the men before, that he's also someone prominent, someone important. Then I slip my phone back into my tabard and feel something in the pocket. It's that letter, the one written in Helen's handwriting, saying how she couldn't go on. I forgot I put it there.

I hurry from the room, lock the door behind me and begin the arduous process of replacing the books, praying that no one will come in and rehearsing what to say in my head if they do. Finally, with all the books back in their rightful places, I exhale loudly and swing round to leave.

'Oh my life!' I gasp; clutch my chest. 'You scared the hell out of me!'

Carmelita. She's standing opposite me, all four-foot-nothing of her, those strange, steely eyes staring right into mine. Dread hits the pit of my stomach and explodes like a mushroom cloud.

'I... I was just... An earring!' I splutter, remembering Helen's excuse when she visited my house before. 'I lost an earring down here last week, and I was just looking for it, and...'

I want to ask her why she first brought me down here, to the library. I think she wanted me to discover the secret room, but I don't have time now. She stares silently at me for a moment before she opens the door and looks out, starts checking left and right. Suddenly, she shoos me back into the room. I hear voices approaching. After physically pushing me behind the door, she swings it open.

'Ahh, Carmel!' I hear Bryan Levinson's voice project as he enters. 'We were just about to show Detective Riley and his colleague here our spectacular library room! Come in, Dan – have a look round!'

My eyes are screwed tightly shut as they come through, terrified someone will hear my heart pounding.

'Wow! Well, now this is certainly impressive,' Detective Riley replies with a little whistle.

'Over 30,000 books in here,' Bryan boasts. 'Are you a reader?'

'I'd like to read more than time allows.'

'Yes, well, too busy catching the bad guys, eh?' Bryan guffaws. 'We love this room, don't we, darling? It's a very *special* place for us.'

I hold my breath. *Helen*. I'm now convinced that it *was* her who paid off Mum's fees in some disturbing and absurd plan she concocted to – and I'm still struggling to believe it – steal my husband. She's sick, and I'm worried she might actually be sick enough to carry such an absurd plan through. Only now I have something that *I* can potentially bargain with. I'm going to fight fire with fire because what else can I do? I don't *want* to blackmail anyone, but everything I love and have is at stake. Helen started it, so I have no choice but to try and finish it.

'Yes,' I hear her reply, though her voice sounds tight. I detect the strain behind it. *'Very special.'*

'We all simply *love* to come down here as a family together and indulge our favourite... pastimes. There's a chess board and backgammon if you're any good?'

I can see Carmelita's small feet in the left of my peripheral vision and pray they don't ask her to leave and close the door behind her.

'Paris often gives me a run for my money, don't you, sweetheart? Good little chess player this one... I taught her well.'

I hear Paris murmur something incoherent in response to her father.

'Anyway, let's take a walk through the back of the house on our way out,' Bryan says. 'We have a stunning sunroom where a lot of our charity events take place. This summer we're planning on hosting an auction in aid of children with leukaemia.'

I exhale long and hard as their voices gradually fade and the door closes behind them.

Carmelita faces me with those steely eyes. 'Wait here five minutes, then go,' she says, suddenly seemingly more capable of speaking English than I'd thought, before disappearing through the door as quickly as she arrived.

I blink at the blank space she's left behind. Is she trying to help me? It feels like it, though I'm not sure why. Maybe she feels guilty for contacting the police. Maybe Helen forced her to do it... or maybe it wasn't Carmelita who called them at all.

Of course! It hits me like a comet. It was *Helen* who'd encouraged me to drink the champagne, practically forcing it down me, topping up my glass every few minutes... She must've planned to get me tipsy and then try to have me arrested for drink-driving! Maybe she thought that if I spent the night in a cell, then she could spend the night with my husband! I try to shake such an abhorrent thought from my mind. This is getting even more screwed up by the second.

By the time I'm driving back from the Levinsons' – having escaped without detection – on my way to Sunnyside once more, I've already decided what I'm going to do. I can't let anyone know my plan, not even Ed. *Especially* not Ed. I'm not going to allow Helen Levinson to hold us over a barrel. I won't go down without a fight...

Tonight, Helen is expecting to see my husband when she opens the front door of her Brighton beach house. I've never been to the house in person, but I have seen images of it – photos on the walls of past summers spent, of fancy garden parties and family beach days with posh picnics. There's a painting of it too, in the hallway, the work of some famous artist they commissioned apparently.

The house itself looks like something from a Jane Austin novel, majestically perched on a clifftop, surrounded by sprawling landscape, the sea licking the rocks below it. Helen thinks she's been cunning and clever – that she saw an opportunity in our shared predicament and took advantage of it, using her money, power and sway to manipulate, to coerce and blackmail in the most sinister and sickening way to get what she wants. But Helen Levinson has seriously underestimated me. And tonight, I think as I swing the Fiat into Sunnyside's car park, she'll find out just how much.

THIRTY-SIX

HELEN

She breezes into the kitchen, her hair bouncy from her blow-dry, carefully dressed in a plissé silk pantsuit co-ord. She's even spritzed herself in new perfume she treated herself to, Flower Bomb. The same one she saw on Christine's dressing room table in her bedroom that time.

Bryan gives her the once-over; curls his lip. 'You're in a good mood this morning,' he remarks sardonically as he pours himself a – very early – Scotch on the rocks. 'Have you been avoiding the mirrors again? A smile like that could light up a whole psychiatric ward!'

And there it is right there. One of the reasons she fantasises regularly about his death.

'Now remember what I've said.' His voice takes on a condescending, patronising edge, even more so than usual. 'He's here to talk to Paris, not *you*. Let me do most of the talking, and if he asks you any questions, try to give intelligent answers.' He smirks, adding, 'So let's hope he doesn't ask you too many, eh?'

Helen's hatred of her husband is the gift that keeps on giving. She glances at the knife block on the island's granite surface and imagines slitting his throat from ear to ear with it in one swift move. It makes her smile for a second.

'I've spoken with Commissioner Lennard, with Guy, and he says it's all routine and there's nothing to be concerned about. They just have to be seen doing their jobs and it'll be over soon enough, and she'll be ruled out of the inquiry. Though we're to keep an eye on this Daniel Riley character. My people tell me he can be quite the tricky customer – doesn't easily let things go, very principled...'

'Positive attributes in his profession, I should imagine,' she comments, forgetting herself for a moment.

Bryan shoots her a look. 'Did you not *hear* me? I said, don't speak unless someone asks you a direct question. Because, you see, the more you open that stupid fat mouth of yours, the more likely problems will occur. Have you taken your pills today?'

Helen feels the bolt of hatred run through her so deeply that it bends her body out of shape.

'You know what happens when you don't take them. You become even more unhinged than you already are. Let's just get this over with, and then we can bloody well forget all this nonsense and get Paris away from that Carter boy.'

'Conor Carter is training to be a professional footballer actually,' she finds herself saying. 'Ed tells me he's very good on the pitch.'

Bryan snorts derisively. 'Ed? *Ed.*' He mimics her. 'Yes, well, I don't trust *that* criminal as far as I could throw him. Anyway, I'm not worried about the Carters.'

No, and he clearly isn't worried about the dead man either, not that she ever expected him to be. She had to physically leave the room in disgust when she heard him giving a quote to his PR officer about the 'despicable, senseless tragedy' that had occurred in 'our' community and how 'we' were all pulling together, united in our strength against crime and violence.

How he extended his deepest condolences to the Reynolds family, especially Mathew's mother, a woman whose name he had to be reminded of at least twice during the conversation.

'They're only a minimum-wage slip away from being benefit scum, the lot of them. Won't take too much to keep them happy, I'm sure,' he says, rubbing his thumb and middle finger together, 'and then all this hideous mess will be over.'

Helen thinks of the £21,000 she took to pay off Christine Carter's mad mother's care-home fees. He'll find out about it eventually, but she'll just have to cross that particular bridge when she comes to it. Nothing and no one is going to kill her buzz today because soon she will be in Ed Carter's strong arms, safe and untouchable. He will protect her. He is a good man – she can feel it; she senses it deep inside. He understands her, can even read her mind! He can see who she really is and what she needs – those invisible threads that bind them together are strong as fishing wire. It really has all happened the way it's supposed to.

There is one thing troubling Helen though. She can't work out why Bryan hasn't simply thrown Paris to the wolves and allowed the police to cart her off already. He's wanted rid of her for so long now, so why hasn't he seized the opportunity to have her locked up? Perhaps he's terrified that she'll talk. But Helen knows Bryan has more than a few ways of ensuring silence. Even if Paris *did* talk, Bryan would make sure that no one would believe her anyway. He'd have her sectioned and follow it up with some damage-limitation PR stunt. There has to be another reason he's spared Paris and is prepared to protect her like this, but Helen isn't yet sure what it is.

'I appreciate you taking the time to speak to us, Paris.' Dan Riley smiles as he squeezes her daughter's arm. Helen's heart sinks in her chest as Paris visibly flinches, sucking air in through her teeth.

'Oh, I'm sorry...' A look of concern flashes across the detective's admittedly rather handsome face. 'Are you injured?'

Paris shakes her head as she glances nervously in Bryan's direction. 'Gym... I think I must've overdone it at the gym,' she replies. 'It's nothing.'

In truth, Helen has only really been half listening as Dan Riley and his colleague spoke to Paris about the events of Saturday night, asking her to take them through it step by step. She caught something about needing to take the clothes for forensics and some swabs for DNA, and of course she heard Bryan's verbose contributions as he cut in and spoke over everyone like he usually did.

Her thoughts are preoccupied by her dinner date this evening, and she can't much focus on anything else. She still needs to pack! Oh God, what to pack! Helen loathes packing ordinarily – it's such a chore and she never seems to get it right, but high on anticipation, the thought no longer dismays her. In fact, she's rather looking forward to it! And she's decided to cook the meal she has planned for them herself, or at least she's arranged to have it prepared and delivered before she'll throw it in the oven last minute to finish it off.

She pictures herself standing at the Aga in the beach house kitchen, dressed in a floaty, thin silk kaftan, her carefully chosen underwear a touch visible beneath the sheer fabric as she flambés filet mignon in a hot pan with the Courvoisier – she suspects Ed is the carnivorous type – imagines his arms linked through her waist, squealing with delight as brandy-scented flames lick their respective faces...

'Let me show you around some of the house, Dan, Lucy...' Bryan is already standing, signifying their time is up and to follow him, which they duly do. She knows exactly why her husband wants to take the police to the library. It'll give him a sense of duping delight to get one over on them without them knowing.

Carmelita opens the library door from inside just as they arrive, startling Bryan – and herself – in the process.

'Ahh, Carmel!'

Bryan is in conversation with the female detective, Lucy, as they eventually leave the library and head off to the west wing of the house to see the sunroom, like some bizarre estate agent's grand tour. She's glad to be able to leave the library. She hates that room now, and yet it was once her favourite place to spend time in. He's even taken that from her.

'How are you, Helen?'

Suddenly, he's there beside her, Detective Riley. She was too busy daydreaming to notice.

'Me? Oh yes, yes, I'm fine, thank you.' She smiles politely at him. 'We just hope all this terrible, unfortunate... tragic business will soon be...' What should she say next? Over? It'll soon be over? No. That sounds callous, lacks empathy. *Think, Helen...* She glances at Bryan ahead of her, but he's still engaged with the female officer, a look of deep concern on his face as he talks at her.

'... *solved*,' she says. Well, it's marginally better than 'over' she supposes.

'Yes.' He nods. 'Well, all we can do is follow the evidence where it leads us, try and bring justice for the Reynolds family, some closure for them, help them to grieve the loss they've suffered...'

'Absolutely,' She nods, avoiding his eyes.

'Actually, Helen,' he says, 'I wanted to ask you about something, something a bit delicate, something quite personal that you may not want to discuss and are under no obligation to, but...'

Helen feels her sphincter muscle almost collapse. 'Really, gosh... what could that possibly be?' Her laugh is a nervous one, even to her own ear. She looks over at Bryan in desperation now; raises her head a touch in a bid to catch his attention. Thankfully, it works.

'What would you say if I said the name Aaron Young to you, Helen?'

But Bryan is behind him now, slapping him on the back. 'Sorry to hurry you along, Dan, but I've got back-to-back meetings this afternoon. I'm due in parliament tomorrow. We really appreciate you coming...'

Helen immediately drops back from them and joins Paris; places an arm round her daughter which she instantly brushes off. She only hopes the detectives haven't seen. Helen tries to temper her panic. Why is Dan Riley asking her about *him*? What have they been digging into? She thought Bryan buried all that a long time ago. He told her he had. And what did it have to do with anything anyway? It was all just a misunderstanding that had happened years ago. She hadn't been so well at the time and—

The sound of the door slamming wrenches Helen from her anxious thoughts.

Bryan stands behind it, staring at both her and Paris, his eyes aflame.

'They saw that!' he booms. 'They saw you pull away from your mother!'

Paris is shaking her head.

'No... no they didn't,' Helen quickly interjects, attempting to placate him. 'They were too busy talking to you – too interested in what you were saying.'

He casts her such a look of disdain that it feels like a slap in the face. 'Seven p.m.,' he says after a pause, nodding at Paris, 'in the library. Be ready and prepared – we have some very important guests tonight.'

Paris's head shaking is becoming faster. 'No – no. I won't be there. I'm not coming. I won't do it.'

Bryan rolls his eyes. 'Tell her, Helen.'

She swallows painfully; looks at her daughter's distraught face. 'Do as he says,' she replies. 'It's for the best.'

THIRTY-SEVEN

DAN

'You saw it?' I turn to Davis as we get into the car.

She nods. 'Yes, gov. I saw it.'

'The way Paris shrank away from Helen when she tried to comfort her? And when I deliberately squeezed her arm – to check for those bruises Conor Carter told me about – she winced in pain.'

'You really think they're abusing her? *Both* of them?'

I don't reply. I'm busy thinking.

'I mean, Helen Levinson is clearly terrified of her husband,' Davis surmises. 'She practically vanishes in his presence. It's obvious he's the one in control. God.' She shudders. 'I don't envy her being married to him. Up close you can see what a snake he is.'

I don't disagree with her. Bryan Levinson – despite his undeniable charisma, which has actually fooled a great number of people – is quite an odious man beneath the thin veneer of respectability. His air of superiority is annoying, his arrogance unpalatable after a short while in his company. Strip him of all the millions he owns and he's as insignificant and powerless as the next man, but there's something about Helen Levinson that disturbs me too. A man is dead, a young man. It's an atrocious crime, one of the most vicious I've seen in my career, and yet Helen Levinson appears completely unfazed by it. Or by the fact that her seventeen-year-old daughter may be involved in some way, if not jointly responsible. She's shown no real emotion, no concern or remorse.

'I asked her.' I glance sideways at Davis, who's behind the wheel. 'I asked Helen about Aaron Young.'

Her eyebrows raise. 'Jeez, gov, that was a bit risky, wasn't it? What if it gets back to the commissioner? Archer won't be happy. We're not supposed to be digging for dirt on the Levinsons.'

'We're not digging for dirt, Lucy; we're conducting a murder investigation. And I know and you know and *they* know that we know that they're covering something up – maybe even more than one thing. Conor Carter and Paris Levinson saw Reynolds that night. I'm convinced they came into contact with him. You saw Paris's face as she glanced over her shoulder on the CCTV footage. I think she knew him.'

'OK,' Davis indulges me, 'so how did she know him? What's the link?'

'What if Reynolds was procuring girls for Bryan Levinson, and Paris found out? Fiona told me about these historic rumours of him paying sex workers for the privilege.'

The look on Helen Levinson's face when I asked her about the name Aaron Young told me more than any verbal answer she couldn't give at the time, thanks to Bryan's intervention. I'm sure it was deliberate – that he came over to cut the conversation short. What is she hiding? Why was she at the Carters' yesterday all dolled up, alone with Ed Carter? I wanted to ask her about that too, though I hadn't had the chance – though of course she would know then that we've been following her, keeping tabs on her. What is she planning? I'm not sure, but I get a very strong feeling that it was *something*. And I don't like it.

'I want a super fast-track on the clothing, Lucy. If it comes back a match, if Paris Levinson's DNA is linked, then I'm bringing them in. And I'll want a search warrant for both the Carters' *and* the Levinsons' addresses.'

'They still won't *give* you one, boss,' she says, her voice a slight whine. 'Conor Carter will be the scapegoat for this, and you know it.'

'They can't stop me, *stop us*, from doing our jobs.'

'Yeah, but they can ensure you don't have one at the end of it,' she remarks sardonically.

'Well then, I'll go out the way I came in.'

'And how's that?'

'As the good guy,' I reply as we pull up outside Sunnyside care home.

'Why are we here, boss?' Davis trots up behind me as I approach the door.

'Christine Carter's mum... maybe she can tell us something.'

'She's got dementia. She'll never be a credible witness.'

'She doesn't need to be,' I reply.

My phone beeps as I push through the doors to the care home. It's my wife.

We have a hearing screening tomorrow – 3 p.m. at St Cat's. Can you be there? X

My stomach lurches, and I squeeze my eyes tightly together.

Of course. Send me details.

I delete the last part. 'Send me details' sounds formal,

maybe even a bit glib, but I can't think how else to word it right now.

It's gonna be OK. X

I replace my phone in my coat pocket.

'Hello!' The large, lovely-looking lady behind the desk greets us jubilantly. Her name tag reads, 'Joy.' Seems apt.

'Detective Dan Riley, and this is DS Lucy Davis.'

Davis nods her greeting with that smile of hers that seems to instantly put people at ease.

'Oooh, detectives?' Joy appears more intrigued and excited than concerned, which tells me something more about her character. 'So what do we owe the pleasure?' Suddenly her expression changes, like she's just realised that we could be here to impart bad news. 'Has something happened?'

'It's nothing to worry about, Joy, just some routine questions regarding an ongoing enquiry.' Admittedly, it's an evasive answer, but thankfully she seems to accept it. 'Do you have a resident here by the name of Cynthia... she's the mother of Christine Carter?'

Joys smooth brow wrinkles. 'Yes, Cynthia is one of our residents. Why?'

'We'd like to talk to her if that's possible?' Davis interjects.

'Has Cynthia done something?' Joy pushes, though I respect the fact that it's her job to. 'Does Christine know you're here?'

'We'll be five minutes,' I say. 'You can accompany us of course.'

She pauses, her brow still fixed in a furrow of concern.

'OK' she says after a moment. 'Follow me.'

. . .

'She's very confused a lot of the time, and sometimes that can be overwhelming for her,' Joy explains as she opens the door. 'So please...'

I lift my hands up; walk over to the bed.

Cynthia looks up at me with a warm smile. 'My Bradley! My boy! You came!'

I sit down next to her on the bed. 'Hello, Cynthia. How are you?'

She glares at me. 'Cynthia! *Cynthia*! Get away with you!' She pushes my leg – which is perched against the mattress – with a grin. 'It's "Mum" to you, thank you very much!' She places her hands on my face, then squeezes my cheeks between her thumb and forefinger. 'I always wanted to know what you looked like, and here you are, you handsome little devil, you!' She starts chuckling, and admittedly it's slightly contagious. 'I knew I'd see you again.'

I have no idea who Bradley is – the son she never had perhaps? – but she seems happy to see him.

'Cynthia, I'm Dan Riley of the Metropolitan Police. I'm a detective chief inspector and—'

'She took them,' Cynthia quickly states as she helps herself to a biscuit from the pack on her bedside table and flicks on the TV.

'Who took what, Cynthia?' Davis says. 'Who are you taking about?'

'Sonia!' She's back to watching the TV now; doesn't avert her eyes.

I look over at Joy, and she shakes her head.

'The new girl. She came and took the clothes from under my bed... and things from the wardrobe.' She pauses. 'Is Christine OK?' Her voice sounds different for a moment, and I witness it clearly then, this horrible disease she has.

'We've been through this, Cynthia.' Joy steps forward now; joins us on the bed. 'She was on about this yesterday as well,

you know, this Sonia woman, whoever she is!' Joy informs me.
'What clothes do you mean, Cynthia?'

'The one that was here on Monday. Gave me the fruit pastilles... the red ones... She took the clothes away that Christine put under my bed and in the wardrobe. Her name is Sonia!'

Clothes? Could she be talking about the same clothes Conor and Paris were wearing on the night of the murder? Did Christine hide them here?

'Sonia doesn't work here, Cynthia,' Joy tells her gently. 'Are you thinking of Sylvie maybe, or Shannice?' She turns to me. 'They were the carers on duty that day.'

'Not Sylvie, not Shannice, *Sonia*!' Cynthia tuts crossly. 'I'm not stupid! It was right there.' She bangs her small chest with a fist. 'On her name badge! *Son-i-a!* Though to be fair,' she adds, 'I suppose she did look a lot like that whatshername woman who my Christine works for.'

My eyes lock with Davis's widening ones.

'What woman is that, Cynthia?'

Joy's brow is still creased, but her expression has changed. 'You don't mean Helen Levinson, do you?'

'Yes! That's her! The one from the magazines, the one who's married to that MP with all the money... never liked the look of him much either.'

'We can check on the CCTV.' Joy stands. 'We have cameras all over the building, both inside and out – standard practice here at Sunnyside. If she was here, then she'll be on camera.'

I feel a sudden energy surge as potent as eight hours' sleep.

'Your name really suits you, do you know that, Joy?' I smile at her.

'Funny,' she says, 'you're the second person that's said that to me in as many days.'

THIRTY-EIGHT
CHRISTINE

I glance down at my phone in my handbag on the passenger seat next to me. It's fully charged, but it's switched off. I know Ed and Con will be blowing it up, wondering where the hell I am and what I'm doing, and I can't have the distraction – or give them the chance to talk me out of anything.

I check the clock on the dashboard. It's 6.45 p.m. I'm making good time; should be there by 7.40 p.m. according to the satnav, which will give me twenty minutes or so spare to gather myself. I'm driving Ed's van down to Brighton. I had to take it, plus the keys to my own car, so that he won't have access to any transport to try to come after me like I know he would. I knew I couldn't just take off without any explanation though – he might think I'd been abducted or something and call the police – so I left him a note.

> *I have to put an end to this mess, Ed. Please don't be cross with me. I'm doing this for us, for you, me and Conor, for Mum. Please don't try and come after me. It will be OK, don't worry. Trust me, just let me finish this. I love you with all my heart, Teddy. Yours forever, Tee xx*

Guilt burns inside my chest as I imagine what'll be going through his mind when he reads it. He'll be worried sick above everything, no doubt angry at me for taking matters into my own hands. But I can't let him go through with it; can't just sit back and watch helplessly while Helen bloody Levinson blackmails my husband into spending the night with him, forcing me to forsake the man I love to save our son. The guilt backslides into bitter anger with a healthy sprinkling of disgust as I hit the M23. Helen Levinson is one sick puppy who needs putting down, figuratively speaking, and I'm volunteering for the job. I'm not going to let her win. Maybe it's David versus Goliath, but I have to try.

My eyes feel gritty and tired as I take the long and winding road, making my ascent towards La Casa del Acantilado – The Clifftop House. I can see it on the horizon as I approach, positioned high on a private clifftop landing, an incredible location with panoramic bay views. The sea, a moving black mass, rolls beneath it.

I did a little research on the imposing Victorian residence before embarking upon my journey – incidentally, just one of many in the Levinsons' impressive portfolio of property around the world. It was built circa 1886, originally for a well-heeled family who went on to house military personnel during WWI and WWII. The Levinsons purchased the house back in the late nineties before lovingly restoring it, and the photos on Google were awe-inspiring. No expense has been spared on the grand interior, a sympathetic and slick mix of modern and traditional with a nod of nostalgic seaside glamour thrown in.

The gravel crunches satisfactorily under the tyres as I pull up onto the impressive crescent-shaped driveway and park the car to the left side of the property where it's more or less hidden from view behind imposing dark green shrubs and tall bushes. I arrive almost bang on the sat NAV's ETA, with seventeen minutes to spare.

Switching the engine off, I'm suddenly aware of my own breathing, the adrenalin coursing through me making me feel lightheaded and a little high. I look out onto the fascia of the tall, imposing house that appears almost gothic in the freezing, inky blackness, like someone hand-painted it in a nightmare. A sliver of self-doubt sneaks its way into my head. What the hell am I doing here? What was I thinking?

Just go to the police, Christine. Speak to that Detective Riley. Tell the truth, explain. Only it's the same old internal battle, and soon I'm back round to: *I must do this, I have to for the sake of my family.* I don't want my son's life blighted, even if he is somehow responsible for the death of another, even though I've practically convinced myself that he isn't and that this whole sorry story is all just some terrible mistake. It's never too late to do the right thing. But it's too late to turn back now.

I glance at the clock again. It's 7.51 p.m. I'll wait a couple more minutes and then I'll make my way to the front door. There's a downstairs light on and one on the second floor. Is it Helen's bedroom? I imagine her inside it, spritzing herself with perfume in the mirror, humming a familiar tune as she prepares herself for my Ed's arrival, feelings of anticipation dancing in her belly...

I snatch up my handbag and shake my hair out, then check my reflection in the rear-view mirror; apply a slick of lip gloss for a momentary confidence boost. It's now or never.

Stepping up to the large black front door, I wrap my puffer jacket tightly around me and pull the butler's bell. It feels like minutes pass before I hear someone approach on the inside, though it can only be a few seconds at best.

I watch her face collapse as she opens the door, that split second between expectation swiftly followed by bitter disappointment and, perhaps, even a touch of fear. Rightly or wrongly, it gives me a brief feeling of satisfaction.

'Helen!' I smile at her; show teeth. 'I hope you don't mind me turning up unannounced?'

THIRTY-NINE
CHRISTINE

She takes a visible step backward, blinking at me, her eyes wide like I've flashed a torchlight directly into them.

'Christine! I... I wasn't expecting to see you here!'

'Can I come in?' I've practically got one foot in the door already, and she's forced to stand back as I stride through it with purpose.

'It's freezing out there,' I say with a shiver, uncoiling the thick scarf from around my neck like a snake. I take my coat off without being invited.

'Won't feel the benefit otherwise,' I explain, slinging it over my arm.

I observe her more closely now. She's wearing that red dress, the one I saw in her walk-in closet the other day, the same one she told me she'd been wearing the night Paris was conceived. She's teamed it with a sheer open silk robe and black heeled sandals. They look uncomfortable because they're too tight. The whole outfit is one exhalation away from a busted zip.

Warm, fragrant and inviting cooking smells suddenly reach my nostrils, reminding me that I've hardly eaten a scrap in days.

'Oh, I'm sorry, were you – *are* you – expecting someone?'

Her eyes dart from left to right nervously before they settle upon mine.

'Actually, yes I was – *am*. Perhaps you can tell me why you're here? It's a surprise to say the least. I didn't know you even knew where the beach house was.'

I follow her as she begins walking down the beautifully tiled entrance towards the cooking smells. 'In fact, how *did* you know?' she asks as she glances up at the huge clock on the wall. It's 7.59 p.m.

'I couldn't have a drink, could I?' I've had the heating blowing on maximum the whole journey here and my mouth is as dry as sandpaper.'

She swings round. 'I'm terribly sorry, but this is all, well, a bit... inconvenient. I'm awaiting a guest, you see – they should be here any minute.'

'Where's Bryan?' I'm still smiling at her, careful to keep my tone neutral. 'And I'd just like a glass of water, if that's OK? It's been a bit of a drive.'

I spot the champagne bucket on the granite kitchen island, the two long-stemmed flutes positioned next to it. There's a platter of canapés too, blinis topped with smoked salmon, caviar and a sprinkling of chives. For a brief second, I think about taking one.

'Who's the lucky guy?' I ask, nodding in their direction. 'Oh that's right!' I tap my forehead. 'It's your wedding anniversary, isn't it? I remember you telling me the other day... and isn't that *the* dress you're wearing? The one you wore when you met that handsome bereaved stranger you told me about, the night Paris was conceived?'

She glances down at herself, suddenly self-conscious as she pulls her silk robe around her billowing chest. The idea that she's dressed herself up in such a provocative manner makes me feel nauseous. Clearly it's all for Ed's benefit.

'Um, yes, do you know actually, I think it might be. I've lost a few pounds recently; wanted to see if it still fitted...'

'Odd choice for your wedding anniversary, isn't it? The dress you wore the night you cheated on your husband?'

She's silent as she places a glass of water down in front of me; looks over at the clock once more. It's 8.02 p.m.

'He's not coming, Helen,' I say flatly.

'Who isn't...?' She doesn't turn round.

'Ed. *My* husband. The one you're trying to blackmail into' – I gesture at the champagne and canapés – '... spending the evening with you.'

She drops her palms down onto the work surface but still doesn't face me.

'I've no idea what you're talking about. I think you'd better—'

'Yes, you do!' I interrupt her angrily. 'You know *exactly* what I'm talking about!' I take a breath. 'What is going on, Helen? What in God's name do you think you're doing?' My voice rises as I demand explanations. 'Paying off our debts, bugging our *house*!' I walk towards her until I'm close behind her, but not so close as to invade her personal space. I sense the nervousness coming from her now; can feel the vibrations.

'I hid the clothes Conor and Paris were wearing last Saturday night in Mum's care home, underneath the mattress on her bed. I'm not proud of it.' I drop my head for a second. 'I'm not proud of *any* of this mess. But you took them, didn't you? You followed me to Sunnyside that day. You knew I'd hidden them there; you filmed me disposing of the holdall! And... and I think you tried to get me arrested... attempted to get me to drink more alcohol than I should before getting into my car. *You* called the police! Why did you do that, Helen? Why are you doing this to us? I thought we all agreed to stick together, to try and keep our children out of trouble... I thought we were *friends*.'

'I must ask you to leave, Christine,' she says quietly after a moment, though I detect no real malice in her inflection. 'He'll be here any second. He *promised* me.'

'No, Helen.' My voice sounds detached, not much like my own. 'He promised *me*, twenty-seven years ago, in sickness and in health, for richer or poorer, *forsaking all others*... What you're doing is absurd! It's sick! Does Bryan know about this?'

His name clearly triggers her as she pivots round, her eyes aflame.

'I'm afraid I'm going to have to *insist* that you leave *now*,' she says, walking past me through the kitchen and back down the hallway towards the front door. I follow her, but I've no intention of doing what she asks.

After swinging the front door open, she turns to me; gestures for me to walk through it.

'I'm not going anywhere – not until I have your word that all this madness stops! You can't do this!'

'I'll call the police!' she shrieks suddenly, taking her shoes off and replacing them with a pair of Wellington boots from a rack by the door. Then she grabs a large padded coat from the antique stand and puts it on.

'And tell them what? That you're blackmailing us? That you bugged our house... that you paid off my mum's care-home fees in some twisted plan to make it look as though *we* were blackmailing *you*... and that you tried to have me arrested, made up some cock and bull story suggesting Ed is Paris's biological father?'

'Tell them what you like. They won't believe you,' she says, walking out the front door and down the driveway, the crunching sound of gravel underfoot as she marches ahead.

'Helen! *Hel-en!*' I have to trot to keep up with her. There's a cold, icy drizzle in the air tonight, the kind that stings your eyes. I zip my coat up; wrap my scarf back around my neck. 'You have to stop this... *please*.' I can hear myself begging and hate myself for it. 'Ed isn't going to leave me *for you*; he isn't going to leave me full stop. We don't want your money; we just want to keep our family together. I realise that maybe you're unhappy, but—'

'Unhappy? *Unhappy*! Ha!' She snorts with derision. 'You don't know the meaning of the word!'

Anger suddenly ignites inside me. This woman knows nothing about me, nothing about my life – or my losses!

'Don't I? Helen, I lost my first child, a daughter, a beautiful baby girl that I, that *we*, adored, to a terrible disease when she wasn't even a year old! A daughter we'll never get to see grow up, go to school, reach her first milestones, get a job, marry, have her own babies. Ed was in prison when she died. I'd lost my husband *and* my daughter… and the person who got me through all of that hell, that horror, that grief and anguish, is now a shell of who she once was, lying in a care home, losing a tiny piece of herself slowly, day by day.'

She's steaming ahead now, pacing along the path that verges the cliffs with purpose, though I've no idea where she's heading.

'I know about unhappiness. And you used my daughter's name to give your elaborate story, your lie, some credibility. My dead daughter, Helen! How could you do that?' My trainers are slipping a little in the wet, icy conditions as I attempt to keep up with her. It's dark, and only the reflected light from the house enables me to see where I'm putting my feet.

'Are you listening to me, Helen? Why are you running away?' I'm breathing harder now as I trace her steps until we come to a small clearing at the top of the cliff. I can hear the sea below, roaring and crashing against the rocks, but I don't look down. I'm terrified of heights.

'You have everything anyone could ever want.' I'm struggling to catch my breath as I face her, yet she doesn't appear to have even broken a sweat. 'Look at you – look at your life,' I splutter, my chest heaving with exertion and adrenalin. 'The houses, the cars and holidays... Never a day's worry or a day's work! Is that why you're doing this? Is it some form of self-entitlement? Are you so used to getting what you want that you'll even resort to blackmail to get it?'

Her face is lit up like the moon, pale and round, as she blinks at me through the blackness.

'Is it even true? The story you told me about Paris not being Bryan's biological child? Talk to me, Helen.'

Finally she speaks. 'Yes. It is true. Bryan isn't her biological father.'

'So who is?' I interject. 'Because I know it isn't my Ed! Why would you make up such a twisted story? Why would you plant a bug inside our bedroom? It's... *perverse!*'

'You don't understand!' she shrieks suddenly, causing me to take half a step backward. 'You have *no* idea what my life is *really* like, what it's like being married to Bryan Levinson.' She spits his name from her lips like poison. 'You have no idea what kind of man he is – no one does – the things he does, the things he's made me do...' She edges a little closer towards me. 'All my life, all I ever really wanted was a family, to be a proper family... and that day at your house, I saw it. I *felt* it.' She bangs her chest with a fist. 'Like I could reach out and touch it, the love and unity, the closeness, the loyalty and support and care and the passion... right there, in your tiny living room, everything I *don't* have. I may be rich, Christine, but you are far richer. You have the things money can't buy.'

'Why don't you just divorce Bryan then, if you're so unhappy? You'd still come out of it a wealthy woman! You don't need to resort to this... this madness!'

'Ha! Divorce!' She throws her head back; starts laughing manically. It's unnerving. 'You don't divorce someone like Bryan Levinson! He would rather have me sectioned than ever leave him. He'd make sure I was locked away, branded mentally unstable. He's a sadistic narcissist. You can't win against the likes of him.'

I open my mouth to speak but decide against it. Clearly Helen *is* unstable, so I don't want to say anything that may trigger her further.

'He'd never let me go. Not because he loves me,' she adds, looking directly at me now, 'but because he *hates* me.'

'Why does he hate you?' I look around me, at the clearing. It's dark and extremely cold, and the wind is biting my ears. 'Let's go back to the house – talk about this there. It's freezing up here, and—'

'Bryan is impotent,' she announces. 'He can't have children because he can barely rise to the occasion, and whenever he does, it isn't even half-mast. All I wanted was a child.' Her tone switches to something pleading, pitiful. 'Only he wouldn't, couldn't, accept his... shortcomings, shall we say? He was reluctant to undergo IVF treatment. "'I don't want a test-tube baby, Helen!"' She mimics his condescending tone, accurately in all fairness. 'He thought it was beneath him somehow, couldn't put his own inadequacies to one side to give me what is most women's birthright. And so that was that. Only the desire to become a mother became all-encompassing until, in the end, I couldn't ignore it any longer, couldn't compensate for it with clothes and jewellery and cars... so I took charge and had a sweet night with a stranger – a young, handsome stranger.'

Her eyes glaze over as she reminisces with a wistful smile. 'He was a solider on leave, and he was tender and loving, nothing like Bryan.' Her lip curls at the edge. 'For years I'd been trying to conceive, on the rare occasion he could manage it,' she adds disdainfully. 'And yet it took just that one time for me to fall pregnant by a total stranger... I was over the moon!'

She looks up at me; her smile has a melancholy edge to it now though. 'Bryan was too. He thought it must've been a fluke, a happy accident, rather than the miracle it would've been, but I wasn't about to pull him kicking and screaming from his denial. I intended to take my secret to the grave with me, and when Paris was born, he doted on her, for a while anyway. He lavished us with gifts and holidays and days out – he adored spending time with his little girl. But then a terrible accident happened that changed *everything*.'

FORTY

CHRISTINE

'What accident?' I wrap my coat tighter around my frame. The wind is rendering me practically blind as it violently whips my hair about. I want to go back to the house where it's warm and dry. I don't feel safe up here on the clifftop in the dark, exposed to these elements with someone who's clearly unhinged, but I can't stop myself from asking the question.

'When she was eleven, Paris was hit by a car. She suffered serious injuries – broken ribs, a fractured leg and skull, external and internal bleeding...' I'm struggling to hear Helen's words over the high-pitched scream of the wind. 'She had to be airlifted to hospital; needed emergency surgery to save her life. It was touch and go... we almost lost her.'

I'm not sure where this story is headed, or what relevance it has, but I let her continue. 'She'd lost so much blood that she needed a transfusion. And that's what blew it all apart.'

I stare at her through blurry eyes, standing there, all dolled up in her fuck-me dress and wellington boots, her red sheer robe flapping beneath her oversized coat in the harsh wind. She looks bizarre, like a child who's raided her grandmother's old dressing-up box. 'I have type O blood, you see, and Bryan is type B. I had no idea what blood type the soldier was, but it turns out that O and B parents cannot produce an A blood-type child together – and that's what Paris was, blood type A. And that's how Bryan discovered she couldn't possibly be his biological daughter.'

'Why are you telling me this? What does this have to do with me, with my family?'

'When Bryan discovered the truth,' she continues, 'I was forced to come clean about that night, how I had intentionally betrayed him in a bid to become pregnant. He slapped me hard across my face, called me a whore, said that he'd married no more than a common prostitute, a filthy slut, and so that was exactly how he was going to treat me from now on. He wanted to punish me for my betrayal, and he did – *relentlessly*.'

I think of the letter then, the one that's currently inside the handbag on my shoulder. I scrabble to open it.

'Is that what this letter is about?' I hold it up in my hand, the strength of the wind and rain almost snatching it from my grasp.

'"I can't go on... The pain torments me on a daily basis. Please release me..."'

Her expression changes suddenly. 'Where did you get that?' She lunges forward slightly, but I quickly stuff it back into my handbag.

'Where you left it,' I reply. 'In the library. It was hidden between the pages of a book, *Gone with the Wind* – one of my favourites actually. There was a key too that unlocked the hidden door behind the bookshelves. I let myself in, Helen... I *saw* what was inside that room.' I pull my phone from my pocket; switch it on.

'What are you doing?' She comes towards me again, but I turn away from her; grip my phone tighter.

'You call the police now and I'll press send!' Her voice is shrill and pitchy as she takes her own phone from her coat pocket and holds it out in front of me. 'One touch and the police will have the footage of you hiding the clothes and disposing of the holdall and—'

'Where are the clothes?' I demand, though the force in my tone doesn't hide the panic that's swelling inside me. I have no idea what this woman is capable of. 'What did you do with them? Please, Helen, can't we resolve this amicably – like two adults, two women, *two friends?*'

I think I see her resolve wavering momentarily, as though she's considering my words carefully. 'I took screenshots,' I tell her, 'screenshots of the photographs and visitors' book I saw in that room... names of people, hundreds of them, different dates and times. Men – important, famous, powerful men I'm certain wouldn't want their names or faces made public, consenting adults or not...'

Her eyes narrow to slits.

'Two can play the blackmail game, Helen,' I say, my confidence building with each word. 'It's not going to reflect well on you and Bryan if it comes out that you throw wild sex and drugs parties in a secret dungeon in your house?'

I'm soaked to the skin now, the fine, driving drizzle insidious, but I'm past caring. I just need to finish this once and for all.

'You don't know the half of it!' She's animated now, turning in circles now she's realised she isn't holding all the cards. 'After Bryan found out that Paris wasn't his child, he forced me into—' She stops short; takes an audible breath. 'He forced me into performing for his "friends", *forced* me into doing terrible, unspeakable things with his "specially selected" guests – *while he watched.* Sometimes he even filmed it. The sick bastard liked me to watch myself being abused on camera.'

My hand covers my mouth in horror.

'For years this went on – two, three, sometimes four times a week,' she continues. 'Guests and girls, young girls – prostitutes he'd hire in for the night – would come to the house, to the secret room, where they would engage in' – she swallows, as though the words are stuck in her throat like glass – 'all manner of sexual acts. Demoralising, abusive, depraved, *disgusting* acts. I was made to endure the most sickening, unspeakable degradation all while *he* looked on, enjoying my humiliation, relishing my pain... Five whole years it continued.'

I think she's crying, though it's impossible to tell. The rain is coming down heavier now, the drizzle turning more substantial.

'Why didn't you go to the police? Why didn't you tell someone what was happening, Helen?'

To my shock, she starts laughing, a horrible, incredulous, manic cackle that causes the hairs on my arms to stand to attention beneath my coat as it rings out across the landscape.

'That man has more coppers in his back pocket than a scrap yard owner! He *is* the police! He told me if I ever told anyone, if I ever went to the authorities or tried to divorce him, then he'd have me sectioned, he'd ruin my reputation, make sure I was left homeless and penniless, that *he'd kill me*. The police couldn't help me because half of them were "special guests" of his at some point in time! They were – are – all in on it together, their sordid, sexual deviancies indulged without impunity or fear of detection or punishment.'

I'm still gripping my phone tightly, unable to look away from her, horrified to the calcium in my bones.

'When did it stop, Helen, this abuse, or did it ever stop?' I feel protective of her suddenly, concern and shock ameliorating my primary reasons for being here on this clifftop in the first place. If what she's saying is true, then it's abhorrent beyond comprehension.

'When Paris reached the age of sixteen...' Her voice drops low, almost inaudible. 'Once Bryan knew that she wasn't related to him by blood, he began to treat our – *my* – daughter, with utter contempt. He was cruel and cold towards her. She had no idea why – she was just a child – or what she'd done to make her once loving father turn on her so dramatically. She couldn't understand it, and he'd forbidden me to tell her – he never wanted it to come out; his ego couldn't stand it. And then on her sixteenth birthday – when she reached the legal age of consent – he made me an offer...'

I'm shaking now, my whole body vibrating uncontrollably. I want to run, but my feet are frozen solid to the ground. *Age of consent?* I think I know what she's about to say, only I'm not sure if I can bear to hear it.

'An... offer?'

'To let her take my place,' she states. 'I could continue to engage in those degrading acts with his chosen "friends" and spare my daughter, or I could relinquish my role and allow her to follow in my footsteps.'

I gasp. 'Oh my God...' I feel physically sick, like I've been punched in the stomach. 'No... no, Helen.' I'm shaking my head, my voice muffled beneath my scarf. '*Please* tell me you didn't do that to her, to... *your own daughter?*' I think of Paris's pretty young face then and the hint of melancholy I've often detected behind it – the sadness and fear and pain that must be so deep inside her it's impossible for it not to subconsciously leak through to the surface – and let out a small whimper.

'I should never have had that child,' she suddenly says. 'It was a mistake – *she* was a mistake! Until then our lives had been perfect, you see, everything I'd ever dreamed of, but then she went and had that accident. If she'd been looking both ways, none of it would ever have happened... *stupid girl!*'

'Helen, how can any of this be Paris's fault? She was just a child, an innocent child! How could you let this happen to her? Allow Bryan to do these despicable things? She was sixteen years old! What kind of mother *are* you?'

I feel the blood rise in me then, the anger and disgust and disbelief rushing to the surface of my skin.

'I just wanted it to stop,' she says pitifully, looking like the pathetic wretch I now know she is. 'If it hadn't been for her, then Bryan wouldn't have made me do all that... I've only ever wanted to be loved, truly loved and respected by a man, by my husband. Someone who saw the true me, saw how much love I have inside of me to give and—'

I snort loudly in derision. 'The *true* you? The true you is a weak, heartless, self-centred woman who allowed her teenage daughter to be abused by a man she loved and trusted, a man she thinks is her real father!' I exhale in short, sharp bursts. 'You're a pathetic excuse for a mother! For a human being!'

The anger explodes out of me before I can think about the consequences.

'*I'm* a victim too!' she screams in protest. 'You don't know what it's like, how trapped I've been, what years and years of physical and emotional torture does to someone, how it breaks you down piece by piece until there's nothing left of you...'

'You could've got help – for yourself and more importantly for Paris!' I shriek back. 'You could've run away together. You had money! You could've emigrated, changed your name, got a new identity for yourselves. Anything! You had *choices*, Helen, and you *chose* to let your daughter suffer in the worst way possible, in a way you understood because you'd suffered it too – your sixteen-year-old daughter, who you should've instinctively wanted to protect!' I reach for my phone again. This is done. It's over. 'I'm calling the police.'

'What about your precious son?' she rages back. Her mascara and red lipstick has run in the wet, making her look bizarre, like a clown from a horror film. 'He'll go to prison, Christine. He'll take the rap for whatever it is they both did to that reprobate Reynolds! Bryan will make sure of it – they all will. And you're right: his "special guests" don't want their sexual depravities made public. They'll lock your boy up and throw away the key before that ever happens! You can't take on someone like Bryan Levinson, Christine. Try, and you *will* lose.'

My finger is hovering over the number nine on my phone. I only have one bar of a signal showing, but I can only hope – *pray* – it's enough.

'I should've done this from the beginning,' I say, as much to myself as to her. 'This stops here, Helen!' But now she's holding her own phone, her finger mirroring mine as it hovers over the keypad.

'One touch is all it will take,' she says, 'and you can kiss goodbye to that talented, well-adjusted young son of yours forever. He'll never be the same after a stint in prison. Imagine what would happen to a good-looking boy like that! One night, Christine, one night was all I wanted, just to feel alive again, to feel love and warmth, and desire, to be part of something happy and untainted!'

I see it then, the visible switch in her, the darkening of her eyes, black like the night closing in on us. I see the hate and malice and pain and anger in them, the emptiness.

'Why should you have it all and not me? You're selfish!' Spittle flies from her lips with the force of her words. 'You're a selfish, greedy woman!'

A protracted note rings out across the black abyss as I press the number nine. My wet fingers are shaking as I make to repeat it, so much so that my phone momentarily slips to the ground. Instantly, I crouch down to pick it up, but she's right here in front of me, on her knees.

'Helen! What the— what are you doing? Stop!'

We're both on the ground now, scrabbling for my phone, the screen illuminated in the dark. I get a grip on it, but she tears at the skin on my hands with her red nails, causing me to drop it again.

'Ha!' She holds it up in the air, triumphant as she backs away from me. 'What are you going to do now, Christine? Shall we call Ed? Oh, look, there's sixteen missed calls from him already! I know! Let's call... Cora, shall we? See how she's doing? Oh!' She slaps her own forehead; tuts. 'Nope! Sorry! Can't call her, can we? *Because she's dead.*'

I don't know where it comes from, the rage inside me; all I know is that it's a driving force so powerful that it takes over. Suddenly, I'm on my feet and I'm charging at her, pushing her as hard as I can. And I can hear Cora's voice in my head, the scream that came to me that night in my dream.

'*No, Mummy, no!*'

FORTY-ONE

DAN

'They've come back a match!' Davis bursts into the incident room as Parker and I are running back through CCTV footage from the night in question. 'Paris Levinson's DNA is confirmed as the third set on the deceased,' she announces, slightly breathless. 'We've got a hat-trick, boss!'

'Right!' I clap my hands together as I stand. This is the kind of news every homicide team dreams of. 'Let's start getting an arrest plan together.' There's a renewed sense of energy in the room now that Davis has come bearing gifts. 'Parker, Harding... I want you both on hand for this, so' – I shoot them an empathetic, that's-the-way-it-is kind of look – 'cancel any foreseeable plans. And I want you and Davis to conduct the initial interviews, Parker, OK?'

'Me, boss?' Parker blinks in surprise.

'Yes, you. You didn't think you could join homicide and just stand there looking pretty, did you?' I'm smiling. Not because we're planning to arrest two extremely young people for murder, but because I *knew* they weren't telling the truth. And that's what I care about, getting to the truth, however brutal, however sad and disturbing, however unjust or unfathomable or unthinkable, *just the truth.*

The door to the incident room swings open again.

'Dan...' Archer beckons me with the slightest twitch of an eye.

'Uh-oh...' Davis purses her lips.

I turn to Parker. 'Get Mitchell on the phone – find out where Helen Levinson is.'

He lowers his eyes sheepishly; glances nervously at Davis. 'We were told to abort the surveillance, boss.'

'What? When? By who?'

He points in the direction of the door where Archer had stood a second ago.

'*Jesus*... OK, see if you can locate her current whereabouts. We need to find her *now*,' I say, already halfway out the door.

'We got a match, ma'am.' I don't give her the opportunity to speak first as I close the door behind me. Archer is standing with her back to me, staring out at the car park vista from the window. 'The third set of DNA recovered from Reynolds belongs to Paris Levinson. We'll need to get an arrest strategy in place, apply for search warrants – we need to locate the items they were wearing last Saturday, if they haven't already been destroyed. We do that and we've more or less got them.'

An unnerving silence follows.

'Ma'am?'

'Commissioner Lennard came to see me earlier,' she says, without turning round, 'in person.'

My guts drop. 'And?'

'And... sit down, Dan.'

'Haven't got time, ma'am – I've got to brief the team.'

'It wasn't a request,' she says flatly.

Reluctantly, I pull up a chair. I suspect I might need it, judging by the edge in her tone.

She sighs heavily as she finally turns round. 'Why did you put surveillance on Helen Levinson?'

I open my mouth to speak, but she continues. 'You knew about the sensitivity surrounding this case. Lucky for you, it doesn't appear that she was aware of it, or I dread to think what might've happened...'

'Such as? And how did you find out I'd put eyes on Helen Levinson?'

She drops down into her swivel chair suddenly, the momentum unsettling the collection of pens and office memorabilia on her usually pristine desk. I blink at the scattered items, items she would usually have had the compulsion to reorganise by now.

'I don't know, is the truthful answer to your question, Dan. Commissioner Lennard knows about it somehow though. He instructed me to call them off immediately.'

'I see.' I pick up a pen from the selection on her desk; start flipping it up on its nib before turning it on its head and then repeating the motion. It's the influx of all this nervous energy – and this conversation – making me twitchy.

'So?' She nods. 'Are you going to tell me why?'

'Just a hunch, ma'am.'

It's not a lie. I *do* have a hunch about Helen Levinson. Only it's not just that I think she may have helped dispose of evidence in a murder case, ergo perverting the course of justice; it's something else.

It's the way she seemed so distracted, so disinterested that Sunday morning we met at the Carters', the day after the murder. It's the way I caught her looking at Ed Carter that time, the historic non-molestation order Aaron Young took out on her for stalking and harassment, how she tried blackmailing him into being with her, convinced he was her soul mate. It's the fact that I've also learned she paid Christine Carter's mum's care-home fees to the grand total of £21K and, I'm convinced, took the evidence I suspect Christine hid in her mum's room at Sunnyside. It's also Conor Carter's suspicions about Paris being abused by her parents and how much she appears to hate them – that flinch when Helen placed an arm around her daughter. It's Helen's voice on the 999 call, reporting Christine's alleged drink-driving. It's the rumours Fiona mentioned about Bryan Levinson's involvement with prostitutes, about the NDAs and the sex worker who said Reynolds was procuring girls down by the arches... It's *everything*.

I know it's all linked together somehow, a complex interwoven puzzle, only there are still pieces missing.

Archer looks up at me, though her expression is unusually soft. 'The commissioner wants you off the case with immediate effect. I'm sorry, Dan; this is out of my hands. I tried to warn you what you were dealing with.'

'I know what I'm dealing with, ma'am,' I say, inwardly losing my cool. 'A murder investigation.'

'I told you to stop digging, but as usual you wouldn't listen,' she snaps, back to her default setting. 'You'll get your arrests tomorrow, and the search warrant for the Carters'. Then you're going to charge Conor Carter, if the evidence allows it, and you'll release Paris Levinson without charge.'

'I thought I was off the case,' I say.

'You are. I'm just telling you what's going to happen, and how it's going to happen.'

I don't say anything for a moment before I fix her eyes with my own.

'Just how deep does this corruption go, Gwen?'

She drops her head slightly; doesn't object to my addressing her informally.

'Look, Dan, I...'

'And just *how* well does Bryan Levinson know the commissioner? Or is it that he has something on him?'

She looks away sharply.

'What do you know?'

'All I know is that this is bigger than you think.' Her voice is loaded with gravitas. 'There's nothing we can do about it.' She suddenly leans forward at me across the desk, her face close to mine. 'There's too much at stake, too many powerful... *men*' – she turns her head almost in disgust – 'too many bloody filthy-rich, powerful, egotistical, tyrannical men! If you want to be a whistle-blower, then go ahead, but it'll be your funeral.' She averts her eyes for a moment; drops her tone. 'And that could even mean literally.'

'Well, well.' I cock my head to the side. 'I never had you down as a corrupt copper. Never found you to be lacking in professional integrity, to be a coward... *until now.*'

'For the love of God, Riley, I'm none of those things,' she protests, 'and let me remind you who you're speaking to!' She stands then; rakes her hand through her perfectly neat hair. It springs back into shape instantly, impressively. 'I'm not a coward; I'm a survivor, and if you've any sense – which has been proven doubtful at times – then you'll be one too. You can't mess with these people. The only way to win is to play the game.'

'And what if I don't feel like playing?' I shrug. 'They'll have me killed? Is that what you're saying?'

There's a knock on the door before she can answer me. Davis pokes her head round it.

'Yes, DS Davis, what is it?'

'Sorry to interrupt, ma'am. Gov, I need a word.'

The look on Davis's face causes me to stand instantly. 'What is it?'

'Whatever you have to say, you can say it here in front of me,' Archer barks at her.

I look at Davis; blink my affirmation.

'There's someone downstairs asking to see you, boss. Says they have some very important information about the Reynolds murder, but they only want to speak to you.'

My heart starts banging against my ribs as I gather myself. 'OK. Does this person have a name?'

'Yes, boss.' Her eyes are lit up like Catherine wheels. 'Her name's Katya.'

FORTY-TWO

DAN

The first thing I notice as I enter the interview suite is the smell. It hits me like a brick wall, the stench of bad hygiene. Katya looks up at me with wide, dark brown eyes as she sits cross-legged on the plastic chair. Her long hair is unbrushed; her clothes, though designer from the looks of them, are filthy and covered in stains; and her fingernails, long and painted, are broken off in places. She looks as if she attended a posh party some days ago and never came home again.

'Hi, I'm DCI Riley – Dan Riley.'

She nods nervously; slides a small hand across the table. 'Katya – Katya Volkova. Though I'm best known as Kat.'

I smile at her. 'So what can I do for you, Kat? You asked to see me.'

She nods; shifts her small frame in her seat. 'You'll have to excuse the state of me,' she apologises. Her voice is soft, her accent British, despite the Eastern European-sounding name, and I can already tell that she's articulate. 'I haven't been home in a few days. I haven't been able to go back there. They'll find me and kill me if I do.'

'Who will?'

She lunges across the table. Grabs my hand suddenly, unexpectedly.

'You *have* to help me!' I can feel her broken fingernails digging into my flesh as she grips my hand in fear. 'I didn't know what I was getting myself into.' She sits back. 'Can I smoke in here?' She glances around the room, empty but for the chairs and table.

I shake my head, and she exhales.

'Look, I saw an opportunity, and I took it. I know it was wrong, I know I shouldn't have done it, but... but sometimes life throws you these gifts, know what I'm saying? I just thought it was a chance to make money – proper money, you know. More money than I'll see in this lifetime, and certainly more money than I could ever make standing up! But like I say, I didn't know exactly what I was getting into...'

She looks up at me again; wipes her nose with the sleeve of her coat. I take a tissue from my jacket pocket and hand it to her. She nods her appreciation; blows her nose loudly.

'I've got a cold,' she explains. 'I've been on the streets these past few days, sleeping rough.' Her head drops. 'I had no choice. They knew all my haunts, friends' addresses, everything! They knew where to find me, so I had to go underground. They froze my bank account too, so I couldn't get access to my own money. Bastards!' she hisses.

'Who are you talking about?' I ask calmly, softly. 'My colleague said you had information, information about the recent murder of Mathew Reynolds?'

She places her arms onto the table and drops her head down onto them. 'Matty... Jesus... he was about to become a father, you know – his kid's just been born! He was only trying to make money like I was... but we didn't know what – didn't know who – we were really dealing with.'

'Just take your time.' I smile at her encouragingly. 'Start at the beginning. How do you know – *did* you know – Mathew Reynolds?'

'He was a dealer; weed, coke, pills, nothing too major. He sold to the girls and the druggies in the area – that's how I originally met him. I'm a working girl, you see.' She averts her eyes for a moment. 'An escort, a sex worker, a brass, a prostitute, call it what you will. But I never worked the arches. I wasn't *that* kind of girl. I had proper clients, decent clients, men with money and high-powered jobs. Matty was my coke dealer. I put some serious money his way, not least when I was booked to do one of the parties.'

'Parties?' Adrenalin explodes inside my solar plexus, and I feel my heart rate increase.

'He has this room, this sort of secret private room in his house, hidden behind the books in his library. That's where it all took place.'

'Who had a room? Where what took place?'

'The Levinson parties,' she says again, as though I should know this already. 'The sex parties Bryan Levinson threw.'

'OK...' My heart is beating so loudly I'm certain she can hear it.

'I started getting booked for them regularly through the escort agency I was working for at the time. He liked me, that piece of shit Levinson, liked girls like me: foreign sounding, young – the younger the better really.' Her lips curls contemptuously at the edge. 'In the end, I started recruiting girls for him. He needed a steady supply of them, and even though he's, like, the richest man alive or something, he didn't want to keep paying the treble figures it cost each time... so I did a deal with him. If I got the girls for him at a decent rate, then I'd still get paid my fee for the night and I didn't have to' – her eyes shift from left to right – 'you know, get involved in all him and his associates' sick indulgences.' She looks up. 'And they were... pretty sick I mean.'

'Go on...'

'So I was providing the girls, and Matty was supplying the drugs. Girls and drugs... he couldn't get enough of them. Not in that way I mean – Bryan Levinson is impotent; he can't even get it up! He's a voyeur and a sadist. He likes to watch, likes to inflict pain and humiliation on the girls... even his own daughter.'

'His own daughter?' It feels like a punch to the stomach.

'Yeah. He's one sick, nasty motherfu— The man's a monster, Detective Riley.'

'How do you know this?'

'I saw her there on occasion. He pimped his own flesh and blood out like she was a piece of meat, poor little love... like, *who does that?*'

Bryan Levinson by all accounts. My heart drops like a brick in the ocean. Conor Carter was telling the truth. I knew it.

'Even the mum was in on it. I never saw her at one of his parties, but I knew that she knew about them, knew that she'd once been involved in it all herself. He played videos, see...' She closes her eyes, the memory clearly making her uncomfortable. 'Videos she was in... his own wife and daughter.' She looks down in disgust. Pauses.

'After a few months of this, Matty and I came up with an idea. Let's blackmail the bastard! We only wanted a small slice of the pie.' She shifts awkwardly in her seat again. 'He had all sorts at those parties – his MP friends, doctors, lawyers, judges, policemen like yourself...'

My eyebrow twitches, though I remain silent. The less I say, the more she's likely to keep talking.

'People in high places, people with money and power and position... people whose careers and reputations and families would be left in tatters if it came out what they liked to get up to of a weekend. We're taking off-the-chart scandal, not least for himself! So I started secretly recording footage from the parties, on the down-low of course. Images of the drug-taking and the debauchery, all of it, even images of his own daughter... Do you have kids, Detective Riley?'

I nod. 'A daughter and two sons.'

'Well then, you'll understand. So I sent them, these videos I'd been secretly recording, to Matty, and he...' She visibly swallows; takes a sip of water from the plastic cup on the table. 'He went to Levinson with them, said he was going to release them publicly if he didn't hand over the cash.'

I raise my brows. 'How much, Katya?'

'A million,' she sniffs. '£500K each.'

'Did he pay up?'

She looks up at me. Shakes her head. 'He agreed to pay us £25K each, up front, in exchange for the video footage. I was happy with that I suppose. I mean, it wasn't the half a mil I was hoping for, but twenty-five grand is twenty-five grand, isn't it?' She shrugs. 'Only then Matty got greedy, didn't he, the stupid sod. He took the £25K and gave Levinson the footage in return as agreed. But he'd made copies of the incriminating videos and told Levinson he wanted more, much more...' She clears her throat; sips at the water again. 'But he cut me out of it,' she explains. 'I didn't know about it at first – he went behind my back. I was livid.' Her eyes are suddenly aflame. 'I was the one who did all the work, secretly recording those sordid videos, and now he'd gone and double-crossed me, wanted it all for himself. It was his greed that killed him!' she says, without a hint of irony. 'That and... well, why don't you see for yourself.'

She slides her phone across the table towards me and presses play on her screen, and I start to watch.

FORTY-THREE
CHRISTINE

'Helen? *He-len!*' My screams echo out across the abyss like an alarm bell.

'Oh my God... *oh my God!*' I whisper on loop as I turn in circles, struggling to breathe through the mix of fear and panic and adrenalin that's hitting me like a round of bullets. I can't see her! She's gone. Oh Jesus... oh God! I pushed her and she tripped, fell backward... fell backward off the cliff edge! One minute she was right here in front of me, and then the next... just gone.

'Oh *noooo*... no, no, no... oh please, *Helen!*' I link my hands above my head; drop down onto my knees on the wet ground. The rain is falling heavier now, has turned almost icy, and I can hear the roaring sound of the sea below, crashing violently against the rocks like a living, breathing entity. *You've killed her! You've killed Helen Levinson!*

I don't want to look over the cliff edge – every part of my being does not want to see her body lying there, smashed and broken and dead, and yet I find myself compulsively taking careful small steps towards it, inching closer in the darkness.

'Oh God... oh dear God help me, help me. I didn't mean to do it, I—'

'Did me a bloody favour – saved me the bother of doing it myself!'

I scream in shock as I swing round. 'Oh Jesus!' I clutch my chest, staggering sideways as he comes into view. 'Bryan! Thank God.' I throw myself into him; grip his forearms. 'Something terrible has just happened. It's Helen – she's... she's fallen down the cliff!' In that moment, it doesn't register with me, what he's actually just said – or why I shouldn't be glad to see him.

He slips past me and peers over the edge as I bend double, struggling to breathe. I can't bring myself to look.

'Huh.' He shrugs. 'Well, will you look at that! So she has.'

I brace myself as I peer over the edge, terrified that I'll slip myself somehow and tumble after her. The rain lashes against my cheeks as I look down and see her lying on her front, her head turned to the side on the rocks below. It looks distorted, at the wrong angle, her arms splayed out beside her, her red robe billowing in the water as the tide begins swelling into her, claiming her.

'Helen! *Helllllen!*' I call down to her, glancing back up at Bryan in abject terror. 'We need to get help! Go get some help!'

He doesn't move, and for the first time I ask myself why he's even here, at the beach house. I thought Helen had planned an intimate dinner with *my* husband.

'I shouldn't bother,' he says flatly. 'She's really quite dead.'

I start wailing. 'Noooo, nooo, this wasn't supposed to happen! Oh Helen, oh God...'

She's dead and it's my fault! I should call an ambulance, let the authorities know what's happened. It was an accident. I didn't mean for her to fall. Did Bryan see me push her? I'll go to prison – I'll deserve to! Only I didn't come here tonight with murder in mind. I came to try to get her to stop blackmailing us, to stop playing stupid, dangerous games. I wanted to try to appeal to her better nature, if she had one, only it turns out that she didn't, and now look!

I'm shaking so violently, I can feel my body slipping into shock.

'Bryan...' I look up at him, suddenly afraid. He seems unfazed by what's just happened, gleeful even. 'We have to call the police... an ambulance. She may still be alive. We can't be sure... we have to help her.'

'You pushed her,' he says. 'You did me a favour. I'd come here tonight to do the same thing myself. You see, because of that stupid bitch, everything's messed up now, isn't it? Her and that bastard daughter of hers, that illegitimate little whore, ruining everything.' He exhales heavily; waves away the icy rain from his face.

I move to go past him. I need to get back to the house, call the emergency services, but he blocks my path.

'Let's not be too hasty, shall we, Christine?' His voice now has a menacing edge to it. I glance up at the house, almost leering at me from behind him in the fading light.

'This is how it's going to go. It's nothing personal you understand,' he states, almost apologetically. 'But none of this can ever come out. Whatever Helen's told you, it's all a pack of lies. The woman was mad, sick in the head, mentally deranged, a complete fantasist. Some of the stories she came up with...' He glances at me, his eyes shining in the low light like two tourmalines. 'I mean, it's dreadfully sad really...'

'Whatever she told me? About the abuse you mean?' I find myself saying. Though I don't know why – it's bound to inflame him. 'The sexual, physical and mental abuse you've been inflicting upon your wife and daughter, or the escorts you hire to degrade and torture along with your high-flying friends in that sex dungeon you have hidden in your library?'

Shut up, Christine! Seriously, just shut the hell up! Only I can't seem to stop myself now – something else has taken over.

'I have images, images of friends of yours with those young women, and that visitors' book you keep down there, the one with all the names of those "high-flying" friends who attend your sadistic sex parties – ha!' I sneer at him in contempt. 'Oh, it's all going to come out all right, Bryan, who you *really* are.' The rain is affecting the clarity of my vision. I can barely see.

'Let me get past,' I say, adding, 'please.' I've antagonised him enough. He's a very rich and well-resected powerful man whose life is on the point of imploding, and that makes him very dangerous.

'I can get your boy out of trouble,' he says suddenly. 'I can get them to drop the charges. One phone call and poof! Just like that, it's all gone. Evidence can get misplaced. Then it's no more police, no more suspicion, not even a slap on the wrist. That's what you care about, isn't it, Christine? Keeping hold of that talented only son of yours? Making sure your sick mother is cared for adequately. That's why you've been on your hands and knees scrubbing my house for pennies, isn't it? To prevent yourselves from being evicted from that public toilet you live in?'

'Let me past, Bryan.' I blink at him in a mix of contempt and fear. 'It's over. It's finished. Did you think it wouldn't all ever come out, what you made Helen do – made your own daughter do?'

'Only she isn't, is she? My daughter I mean. She's the bastard spawn of some soft-headed Neanderthal dog my tramp of a wife randomly fucked in a toilet. She hasn't got any real Levinson in her. Pathetic and ineffectual, emotionally deranged' – he snorts in derision – 'just like her mother. Her dead mother now, as it happens.'

He's slowly edging towards me now. I move myself away from the cliff edge, and he swings round on me suddenly. I gasp; leap back.

'Think about it, Christine – never a moment's financial

concern again. Finally being able to care for your family in a way they deserve, in a way *you* deserve after sacrificing so much...'

I'd be lying if I said I didn't think about it for a split second; how that kind of life might be, what it would feel like without the eternal stress and financial burden, never having to graft day in and out and still only be treading water for all the effort you put in, forever chasing your tail. Only it would never truly be 'ours', would it – a life like the one he's trying to sell me? Not this way, never like this.

Just then I think I see something in my peripheral vision, coming from behind him, back up towards the house. Lights? It was just a brief flash, but maybe? I say a silent prayer.

'Bryan' – I try to keep my tone as level as fear and the freezing temperature will allow – 'let's go back up to the house, shall we? Let's have a drink together; talk about it properly.' I reach for my phone, but it isn't in my pocket. Panic pierces my guts. Perhaps it went over the cliff with Helen! Oh my God, *Helen*.

'Everyone has a price.' Bryan's voice is low with gravitas. 'They all do, every single stinking one of them, and you are no different. So name it.' He clasps his hands together then opens them out to me. 'Tell me what you want. Or shall I make that phone call and have your son banged up faster than one of those sponging council-estate sluts I regrettably have to see and sympathise with on a daily basis.'

He's getting closer.

'You do that and neither of us gets what we want then, do we, Bryan?' I muster up the confidence to say. 'My son is in jail and you're exposed as a sexual predator, a pervert, an abuser. We both lose.'

A slow smile creeps across his features then. 'I never lose.'

He says it with such conviction it's almost impossible not to believe him.

'I honestly don't want to have to do this, Christine,' he says, still smiling. 'I never did.'

'Do what? What are you going to do?'

He's still coming towards me.

'I'll tell them I saw you push Helen, which isn't even a lie – and, once again, thank you for saving me the effort – and that we were grappling. I tried to prevent you from pushing her, the rich woman you worked for, the one you were blackmailing for money to pay off your debts. I had no choice.' He shrugs. 'It was self-defence – you killed my wife right in front of me, my darling, *dearest* wife, Helen.' He pretends to cry then; mimics emotion with exaggerated crocodile tears.

'Stay back, Bryan, keep away...' I hold my hands out at him, try to angle myself so I can turn and run, only he's blocking my way, shadowing my every move. I'm convinced he's going to kill me. He's going to push me off the cliff, just as I pushed Helen. It would be instant death. *It would be instant karma.*

'What about Paris?' My voice is hoarse. 'She still knows the truth, even with Helen' – I close my eyes for a few seconds – 'even with Helen gone, even if you kill me, how will you then silence her?'

'Kill you?' He chuckles, as though I've tickled him. 'I don't want to *kill* you, Christine. Well' – he drops his voice lower – 'I'd rather not *have* to. And don't worry about Paris. I'll take good care of her. She'll not say a single word. Not unless she'd like to spend her entire youth in a psych ward, pumped stupid full of pills, a dribbling zombie.' He smiles, like the image pleases him. 'Or I suppose I could keep her at the house for' – he shoots me a look that could chill the ice in the air – '*other* uses. *Orrrrr*' – it seems he's enjoying himself now – 'I could just kill the wretched little bitch?'

She appears then – steps right out of nowhere from the darkness and runs right at him.

'Not if I kill you first, you sick, evil bastard!'

FORTY-FOUR

CHRISTINE

We both stand there paralysed for a moment, like someone hit the pause button. Oddly, the wind seems to instantly drop somehow, and the rain starts to ease off, like something has passed.

I glance over the rock edge. 'He's dead.' I turn to Paris; see as something shifts in her terrified young face. 'He's gone.'

'Are we going to go to the police?' she says as we make our way back up to the house. 'Are we going to tell them everything?' Her voice sounds thin and defeated, broken somehow. 'We'll all go to prison, won't we? And everyone will know what's happened to me.'

I take her hand in mine; squeeze it tightly. 'Let me handle the police,' I say, bringing it to my lips and kissing it.

The heat hits me as we enter the house, those delicious cooking smells from earlier now acrid and burned in my nostrils. I turn the oven off. Run a glass of water from the tap and swig it.

Helen and Bryan Levinson are both dead. When I looked over the cliff edge, I saw that Bryan's body had fallen practically on top of Helen's, suffocating her in death, just as he had in life. I knew then what I was going to do.

'There was supposed to be a... a party tonight, but he called it off so he could follow her out here,' Paris says. 'He suspected she was up to something, and so he followed her. And then I followed him.'

She wipes her eyes with her sleeve; turns to face me.

'Mathew Reynolds knew who I was that night, down by the arches, the night it happened. He'd seen me at the house, at the... parties.' Her head lowers, and I reach out to take her hand again. 'I think he was blackmailing my—' She suddenly stops herself. 'He isn't even my real dad, is he? He never was.'

She starts to sob then, and I pull her to my chest.

'Are you able to drive, love?' I stroke her hair. 'If you think you can manage it, I want you to drive to my house now. Follow me, and if you arrive before me, just wait for me there.'

She nods and looks up at me, her eyes glassy with tears, and in that moment, I'm ashamed to say that I'm glad both Helen and Bryan were dead.

I don't know what will happen with Con and the death of Mathew Reynolds though. Even with this evil, wretched pair gone, it doesn't change anything much. The police will still investigate, won't they? And now I'm about to make things even worse.

I take the letter, Helen's letter, the one I found tucked inside the pages of *Gone with the Wind* in the library and place it on the kitchen table, next to the ice bucket and the two champagne flutes, one for her and one for my Ed. *Ed.* He'll literally be bouncing off the walls by now, worried sick about me. But I can't call him. My phone is gone. I think it may have gone off the cliff with Helen. I can only hope it's at the bottom of the sea by now.

The drive home feels like a dream in itself, like I've slipped into a twilight zone where nothing feels real or familiar. But I know what I have to do. And so does Paris.

Relief floods through me like a hot spring as I hit the top of our street, so much so that I burst into tears again and start whispering Ed's name. But then I see the police cars outside our house.

My guts drop as I exhale into the ether. Why are they here? Surely they haven't found the bodies already? Or are they here for Conor? Maybe they've come to arrest my boy and all of this... it's all been for nothing! I check behind me in my rear view mirror, see Paris's fancy car pulling up behind me.

I park the van and turn my key in the lock, my stomach an empty pit of impending dread as Paris silently follows me.

They're in the living room as we enter, the four of them, the detective fella, Dan Riley, and his colleague, the female one. Ed and Conor are standing opposite them.

'Tee!' Ed lunges at me the moment he sees me; swoops me up in his arms.

'Where the hell have you been?' he whispers in my ear. His eyes are lit up, and he's smiling. 'You are not going to *believe* what's just happened.'

FORTY-FIVE

DAN

As soon as I start watching that secret footage on Katya's phone, everything turns on its head. That's all it takes in this game – and in this life I suppose – a split second and everything is upside down, back to front, left to right, on its head.

I curse under my breath as I watch the video play, but Katya must hear me because she nods slowly at me and says, 'Exactly. Now are you lot going to protect me or what?'

I rush the phone straight up to Archer, taking the stairs two at a time. This is something quite unbelievable, something so shocking I'm not sure how to even feel about it yet. In truth, I didn't see it coming. But now that I *have* seen it, it's all started to slot together to make perfectly horrible sense.

'Ma'am, you have to see this! You have to see it right now!'

I burst into Archer's office without knocking, holding Katya's phone up like a trophy. She's in the same position she was in before, looking out across the car park from the window, like she went straight back there as soon as I left the room.

'I already know, Riley.' She swings round. 'I just got a call from Commissioner Lennard. And no one can locate Bryan *or* Helen Levinson. We think they may have gone to their beach house in Brighton. I've despatched a squad car to go down there now, break the good news to them.'

Boom! I stop dead; freeze like a musical statue.

'He'd already been tipped off,' she says. '*Someone* on the inside must've let Bryan Levinson know that Katya Volkova came in to see us. He knew why she'd come; he knew the game was up.' She exhales loudly. 'So,' she says, sucking in her breath, 'let's see this footage then.'

It starts off a little shaky as Katya positions herself from a safe distance, undetected. A few seconds in, we see Conor Carter and Paris Levinson come into view, arm in arm as they walk along the path that runs against the river's edge underneath the old railway arches. Conor disappears for a few minutes at one point, and we then see Reynolds conversing with Paris until Conor returns. The exchange between Paris and Mathew Reynolds looks heated, though Katya's positioned too far away to pick up the conversation, but it's obvious that Paris is intimidated given the way she backs away from him, her body language clearly signalling distress. You can hear Katya's breathing as she holds the phone steady; zooms in further on them.

Next, we see Conor come back into frame. He approaches the pair with purpose, clearly demanding to know what's happening, suspecting, I imagine, that his girlfriend may be in danger. While the footage is shadowy, rudimentary, we see an altercation break out between the two men. Conor Carter shoves Reynolds, causing him to lose his footing momentarily before he's up on his feet again. He punches Conor, and a fight ensues. At one point, Paris joins in and begins kicking Reynolds, sticks the boot in him as he's lying on the ground until Carter pulls her away and they hurry off, out of view.

I finally find my voice. 'Katya was keeping tabs on him. She thought Reynolds was cutting her out of a blackmail deal, so she wanted to keep an eye on her investment.' And thank goodness she did, otherwise we might never have known the truth of what really happened that night, like I suspect Archer would, in this moment, probably prefer.

Reynolds picks himself up off the ground within a few moments of Conor and Paris's exit. He doesn't appear to be seriously harmed; looks compos mentis. He begins pacing up and down for a few minutes; takes his phone from his pocket and starts reading something on it, and then suddenly...

Archer gasps, something I've never heard her do before, or certainly not with as much emphasis.

'*Levinson...*' she whispers, unable to look away from the gruesome scene playing out on screen.

He comes into frame from the left, taking Reynolds by surprise. He's wielding what looks like a bottle in his hand and smacks it over his head, causing him to collapse onto the ground, I suspect, unconscious... and then he sets about getting to work on Reynolds's face.

'Turn it off, Dan.' Archer turns away, visibly horrified. 'I've seen enough.'

I have a dreadful sensation in the pit of my empty stomach though as Davis and I make the drive to the Carter's house, several hours later than I would've liked. Where are Helen and Bryan Levinson? Why can't anyone get hold of them?

Ed Carter opens the door. 'What's happened?' he asks, his eyes desperately searching mine. 'It's not Tee, is it?'

'Can we come in, Ed?' Davis says.

He looks genuinely spooked as he immediately stands back and lets us through into the lounge.

'Christine isn't here?' I nod at Conor Carter – he's standing next to his father with a pensive expression on his face.

'No... er, no, she's not here currently,' Ed says, glancing

nervously at his son. 'I'm sure she won't be long though. Has something happened?' he tentatively enquires again.

I can tell he's doing his best to hold it together, but he's only a man like the rest of us. He probably thinks we're here to arrest Conor, arrest them both even. I need to put him out of his misery.

'Some new, and rather upsetting, information has come to light that's changed the course of our investigation. Conor.' I turn to him; see the fear in his young eyes reflecting back at me. 'A witness came forward today with some video evidence.'

'O... OK.' He fidgets nervously on the spot. 'What video evidence is that?'

'S'all right, son.' Ed Carter grips his forearm. 'It'll be all right.'

'Maybe it's best we play you the footage – see for yourself,' I say. It's unorthodox, I know. This should be done down at the station. But Archer made it clear to me that there were to be no charges against Conor Carter, even though he, and I suspect both Ed and Christine too, have perverted the course of justice.

'The commissioner wants it all packed neatly away,' Archer told me, a few hours after I'd shown her the footage. 'This is already going to cause a media sensation. Bryan Levinson – MP and "man of the people" Bryan Levinson – a sadomasochist, deviant voyeur who throws wild sex parties for his important friends in a specially modified secret room in his house... A man of his standing being blackmailed by a drug dealer and an escort, a man who used his own daughter, pimped her out to his disgusting cohorts!' She paced the room, chewing at her thumbnail. I noticed her pens were still scattered all over her desk.

'Lennard will do his best to limit the damage here. They'll spin it somehow,' she spat angrily. 'Forensics found very incriminating photographs and a guest book in that room, a visitors' book containing the names of men, many men, many very important men.' She looked up at me, met my eyes with her own, adding, '*Commissioner Lennard being one of them.*'

I watch, admittedly with a touch of morbid interest, as Davis plays Ed and Conor the footage extracted from Katya's phone; wait for the horror to creep across their faces with an uncomfortable anticipation.

'Oh, Jesus.'

Ed Carter bends forward; places his hands on his knees, as though all the wind has suddenly gone right from him. 'Oh my days... oh thank God...'

Conor appears frozen in shock.

'What about Helen?' Ed says. 'Where's Helen? Does she know what's happened? Has she seen this video?'

'We think she may be at her house in Brighton – the beach house.'

Davis's phone rings then, and she walks through the lounge into the tiny kitchen to take it. Sensing it may be important, I follow her. She holds a finger up as she listens, her eyes growing wider.

'The Levinsons, gov. Seems like they're missing from the beach house. Uniform are down there now. Their respective cars are still there, but no sign of them at the house, though they were clearly there at some point. They found champagne on ice, two champagne flutes and a fancy meal delivery, also for two... It was their wedding anniversary apparently, twenty-fifth, silver.'

Instinctively, I glance over at Ed Carter in the living room, busy having a hushed conversation with his son.

She cuts the call off.

'They've found a letter, possible suicide note, gov. Looks like it was written by Helen Levinson! Jesus, we could have a double suicide on our hands here.' She shoots me a grave look. 'They're bringing the choppers out to look for them now.

Maybe they couldn't face it all coming out in public – made some sort of pact to do themselves in.'

Ed Carter is right behind me when I turn around. I suspect he's overheard our conversation.

'Is everything OK, Detective Riley?'

'I think we ought to sit down, Ed.'

We move back in the living room, then I hear a key turn in the lock, and Christine Carter walks through the front door with Paris Levinson behind her. Their sudden presence is like a gust of wind entering the room and instantly changes the energy. I smell fear on them.

'We've just come from the Brighton beach house,' she says, swallowing hard. 'Helen asked me to go up there and give the place a spruce up before their anniversary dinner this evening. Paris turned up a little later, didn't you, love?'

She nods. 'Yeah, Mum wanted me to join them both, you know, help them celebrate? But we couldn't find them when we got there, could we? Maybe they went for a walk or something,' she adds softly.

I glance at Davis. I know she's thinking what I'm thinking, or at least I think she is.

'You are *not* going to believe what's just happened,' I hear Ed say to his wife as he embraces her like he hasn't seen her in over a year. 'There's been a terrible mistake.' He holds her by her shoulders. 'Con never murdered anyone – you were right all along! *It was Bryan Levinson who killed him.*'

FORTY-SIX

CHRISTINE

What have I done?

The words are looping round and round my head as I fight to stay upright, to process everything I've just heard. Cognitive dissonance clouds my aching mind. I'm elated that our Conor has been exonerated, that he isn't a murderer, and distraught and despairing that now, however, *I am*. It's just been a dreadful mistake from beginning to end.

Conor is innocent. The fight he and Paris had with Reynolds wasn't enough, it transpires, to have killed him, even though, in the heat of the moment, it may have seemed like it. Instead, it was that sick monster Levinson who'd committed such an unspeakable act. And yet still I couldn't comprehend it! Even with a few drinks inside him, Conor must've known he hadn't caved Mathew Reynolds's face in and stabbed him in the neck; that someone else must've been responsible. Had he thought that someone else could've been Paris? Had he, in a diabolical twist of irony, just been doing what we'd always taught him to do and been protecting the person he loves, just as we thought we were doing, only needlessly now as it turns out?

I collapse onto my tatty old sofa. For reasons I can't explain, not even to myself, I start to laugh – the incredulity, the disbelief, the regret spilling from me in a half-laughing, half-despairing sound.

It all started with a lie – an unwitting lie at that – and then one had followed right after the other, multiplying like lemmings until they'd taken over completely and become something else entirely.

I feel brittle, like the slightest move might cause me to shatter.

'The helicopters are out now, looking for them. And you definitely didn't see them, either of them, when you were at the house?' Dan Riley addresses me.

Can he tell? Does he know what I've done?

We shake our heads in unison.

'No. We were both surprised that they weren't there.'

'Paris.' Detective Riley moves towards her, and instinctively I put a hand out to stop him.

'I'm sorry.' I catch the expression on Ed's face. 'But this is all such a shock for her, for all of us. *Bryan* killing Mathew Reynolds. For the love of God, why would he do that?'

'It's OK, Paris.' Detective Riley smiles warmly at her. 'We know what's been going on, what's been happening. It's OK. Please let us help you...'

He knows about the abuse somehow – someone has told him.

'We found a note on the kitchen table; we think it may be your mum's handwriting, Paris.' He places a hand gently on her forearm. 'We think it could be a suicide note...'

Paris gasps, and Conor goes to her then, envelops her in his arms, and I wonder if – I hope – it will become her safe place, just as mine is in Ed's.

'What did they do to you, babe?' he breathes against her hair as she begins to cry into his chest.

I stifle a gasp with my hand. 'Oh my God... This is just... awful. Do you think they may have *both* killed themselves?'

'The beach house is high up on the cliff's edge, isn't it?' Detective Riley looks right at me, his eyes like scanners trying to read me.

He suspects something – I can tell.

'Yes, yes it is. You don't think they... *The cliff?*' I recoil in horror.

'Like I say, the helicopters are out searching for them. We'll get a forensic team down there too, if they don't turn up alive and well soon.'

Forensics? A chill runs through me. The letter! My fingerprints will be on it, won't they? I touched it and held it numerous times, folded it and placed it into my handbag. I drop my head into my hands. I don't need to act upset and distressed – it's coming out of me as naturally as breathing.

Detective Riley looks at me for a moment longer than I'd like him to.

'Was Helen suffering with depression, do you know? The two of you were friends – did she ever confide in you about anything, about how she was feeling?'

'She did tell me something,' I say before my brain can advise me not to. Ed's arm is around my waist. He knows what I've done. That man knows every inch of me inside out. I think of the note *I* left *him*. Ed knows I drove down to Brighton to confront Helen. He knows I would fight to the death for him, for Conor, for them, my loves, my everythings.

'Oh?'

'She told me that Bryan wasn't Paris's biological father. That he was impotent and couldn't have children.' The words splutter from my mouth. I'm shaking. 'She had a one-night stand with a stranger, a soldier on leave so she said, though she never told me his name. Bryan believed that Paris was his until there was an accident and she needed an emergency blood transfusion. That's how it all came out... her blood type. He couldn't possibly have been her biological father...' I swallow back the regret that's pushing its way up through my larynx; drop my gaze. 'She told me that things changed after that, after he found out...' I don't want to say anymore, lest I incriminate myself somehow.

He blinks at me. 'Right, I see. Well, thanks for telling me, Christine. That could prove helpful.' And he and his companion start to leave.

I follow him out the door, leaving Ed and the others behind. 'Paris can come and live with us,' I blurt out, unable to stop myself.

He turns to look at me.

'We can give her the support she needs. She's been through so much and...'

He nods at the female detective, and she gets into the car, leaving the two of us alone together.

'I think I know what you did, Christine,' he says, though his tone is soft, gentle even. 'And why,' he adds. He meets my eyes then; looks right into them with his own. He has such kind eyes, like you can see the good shining right out of them.

I attempt to look puzzled, surprised, unsure of what he means, though I've never been a good liar – or a great actress for that matter. I'm just a mother and a wife and a daughter who loves her family and wants to protect them at any cost, however high the price may be.

'Take care,' he says, placing a hand on my coat sleeve – still wet, despite me blasting the van's heater all the way home – before he turns to get into the car. 'I'll be seeing you.'

'You too, Detective Riley,' I croak back, my voice a hoarse whisper.

Yet something deep inside me tells me that he won't.

FORTY-SEVEN

DAN

It's cold in the ENT waiting room.

I take Fiona's small hand in mine as we sit patiently. It feels cold, and I squeeze it tightly, silently.

The helicopters were out all night searching for the bodies of Bryan and Helen Levinson, but to no avail. If they did, as I suspect, fall from the cliff edge, then in all likelihood they're both dead. There's still time of course – they could wash up somewhere along the coastline in a few days, weeks or even months to come. By then however – and there's no nice way of putting this – they'll have been gnawed upon by every sea creature imaginable, fish food, their remains absorbed by the ecosystem, their bones just another recruit of Davy Jones's locker.

Did Christine Carter drive to the Levinsons' Brighton beach house to confront Helen about the blackmail, about what I suspect was her obsession with Ed, to try and put a stop to it? Did she, in a moment of confrontation, in a moment of despair, push Helen off the cliff, intentionally or otherwise? Did Bryan turn up and try to intervene and somehow meet the same fate? Did Paris finally have her moment of retribution on the man who'd inflicted such abuse on her – the man she believed to be her own father? Was that how it went down? I suspect so, though without any solid evidence, or a body, or a confession, it's all just hearsay, circumstantial, unprovable beyond reasonable doubt.

I knew what Archer was going to say when I briefly returned to the nick and verbalised my true suspicions.

'Commissioner Lennard is going to hold a press conference this evening, right away,' she informed me. 'He's going to tell them that the Levinsons' marriage was in difficulty, and that Bryan was struggling with his wife's mental health issues...'

I felt the skin on my face pull taut as my eyes widened.

'I know, Riley.' She gave me a withered look. 'But that's how it's going to be.'

'What about Reynolds? What about *his* family? They'll want a resolution to this, to see a culprit behind bars; they'll want justice to be done and—'

'And it's amazing what price some people place on their loved ones, Riley.'

I blinked at her, not entirely sure what she meant. 'A price?'

'Money talks – you know that. They'll receive the appropriate' – she cleared her throat, like the words were sticking in it – 'compensation. In due course obviously. Same for the Volkova girl.'

'But what about the Carters?' My voice rose with incredulity. 'I'm convinced Christine may know much more than she's telling us...'

Archer exhaled. 'Even if she does, she's not going to make it public, is she, and potentially incriminate herself? Besides, there's not enough evidence to convict her of anything.'

'But I think she knew – knows – what went on in the Levinson household, ma'am, the things both Helen and Paris were forced to endure. I suspect she knew about the secret room in the library; maybe she even had evidence and—'

'And that's the end of it, Riley,' she interjected with a cold stare. 'And the end of Lennard's career too incidentally. He informs me he'll be resigning within the month, after this has all blown over.'

I noticed that her pens were back in order on her desk once more, perfectly lined up together like little soldiers.

'And good riddance to bad rubbish,' she added contemptuously.

It was the only part of the conversation I found myself agreeing with.

I feel cheated somehow, straightjacketed. Commissioner Lennard was involved in the depravities Levinson engineered. Someone high up in the force, someone with power and sway and control; someone trusted and admired and respected. Bryan Levinson, who I'm certain is now dead, has escaped justice, his apparent 'suicide' blamed on his long-suffering, and clearly mentally unhinged, wife, his untarnished reputation still intact, his depraved secrets taken with him to his no doubt watery grave. I feel as if I have to do something, but I don't know what. The corruption ran so deep. And yet all I can think about, as I sit next to my worried wife – our son, Jude, asleep in the pram next to us – is the truth.

I like the Carter family; can tell how much they care about one another, how close they are as a unit, and I understand *why* they did what they did, trying to cover up what they – and indeed I – believed had happened, the crime they believed their beloved son had committed. But I couldn't just let it go, could I?

'Come in please.' Dr Rowan, an otolaryngologist – a doctor who specialises in hearing issues – beckons us into his office, and we follow him in nervously.

'Thank you for waiting.' He smiles warmly, though I see something in his eyes as they meet mine. Maybe it's because of my profession, the experience I've garnered over the years, my ability to read other people, but in this moment I know what he's about to say.

'I'm afraid it's not the best news. This little man here...' He peers into the pram with what looks like genuine sadness. 'Your son is deaf, pre-lingually deaf, which means...'

Ironically, I don't hear the rest of what he says. I only hear Fiona start to cry as he talks in the background, his voice becoming white noise as I hold on to her.

We're both silent on the journey home, Fiona and I, as our baby boy sleeps soundly in the car seat behind us.

'I'll put the kettle on,' Fiona says, her voice heavy with sadness, as I carry our sleeping son from his car seat back into the house. 'Then we can talk.'

Jude never even stirs as I remove him from his seat and place him down gently into his cot, his small body warm and soft to the touch. And it hits me then, as I look down upon him.

My son is deaf.

Never will he hear the sound of my voice, or his mother's or sister's or brother's. He will never be uplifted by the melody of music or hear a lover's whisper of affection in his ear. He will forever be denied the beauty of morning birdsong, or the satisfying sound of crickets on a warm summer's night...

I watch him, his eyes closed like two ticks on a page, as he sleeps peacefully, unaware of what the world will mean to him, a world of silence, and the need to protect him overwhelms me to the point that I find myself crying too. Hot, salty tears that streak my cheeks then drip onto his fleecy blanket.

In this emotionally charged moment, I suddenly understand it all so perfectly, the instinctive need within me to protect this little man at all costs, not least now that I know this life will present him with more challenges than most, a feeling so all-encompassing, so powerful, that I know I'd do anything I had to do to keep him forever safe from harm, just as the Carters had done for their remaining precious child.

I hear Fiona enter the nursery. She's carrying two steaming

mugs of something; places them down onto the table before joining me at our son's cot.

'Oh, Dan,' she says as she places an arm around my waist and drops her head onto my shoulder. I don't think she's ever seen me cry before. 'It's going to be OK.'

I smile through the pain. I have to be strong for her, and for Pip and Jude and Leo, but another tear escapes and splashes down onto Jude's tiny face, waking him up.

He opens his brown eyes wide, as though surprised, and, looking right up at me, he does something incredible.

He starts to laugh.

I look down on my beautiful boy with a heart so heavy, so filled with love for this tiny little human being I helped to create, and open my mouth to speak, to tell him I love him more than anything else in the world, only I realise that he won't, that he *can't,* hear me, so instead, I bring my hands together in the shape of a heart and show it to him. Because when it comes to love, what good are words without actions anyway?

A LETTER FROM ANNA-LOU

My dearest reader,

I'd like to thank you so very much for choosing to read *What Kind of Mother*. Without you, this book wouldn't have been written, and I'm honoured that you picked it. All the time you continue to enjoy my books – and DCI Dan Riley's escapades – I will continue to write them. If you want to keep up to date with all my latest and former releases, please sign up at the following link. Your email address will never be shared, and you can unsubscribe at any time.

www.bookouture.com/anna-lou-weatherley

If you enjoyed *What Kind of Mother*, it would be wonderful if you could spare the time to write a review. It means everything to me to hear what you think, and it makes such a difference in helping new readers discover my books for the first time. So please do share the love!

I truly LOVE hearing from my readers and will always do my very best to reply personally to everyone – you can get in touch on my Facebook page, through Instagram, X, Goodreads, or on my website any time.

With much love,

Anna-Lou

KEEP IN TOUCH WITH ANNA-LOU

facebook.com/annalouweatherleyauthor
x.com/annaloulondon
instagram.com/annalouwrites

ACKNOWLEDGEMENTS

As ever, I have many wonderful people to mention, so without further ado, thank you to all the brilliant publishing team at Bookouture, in particular, my lovely editor, Jessie Botterill, for all your help, patience, support and encouragement – wishing you love and luck with the new addition! I'd also like to thank all my awesomely talented fellow authors for their continuing support – too many to mention, but a special shout out to Casey Kelleher, Kim Nash, Victoria Jenkins, Angie Marsons and Sue Watson.

Thanks to Jan and Lawrie and Bridget and Bob, to my wonderful, amazing, and supportive friend, Sue Traveller, and to John and Sam too – thanks for all the laughs and love. A very special thank you to my friend Kelly for always being here for me, our friendship means so much. Also, my beautiful, stylish sister, Lisa-Jane – you are always an inspiration and I love and admire you! Mummy: you are my everything, my biggest supporter, my best friend, my sanity! I don't know what I would do without you. Thank you so much for being the best mum a girl could ever wish for. Thanks to the boys, Lz and Joe – I love you both with all of my heart and soul (and pocket!) – and to my darling Iggy, forever next to me. Thanks to Luca Paollini, Andrea 'Droppy', and all my Senigallia friends. Thanks also to Dementia UK.

My biggest thanks to my incredible agent and friend, Mr Darley Anderson. Your guidance and belief in me have been immeasurable, and to the wonderful Rebeka Finch at Darley

Anderson for everything you've done and continue to do in championing me and helping me survive! I'm very lucky to have you!

Lastly, a special mention to all the PW crew, Krasi, Demi, Mark, Marieke, Greta, Emma, Stacey, and of course, my Stevie P – I will always be here for you, the best is yet to come.

PUBLISHING TEAM

Turning a manuscript into a book requires the efforts of many people. The publishing team at Bookouture would like to acknowledge everyone who contributed to this publication.

Commercial
Lauren Morrissette
Hannah Richmond
Imogen Allport

Contracts
Peta Nightingale

Cover design
Lisa Horton

Data and analysis
Mark Alder
Mohamed Bussuri

Editorial
Jessie Botterill
Ria Clare

Copyeditor
Laura Kincaid

Proofreader
Claire Rushbrook

Marketing
Alex Crow
Melanie Price
Occy Carr
Cíara Rosney
Martyna Młynarska

Operations and distribution
Marina Valles
Stephanie Straub
Joe Morris

Production
Hannah Snetsinger
Mandy Kullar
Jen Shannon

Publicity
Kim Nash
Noelle Holten
Jess Readett
Sarah Hardy

www.ingramcontent.com/pod-product-compliance
Ingram Content Group UK Ltd.
Pitfield, Milton Keynes, MK11 3LW, UK
UKHW040621090125
453151UK00012B/105